GREYBACK GOLD

SERIES BY NELLIE H. STEELE

Cate Kensie Mysteries
Shadow Slayers Stories
Lily & Cassie by the Sea Mysteries
Pearl Party Mysteries
Middle Age is Murder Cozy Mysteries
Duchess of Blackmoore Mysteries
Maggie Edwards Adventures
Clif & Ri on the Sea Adventures
Shelving Magic

GREYBACK GOLD

A MAGGIE EDWARDS ADVENTURE

MAGGIE EDWARDS ADVENTURES
BOOK FOUR

NELLIE H. STEELE

This is a work of fiction. Names, characters, places, and incidents either are the product of the author's imagination or are used fictitiously. Any resemblance to actual persons, living or dead, events, or locales is entirely coincidental.

Copyright © 2023 by Nellie H. Steele

All rights reserved.

No part of this book may be reproduced in any form or by any electronic or mechanical means, including information storage and retrieval systems, without written permission from the author, except for the use of brief quotations in a book review.

Cover design by Stephanie A. Sovak.

❦ Created with Vellum

CHAPTER 1

"What do you think about King Solomon's diamond mines?" Maggie asked as she flipped through a book. She settled on a page, letting her elbows rest on the glass countertop of Maggie's Books and Baubles Boutique.

"I don't," Henry answered from the armchair across the shop, staring down at a magazine in his lap.

Maggie flicked her gaze into space, her finger tapping her lips before she turned to the next entry and puckered her lips at it. "Where do you think they are? Where would we look?"

"I don't know," Henry murmured, flipping the page and eyeing the latest rifles available.

Maggie straightened, placing her hands on the counter and narrowing her eyes at Henry. "Are you even listening?"

He kept his gaze fixed on the glossy paper in front of him. "Of course I am, Princess."

"Then why aren't you more interested?"

Henry flicked the magazine closed and dumped it on the table next to his armchair. The leather creaked as he pushed himself to stand and shuffled across the shop toward her.

"I'm listening to every word you say. But I'm not sure what you're getting at."

Maggie flicked the open book toward him, tapping the page. "I'm searching for King Solomon's diamond mines." Maggie flicked her gaze back to the printed words. "Do you think Agent Thomas would approve us to go looking for it?"

"Why are you so adamant about this?"

Maggie lifted her shoulders as she let the book thud against the glass. "I'm just…looking for some adventure. It's been three months since we went to Scotland. I feel like nothing's happened since then. I'm part of a special government asset retrieval team, and we're retrieving nothing."

Henry grabbed her left hand, tugging her ring finger toward the light. The diamond he'd slipped on it before finishing their vacation in Scotland sparkled in the light. "I thought we had plenty of excitement to look forward to."

Maggie sighed, cocking her head and staring at Henry as she tugged her hand away. "That's not what I meant, and you know it." She grabbed the feather duster and flitted from behind the desk to dust the bookshelves.

He spun to face her as she departed, leaning his elbow against the counter. "Maybe you could spend some time, I dunno, planning the wedding."

"We only got engaged three months ago. There is plenty of time," Maggie answered, without looking at him.

"But you'd rather search for diamond mines."

"You know, when I met you, you only wanted to spend time in a dusty tomb."

Henry straightened and crossed his arms over his muscular chest. "I'm starting to become concerned you don't want to be Mrs. Henry Taylor."

Maggie whipped around to face him, thrusting the feather duster toward him. "Okay, let's get this conversation over with right now. I am Maggie *Edwards*. I will always be

Maggie Edwards. If you expect me to walk down the aisle, put a ring on my finger, and become someone else and lose all of my own identity, you've got another thing coming."

With a huff, she spun back and frantically dusted the shelf.

"Of course not, Princess. If you want to stay Maggie Edwards, stay Maggie Edwards. But I'm being serious. I'm a little worried you don't want to get married."

"That's ridiculous."

"Is it?"

Maggie spun to face him again. "Yes. Of course it is. A gigantic party, a big dress, all the attention on me. Why wouldn't I want to get married?"

"Because after the gigantic you-centered party, you're stuck with me for life."

Maggie rolled her eyes and returned to her dusting, disappearing around a corner. "I'm perfectly fine with that."

"Are you?"

She poked her head from behind the shelf. "I said yes, didn't I?"

"Yeah," Henry admitted. "But–"

"So quit badgering me about it, okay?" Maggie's phone chimed from under the register. Her eyes widened, and she hurried toward it.

"I've got it," Henry said, reaching his arm over the counter.

"No!" Maggie exclaimed as she dove around the side and snatched the phone. "I've got it."

"Okay," Henry said, his eyebrows and arms raised in surrender.

Maggie perused the screen before she tucked the phone into her pants pocket. "Nothing. Junk mail."

Henry arched an eyebrow at her. "That was some sprint for junk mail."

"Well, I thought it was Piper. I didn't know it was junk mail."

Henry gave her a dubious stare. "You ran across the store for a text from Piper?"

"Oh, speaking of Piper," Maggie said as she wandered away again, disappearing in the stacks, "you remember we have her and Charlie's costume party on Friday, right?"

Henry sighed, pausing for a moment before he answered.

"Henry?" Maggie questioned, poking her head from around the corner again.

"Yeah, I remember."

Maggie disappeared between the stacks, sliding her phone from her pocket and reading the message. She swiped to unlock her screen before her thumbs pounded out an answer as she glanced over her shoulder. "You have a costume, right?"

"Of course."

She clicked off her display and slid the phone into her pocket as Henry rounded the bend. "What is it?"

Henry's eyebrows knit and stared at the phone poking from her pocket. "Huh?"

"Your costume, what is it?"

"Oh, uh, it's uh, I forget."

Maggie offered him an unimpressed stare. "You forget? Or you don't have one."

He avoided her gaze, studying one of the books on the shelf. "I have one."

"You don't. You forgot to get one."

"I did not. I was planning to go as...Indiana Jones."

"No," Maggie said, with finality. She sighed and shook her head, returning to her dusting. "Never mind. I'll get you one."

"No, not going there. I'll go myself tomorrow."

"No, you won't. You'll pick something stupid. I'll get you one."

"I will not. You'll pick something stupid."

Maggie stuck a hand on her hip and twisted to face him. "Seriously?"

"I don't want to go as a sexy vampire or anything that requires makeup."

Maggie lifted her hands in surrender before she grabbed a cart of books and shoved it ahead of her. She stopped and slid a few onto the shelves. "Fine. No sexy costumes, no makeup. Got it."

"How many people are going to this thing?" Henry questioned, grabbing a few books and spinning to another shelf to re-shelve them.

"I don't know," Maggie answered, with a shrug.

Henry flicked his eyes sideways toward her. "You don't know, or you don't want to say?"

"How would I know?"

"Piper works here *and* lives next door to you. Parties are of great interest to you. But you don't know how many people are on her guest list?"

"Ummm, maybe something like…a hundred or something."

"A hundred?" Henry asked, the books dropping to his side.

"Not everyone will come. It'll probably end up being, like, fifty."

"Fifty people? Maggie–"

Maggie sliced a finger through the air. "Don't start. They are our friends, and it's their first big party as a married couple. We have to go to support them."

"What if–"

"And we *have* to wear a costume, so don't even ask."

Henry cursed under his breath as the front door's bell jangled. Maggie hurried from between the shelves to greet her customer, leaving Henry to fume silently while shelving books.

"Tarik!" Maggie exclaimed as the Egyptian man strode into the shop, tucking a lock of his dark hair behind his ear and grinning at Maggie.

"Hello, Maggie."

Maggie wandered behind the register and tossed the feather duster onto the counter. She sank onto the stool, brushing a lock of hair from her face. "Any luck with the job search?"

"Actually, yes," Tarik answered.

Henry popped his head from between the shelves. "You got a job? About time, mate. I thought you were going to sleep on my couch forever."

"I am still planning to sleep on your couch, my friend," Tarik said, shooting a grin over his shoulder.

Maggie dug a lip gloss from her purse and swiped it across her lips. "What's the job?"

"Ollie said a position opened up at the museum, and I applied. I happen to know the assistant director, so I was offered the job on the spot."

Maggie gave him a coy grin. "You don't say. So, you'll be working with Emma. That's great."

"And flexible for any…trips."

Maggie shot Henry a glance as he approached with two books in his hand. "No idea where these go, and I don't want to put them in the wrong spot and get huffed at again."

Maggie tugged them from his hands with an eye roll before flitting into the stacks. "I did not huff."

"You did."

"I didn't. Believe me, you'll know when I'm mad!" she called as she shoved one book into an empty spot.

She spun around and re-shelved the second book before she darted back toward the front of the shop. Henry and

Tarik murmured between them, ceasing their conversation when she appeared.

Maggie stuck her hands on her hips as she eyed them. "What's going on here?"

Henry shook his head. "Nothing."

"He was trying to convince me not to wear a costume to Piper and Charlie's party."

Maggie's eyebrows shot up to her hairline, and she crossed her arms. "Oh, really?"

"Traitor," Henry groused at Tarik.

"And did you agree?" Maggie questioned as she plopped onto the stool again.

"Certainly not. I already have my costume prepared."

Maggie perked up, leaning forward onto the glass counter with a grin. "What's the costume?"

"King Tut," Tarik answered, lifting his chin.

"Nice choice! Aww, babe, you should have been King Tut."

"No," Henry said, with a wave of his hand. "Why can't I be Indiana Jones? I already have everything I need."

"You can't wear the same clothes you wear all the time, Henry. You just can't. Look, leave it to me, and I'll make sure you've got a great costume." She turned her attention to Tarik. "In the meantime, have you heard anything about any...trips?"

"No. Should I have?"

Maggie sighed, her shoulders slumping as she shook her head. "No. I was just trying to convince Henry to go search for King Solomon's mines or something, but he's being a stick in the mud."

Henry leaned across the glass. "Tell you what, we'll go searching for King Solomon's mines if I don't—"

"Don't even say it," Maggie said, wagging a finger at him. "You're *not* going without a costume."

Henry scrunched his nose at her as Maggie's phone

chimed again. She glanced at it before shoving it back into her pocket. The bell over the door jangled as her newest shop assistant pushed through the door.

"Ah, Erin, perfect timing," Maggie said, leaping from her stool and grabbing her purse.

"Hi, Maggie, and everyone," the blonde answered as she shrugged her backpack off her back and strode toward the counter.

Maggie slung her large purse over her shoulder and slid her sunglasses onto her face. "Everything is in order from the day shift, so you're good to go!"

She waved as she tugged the front door open and hurried to the sidewalk outside. Henry and Tarik followed her into the warm afternoon.

Henry shoved his hands into his pockets, giving Maggie a sideways glance. "So…"

Maggie checked her phone again before she snapped a gaze at Henry. "Why don't you take Tarik out for a celebratory drink? Congratulate him on the new job."

"Oh, ah," Henry mumbled, rifling his hair, "really?"

"Yeah," Maggie said, with a wave of her hand, "have fun. Have a few drinks. Enjoy."

"But…what about the costume?" Henry said, with a wince.

"Go," Maggie said, with another wave. "I've got the costume. It's handled. You know how I love to shop."

"Y-yeah, I do," Henry stammered, "but I also know you don't like getting stuck doing my shopping."

"Babe, don't worry about it. Have fun. I've got this," Maggie said, cupping his face in her hands and giving him a light kiss.

"Thanks, Princess," Henry said, with a tentative grin.

"Go, go!" Maggie said, shooing them away. "Tarik, please, take him out of my hair!"

"I've got it covered, Maggie," Tarik said, with a grin, wrapping his arm around Henry and pulling him down the sidewalk.

Maggie stared after them as they continued down the block. Henry gave her one final glance, and Maggie waved at him. She rolled her eyes as he turned back, mumbling something to Tarik, and tugged her phone from her pocket.

She tapped the last incoming message and swiped to initiate a call. "I got your message. I can meet you now." She paused, listening for the response. "Don't worry. I got rid of Henry. He has no idea."

CHAPTER 2

"Do I really need to wear this?" Henry called from Maggie's spare bedroom.

"You said no makeup and nothing sexy. This is neither," Maggie answered from her couch. She glanced at the clock on the mantel before returning her attention to the television. "We're going to be late."

"No, we're not," Henry answered. "We only have to walk next door."

Maggie heaved a sigh as her phone chimed. She glanced down at the message from Piper.

Where you at, boss lady? Trying to be fashionably late?

Maggie pouted at the screen as her thumbs pounded across the virtual keyboard.

Henry's being Henry. We'll be there as soon as he gets his costume on.

She tossed the phone onto the cushion next to her. "Henry! Piper said we're late. Hurry up. It can't be that hard to get into that costume."

Henry clopped out with most of his costume on, though he was missing one key component.

Maggie glanced over her shoulder at him. "Where's the rest?"

His nose wrinkled as he lifted the large headpiece. "Do I have to? Isn't this enough?" He waved a hand to his ensemble, fussing with his frilly cravat and tugging at his blue velvet tuxedo jacket.

"No, that's not enough."

"Maggie, I'm wearing tights. I can't do this."

"It's not sexy, there's no makeup, and it matches mine. Now come on," Maggie said, struggling to stand and letting her bright yellow ball gown flow around her, "put the mask on."

Henry stared at her with an unimpressed frown on his face before he lifted the headpiece and smashed it down over his head. "Happy?" he asked, voice muffled by the massive costume topper.

"Very," Maggie said, with a lift of her shoulder. She strode to the mirror in her entryway and fluffed her hair. "Let's go. I want to make an entrance."

"Don't worry, we will," Henry mumbled from inside his giant beast mask.

They strode from the apartment and took a few steps before pounding against the apartment door next to Maggie's.

"Are you sure–"

Maggie held up a hand, interrupting him. "I could have gotten you the candle. I got you Beast. At least you get the girl."

The door swung open, and Charlie grinned at them. With darkened eyes, a white face, and blood dripping from his prosthetic fangs, his costume was obvious without needing the dramatic black cape and velvet smoking jacket with frilly cravat.

"Velcome to our home," he said in an accent.

Maggie offered a wide smile. "Hi, sorry we're late. Henry had some trouble with his costume."

"Trouble with his costume?" Piper inquired, swishing over in a large Victorian skirt. Blood dripped from two bite holes in her neck.

Henry pulled the beast's headpiece from his head. "I can't wear this."

"What? Put that back on, mate, you look great!" Charlie exclaimed.

"See, I told you," Maggie said as she gathered her skirts and pushed into their apartment.

Charlie looked him up and down as Henry slammed the mask back onto his head. "I never realized what nice legs you've got, Taylor."

Henry waved a paw at him. "Don't start with me, Charlie."

"If you would have just bought a costume ahead of time, she wouldn't have had the choice," Piper told him. "What are you drinking?"

"Anything with alcohol. I need it."

Charlie slammed his buddy on the back and led him toward the bar. "I've got you covered, mate."

Maggie already stood with a mixed drink, scanning the room as she waited for Henry's drink. "Oh, there's Emma and Leo. Let's say hi."

She grabbed Henry's arm and dragged him across the room. "Hi! How are you two?"

Emma stared her up and down. "Good, thanks."

Maggie glanced at Emma's long white dress, and Leo's dark pants and vest over a white shirt. "What are you supposed to be? Why are you wearing cinnamon buns on your ears?"

Emma screwed up her face. "Princess Leia and Han Solo."

"Who?" Maggie asked after taking a sip of her frothy concoction.

Emma shook her head. "You can't be serious."

Henry pulled off his mask, sucking in a breath. "I can't breathe in this thing."

"I see you went for the Disney princess look. I am not surprised," Emma answered.

"People have told me I look like Belle."

"People have told me I look like the guy from *Lost*, and quite frankly, I'd rather have come as him than in this. I can barely hold my drink with these paws on."

"Buck up, man," Leo said, slapping him on the back, "Beast fits your personality." He flicked his gaze to Maggie. "And I always did say you looked like Belle."

Henry glared at him as he wrapped his arm around Emma, who also gave him an annoyed glance.

"Piper and Charlie went full gothic vampire. Very fitting," Maggie said as she continued to scan the room.

Emma clasped her hands together in front of her, rocking on her heels. "So, how are the new assistants working out at the shop?"

Maggie waved across the room at a few other people. "Oh, fine. I'm really glad to have the extra help, though lately I haven't really needed it. How are things at the museum?"

"Busy. We're getting some of the Drakon pieces for a special exhibit."

"Oh, fun!" Maggie said, staring into space. "Gosh, that was so fun, wasn't it?"

"Also, dangerous. We were nearly killed several times, Mags," Leo reminded her.

Maggie breathed out a satisfied sigh. "Yeah, those were the days."

"Who enters my tomb?" Tarik's voice boomed from behind them.

Maggie spun to face him, a smile brightening her features. "Tarik! You look great!"

He threw his arms out to the side to show off his King Tut costume, complete with headpiece. "Thank you. And you, you look like a princess."

"So what else is new?" Emma said.

"Oh, there's Uncle Ollie!" Maggie said, waving to the man Charlie led across the room.

After grabbing a drink, he approached their group, lifting his glass. "Evening, everyone."

"Hi, Uncle Ollie, I'm glad you could make it."

Ollie sipped at his beverage and wiggled his eyebrows. "Me, too."

"Why didn't you wear a costume?" Maggie inquired as she studied his tweed suit and hat.

"I did."

Maggie cocked her head, letting a finger travel up and down. "Those are just normal clothes."

"I'm Henry Jones, Sr." Ollie stuck the hat on his head and waved his umbrella in the air. "See. Complete with the umbrella he used to chase the birds on the beach."

Henry sighed and shook his head. "See, I could have come as Indiana Jones."

"I can't believe you didn't," Leo answered.

"I tried, mate, believe me, I tried," Henry grumbled.

Maggie puckered her lips and shook her head. "You two are boring. Live a little."

"Wearing fake paws and a giant mask is not living, Princess," Henry said.

"Ah, she just wanted to wear the princess dress," Leo retorted after a sip of his beverage.

Henry shook his head. "And no one would have stopped her."

"But it's not a couple's costume," Maggie and Leo replied at the same time.

"Jinx, buy me a Coke," Leo said, pointing a finger at

Maggie, with a grin.

Maggie lifted her skirts with an arched eyebrow and skirted around the other guests to retrieve the demanded soda before she returned and handed it to Leo.

She then spun to face Henry. "And now with that done, put your costume back on."

"I think I see Charlie needing some help over there. I'd better go find out," Henry said, gazing into the distance before he wandered away.

"So, Uncle Ollie," Maggie said as Henry whispered something to Charlie, who then gave him a thumbs up, "anything fun and exciting on the horizon?"

"I've got some grading to do this weekend. How's that?"

Maggie wrinkled her nose. "Neither fun nor exciting."

"You're probably correct, Maggie."

"I meant fun and exciting like…finding a tomb or a treasure. Anything like that you need us to follow up on?"

"You're not seriously looking for more trouble, are you, Maggie?" Leo asked.

Emma held her hands up in front of her. "Whatever it is, don't involve me. Every time you're looking for fun, we end up stuck somewhere or held at gunpoint. Or both."

Maggie stuck her hands on her hips. "What is with you guys? Are you all this dull? Doesn't anyone enjoy the adventures we've had?"

No one answered, avoiding her gaze. She stuck her hands on her hips and narrowed her eyes. "You all are a bunch of stick-in-the-muds. You know that?"

With a huff, she stormed away, pushing through the revelers and onto the deck outside. Warm air surrounded her as she wandered to the railing and leaned against it, blowing out a long breath.

She stared over her town below for a few moments before a strawberry daiquiri floated in front of her face.

She flicked her gaze sideways to stare at the man offering it.

"Thought you could use it," Leo said, with a grin.

Maggie snatched it from his hand and took a sip, giving the town's glittering lights another glance. "Where's Emma?"

"Talking shop with Ollie," Leo said, shoving his hands in his pockets as he stared out over Rosemont.

Maggie glanced over her shoulder before taking another sip of the sweet drink.

"You do make a perfect Belle," Leo said.

Maggie's lips curled into a half-smile at the words. "We never did get to do a party as Belle and Beast, did we?"

"No," Leo said, "I think the last costume party we did together was…uh…" He scratched his head as he tried to recall their costumes.

"Cleopatra and Marc Antony," they said in unison.

Maggie bobbed her head as she took another sip of her drink. "Yep, kind of ironic, wasn't it?"

Leo shoved his hands into his pockets again. "What, that you went on to find Cleopatra's Tomb? Yeah, I'd say it was."

"Those were the days," Maggie said with a reminiscent sigh as a warm breeze tickled her skin.

"Hey, Maggie…" Leo said, turning toward her. She sipped at her drink, flicking her gaze up at him expectantly when Henry stepped out on the deck.

"There you are," he said, his headpiece noticeably missing.

"What happened to your head?"

"Oh, uh," Henry answered. "Must have put it down in the other room when I was helping Charlie and forgot it. Oh, well. Anyway, did you want anything to eat?"

"Uh," Maggie murmured, flicking a gaze up to Leo, who pretended to stare out over the landscape again.

Emma appeared at the door, eyeing the scene suspiciously before she stepped onto the balcony.

"Yeah, yeah, I think I'd like to grab something," Maggie answered, lifting her skirts and ambling toward Henry.

"Everything okay?" Henry asked as they stepped back into the living room.

"Yeah, why?"

"You and Leo on the balcony. I'm surprised one of you didn't go over the edge."

Maggie scoffed as she picked up a small plate and filled it with veggies and cheese cubes. "What? That's going a bit far."

"Come on, everyone knows you and Leo don't always see eye-to-eye. What word did you use to describe your relationship? Explosive?"

Maggie shot him a sideways glance as she scanned the crowd again, dipping a celery stick into ranch dressing. "Complicated. I don't think I ever said 'explosive.'"

Henry tossed a cheese cube into his mouth. "Mmm, I think you did, Princess."

"Never," Maggie retorted before biting into a carrot stick. "Our relationship is explosive. Usually because explosives are somehow involved." She shot him a saucy grin.

"That's my kind of relationship," he purred, leaning in for a kiss.

Maggie shifted her head at the last minute. "Oh, look, it's Karen and Jim!" She waved a hand in the air, grinning widely as she called hello and strode across the room to greet them.

She spent the remainder of the party meeting and greeting Rosemont's other residents, chattering away about her latest accomplishments, and showing pictures of her recent trip to Scotland.

The party wound down around midnight. Maggie plopped on the couch, her massive skirt splaying around her as she sat. "Whew, great party, you two."

"Thanks, chicky," Charlie called as he stuffed soda cans into a black garbage bag.

"Need help cleaning up?"

"Nah, we'll handle it in the morning. I'm just clearing the walkway," Charlie answered as Piper snapped the lid on what remained of the veggie tray and carted it off to the kitchen.

Piper flitted back into the room as Charlie passed her with the trash bag.

"Thanks for having us, Piper," Emma said as she pulled her coat on before wandering over to pull her into a half-hug. "We really enjoyed it."

"You're welcome. Thanks for coming to our first big party."

"I had a most enjoyable time, too," Tarik said, with a grin.

Maggie twisted to glance at them as Henry helped Charlie tug a table from the wall toward the middle of the room.

"Hey, you aren't leaving yet, are you?"

Emma shot Maggie an irked glance. "The party *is* over. That's usually when people leave."

"Come on!" Maggie groaned. "The night is still young!"

"It's after midnight!" Emma said.

Maggie screwed up at her face and climbed off the couch, lifting her skirts as she stomped toward them. "Oh, I'm sorry, Cinderella. I didn't realize you turned into a pumpkin."

Emma rolled her eyes and crossed her arms. "It was the carriage that turned into a pumpkin, not Cinderella."

"Whatever, Grandma," Maggie said, with a groan, "no one's turning into a pumpkin. No one's car is turning into a pumpkin. Stay! Let's play a game or something!"

"Maggie! I don't think we should invite ourselves to stay at Piper and Charlie's place. Maybe they're tired."

"Umm, I'm right here," Piper said, raising her hand before she pointed to herself. "Also, I'm not a grandma, so it's all good." She turned her head to call over her shoulder. "Hey, babe!"

"Yeah?" Charlie answered from the kitchen.

"We're doing a game night after-party. Bring the good stuff."

"Yay!" Maggie said, bouncing on her toes and clapping. She hurried across the room and plopped on the couch again.

Emma's shoulders slumped, and she fluttered her eyelashes. "I would love to stay, but I'm just…this costume isn't the most comfortable."

"You're right," Maggie groaned.

Piper flicked her gaze between Maggie and Emma. "So, is this not happening then?"

"Oh, it's happening," Maggie said as she rose to stand. "We'll be right back. Tell Henry to change and tell Tarik and Leo to borrow some sweats from Charlie."

Maggie grabbed Emma's hand and tugged her toward the door.

"I'm not wearing your clothes, Maggie," Emma argued as she stumbled after her.

"You will, and you'll like it. They'll be the best clothes you've ever worn."

Emma groaned as Maggie dragged her into the hall and down to her door. She pushed inside and continued to her bedroom, her dress swishing as she hurried into her walk-in closet.

"What do you want? Yoga pants? Sweats?" she called as she shimmied out of the dress.

"Does it matter what I want?" Emma shouted back.

"Just come in and pick what you want, then."

Emma hovered at the doorway, her eyes scanning the space. "Of course your closet looks like this."

"Oh, shut up," Maggie said, with a roll of her eyes, "and get some clothes on, and let's get back over there."

Emma wrinkled her nose as she scanned the array of sweatpants. "What's with you?"

"I don't know what you're talking about. Pull this skirt off me, I'm stuck."

Emma scoffed at her, half-in and half-out of her massive hooped skirt. She batted at the dress, trying to knock it down on the floor. "Step out. You gotta help me out here."

"I'm trying. My leg is stuck."

"You are so needy. Whenever there's trouble, Maggie Edwards is always at the center of it."

"Unfortunately, this is only trouble with a stupid dress," Maggie said as her ankle finally found its freedom. She tumbled backward, knocking a designer bag into Emma's head.

"Ow! Seriously?" she asked, rubbing her head as she stood.

"Yes, seriously," Maggie fumed, snapping a T-shirt from a shelf and unraveling it before tugging it over her head. "I'm not at the center of anything anymore."

Emma grabbed a pair of sweatpants and tugged them up under her dress. "I meant 'seriously, did you just knock that bag on my head?'"

"Oh," Maggie groaned, sliding into a pair of yoga pants before she plopped down on a backless bench with a pair of sneakers.

"What's going on with you? You're acting weird."

"Am I?" Maggie tugged her laces tight before tying them.

"Uh, yeah. Do you have any T-shirts that aren't 'ladies fit?'"

Maggie screwed up her face. "Why would I have that? That's gross. Put on a ladies' tee and show off your curves, Emma."

Emma wrinkled her nose at a tiny pink T-shirt that read "Divalicious." "There are a few curves I'd rather not show off, thanks."

"Oh, stop," Maggie said as she tugged her second shoe on and tied it. "You're fine."

"Are you?" Emma asked as she picked the least fancy shirt she could find on the shelf and pulled her dress off before donning it.

"I'm not fat. Wait, are you saying I'm fat?" Maggie pinched her waist.

"No, duh. You're moaning about not being in trouble, not being the center of anything, and you're acting weird. What's up with you?"

Maggie dropped her foot to the floor, her shoulders slumping as she rested her elbows against her thighs. She bit her lower lip as she considered her response. Should she tell Emma the truth?

CHAPTER 3

Maggie blew out a sigh as she stared into space. "I dunno. Just...things feel so...boring."

Emma screwed up her face as she pulled on her sneakers and tied them. "Are you kidding me? You just got home from Scotland. And you're *engaged*."

"I know." Maggie sighed. "That was, like, three months ago."

"Aren't you busy planning the wedding?"

"Yeah," Maggie murmured, her chin resting in her palm as she stared blankly ahead.

Emma's eyebrows shot up as she glanced sideways at Maggie. "You're not?"

Maggie lifted her shoulders, her top lip lifting into a sneer. "I am thinking about stuff." Maggie rose to her feet and ran her fingers through her hair, reaching down to pull Emma to stand. "Come on, let's go. This game night is the best thing that's happened in weeks."

Emma offered her a confused glance as Maggie trudged from the room. She rummaged through a cupboard, pulling a bottle of wine from within before she swung open the front door, meeting Henry.

"I'm supposed to change?"

"Yep, then hurry back! We're playing games!"

"What's with her?" Henry asked Emma.

"No idea," Emma said, following Maggie back to Piper and Charlie's apartment next door.

Piper tossed a few pillows onto the floor around their coffee table. Charlie handed beers off to Tarik and Leo before he plopped onto one of the pillows.

Maggie waved the wine bottle in her hand before she collapsed onto the sofa.

"I'll grab some glasses," Piper announced as she pulled her hair up into a messy bun on the top of her head.

"Great!" Maggie said, with a grin. "This is great. What games do we have?"

Charlie picked up a stack of boxes and set them on the table. "We've got two different Clue escape games, Trekking the World and Spy Alley."

Maggie wrinkled her nose at them. "What's with you two and Clue games?"

Charlie lifted a shoulder, tugging the boxes to the side. "Okay, Clue's out."

"No," Maggie groaned, "Clue's not out." She tapped a finger on top of a box. "Trekking the World, out!" She tossed her thumb over.

"Says who? That looks like fun," Emma said.

Maggie yanked the box from the table and tossed it underneath. "If you want to trek the world, trek it. Don't do it from your couch with a board game."

"Hey, you can't toss board games in our house," Piper said. "Though I'm with you on this one. Trekking the World is meh. Let's go for a Clue one. Do we want to be stuck in the Tudor Mansion or solve the Robbery at the Museum?"

Leo sipped his beer, kicking his feet up. "Robbery at the Museum hits a little close to home, doesn't it?"

"Perfect. Memories of great times," Maggie said, sliding the top off the box. "We'll pretend it's Rosemont's museum."

Henry strolled into the apartment with his street clothes on. "Oh, this is so much better. Please, mate, don't have another costume party, huh?"

"Just in time," Maggie said, sliding onto the floor as she emptied the box. "We're solving a museum robbery escape room style."

Henry screwed up his face. "Didn't we do that once already?"

"We did. Like, forever ago," Maggie said as she unfolded the board and laid it flat.

"It wasn't that long ago," Henry replied, easing into a chair. "And besides, I thought when we went to Scotland, you wanted away from the whole adventure thing?"

"I wanted away from the bad guys who ended up finding us in Scotland. And I'm over it now."

"Over not wanting bad guys to follow you?" Emma asked as she snagged the instruction sheet and perused it.

Maggie set out the game pieces. "Yes. I'd kill for some bad guys right now."

Leo sipped his beer, his brow furrowing. "Like gun-toting bad guys, Mags?"

"They could leave the guns, but something fun and intense."

"Mmm, pass," Emma said, flipping to the second page of instructions. "Every time you want something fun and intense, I end up trapped somewhere I'd rather not be trapped."

"That's not true," Maggie said.

"Yes, it is. Cleopatra's tomb, not once, but twice, and that secret passage in Scotland."

"Lighten up, Emma. Those were the best times of our lives." Maggie grabbed the bottle of wine and poured herself a glass.

"Okay, here's the deal," Emma said, turning back to page one of the instructions. "Mr. Boddy wants us to take part in a heist."

Piper waved a hand in the air. "Wait, we're not solving the heist? We're, like, stealing stuff?"

"Good thing I'm here," Charlie said. "Right up my alley. Eh, mate?" He shot a finger gun at Henry, with a wink.

"Been there and done that on multiple occasions," Henry said.

"Right, like the other time you got me in major trouble by stealing something from the Cairo Museum and using me to do it," Emma said, with a nod. "And how am I not always in trouble when you're around?"

"Give me a break, Emma," Maggie said, with a roll of her eyes. She slammed the wine glass onto the table before she cracked her hand against it, rattling the game pieces. "What's wrong with all of you?"

"Huh?" Emma questioned, her nose wrinkled.

"You okay, Maggie?" Tarik inquired, leaning forward to balance his elbows on his knees.

"Yeah, chicky, you seem tense," Charlie said after a sip of beer.

"I'm not tense."

"Mmmm, seems like you are, Boss Lady," Piper said, one eyebrow arched.

Leo nodded, his lips puckered. "Definitely agitated. Classic Maggie tension."

"Will you all stop piling on me? Is it that crazy that I want a little adventure?"

"I would just like to note I've not said anything," Henry added as he cracked open a beer.

"I thought that's what the impromptu game night was for?" Emma asked.

Maggie pushed herself up from the floor, threading through the room's other occupants and pacing behind the sofa. "Is it too much to ask for a little adventure?"

"I feel like we've had plenty," Emma retorted.

"Oh, come on," Maggie said, slapping her thigh. "Tell me you don't want to discover something new."

Emma opened her mouth, but Maggie continued. "Henry," she said, tapping his shoulder, "tell me you don't miss schlepping through the desert in search of a lost something or other."

Henry's eyebrows raised as she rushed toward Tarik and knelt in front of him. "Tell me you didn't expect life in the States to be wilder than getting a job at the museum."

Tarik lifted his shoulders, but before she could answer, Maggie spun to face Charlie and Piper. "Can you two honestly tell me your honeymoon wasn't exciting and you're not burning for a new challenge?"

"And you," she said, flinging a finger toward Leo, "I *know* you want more of that Mario Andretti action."

She stood and flung her arms out. "Come on, people! I think we could *all* use another adventure. Get the team back together. Work on something more than a fake escape room with a paper game board." Maggie grabbed ahold of the Clue board and waved it in the air.

Silence filled the air before Piper slowly began nodding her head. "Yeah. Yeah, I could use some action."

"Me, too, chicky. Old Charlie is always ready to conquer the unexpected."

Maggie nodded, her eyebrows shooting up. "Yes, yes, that's what I'm talking about. Who else?"

"I am always up for a team-building exercise," Tarik answered.

Maggie clapped her hands together and shook them at Tarik. "Yes!"

She spun to stare expectantly at the others in the room.

"I suppose a good discovery wouldn't be unwelcome," Henry said. Maggie grinned and nodded.

"I'm not sure I want–" Emma began.

Leo raised his beer in the air. "I'm with you, Mags."

Emma crinkled her brow and glanced at Leo before she sighed. "Okay, I guess we could do something bigger than a board game."

"Yes!" Maggie exclaimed, leaping in the air and pumping a fist. "Let's do this!"

"Yes!" Piper said, tossing her arms over her head. She high-fived Charlie as they grinned at each other.

"Hey, I hate to be a super huge pain here," Emma said as she tossed the instruction manual down on the table, "but what exactly are we doing?"

Maggie winced, crinkling her nose. "I don't know. But at least we're all on board with this plan. So as soon as we find something to do, we're going all in."

Maggie plopped on the couch between Leo and Emma, sinking her chin into her palm. "Let's see. Oh, umm, King Solomon's mines. Anyone want to go searching for those? I just saw an article on it a few days ago."

"Are you kidding?" Emma asked. "That's…insane."

Maggie cocked her head. "Really?"

"Uh, yeah. We all have to go to work Monday."

Maggie shook her head. "*Not* if we find a lead. Frank will okay it."

"Also, my boss is super laid back," Piper said, "and she'd totally give me the time off."

"I work remotely, baby, I'm good," Charlie said, with a grin.

Emma shrugged a shoulder. "Maybe we can come up with

something closer to home. Something reasonable, but enough to whet Maggie's adventurous appetite."

"What could there possibly be in Rosemont that's adventurous?" Maggie questioned. "Don't get me wrong, I love it here, but it's not the most exciting town on the planet. Rosemont doesn't have any secrets."

"What about the museum?" Henry suggested.

"What about it?" Maggie asked.

"We'll go there and dig around in the storage and see what we find. That'll be fun, right?" Henry splayed his hands to the sides.

Maggie screwed up her face. "No! Digging around in Emma's basement? Not fun. Not exciting."

"I've got it," Tarik said. "We'll draw straws, and half of us will pretend to be an opposing team after an artifact. First ones to retrieve it win the game."

"Are you saying you'd be fake bad guys?" Maggie asked, leaping from her seat and pacing the floor.

"Yes," Tarik said.

"Real-life Clue, man, I like it," Charlie said, with a nod.

"Well, I don't," Maggie said, a frown forming on her lips. "I don't want to play a fake game for a diorama set."

"We don't have dioramas anymore," Emma said, with a shake of her head.

Maggie offered her an unimpressed stare.

Emma held her hands up. "Just sayin'."

"Come on, people! *This* is the best we can do? We found Cleopatra's tomb. We found the Library of Alexandria! We found a lost Viking treasure. And now you want to run around the museum after hours for a fake prize?"

"I don't really know what else we could do, Maggie, but it's not like there's anything else on the burner right now. Frank hasn't sent anything on. Ollie's got no leads," Henry said.

Maggie slapped her hands against her forehead, with a groan.

"Take it easy, Maggie. We don't need to live in the fast lane all the time. And like you said, it's Rosemont. It's not that exciting," Emma said.

"Yeah, Boss Lady. Nothing exciting happens here like ever. Except for that one time you almost got run over in the museum parking lot after it got robbed."

Charlie wiggled his eyebrows at her. "You make Rosemont exciting, chicky."

Maggie slumped into an empty armchair with a sigh. "Fine. There's nothing exciting to do here. Let's just play the stupid Clue game."

"I can't believe I'm the only one who knows the really exciting thing about Rosemont," Leo said, with a shake of his head before sipping his beer.

"What?" Maggie crossed her arms over her chest. "That there's a twofer on popcorn at the Grand Theater if you ask?"

"Nope," Leo said, staring up at the ceiling with a cat-who-caught-the-canary grin on his features.

"Well, are you going to tell us or just hold on to it?" Maggie asked, waving a hand in the air.

"Mmm, maybe I'll hold on to it," Leo said smugly.

"Oh, come on, Oscar," Piper said, "you can't drop a 'Rosemont has a super cool secret' bombshell and then take it back."

"I really don't think I should tell someone who calls me Oscar. I am not a grouch."

"Says you. You're almost always crabby," Piper shot back.

"He doesn't know anything," Charlie said, leaning back to rest on his palms. "He's bluffing."

"I'm not," Leo promised in a sing-song voice.

"Well, tell us this exciting secret!" Maggie said, leaning forward.

Leo shot her a sideways glance, arching an eyebrow. "Only if *everyone really* wants to know."

"Are you kidding me?" Maggie asked.

Leo raised both eyebrows and stared at her.

"Fine," she said, with a tensed jaw. "I *really* want to know."

Leo slid his eyes to Piper and Charlie, across from him on the floor.

Piper fluttered her eyelashes. "I totally want to know. This is the one time I've found a conversation with you interesting."

Leo tipped his beer bottle to point at her. "Outside of that date we went on, right?"

"You wish, Oscar. That was a mistake."

"Wait, you dated him?" Charlie asked.

"Not really," Piper said. "I'll explain it later. Just tell him you want to know about his secret."

Charlie offered Piper a dubious glance as Maggie stepped in to explain. "He tricked her into taking him to the museum gala that got robbed. It was no big deal, trust me."

"All right, since chicky is vouching for you," Charlie said, with a nod, "I, too, want to know the big secret."

"Three for three." Leo pointed at Tarik.

Tarik raised his hands and nodded. "I'm new here. I'd love to know the town's secret."

Leo slid his eyes to Henry, who sipped his beer. "Is there anything I can actually say that won't make you mad?"

"I don't know, Indiana Jones, try me."

Henry narrowed his eyes at Leo. "I really want to know the secret."

"Gonna have to do better than that," Leo said, cocking his head.

"Seriously? Come on, mate, there's no way I can convince you."

"Henry!" Maggie hissed between clenched teeth. "Do a better job."

"I'm really curious," Henry said, his head bobbing up and down. "Honestly. I'm intrigued."

"All right, good enough, I believe you."

Leo glanced at the remaining person in the room.

"I'd like to know," Emma said, with a shrug.

Leo slapped his hands together and rubbed them. "Looks like we're in business."

"Wait, that's it? She shrugged and said, 'I'd like to know,' and that was good enough?" Henry asked, flailing a hand at Emma.

"Henry!" Maggie growled, her eyes going wide. "Don't mess it up!"

"Yeah, Dr. Jones," Leo said in his best German accent, "don't mess it up."

Henry shot an irritated glance at Maggie. "Well, she seemed less than enthused. I had to practically kiss the bloke's a–"

"Never mind what you almost had to kiss," Maggie said, flailing a hand in the air. "We're about to finally get to something exciting. Let's get on with it. I want some adventure!"

"Do you really think it'll be something *that* exciting?" Henry questioned.

"Really? Are you *trying* to tick me off?" Leo questioned.

"Henry," Maggie growled, shooting an unimpressed-verging-on-angry stare in his direction.

"He has a point," Emma responded.

"Emma!" Maggie exclaimed.

"Yeah, come on! Whose side are you on?" Leo retorted.

"Well, I'm just saying," Emma answered, with a shrug. "It's Rosemont. Lovely small town, great shopping, great dining, great living, but Earth-shattering secrets? Eh, I'm not so sure."

"I grew up here, remember? I know everything there is to know about Rosemont, and there's a secret," Leo assured them. "And it's big. It's a local legend. With the influx of newcomers in the last few decades, it's kind of died off. But the locals still know about it. And some of the old-timers still believe it's pretty powerful."

"Old-timers?" Piper asked, with a chuckle.

"Yeah, fair maiden, old-timers," Charlie said, leaning forward to mime holding a cane and pulling his lips into his mouth to mimic losing his teeth. "There's a secret in this town, young lady."

Piper shoved him playfully. "I know what an old-timer is, duh. I just can't believe Oscar uses the phrase 'old-timer.'"

"I can't believe you dated a guy who uses the phrase 'old-timer.'"

"Honestly, they didn't really date," Maggie said, with a roll of her eyes and a shake of her head. "Now, can we please get on with it? What's the secret?"

Leo set his beer on the table and leaned forward, balancing his elbows on his knees. He licked his lips, his eyes sliding around the room to each of their faces. He arched an eyebrow, a twinkle in his eyes as he opened his mouth to share the secret.

CHAPTER 4

Butterflies fluttered in Maggie's stomach as she leaned forward, staring at Leo's lips. One of her eyebrows arched as the corners of her lips turned up. She sucked in a breath, awaiting his response.

"Everyone knows of the Rose River, right?" Leo flicked his gaze around the group.

No one answered. Leo paused, his eyes going wide as he scanned the crowd again. "Well?"

"Yeah, of course. That's obvious," Maggie said, bobbing her head up and down. "Edge of town. The Rose River Walk. Everyone knows it. It's almost as famous as the Sienne."

Emma scoffed. "As famous as the Sienne? Maggie, are you serious?"

Maggie sipped her wine. "What?"

"I think the Sienne is just a little more famous."

"I said *almost*," Maggie said, with a raise of one shoulder.

"Famous or not, all of us in this room know the Rose River. But did you know that Rosemont actually has two rivers?" Leo raised his eyebrows and settled back into his seat.

Maggie's features scrunched. "Two rivers?"

"Yeah, what?" Piper asked.

Henry slouched in his chair and sipped his beer. "Two rivers? That makes no sense."

"I'm not seeing it," Emma retorted. "Is this some sort of joke? Like the Rose River runs backward, so it's considered two or something?"

"Runs backward? Now who's talking ridiculous?" Maggie asked.

Emma threw a hand out. "Well, I don't see how that makes sense."

"I don't see what this has to do with the stupid secret," Maggie huffed.

"Hello? Guys! I just told you there's a second river in Rosemont."

"What are you getting at, sourpuss?" Charlie inquired.

Leo gave him a pointed look. "Are you kidding me?"

"I am not, sir. You are quite sour," Charlie answered, leaning back on his hands and stacking one foot on top of the other and swaying them.

Leo rolled his eyes and slouched further down the couch. "You can't be serious. I don't know why I waste my time on you guys."

"It's not a waste," Maggie said. "I just don't think anyone understands what you're saying. Are you saying there's literally a second river? Where? Like on the outskirts of town or what?"

Leo lifted his shoulders, the glimmer returning to his eyes. He waved a hand in the air. "No one knows."

"Wait, so the deal is, there's a secret river, and no one knows where?" Henry questioned.

"Sort of."

"What the bloody hell does that mean?" Henry shot back.

"All right, listen," Leo said, leaning forward again and

taking another swig of his beer, "let me sweeten the pot. This hidden river, buried somewhere underground, is not just any river."

"No kidding, if it's underground, duh," Piper said as she raised her wine glass to her still-blood-red lips.

"No," Leo said, with a shake of his head, "it's not just underground. It's a river…of blood."

A breath of silence filled the air before Maggie started to laugh. Her chuckling proved infectious, spreading first to Charlie, then Piper, then Henry and Tarik, and finally even Emma covered her lips as she tried to hide a giggle.

Leo's eyebrows shot up as he stared at them. "Are you serious? You're laughing?"

Henry slapped his thigh. "A river of blood," he repeated between snickers. He wiggled his fingers in the air. "Wooooo. Are there ghosts down there, too, mate?"

Leo wrinkled his nose and snatched his bottle of beer from the table. "No, there are not."

"OMG, you're serious," Maggie said as she wiped tears from her eyes.

"Of course I'm serious," Leo said, with a frown.

Maggie's expression snapped to serious, and her nose wrinkled at the detail. "There's a river of blood running under Rosemont?"

Leo slouched down, kicking his feet onto the table. "That's what they say."

"Okay, say we believe you," Piper said, holding a hand up as she sloshed her wine in her glass. "Why would we want to find it?"

Leo flicked his eyebrows up. "Because the lost river of Rosemont contains the first clue to finding the biggest cache of Confederate gold ever hidden."

"What?" Maggie said, with an incredulous expression as Charlie said, "Come on, mate."

"Really, do you expect us to believe that?" Henry asked.

Emma shrugged her shoulders. "Why would there be a clue in Rosemont?"

Leo shook his head. "I really do not understand how you have managed to find three different lost treasures when you do not believe anything anyone says. Why wouldn't there be a clue to the treasure here? For what reason would there not be a clue?"

"Because it's Rosemont," Maggie answered. "Don't get me wrong, I love Rosemont. But it's not exactly the hub of…well, anything. Certainly not the hub of the south."

"Or the north," Emma added.

"Right!" Maggie said, jabbing a finger at the strawberry blonde across from her.

"Which makes it a perfect place to hide a clue about Confederate gold. Who would look here?"

"He has a point," Maggie said as she pulled her phone from her pocket.

"Don't tell me you believe this story," Henry groused before sipping at his beer.

"Doesn't hurt to check it out," she answered, tapping around on her phone.

"Okay, say we buy into this river of blood stuff and the whole Confederate gold thing," Piper said. "Where is this place?"

Leo bit his lower lip as he raised a shoulder. "That's the point of this little game, isn't it?"

"So, the challenge is that we need to find the Rosemont River of Blood?" Charlie inquired.

"To start with," Leo said.

"The real challenge is to find the Confederate gold," Tarik responded.

Leo pointed a finger gun at him. "Bingo."

"If it even exists," Henry retorted.

"There's a *ton* of information on this, apparently," Maggie said as she scrolled through her phone.

Leo raised his eyebrows, taking another swig of his beer.

"Really?" Emma asked, climbing over Piper and Charlie to peer over Maggie's shoulder.

Maggie shifted the phone to allow her to view what she'd found.

Piper pulled her legs under her and set her wine glass on the coffee table. "All right, well, if you expect us to find this, you've got to give us more of a clue, dude. I mean, we're super smart and all secret-agent-y and stuff, but we need more to go on."

Leo rolled his eyes. "You found a Viking treasure based on a story and a carving. Are you serious?"

"Exactly, mate," Charlie said. "A story. Where's the story? You just plopped a random idea down. Hey, there's a secret river, but what led to the fact? You gotta provide details, man."

"Yeah, Oscar. This is weak. Entertain us."

"Tantalize us," Charlie said.

"Ti–" Henry began.

"Don't say it. I do not want to hear that word from you, thanks," Leo said, waving his bottle toward Henry.

Henry screwed up his face. "It literally means–"

"I don't care what it means, it sounds gross. Especially from you."

Maggie shot Henry a glance and shrugged. "He hates that word. It's like his version of 'moist.'"

Charlie tugged his lips into a grimace. "Ugh, please don't say it, chicky. That word is just nasty."

Emma's features scrunched. "Really?"

"There is an entire camp of people who hate the m-word," Piper said, with a nod.

"Whatever, that's neither here nor there. Please, continue," Maggie said, returning her attention to Leo.

He wiggled his eyebrows, his gaze stuck on Maggie for a moment as his lips curled up at the edges. "All right. Since you asked so nicely. I'll tell you what I know."

Leo glanced around at all of them, a grin broadening on his lips. "Settle in, kids. Dim the lights. Grab your popcorn and your drinks, because I'm going to tell you the tale of Thomas Tilton and the Confederate gold."

"What the hell kind of intro is that?" Henry groused. "'Grab your popcorn?'"

"I was into the popcorn aspect. Anyone want some?" Piper asked.

Maggie climbed to her feet. "Oh, yes. Wait, don't say anything yet. We need snacks. We need the lights down. We need atmosphere. Charlie, build a fire!"

"It's a gas fireplace. I just have to use the remote."

"Then use it! Piper and I will make the popcorn. Emma, get the lights. Tarik, just relax. Henry…don't antagonize him while we're gone."

Maggie pulled Piper to her feet and dragged her to the kitchen. They returned a few minutes later with a large bowl of popcorn. Piper killed the lights, leaving only the flickering flames from the fireplace for light. Maggie set the snack on the coffee table before she plopped onto the cushion on the floor.

She tugged a flashlight from her pocket and handed it over to Leo. "Here, use this for dramatic flair."

Henry clicked his tongue and rolled his eyes.

With a smirk, Leo grabbed it from Maggie and flipped it on. He held it under his chin and leaned forward. Maggie grabbed a handful of popcorn, tossing a piece into her mouth as her lips curled up, and waited for the tale.

Lit from below, Leo's features gave an ominous vibe as he lowered his voice to a gravelly growl. "Centuries ago…"

"Wait, stop," Henry said, with a wave of his hand. "I know I'm not American, but even I know the Civil War wasn't *centuries* ago."

"Henry!" Maggie scolded.

"He has a point," Emma said. "I mean, the *start* of the Civil War was only one hundred and sixty-one years ago. Not even two centuries."

Maggie scoffed. "Way to nitpick! Let the man tell his story."

"Fine, fine, fine," Leo said, lowering his voice again. "One hundred and fifty-some years ago, a young Confederate soldier named Thomas Tilton was tasked with moving the largest shipment of Confederate gold from the war-ravaged South."

"From what city?" Henry asked as Leo paused.

"I don't know."

"What state?" Charlie questioned.

"I don't know!"

"Come on, Oscar, what kind of story is this?" Piper said with a scoff before grabbing a handful of popcorn.

"One I heard a hundred years ago and didn't think I'd have to memorize every detail of, okay?"

"An actual hundred years, my friend, or no? Maybe you were alive when it happened," Tarik said, with a loud laugh.

The group chuckled as Leo's arm dropped toward the floor, and he shook his head. "You guys are all idiots."

"Oh, come on, that was funny," Maggie said, patting Tarik on the arm. "Keep going."

"Wait," Emma said, waving a hand in the air, "why was this young soldier tasked with this instead of someone more senior?"

Leo waved the flashlight at her. "Great question. And that's where the story gets interesting."

He flicked the flashlight under his chin again. "You see, Thomas's regiment was trapped and taking heavy fire. As bombs exploded all around them–"

"Bombs? Did they have bombs like that in the Civil War?" Charlie asked.

"Will everyone please stop interrupting me?" Leo asked. "Obviously, there was artillery of some kind, and it was exploding everywhere, okay? It doesn't matter what kind of bombs they had. They were in dire straits. And Thomas's commanding officer was tasked with taking a small team of men and removing the gold in an ironclad."

"What's an ironclad?" Tarik asked.

"Ships with a protective outer armor, usually of iron or steel," Emma answered, and Tarik nodded his thanks.

"I thought you said Thomas was tasked with it? Now it's Thomas's commanding officer," Henry said.

Leo continued. "I was getting to that. Thomas's commanding officer had the gold loaded…then took a bullet straight to the brain." Leo pointed a finger at his temple.

"Leaving young Thomas to transport the gold," Maggie said.

"Bingo," Leo answered, waving the flashlight at her.

"Where was the ironclad headed?" Henry asked.

"And how did it get to Rosemont?" Emma added. "There's no way one of those could have made it up the Rose River."

"It didn't. The ironclad docked somewhere, but no one knows where. The gold was unloaded and hidden, with a trail of clues leading to its location. The first clue is right here in Rosemont's bloody hidden river."

Piper crossed her arms. "How do we know that's true?"

"Because Thomas himself told the tale about it on his deathbed." Leo arched an eyebrow at the detail.

"Did he die here in Rosemont?" she questioned, leaning forward, with her jaw hanging open.

"He did. He's buried in the old cemetery on the hill."

"Rose Fields?" Maggie asked.

"That's the one," Leo answered. "He wandered into town, bloodied and battered. In his final breaths, he imparted the knowledge to a young boy. And then he died."

"What did he tell the boy?" Charlie asked.

"That he'd seen a river of blood flowing through the heart of the city. It reminded him of the bloody massacre he'd endured that had robbed him of most of his friends. So, he'd hidden the first clue to the gold there. The war had cost the country greatly. He'd lost brothers, cousins, and friends. 'When the time is right,' he told the boy, 'you can search for it. When the country is healed.'"

"How old was the kid?" Henry asked. "Are we talking someone who could have messed up the details or old enough to get most things correct?"

"Twelve," Leo answered.

"Do we know who the child is? Is there any information we can learn by seeking him out?" Tarik questioned.

Leo nodded. "Yep. William Hamilton."

A knowing expression crossed Maggie's face as realization dawned on her. "Your ancestor. Thomas Tilton told the tale to your ancestor."

Leo settled back into the cushions behind him, with a satisfied smile. "And that story has been passed down through generation after generation."

"And no one found this river? None of your ancestors ever looked for it?" Piper asked.

"No."

"Maybe just a fun family tale to pass the time?" Henry suggested.

"It's not," Leo answered, annoyance creeping into his

voice as he let the flashlight flop onto the cushion next to him.

"Says you," Henry retorted.

"Well, there's some urban legend about this on the Internet," Maggie said, waving her phone in the air. "So, people know about it."

Henry waved a dismissive hand in the air. "Yeah, from his family spreading the tale. That doesn't make it true. The fact that no one's found it despite the stories makes it even less likely it exists."

"Oh, come on," Maggie said.

"Yeah, Mr. I-found-Cleopatra's-tomb-with-a-scarab-that-no-one-thought-existed." Leo bobbled his head around as he frowned at Henry.

"Ollie would believe you, I'd wager," Charlie said, with a nod.

"Well, I do have proof it's true."

"Proof?" Henry questioned.

"Proof," Leo said.

"All right, mate. Let's see the proof."

Leo offered them a broad grin. "Who's up for a field trip?"

CHAPTER 5

Maggie palmed her keys before darting out into the hall. "Okay, ready. Who's in my car? Did you figure out carpools?"

Henry followed behind her as she hurried toward the elevator bank. "You, me, Piper, and Charlie. Leo's taking Tarik and Emma."

"Perfect," Maggie said as she jabbed at the elevator button.

Leo grinned at her. "You remember the way, don't you, Mags?"

"To your parents' house? Yeah, of course."

Emma flicked her gaze between the two of them before fluttering her eyelashes. "What?" Maggie questioned. "It hasn't been *that* long, and I was there a lot."

"And you know the passcode is-"

"One-one-zero-seven, yep," Maggie answered as the elevator doors whooshed open. She hurried inside, pressing herself against the back wall as the others piled into the car.

Emma sidled next to her. "You still remember the code to his parents' gate?"

"Yeah, of course. Don't worry, you'll remember it after a

few holidays," Maggie said with a wave of her hand as the elevator doors slid open to reveal the lobby of her apartment building.

They crossed the large art-deco-themed lobby and headed to their vehicles, making the short trip to Leo's parents' home on the outskirts of Rosemont. Maggie eased her car to a stop outside their electronic gate as Leo's car wound up the long driveway ahead of them toward the stately home. She tapped in the code, and the gates swung open.

"It sort of bothers me that you still know the code to his parents' gate," Henry said, with a wrinkled nose.

"What's the big deal? We dated for a really long time. I was here a lot," Maggie said with a shrug as she passed through the gates and sped up the long drive.

She pulled next to Leo's car as he, Emma, and Tarik climbed out and tugged on her emergency brake after throwing the shifter into park. "Let's go!"

"Wow, you're excited, Boss Lady."

"I want to see the proof! Come on, this could be a great discovery!"

Henry popped his door open. "I wish we didn't need Mr. Ego for it."

"He's not a bad addition to the team," Maggie said as they climbed the stone steps leading up to the white double doors.

"Addition to the team?" Henry questioned, stopping on the second step and staring up at Maggie. "We're not going that far, are we?"

"He did save our necks in Scotland with those driving skills."

Henry shook his head. "Fine, we'll call him when we need a driver. No, wait, I'm a fantastic driver. We don't need him."

Maggie rolled her eyes. "He's not that bad. Come on." She

grabbed Henry's hand, tugging him into the house after Piper and Charlie, who waited in the oversized foyer.

"Leo!" she called into the darkened house.

"Back here! In the study!" his voice answered from the back of the house.

"This way," she said, leading them toward a back doorway tucked behind a grand staircase.

"Shouldn't we keep it down with all the shouting?" Piper questioned as they stepped into a large library-style study.

"Yeah, really, Maggie," Emma answered, "you'll have the whole house up with your screeching."

"His parents are in London," Maggie said as Leo said, "My parents are in London."

Emma glanced between them again before her gaze settled on Maggie. "Why would you know that?"

Maggie wrinkled her nose. "Huh? Must have come up in conversation earlier. Anyway, where's this proof?"

"Right here," Leo said, lifting a painting from a back wall and setting it aside to reveal a wall safe.

He spun the dial back and forth before he twisted the handle and tugged open the safe. After a minute of rooting around through the contents inside, he removed a small wooden box. With the safe closed, he wandered to the oversized desk and set the antique trinket box down in the middle.

He scanned their faces as his fingertips traced the outline of the box. "I give you proof." With a flick of his wrist, he spun the box to face them and opened it.

Blue velvet lined the interior. Inside, a gold coin stood out against the dark color. Emma's eyes widened as she stared down at it. "Oh, my gosh! Is that what I think it is?"

"Yep,"

"What is it?" Maggie asked. "Is it a special coin?"

Emma snorted a laugh. "Special isn't the word." She glanced up at Leo. "May I?"

"Have at it."

Emma reached toward it before she pulled her hand back. "Oh, do you have gloves or something?"

"Ahhh…" Leo swiped a tissue from the box on the corner of the desk. "Here, use this."

"Thanks," Emma said, with a nod. She carefully wrapped the coin in the thin paper and lifted it.

Maggie peered over her shoulder. "What, Emma? What's so special about it?"

"That," Leo said, jabbing a finger at the object Emma held, "is a very rare, very old Confederate coin."

Piper peered at it, lifting her chin. "Like made from the gold they hid?"

"Yep," Leo said, shoving his hands in his pockets as Emma studied the coin.

"Is it real, Emma?" Maggie asked, studying her friend's face. "Can you tell?"

Emma shrugged. "I have no reason to suspect it's not. But I couldn't tell without extensive testing."

"Bite it," Maggie said.

"What?"

"Bite it."

"That's not how you check if gold is real, Maggie. They only do that in movies."

"It works every time there."

Emma shot her an unimpressed glance before she returned to studying the coin, pulling it closer to her eyes.

"All right, under the working assumption this is real," Piper said, "we have proof that somehow Oscar's ancestor had contact with someone who had Confederate gold."

Charlie poked a finger at Emma. "Right, and the Confederate dude hid a clue in some unknown underground river right here in Rosemont."

"Which no one knows how to access or find," Henry said.

"And has become the stuff of urban legend," Tarik said.

Maggie raised her eyes to Leo. "Challenge accepted." She grabbed the gold coin from Emma. "Mind if we keep this?"

Leo offered her the box, and she dumped it inside. "All right, team, let's divvy this up. Charlie, Piper, Henry, and Tarik, check the urban legends, maps, etcetera, and see what leads you come up with. Emma, Leo, and I will work the Hamilton angle. Check out anything we can about his ancestor."

"Wait, are we seriously searching for this?" Henry questioned.

"You asked for a challenge!" Leo shouted, flinging his hands out.

"Technically, boss lady asked for the challenge. We were cool playing Clue."

"Are you guys serious?" Maggie asked.

Leo crossed his arms. "Yeah, I'm with Maggie on this one. Now that I've told you the story, I kind of feel like you owe it to me."

"Of course you do, mate," Henry said.

"What's that supposed to mean?" Leo questioned.

"I don't feel like we owe it to you, sourpuss, but I'm sufficiently intrigued," Charlie said.

"I must admit to having a twinge of curiosity," Emma added.

"I'm down for whatever," Piper said, with a shrug. "If my good sir is intrigued, then color me titillated."

Henry waved his hands in the air as Leo offered a satisfied smirk. "I thought we weren't allowed to use the t-word?"

Leo smirked at him. "It sounded better from her than you."

Maggie's phone chimed, and she tugged it from her pocket and swiped it open. She flicked up her eyebrows, the corners of her lips turning upward. "Intrigued or not, buckle in, because this is now official business of the United States of America." She flashed the phone toward the others, revealing the message from FBI director Frank Thomas greenlighting their operation to search for the Confederate gold.

Henry grabbed the phone and tugged it closer to him. "You're kidding?"

"Nope. Looks like we're back, baby!" Maggie said, with a fist pump. "All right, so like I said: Charlie and Piper, run down urban legend on the web. Piper, help him sort fact from fiction. Tarik and Henry run down leads on the locations. Maybe check old city maps. Uncle Ollie can probably help. I'll text him. Emma, Leo, and I will follow up on the Hamilton side of things. We'll check out the Confederate's grave, too."

"I'll get started as soon as we get back to the apartment," Charlie said. "I'll get a crawler running to find anything on the web, and we'll start sorting it in the morning."

"Sounds good."

"Ah, I guess Tarik and I will check maps tomorrow morning and connect with Ollie," Henry said.

"Perfect. Emma, Leo, how about coffee tomorrow morning, and then a trip to the cemetery?"

"Wait a second, I want to go to the cemetery, too," Piper said.

"Okay, that's fine. Tomorrow morning around ten good for everyone? We'll meet at Cafe au Lait."

"Why don't we all go? Tarik and I won't be able to get access to any maps tomorrow anyway," Henry said.

"Field trip, then," Maggie said. "Tomorrow at ten."

* * *

The lace curtains did little to veil the bright sun that shone through the windows of Maggie's bedroom window early the next morning. Her eyes popped open, and she groaned as she stared at the clock.

"I hate mornings."

She let her head thud back to the pillow before she opened her eyes to slits. She turned sideways toward the wooden box on her nightstand. With a deep inhale, she tugged it onto her chest and popped it open.

The gold of the coin glinted in the morning sun. Maggie pinched it between her thumb and forefinger and studied it.

"Where are your friends?" she asked it. "Time to find out," she whispered before dropping it back into its box and swinging her legs over the side of the bed. "After coffee, of course."

She padded into her kitchen and made a fresh mug of coffee, sipping at it as she returned to her bedroom to dress for the day. After grabbing her purse, she strode to the door and pulled it open, finding Piper and Charlie emerging from the apartment next door.

"Hey, Boss Lady, I thought you'd be late," Piper said as she slid her pink shades on before poking at the elevator call button.

"When am I ever late?" Maggie asked.

Charlie opened his mouth to answer when the elevator doors whooshed open in front of them.

"Never mind," Maggie said as she strode into the elevator. "Let's go."

"I can't believe you're this cheery before your morning coffee," Piper said as she strode into the car behind Maggie.

"I had coffee, that's why."

"You had coffee before your coffee, chicky?" Charlie asked as they descended to the lobby below.

"I did," Maggie said as she dug through her purse for her keys. "Ugh, I can't find my stupid keys. They must be buried."

Charlie dangled a set of keys in front of her. "Never fear, Charlie's got his keys. You can ride with us."

"Please tell me you don't drive like Henry."

"No, chicky. I have only ever driven at breakneck speeds once. And it was the time Henry and I–"

"Had to be evac-ed in a helo, I remember," Maggie said with a nod as they strode across the lobby and into the bright sunshine outside.

"Hey, speaking of," Piper said, popping the passenger door open on Charlie's crossover, "when's the big day?"

Maggie plopped into the back seat and tugged on her seatbelt. "Huh?"

"Wedding day, chicky," Charlie said, flashing her a glance through his rearview mirror before he eased the car from the parking space.

Maggie crinkled her nose and glanced out the window. "Oh, that. Not sure."

"Oh, that?" Piper asked, spinning around in her seat to face Maggie. "*That's* what you refer to your upcoming nuptials as?"

"What else do you want me to call them?"

Piper's eyes darted from side to side. "Ah, I mean not…*that*. Sounds like a colonoscopy."

"Ew," Maggie said, screwing up her face. "Okay, fine. I don't know when the wedding is. I haven't picked a date yet."

Charlie eased the car to a stop at a red light and flicked on his turn signal. "Bit of cold feet, eh?"

"No," Maggie retorted. "What's the big deal? I haven't picked a date, okay? It's not a crime. We don't all have to get married in two seconds, like you two did."

Maggie crossed her arms over her chest and slammed herself back into the seat behind her, a frown forming on her lips.

"Oh, someone's touchy," Piper said, swiveling to face front.

"I am not touchy. I'm just saying I don't know why everyone has to rush me."

"I'm just saying this isn't like you. I'm surprised you didn't have a hall already rented, Boss Lady."

"And I'm saying maybe you aren't quite so sure," Charlie added, reaching over to grab Piper's hand as they pulled onto another street. "I mean, I did not hesitate when it came to marrying my lady."

Piper grinned at him before leaning over to kiss his cheek.

"Great for you. Some of us like to plan."

"So start planning," Piper said.

"Can we just drop this? We've got a case. And it's important."

Charlie and Piper shared a glance before they shrugged at each other.

"What was that?" Maggie questioned.

"I invited Ollie this morning. Hope that's okay," Charlie said.

Maggie waved a finger in the air between them. "No, wait a minute. Why did you two look at each other like that?"

"What?" Charlie asked, his eyebrows shooting up.

"I don't know what you're talking about. We had no such look," Piper answered.

Maggie huffed, slamming back into the seat again. "I should have driven myself."

Charlie eased the car to a stop at another red light. "Anyway, I invited Ollie. I think he'll be of great help in sorting through the bevy of information I've already managed to find."

"Really?" Maggie asked, perking up at the conversation. "Anything promising?"

"A few interesting things," Charlie answered, turning into the coffee shop's parking lot and pulling into a parking space. "If you don't mind, I'll wait to enlighten you when everyone's here."

Maggie unbuckled her seat belt and threw open the door. "Leo's already here."

She hurried to the patio seating, where he waited for them. A grin formed on his face as he spotted Maggie hurrying toward him. He stood to greet her.

"Mags, I'm glad you're…" His voice trailed off and the smile faded from his face as Charlie and Piper strolled up behind her. "Here," he finished, with a note of dejection in his voice.

"Nice to see you, too, Oscar."

"You all came together?"

Charlie dragged an extra chair over to the table for Ollie. "Well, we live in the same building, mate. It just makes sense. Besides, then we can get all the latest wedding gossip."

"Wedding gossip?" Leo questioned as he eased into his seat.

"Dates and the like," Charlie said, plopping into a chair next to Piper and pulling his laptop from his backpack.

Leo shot Maggie a surprised glance. "You set a date?"

"I–" Maggie's eyes grew wide and she glanced around the patio when three figures approaching caught her eye. "Henry, Tarik, and Uncle Ollie are here. Oh good."

Maggie leapt from her seat and hurried over to pull Ollie into an embrace.

"Heard we have a case," the older man said as he sat down at the table.

"We do. Exciting!" Maggie said, waving her fists in the air. "Can I get everyone coffee?"

"Aren't we waiting for Emma?" Henry asked.

"Oh, I'll just order her a coffee. I know what she drinks," Maggie said, with a wave.

She darted into the shop to place the order, returning with two carriers laden with hot and iced coffees and distributing them as Emma joined them.

"I already got you a coffee, just the way you like it," Maggie said.

Emma flicked her eyebrows up over sunglasses. "Wow. Maggie Edwards arriving first to a meeting?"

"Technically, I was first," Leo said.

"And she was early because she came with us," Piper said, before sipping her iced latte.

"Okay, who cares?" Maggie said, waving the comment away as she opened her to-go lid. "What did you come up with?"

"Calm down, chicky. Let me get a sip of my coffee. I haven't had any, unlike you."

"Well, sip it! Let's go!" Maggie said, snapping her fingers.

"All right, all right," Charlie said, slurping a sip of his coffee as he tugged open his laptop. "My little web crawler found loads of information about this mysterious river, ranging from complete and total nut-job ideas to actual information that could be useful. We haven't taken a close look at many of these leads, and Ollie, I'll be relying on you for your expertise."

"I know a little of the legends about the river, though I never followed up on it," Ollie said, clasping his hands as he leaned back in the chair.

"Really? You were that close to an urban legend like this and never explored it?" Maggie asked.

"I was searching for Cleopatra's tomb, remember?" he answered, with a chuckle.

Henry sipped at his coffee. "Well, it looks like you'll make up for that now, Ollie."

"So, should we just divvy up what your program found and start ruling things out and listing possibilities?" Emma asked.

"We may need to do that, yeah. At a glance, there are several redundancies in what's been picked up. But I thought we could start with one very interesting lead I happened to spy in the output this morning."

Maggie sat up straighter, her eyebrows raising. "What is it?"

"There was a bit of chatter a while back, when a certain building project was being completed in the early two thousands. Strange things happening and all that. And the legend of the second river reared its head. Nothing much came of it, and the building project was completed. Then the whole thing died down."

"What building project?" Maggie asked.

"What was the chatter?" Ollie inquired.

Charlie pointed a finger at Ollie. "I'll answer him first and save the most delectable part for last." He pulled up a window on his laptop and read a few snippets.

"Air coming from nowhere. Odd, unexplained sinking at the building site. The sound of rushing water."

"The article claims it was all explainable," Piper chimed in. "The cement was subgrade and when repaired was fine. The air came from a leaky pipe. The sound of water was a sewage leak."

"Right," Charlie said, "but of course, some people insisted it was all a cover-up for the location of the lost river."

"Sounds like a promising lead," Maggie said, with a grin. "Where is it?"

"Wait a minute. If it's all explainable, it's not *that* promising," Emma replied.

"The thing is," Piper answered, "people said none of those explanations added up. Like the people who poured the concrete said it wasn't subpar."

"What else are they going to say?" Leo chimed in.

"The air came from a pipe that didn't exist, according to city plans," Piper said.

"An oversight on the drawing, maybe," Henry answered.

Piper raised her eyebrows and settled her arms on the table, glancing at all of them. "There was no sewage leak on the day the water was heard."

Maggie tapped her hand on the table. "The plot thickens. Okay, so where are we checking first?"

Charlie tapped around on his laptop, a brash expression forming on his features. He spun it around for everyone to see. They all leaned in to look at the picture of the finished building.

Maggie's jaw dropped open, and she flicked her gaze to Charlie. "Rosemont Terrace?"

Charlie settled back in his chair, the smug smile still on his face. "That's right, chicky. None other than our home."

CHAPTER 6

Maggie stared in disbelief at the image on the screen. The sun lit the windows of her Art Deco-style building, pictured shortly after it had been restored and opened.

"So, there's a rumor the hidden river is what? Under our building?"

Charlie pointed a finger at her. "One hundred points for the smart, chicky."

"Actually, there are a lot of rumors about that building," Piper said, swinging the laptop to face her and clicking around.

Emma sipped at her coffee. "Such as?"

"Hauntings, satanic rituals, the whole nine. The river of blood supposedly running underneath it only adds to that."

"So, why do they think it's under that building outside of the odd coincidences?" Henry asked.

"That's a great question," Charlie said. "And I've only got limited knowledge to answer at the moment, but–"

"The placement is correct, from what little I know of the stories," Ollie finished for him.

Emma shot him a glance. "Sounds like you know more than a little to make that statement, Ollie."

"Well, you live long enough that you start to know more than a little about everything," Ollie answered, with a chuckle, "but I believe Thomas Tilton was found on the brink of death very near to the spot that building would be erected on. He was two streets over from what was then the edge of town."

"That's right," Leo said, with a nod. "At that time, the town stopped at what's now Fletcher Street."

"And," Ollie continued, "he was found just outside the old brewery that used to be on Vine Boulevard. You know, in all these years, I have never put two and two together and realized you were descended from the Hamilton who stumbled on Thomas."

"That's weak, Ollie," Charlie said, with a wink. "You could have solved this years ago."

Ollie snapped his fingers and sighed. "I suppose if I hadn't wasted all that time with the greatest archeological discovery of the modern world."

After a round of chuckles, Maggie refocused the conversation. "Okay, so let's suppose this is true, and the river is accessible from our building. We need to start searching for a way to enter."

"Likely in the basement," Henry said.

Leo wiggled his eyebrows, feigning surprise. "Wow, very astute, Indiana Jones. The underground river is…underground."

"We likely must find a hidden entrance, unless they left an accessibility panel to it when they updated the building," Tarik answered.

Henry waved a finger in Tarik's direction. "He's got a point. No one knew this existed, so why would there be access from the building?"

"Maybe they did know it existed." Emma narrowed her eyes, staring into space.

"What makes you say that?" Maggie asked.

Emma shrugged as she sipped at her coffee. "Didn't Piper say something about satanic cults or something?"

Piper glanced at the laptop before she raised her eyes to Emma. "Yeah, totes. The article said something about rumors of satanic rituals in the original building before it was converted to apartments."

Maggie waved a hand in the air. "Those are just rumors. There are rumors of satanic rituals and ghosts all over the town."

"Or it's not. And they knew a river of blood ran under that building. Maybe even accessed it for their rituals. And there is access," Emma posed.

Maggie wrinkled her nose, her lips parting as she considered it. "Ew. That's horrible."

"Horrible or not, it does happen," Ollie said. "And Emma makes an excellent point. It's certainly worth checking into, given the access to the building we have."

"Okay," Maggie said, with a bob of her head. "We should keep other things in play, but I'm game to check it out."

"Doesn't hurt to take a look, I guess," Leo said.

Henry drained the rest of his coffee. "All right. Sounds like a good place to start. Charlie, can you forward us the list of other places in case we need it?"

"Done," he said as their phones chimed in rapid succession around the table. He slammed his laptop closed. "Well, should we have a look-see 'round the old Terrace?"

"Sounds like a fun Saturday afternoon," Tarik answered.

Maggie finished her coffee and slapped a hand on the table. "I'll grab flashlights."

"We can grab a few, too, and meet everyone in the lobby," Piper answered.

"Sounds like a plan!" Ollie answered.

They filtered back to their cars, with Maggie switching to Henry and Tarik's vehicle for the drive back to Rosemont Terrace. She walked into the lobby, scanning it with new eyes. Had there been satanic cults meeting in the basement? Did a river of blood run underneath?

She stared down at the shiny tile floor, arching an eyebrow before she grabbed Piper's arm and tugged her toward the elevators. "We'll run up for the flashlights."

"I'll come with you," Henry offered.

Maggie poked the call button for the elevator and waved a hand in the air. "Oh, I've got it."

"I'm not really doing anything, Princess."

The doors whooshed open before Maggie could answer, and the trio stepped inside. Piper pressed the button for their floor, and the rest of the group slid away from their view as the doors closed. The elevator started its slow journey upward.

"I've got two or three flashlights, I think," Maggie said, shifting her weight from one foot to another as Henry slid his arm around her.

"We've got tons. I'll grab four more," Piper answered, flitting out of the elevators and heading straight to her door.

Maggie stepped to the next door down and slid her key into the lock, pushing inside and leaving the door hanging open as Henry stepped in behind her.

"I'll just be a minute," she called over her shoulder as she tugged open her junk drawer and rooted around for a flashlight. Her fingers wrapped around the cold metal of a pocket-sized flashlight, and she pulled it out, clicking the button to check its light. "There's one."

She slid it into her pocket and stepped toward the living room. Henry blocked her from moving from the kitchen.

"I'll just be a minute," she repeated.

"Easy, Princess, I'd just like a minute alone."

Maggie screwed up her face and shook her head. "What?"

"A minute. We've been running around all week, and I barely saw you this morning. I just wanted to give you a proper hello."

He laced his arms around her waist and leaned in for a kiss. Maggie squashed her hand across his face. "There's no time for proper hellos. Everyone's waiting on us."

She pulled away from him and headed for the living room, searching a few drawers for another flashlight. She groaned, blowing a lock of hair from her face as she scanned the space, trying to remember where she'd put the large flashlight she kept there.

"Maggie, can we talk?"

She pressed a palm to her forehead. "Have you seen the flashlight I normally keep in here? Do you remember if I put it somewhere else?"

"I don't know."

Maggie squashed her lips together before she hurried across the room and tugged open a cupboard. "Here it is! Two down, one to go."

She flitted into her bedroom, pulling open her nightstand drawer. She removed a flashlight and waved it triumphantly. "And three."

She spun and darted across the room. "Come on, let's go."

Henry thrust his arm across the doorway, his muscles rippling as he pressed it against the jamb. "Just a minute."

"What now? Come on, Piper's probably waiting for us."

"We can take a minute."

Maggie knit her brows. "A minute for what?"

"We need to talk."

"About?"

Henry narrowed his eyes at her, tilting his head. "Is there something going on with you?"

Maggie screwed up her face and shook her head. "What? No. What would be going on?"

"I don't know. You're acting strange."

"What?" Maggie said, drawing her chin back to her chest. "No, I'm not."

"Yeah, you are."

"I'm not, Henry. I don't know what you mean." She tried to push past his arm, but he held it firmly against the jamb.

"Come on, Maggie. This past week, we've barely seen each other. You're jumpy. You're avoiding me."

Maggie rolled her eyes, crossing her arms with a huff. "I am *not* avoiding you."

"Yes, you are. You're acting just like you did that night in the desert when you didn't want to admit you had feelings for me. You won't even set a date for the wedding. In fact, you seem determined not to set a date. And to do whatever it takes to avoid doing that."

Maggie let her head fall back between her shoulder blades. "OMG, what is with this wedding date stuff? Will everyone please stop badgering me about it?"

"Is there a reason?"

She flung her hands in the air, then tugged her phone from her pocket. "Fine, fine. Okay. How's…" She tapped around on the screen. "June fifteenth? Is that fine with you? Can I be excused now?"

"Come on, Maggie. What's up with you, huh? Are you having second thoughts?"

"No," Maggie said, casting her gaze at the floor. "I just–"

A knock sounded at the door. Maggie snapped her gaze toward it. "That's probably Piper. We need to go."

"Maggie–" Henry said as she pushed past him and headed across the living room.

"Later, Henry," Maggie said. She shot him a glance as she wrapped her fingers around the door knob. "I promise."

Henry sucked in a breath, running his fingers through his sandy blond hair, jaw flexing.

"Hey," she said as the knock sounded again, "I promise."

"Yeah," Henry said with ice in his voice as he stalked toward the door.

Maggie tugged it open, finding Piper on the other side. "Geez, Boss Lady, what took you so long? I got four flashlights and stood here for five minutes before I wondered if you ditched me."

"I couldn't find one of mine," Maggie said, with a huff. "Come on."

Maggie skirted around her and hurried toward the elevators, tapping the button over and over.

"It won't come any faster if you keep poking it," Henry said as he stopped next to her, with another sigh.

Maggie shot him a narrow-eyed glance. He opened his mouth to speak, snapping it shut as he eyed Piper. Maggie huffed, tapping her foot on the floor until the doors slid open.

"Finally!" she said, tossing her hands in the air as she stormed into the elevator and jabbed the button for the lobby.

"Take it easy, Maggie," Henry said as he stepped inside.

She smacked one of the flashlights into his chest as they descended. "I'll take it easy once I find out if I'm living over a creepy river of blood."

Henry shifted his shoulders, heaving another sigh. Piper's eyebrows squished together as she side-eyed them. The elevator doors opened, and Maggie rushed out to the waiting group.

"Get 'em?" Leo asked.

"Yep," Maggie said, offering a flashlight to him. "Okay, where should we start?"

Ollie rubbed his chin. "We were discussing that while you

were upstairs. There must be access to the basement somewhere. Do any of you know where?"

Maggie raised a finger. "There's a basement button in the elevator." She spun on her heel and raced back to the elevator bank just as Piper and Henry joined them.

She jabbed at the button. "Come on, come on."

The door zipped open, and Maggie raced inside, holding her hand against the cold metal to ensure the elevator did not close. She grinned and waved the others inside.

"Here!" she said, jabbing at the button.

Her smile faded, replaced by a frown as she stared up at the display. She wrinkled her nose. "Insert key?"

"Here," Leo said, rubbing his finger over a keyhole. "You need a key to get the elevator to go to the basement level."

"Ugh," Maggie groaned, her head falling between her shoulder blades. She tugged her head up and snapped her fingers. "Stairs! There must be stairs!"

She hurried from the elevator, leading the others behind her as she scanned the space. An "EMPLOYEES ONLY" door stood in the back corner. Maggie hurried toward it and tugged on it.

"Locked!"

"Can I help you?" a man asked from behind them. They spun to face him. "Oh, Ms. Edwards, hi."

"Hey, Reggie," she said to the middle-aged man. "Yeah, we needed to get to the stairs that lead to the basement."

Reggie crinkled his forehead at the request, adjusting the lapel on the blazer of his uniform. "Basement? Something wrong in one of your apartments?"

"Uh, no, we just wanted to look around."

Reggie shook his head. "We don't let residents down there. There are just too many things you could get hurt on."

"We'll be careful. We have a bet, we just want to see if anything from the original building exists."

"Ah, sorry, Ms. Edwards, I really can't." Reggie pressed his lips together and wrinkled his nose.

Maggie pursed her lips, drawing in a deep breath before she flicked her gaze to him. "No problem, Reg, I understand. Thanks anyway."

"No problem. And if there's anything wrong with your heat or air, just call down, and I'll get it taken care of, okay?"

"Thanks!" Maggie called over her shoulder as she stalked away, waving overhead. She jabbed at the elevator button again.

"What now, chicky? Reggie has effectively rained on our parade," Charlie asked as Reggie skirted past them and returned to his post near the front door.

"We need to regroup and think. We'll head upstairs to my apartment."

"There's got to be another stairwell. Like, what if the elevator breaks or whatever?" Piper asked as they waited for the lift.

"There is," Maggie said as the car dinged and she entered. "But none of them lead to the basement. They end at the ground floor with an emergency exit to the outside."

"Shoot," Leo said as they crowded into the car.

"There's got to be a way. Charlie," Maggie said, poking a finger at him as they rose to their floor, "can you find plans for this building?"

"Chicky, do bears have fur?"

Maggie screwed up her face. "What?"

"Yes, he's saying yes." Emma huffed and rolled her eyes.

"Okay, okay, you don't have to bite my head off."

"Maybe we wouldn't if you weren't so jumpy. We don't have to find this *today*."

"What is wrong with you?" she asked, stamping a foot on the floor. "Why does everyone act like there's something wrong with me because I'm excited about searching for something really interesting? Don't you dig through the sand grain by grain to find teeth or something?"

"I'm not even answering that," Emma said with a disgusted sigh as the doors swooshed open. She stormed from the car and stood in the hall, with her arms crossed.

"Ladies, let's take it down a notch," Ollie suggested.

"I'm not doing anything!" Maggie shouted. "Why is everyone acting like I'm committing a crime?"

"No one's acting like that, Mags," Leo said, clamping his hands on her shoulders and massaging them. Henry drew his chin back to his chest as he eyed the scene, his eyebrows shooting toward his hairline.

"Yes, they are. Okay, fine. Let's just hang out at my place and brainstorm. I'm sure we can figure this out."

"I'll grab my second laptop. Chicky, you up for ordering pizza?"

"On it!" Maggie shouted, waving a hand in the air as she strode to her apartment.

"I like anchovies," Charlie shouted, sliding his key into the lock.

"You do not," Maggie said, with a chuckle.

"Be right over," Charlie said, disappearing through the door.

The remainder of the group followed Maggie into her apartment, taking seats in the living room as Maggie tapped around on her phone, ordering food. She blew out a long breath as she shoved her phone into her pocket and plopped onto the couch.

"Okay, what'd you come up with while I was ordering food?"

The door swung open, then banged shut as Charlie walked in, carrying an open laptop. "I hope you got several pies, chicky. I am starving."

"I got plenty of food. Did you get the plans pulled up?"

Charlie took a seat on the floor next to Piper, who had his laptop open, and perused articles about the river and any connection to their apartment building.

"Of course I did. I pulled them on my way over."

"Seriously?" Emma questioned, her nose wrinkling.

Charlie shot her a surprised glance. "Who do you think you're dealing with here? Charlie Rivers is an expert. Of course I did. A few taps around into the city's database, and voila!" Charlie spun the laptop around, showing plans for the building when it became Rosemont Terrace.

Maggie stared at them, squinting at the blueprints. "Okay, so how can we get into the basement?"

"Don't look at me," Charlie said, the corners of his mouth turning down. "I'm a hacker, not an architect."

Maggie grabbed the laptop and dumped it in Henry's lap. "You're good at stuff like this, right?"

Tarik rose from his seat and peered over Henry's shoulder. "Looks like there is access through ductwork, and the stairway we were blocked from using."

"Is that the only access?" Ollie questioned. "It seems like there should be more than one access point for a basement that large."

Henry squinted at the screen, flicking his fingers around the trackpad before he leaned closer to the screen. "Here," he said.

"Yes," Tarik agreed. "Very good, my friend."

Maggie peered at the screen over Henry's other shoulder. "What'd you find?"

"A stairwell that has access to the basement, along with every floor in the building," Henry said.

Maggie clapped her hands. "Yay! Next stop: the basement!"

"After lunch, of course," Charlie said.

"Of course," Maggie said, with a grin. Henry slid the

laptop onto the coffee table and slipped his arm across the cushion behind Maggie.

She popped from her seat, skirting around the couch and into the kitchen. "What's everyone want to drink?"

"Oh, we've got tons of soda left from the party," Piper said. "You want me to run over and grab some?"

"Oh, do you have an orange?" Emma asked.

"Yep, we've got an orange left. Anyone else? Cherry, orange, root beer, grape, cola?" Piper climbed to her feet, waving a finger over the others in the room.

After they all gave their requests, she hurried from the apartment, shouting for Maggie to grab ice for the soda. Piper returned and unloaded a grocery bag onto the table just as a knock sounded on Maggie's door announcing the delivery of their meal.

They polished off the pizzas in record time. Maggie leapt from her seat, closing the empty boxes and tossing them onto her kitchen counter. She grabbed a flashlight and spun to face them with a grin.

"Okay, let's go."

Emma leaned back in her armchair, slouching down. "Give us a few minutes. I'm stuffed. I can't move."

Maggie raced across the room and tugged at her arm. "Perfect time to get moving. Naps after meals are awful for you."

"I'm with you, Maggie," Leo said as he pushed himself to stand. "If you all are too tired, we can do some scouting and let you know what we find."

Tarik stood and stretched. "I will go."

"I'll go," Henry said with a sigh, climbing to his feet.

Maggie waved him down. "Don't worry about it, babe. If you're too tired, we can go."

"Let's all go. I, for one, do not wish to be robbed of seeing this supposed river under my abode." Charlie pushed himself to stand.

They rose and stretched, arming themselves with flashlights before leaving the apartment. "Okay, where's the stairwell?"

Henry narrowed his eyes, waving a finger in the air at the elevators before he swung it to his left. "This way."

They passed a few other apartments and turned into a new corridor. Maggie spotted the metal door at the end of the hall, and a grin spread across her face. She dashed toward it and shoved it open.

The lights dimmed in the hall, and emergency lighting sprang to life. Red lights whirled, creating an eerie scene as emergency klaxons sounded overhead.

CHAPTER 7

"What is that?" Maggie shouted, wincing as the klaxons continued to sound.

"You pushed open an emergency door! Close it!" Henry shouted.

"What?" Maggie asked, holding her hands over her ears.

Henry grabbed Maggie's arm and tugged her from the doorway, pulling the door shut.

The klaxons overhead still blared as the door clicked closed. Other doors in the hall popped open, and residents glanced out into the hall.

"It's fine, folks, false alarm," Henry said, waving them back.

A radio crackled to life, and a distant voice muttered something unintelligible.

A man raced around the corner a moment later. He slowed to a stop, staring at the group huddled around the door before pulling the radio up to his lips. "Everything's fine, turn the alarm off."

"Hey, Reggie," Maggie said as the sirens finally stopped blaring and flashing red lights stopped.

"What's going on here?"

"Nothing. We were having a spirited debate about whether or not there was a stairway in this building that was connected to an alarm. I firmly believed there was not. Oops." Maggie shoved her hands into her pockets and raised a shoulder, offering him a grin.

Reggie narrowed his eyes and nodded his head. "You wouldn't have been trying to access the basement, would you?"

"Basement?" Maggie asked. "No. I mean, this doesn't go there, right? Just that one stairwell in the lobby."

"That's right," Reggie said, with a nod. "No access to the basement. Not that you need it."

"Nope. We don't," Maggie said, with a smile. "Sorry to have disturbed you."

"No problem. Heading back to your place?"

"Ah, yep," Maggie said, her voice an octave higher than normal. "Theory tested. Nothing else to do but spend a quiet Saturday afternoon playing board games."

"That sounds like an excellent plan, Ms. Edwards," Reggie said as he walked next to her back toward her apartment.

She swung the door open, hovering in the doorway as Reggie walked backward toward the elevators with a wave.

Maggie offered him a smile, masking her annoyance with the pleasant gesture as she waved and retreated into her apartment. The door slammed shut as the last of the group wandered in, and Maggie let out a muffled scream.

"I can't believe we got caught," she lamented.

Emma tossed her flashlight down on the counter. "Well, thanks for the pizza. See everyone around."

Maggie's jaw dropped open. "What? You can't leave. Wait!"

"Maggie, we're getting nowhere. We can't get to the basement. I'm just going to go home to spread out on the couch and read a book."

"Read a book? Are you kidding me? We need to find a way into the basement now more than ever!"

"Now more than ever?" Piper questioned.

Maggie spun to face her. "Do you not find it strange that Reggie lied to us about where that stairway goes? He said it doesn't go to the basement. That's a lie. What is he hiding?"

"Lack of knowledge?" Leo asked. "Maybe he has no idea that it goes to the basement."

"He knows. He lied. For a reason. What's going on down in that basement that they're so interested in hiding?"

"Who are 'they'?" Emma asked, with a wrinkled nose.

"Maggie makes a decent point. This is rather a simple task, but it has been met with resistance at every turn," Ollie pointed out.

"From one person," Emma argued.

"She's right," Henry said.

Maggie scrunched her nose at Henry's assessment.

He swallowed hard, directing his attention back to Ollie. "What are you getting at, Ollie?"

"I'm getting at the fact that Piper mentioned satanic rituals and other wild tales. There's no telling what may be in that basement, but it is growing clearer that someone wants to protect whatever's down there."

"Or they just don't want people to get hurt," Henry contended.

"Maybe," Ollie said, with a tilt of his head. "Or maybe they're hiding something."

"There's only one way to find out," Maggie replied. "And that's to get into that basement. And we're not going to do that if Emma goes home to read a book."

Emma flung her hands in the air, with an incredulous

expression on her face. "Why are you blaming this on me? I hardly think my presence is required."

"Don't you want to see it? What if there are bodies or ghosts or something?" Maggie asked.

"Take pictures? Look, Maggie, I just don't see why this is so vital to find *today*."

"It's not that it's vital, but…" Maggie's voice trailed off as she pouted at the floor.

Henry wrapped an arm around her and squeezed her shoulder. "Maybe we'll take a break, Princess. Spend a little quality time together and come up with another idea."

Emma shrugged and nodded. "Yeah, we'll brainstorm in our downtime and–"

Maggie pulled away from Henry, stalking across the room as she bit her thumbnail. She spun and snapped her fingers. "Charlie, can you disable the alarm on that door?"

"I can try, though sometimes those are–"

"Internal alarms, not controllable through an online system," Henry said.

Maggie flicked her gaze to Henry. "Can you disable it from here?"

Henry raised his eyebrows and glanced over at Tarik. "We'll have to take a look at the mechanism."

Tarik scrunched his eyebrows as he considered it. "Likely triggered by pressure."

"Yeah, I'd figure the same thing. As soon as the weight of the door is off the trigger, it sounds."

"So, you can?" Maggie flicked up her eyebrows.

Henry stuck his hands on his hips and shook his head. "Maggie, I don't know if we should try again right now. What if we get caught again?"

Leo shoved his hands in his pockets, raising his eyebrows as he rocked on his heels. "Indiana Jones, afraid of getting caught?"

"Stuff it, Leo," Henry said.

"Okay, that was uncalled for. It's just a joke."

Henry jabbed a finger at him. "Well, I'm sick of your jokes, mate."

"Well, I'm sick of your attitude, *mate*." Leo took a step closer to him, squaring his shoulders.

"Enough, stop, both of you," Maggie said. "Leo makes a good point. Why are you so nervous about it?"

"Unbelievable," Henry said, raising his hands in the air as he shook his head.

"What's that supposed to mean?" Maggie asked, sticking her hands on her hips.

"Okay, I think it's time for me to go," Emma murmured.

"It means I can't believe you're defending him of all people, Maggie!" Henry flung a hand out toward Leo.

"I can't believe you're backing down from a challenge, Henry," she shouted back.

"I'm just saying we're all over Reggie's radar, and maybe we should cool it for a day or so until things die down before we try again."

"And I'm saying there's no reason to wait," Maggie retorted. "I'm not taking Leo's side. I'm just pointing out that he has a point. You're just mad because I didn't set a date for the wedding fast enough."

"That is odd for you, Maggie," Ollie said, shoving his hands in his pockets as he considered it.

Maggie shot him an icy glance.

"But understandable," he added.

"I guess the date I set earlier didn't suit you, huh?" Maggie huffed.

Henry cocked his head. "You mean June fifteenth?"

"Yep," Maggie said, crossing her arms as heat washed through her.

"I'm just surprised you'd like to get married…on a *Tuesday*."

Leo's brow furrowed. "You set a date?"

"Why would you pick Tuesday?" Emma questioned.

"That's rather an odd day," Charlie said.

"Almost no one chooses this day in Egypt," Tarik answered.

Piper shrugged, her eyebrows shooting up. "Hey, when you know, you know. Charlie and I got married whenever we wanted."

"Thank you, Piper," Maggie said.

"Though *picking* a Tuesday way in advance seems…weird."

Maggie's jaw tightened as she shot Piper an unimpressed stare. "To answer everyone's questions. I had no idea it was a Tuesday, okay?"

"Because you didn't even look," Henry said, running a hand through his hair.

"Because you rushed me! Okay, look," Maggie answered, pressing her index fingers against her temples, "while you guys figure out how to open that door without setting off the alarm, Emma will help me pick a date. Okay, is that a good plan?"

"Why do I have to help you?"

Maggie shot her an incredulous stare. "Are you serious?"

Emma threw out her hands. "It's *your* wedding, Maggie."

Maggie's features scrunched. "I thought you'd be my maid of honor."

Emma poked a finger at her chest. "Me?"

"Of course! Who else would I pick? You're my sorority sister. We've been through hell and back together. Who did I call when I stole that staff from the museum and needed help? You. Who did I get through the bowels of a tomb with?

You. Who did I pick when I wanted to explore the castle? You. Why would this be a surprise?"

Emma's jaw dropped open, and her forehead crinkled. "Okay, first of all, you had no one else to call in Egypt. Second, we got stuck in the tomb together by accident. And third, no one else was awake."

Maggie's lips formed a pout.

"Awkward," Piper sang as she crossed her arms and stared at the floor.

Emma's gaze traveled around the group before she lifted a shoulder. "And fourth, I guess I would be happy to do it if you really want me."

Maggie's lips curved up into a smile, and she flung her arms around Emma.

The surprised woman stumbled forward a step before she returned the embrace. "Okay, let's pick a date while they solve this door problem."

"Have fun," Piper began as Maggie dragged Emma along with her toward the bedroom.

"You're coming, too," Maggie announced, latching on to Piper's arm with her other hand and tugging her along as well.

"What, why?" Piper inquired as she shuffled along behind Maggie.

"You are a bridesmaid. What is with you people? Have you never been to a wedding before?"

"Wait, no, pass," Piper said, grinding to a halt and clinging to the door jamb to stop her forward progress.

"Are you kidding me?" Maggie questioned.

"Yeah, Piper. We're all in this together," Emma answered, with an unimpressed glance.

"I'm *not* wearing one of those ridiculous dresses that Maggie will pick. No way, pass. Charlie and I will be guests."

"Charlie will probably be one of the groomsmen, duh.

Who do you think Henry is going to pick? Leo?" Maggie chuckled at the suggestion before sobering. "Although, he does look good in a tux."

Maggie waved her hands in the air and shook her head. "Never mind. Just get in here." She grabbed hold of Piper and yanked her through the door before she slammed it shut.

"Okay," Emma said, crossing the room and plopping on the bed. She pulled her phone from her pocket and tapped around. "What are we looking at? Next summer or…?"

"Whatever the date, I am *not* wearing any girly fru-fru frilly dress you pick. I demand a say in this," Piper said, collapsing onto the bed next to Emma and peering over her shoulder.

Maggie leaned against the door, forming an amused expression on her face.

"Maggie?" Emma asked, furrowing her brow and glancing up.

"Who cares? I didn't come in here to plan the wedding." Maggie rolled her eyes as she scurried to the French doors across the room.

Emma screwed up her face. "What? Isn't that the exact reason you said we were coming in here? Didn't we just have a major argument about your bridal party and then you insisted we were in it and dragged us in here to plan while the guys figure out something with the door?"

Maggie tugged open the doors, letting in a whoosh of warm air. She glanced over her shoulder at them. "I have no intention of planning the wedding right now. I've got an idea."

"Idea?" Emma questioned.

"On how to get into the basement," Maggie said, with a grin.

"Maggie!" Emma exclaimed. "Are you kidding? The guys are working on that."

Maggie brushed off her comment with a snap of her hand. "The guys, the guys. They aren't the end all, be all, you know. They're probably out there drinking a beer and gabbing."

"Or Henry is killing Leo," Piper offered, drawing her knees up to her chin.

"Right," Maggie said. "Which is the perfect time for us to do some investigating on our own. Who's with me?"

CHAPTER 8

"You can't be serious, Maggie. What are you planning to do? Walk out past them without a word?" Emma rolled her eyes.

"Of course not, don't be ridiculous," Maggie said. "I'm going to climb down from my balcony."

Piper flung herself back onto the bed, covering her face with her hands. "You deal with this. I can't even."

"Are you insane?" Emma said in response.

"No, why does everyone ask me that?"

"Why don't we just tell the guys you have an idea?"

"Have you not been paying attention?" Maggie questioned as she stepped onto the balcony. "It's like they're completely dumbfounded by this or something. I've never seen Henry less motivated than he is right now. I don't get it."

Maggie lifted her leg and clamored up onto the thick stone railing surrounding her oversized balcony.

"Get down from there before you fall and break your neck," Emma said, wandering onto the balcony.

"I'm not going to fall, Emma," she said as she lowered one

foot to stand on the outside of the railing, wedging her shoe between two balustrades.

"Maybe it's your lack of wedding planning that's got him down."

"Don't be ridiculous. Men hate that kind of thing. Henry doesn't want to hear about color schemes and flower arrangements. He thinks all red lipsticks are the same."

"I think he just wants to get married," Emma answered, with a shrug.

"You're being ridiculous," Maggie said as she clung to the railing and glanced over her shoulder to the balcony below.

"I'm not the one clinging to the outside of my balcony and ready to leap to the ground below."

Maggie rolled her eyes and shook her head. "I'm not going to leap to the ground below. I'm going to dangle from my balcony and gracefully land on the balcony below and *then* leap to the ground below."

Emma flung out her hands. "This is ridiculous, Maggie! Let's just go out through your door!"

"No, we're avoiding both the men *and* Reggie. If he sees me, he'll get suspicious right away. Come on, just follow me."

Piper appeared at the door, leaning against the jamb. "I think Henry's got his knickers in a twist over Oscar being involved."

Maggie pointed at Piper. "Yes. Probably. He hates Leo. So, while they argue with each other out there, let's go solve this."

"This is insane. You're going to kill yourself jumping off the–" Emma's words cut off as Maggie lowered herself down and disappeared.

"Maggie!" Emma shouted, racing to the edge of the balcony and leaning over to scan the area below. Piper joined her, slamming into the stone railing, her jaw hanging open.

"I'm fine!" Maggie said with a wave from the second story

balcony below. "It's super easy. Just climb over, lower yourself down, and drop. It's not that far."

"NO!" Emma shouted. "I'm telling."

"Telling? What are we, five? Just climb over. Come on, don't leave me alone in this. What if something happens to me? You'll feel terrible."

Emma squashed her lips together, her features pinching as she stared down at Maggie on the balcony below.

"Come on, it's safe. This balcony is bigger than mine. It's a straight drop."

"Of course, you'd know that," Emma murmured, sticking her foot onto the stone ledge and swinging over it.

"Why wouldn't I know it? It's an obvious choice. Larger balcony or a better view. I obviously weighed that option when I bought here."

"Wait, you're actually doing this?" Piper said to Emma as she clung to the stone railing and glanced over her shoulder.

"I'll die of guilt if something happens to her, so I may as well go for it. Though I'm certain I'll injure myself. I don't have Maggie's luck."

"Dude, this is insane," Piper said, running a hand through her rainbow-colored hair.

Emma lowered herself, grasping the stone balustrades as she let her feet dangle.

Piper leaned over the railing after Emma let go, dropping the short distance to the balcony below and landing neatly.

Emma straightened her bent knees and glanced around. "Wow, that was easy."

"Told ya." Maggie shielded her eyes as she gazed up at Piper. "Come on, Piper. Live a little."

"No way, dude, no way. This is crazy. I'm not jumping off a balcony."

"You're not *jumping*; you're just dropping," Emma said.

"Come on! We both did it. You don't want to be a chicken, do you?"

Piper paced back and forth, her arms crossed tightly over her chest. "This is crazy. Stop peer-pressuring me into jumping off a balcony."

"Piper's a chicken!" Maggie called.

"Fine," Piper said, flinging her arms in the air as she climbed over the railing. "I hate you two. I'm so glad we didn't go to college together, because who knows what would have happened to me."

"You would have been in a sorority," Maggie said.

"Hell no," Piper shouted as she dangled from the balcony above and dropped to the one below. "I hate that stuff."

"You made it!" Maggie said, with a grin. "Just one more to go, and we're all set. And this one is easier. The hedges will break our fall."

Maggie climbed over the railing and dropped into the thick bush below, climbing out and brushing herself off. Emma and Piper followed, with Piper complaining about the sticks that poked her when she landed.

Maggie waved away the comment. "You're fine. Come on!"

"What's this big plan, Maggie?" Emma questioned as they approached the corner of the building.

"You should have asked that three balconies ago, brainy," Piper said.

Maggie peered around the corner before snapping back. "Coast's clear. There's a window about halfway down this side. I'm pretty sure it leads to the basement."

"'Pretty sure?' We jumped off a balcony, and you're only 'pretty sure?'" Emma asked.

"I'm sure."

"Genius moves, Boss Lady, but how are we going to get into said window?"

"It doesn't latch all the way. I saw Reggie talking to someone about it last week. To my knowledge, they haven't fixed it yet. With a little ingenuity, we could unlatch it and slip inside."

"I think we should have waited for the guys to silence the alarm," Emma said.

"Oh, come on. Don't you want to show them that we ladies know how to get things done?"

Emma shrugged. "I mean, maybe without having to break into a window and slide through it into a basement."

Maggie puckered her lips and shook her head. "Never mind. Come on."

She hunched over and half-ran, half-crawled toward a stone sill poking into the manicured strip of grass. Armed with a thick stick wrangled from a nearby bush, she dug her nails into the window's edge and tugged back. The latch caught, but she managed to stick the branch through the opening.

"This is never going to work," Emma said as Maggie wriggled the stick back and forth.

Maggie wrinkled her nose as she fought with the branch. The bark wore off quickly as she slid it back and forth, trying to loosen the latch holding it shut.

"You're going to break it," Emma warned.

Maggie pinched her brows together. "I'm not going to break it."

"Yes, you are. You're going to break it."

"I'm not. Stop badgering me and keep a lookout."

"Piper's the lookout. Just be careful, because you're going to snap it."

"I'm not going to snap–" Maggie began when the twig broke in two, a piece of it falling into the basement and the other popping back toward her. She cursed under her breath, tossing the fragment down on the ground.

"Told you," Emma said with a shrug as she squatted next to the window.

Maggie ripped another, thicker branch from the shrub and pried the window open again. She shoved the new stick inside and continued her work. After a second, the latch fell, and the window whipped back toward them.

"See, told you I could do it," Maggie said with a triumphant grin as she tossed down the branch and dusted off her hands. "Come on."

Emma puckered her lips as she studied the angled opening. "I'm not going to fit through that."

"Yes, you will. Come on. I'll go first." Maggie stuck her legs through the slim opening and shimmied her way down until she dropped to the floor below. "Next!"

"Go ahead, Piper. I'll stay out here and watch."

"Now who's the fraidy cat?" Piper asked, squatting down and sticking her legs through the opening.

"Come on, Emma!" Maggie called from inside the dark basement. "Just stick your legs through. You'll make it."

Emma huffed, her face appearing at the opening. "If I get stuck, I'm going to kill you."

"You won't," Maggie promised. Emma slid her legs into the opening and shimmied. "Besides, you can't kill me. If you're stuck, I'll run away."

"Very funny," Emma grunted as she pushed to shove her hips further.

Maggie grabbed ahold of her legs and tugged. After a minute, she popped through the opening and landed in a heap on the floor.

"Told you you'd make it," Maggie said with a grin, pulling her friend to stand. She raised her eyebrows and bit her lower lip. "Now, let's see what they're hiding down here."

"Did you bring the flashlights?" Emma questioned.

"No," Maggie said, glancing around the dark space. "There's got to be lights, right?"

Emma tossed her hands in the air. "Then why did we get flashlights before we tried to get in here the first time?"

"In case it was dark in some spots. It *is* a basement, duh," Maggie said, with a shake of her head.

"Then why didn't you bring the flashlights?" Piper asked, crossing her arms.

"Just use your phones!" Maggie exclaimed, tugging hers from her pocket and flicking on the flashlight. "Why do you keep finding problems where there aren't any?"

Emma did the same, followed by Piper. "Oh, I don't know. Maybe because we just leapt off your balcony, then squeezed through a window into a creepy basement that may or may not have a river of blood running through it."

Maggie shined her light around. "Exactly. It's supposed to be *fun*. But you two keep raining on my parade."

"Sorry, Boss Lady. I wasn't aware leaping off a building was fun."

"Me neither," Emma answered.

Maggie rolled her eyes at them. "It's fine. We're all fine. Just…spread out and look around, okay?"

Emma held up her hands and pointed her flashlight's beam toward a distant corner. "I'll be over there in the dark corner, searching for a river of blood."

"I'll take that one," Piper said, pointing to the one across from Emma's.

"All right, I'll start over there and work my way across to this corner."

Maggie took a step toward her designated corner when Emma grabbed her arm. "Whatever you do, don't touch anything, okay?"

Maggie settled her features into an unimpressed frown. "Just go search your corner." She tugged away from Emma's grip and stalked to the wall, shining her light over the cement block. Cobwebs glowed as the light swept over them, and spiders scurried to new hiding spots.

"You know," Maggie called as she pushed against the blocks, testing for any weaknesses or triggers, "this isn't a tomb. It's not like I'm going to trigger some kind of trap."

"You don't know that," Emma shouted from her corner.

Maggie rolled her eyes again. "I kinda do. I doubt my building has a giant stone ball waiting to kill us or a collapsing ceiling."

"Don't roll your eyes at me, Maggie," Emma shot back. "And like I said, you don't know that. You're convinced your building is hiding a river of blood. So, who's to say it doesn't have a trap to keep people out?"

"Fine, fine. Maybe there's a deadly trap down here."

"So, stop pressing on things, so you don't trigger it."

"I'm not pressing on things," Maggie retorted, pulling her hand away from the wall.

"You are, too. I can see you. You keep putting your hand all over the wall."

Maggie crinkled her nose and curved her lips into a sneer.

Piper interrupted the conversation, calling from her corner, where she squatted with the light. "Hey, if you two losers want to quit arguing, I may have found something."

"Really?" Maggie questioned, whipping her head in Piper's direction. "What is it?"

"Come see for yourself," Piper said.

Maggie flashed her light toward the opposite corner and hurried toward her kneeling friend. Emma joined her, peering over Piper's shoulder at something on the floor.

"That's kind of weird," Maggie said as she shone her light on the tiles. "The rest of the floor is concrete, but this is tiled."

"Yeah, and it says something weird, too," Piper said, blowing away some dust and sweeping her hand over the tiles to clear more.

Carved letters adorned the red floor, along with a large crest. Maggie shined her beam across it, her forehead pinching. "*Ordo Sanguinis*," she read. "What does that mean?"

"Order of Blood or Order of the Sanguine," Emma murmured as she studied the crest. A red snake wrapped around a skull.

"Order of Blood? Ew, dude, that's nasty," Piper said, straightening and backing a step away.

"But relevant," Maggie answered, taking her place and squatting lower to examine it. "There are more words below the creepy emblem."

She brushed the dust away with her fingers. "*Intra et per ignem emunda*. What's that mean?"

"Probably means 'don't go in there,'" Piper suggested, with a shrug.

"Basically, yes," Emma answered.

Maggie rose to her feet, shining her flashlight in Emma's face. "Seriously? It says don't go in?"

Emma squinted against the beam's bright light and shoved it away. "No. It says, 'Enter and be cleansed by fire.'"

Maggie wrinkled her nose as she flicked the beam back down to the floor tile and grimaced. "Cleansed by fire. Sounds rough. So, how do we get in, do you think?"

"Are you serious, Boss Lady? I don't want to be cleansed by fire."

Maggie waved the comment away, shining her light at the area around the tile. "Oh, I doubt they mean it literally. It's probably just figurative. Like…be prepared to bear your soul. Or get naked. Maybe they met naked."

"Only you would think 'cleansed by fire' means they met naked," Emma said, with a huff. "Piper's got a point."

"Oh, yeah? If you're so uninterested in entering, why are you still searching for a way to enter?" Maggie asked, motioning to Emma's sweeping flashlight beam as she searched the nearby stones.

"I'm not," she said, with a shrug. "I'm just looking around. That's what we were supposed to do."

Piper crossed her arms. "Yeah, we found something. Let's go get whoever's left alive from the guys and bring them down to be cleansed by fire."

"Or," Maggie said, spinning to face them both, "we could get cleansed by fire and tell the guys about our amazing discovery when we're done."

Piper avoided Maggie's gaze, scuffing her foot against a dirty spot on the floor.

Emma wrinkled her nose. "I mean…"

"Come on, Emma. Really? You need Leo to hold your hand?"

"No," she said, with a sour face.

"No. We are capable people. We don't *need* the guys to get cleansed by fire or whatever. Probably just means it's hot inside. Come on, let's figure out how to open this and see if this really leads to a river of blood or not."

Emma shot a glance at Piper, who shrugged. "Okay, fine. Let's find out if this leads anywhere."

"How could it? Is there a trigger somewhere?"

"There must be," Maggie said, squatting down again and shining her light in the corner. "The tile looks like it goes underneath the wall."

"It does," Emma said, joining Maggie and squinting as she traced a finger along the floor.

"But how do we open it?" Maggie murmured, chewing her lower lip.

"Maybe you have to get naked first?" Piper suggested, with a shrug.

Maggie wrinkled her nose and shook her head as she studied the emblem on the floor. "Nah, I doubt that. How would the trigger know?"

"It was a joke, Boss Lady," Piper said, with a sigh. "Just–"

A whooshing noise sounded, and a burst of hot, stale air smacked them in the face. The floor rumbled underneath them as the wall slid away, leaving a black hole gaping in front of them.

CHAPTER 9

"There," Maggie said, dusting her hands off as she rose to stand. "Let's go in."

Emma rose to her feet, an incredulous expression on her face. "Let's go in? Are you crazy? And what did I say about touching things?"

"How'd you open it?" Piper questioned.

"I pushed the emblem where it said ENTER," Maggie answered. "Come on, we didn't open this to stare at it and not do anything."

"Why has no one else found this and gone in?" Emma asked.

"We don't know that. The way Reggie was making sure we didn't get down here, maybe someone else had found it and goes in and out all the time."

"So, why has no one found the gold?"

Maggie lifted her shoulders. "There's only one way to find out if there's a river of blood and if it leads to Confederate gold, and that's to go inside."

Emma stared down at the snake emblem on the floor, blowing out a long breath. "Okay, let's see what's inside."

"Come on!" Piper shouted, flailing her arms. "I was counting on you to be the voice of reason in this."

Emma shrugged as she shined her light into the hole. "I guess I'm curious, and I've been in enough tombs and excavation sites to know how to explore something."

Maggie grinned at her, shooting a coy glance at Piper, with her eyebrows raised.

"Fine," Piper said, slapping her thighs, "fine, yes. By all means, let's go into the scary, sweltering black hole. That won't be a bad idea."

"It'll be fine, Piper," Maggie said. "We're pros."

"Famous last words. You two 'pros' have ended up stuck too many times to count."

Maggie grabbed her hand and tugged her forward. "And the last time we left you behind, you got kidnapped."

"She has a point," Emma said as they inched forward into the black hole.

"We're doing you a favor. At least you won't get kidnapped."

"Makes me feel so much better," Piper murmured as they crossed the threshold into the darkness.

The small amount of light filtering from the basement disappeared as the wall slid shut behind them.

Maggie tugged her lips back in a grimace. "Oops."

"Great, now we're stuck," Piper said.

Emma shined her light around the newly blocked entrance.

"We can't be stuck," Maggie said. "I'm sure there's a way to open it from this side. Besides, we could just call the guys and tell them to open it from their end. It's fine."

Piper toggled on her phone's screen and stared at it before she spun it to face Maggie. "No service, so that's out."

"As much as I hate to admit this, Maggie's probably right. There should be a way out from this side."

Maggie raised her eyebrows and flung her hand toward Emma, plastering a triumphant grin on her face. "See, I told you."

Emma sighed, letting her hands drop to her sides as she slumped against the closed passage. "But I can't find one."

Piper's frown deepened, and she shot an annoyed glance at Maggie.

"It's fine. We'll figure it out. Let's just keep going. There's some kind of red light glowing down there," Maggie said, pointing forward.

Piper scrunched her nose, directing her gaze to the floor. "Yeah, let's walk toward the eerie red light. That'll solve our problems."

"It can't hurt," Emma said. "We didn't survive being stuck in two tombs *and* a castle because we weren't willing to explore."

Maggie grabbed Piper's arm and dragged her along as they inched toward the dim red light glowing at the end of the passage.

"Good for you two. I personally do not like being stuck in tight spaces, okay? I do not want to run away from a giant stone ball or have a ceiling smash me like a bug."

"Shh," Maggie said, hushing Piper. "I hear something."

"I don't hear anything, you're crazy."

"I hear it, too," Emma whispered. She twisted her ear toward the glowing opening.

Piper shook her head at the woman. "I can't believe you keep agreeing with her. This maid of honor thing has really set you back."

"Shhhhhhh," Maggie hissed. "Quiet!"

Silence fell between them as they strained to listen for the noise. Maggie's muscles stiffened as a hot breeze wafted past them. On it floated the sound she'd heard before.

"There!" she whispered, raising her eyebrows at her companions.

"I hear it," Emma said, her brow furrowing. "What is it?"

"I hear it, too," Piper answered. "Sounds like..." She leaned forward, straining to listen.

"Water," they all said at the same time.

Heat washed over Maggie as she straightened, and her skin turned to gooseflesh despite the warm air surrounding them. "Water," she repeated. "Do you think..."

"One way to find out," Emma said, with a tilt of her head.

They continued toward the end of the corridor. The heat grew with every step.

"Ugh, it's getting hotter in here."

"Yeah, it's really stuffy," Maggie said as the passage spilled into a new chamber.

She scrunched her features as she studied the brownstone making up the walls and rising to the arched ceiling. She rubbed her foot against the cobblestone floor. "Where's the water?"

"I still hear it," Emma said. "But I don't see it."

Maggie stared down at her hands bathed in the red light. "No. Just this weird red glow from...somewhere."

"Hey, there's some kind of grating over here," Piper called from a corner of the long, rectangular room.

Maggie and Emma hurried to join her. "There's the red light," Maggie said, poking her finger at it.

"And the heat," Emma added, waving her hands over it.

Maggie dropped to her knees and peered through the small square holes. "I can't see much, but it looks like there's a room down there."

She reached for the grating, sliding her fingers into the openings before she snapped her hand back, shaking it. "Ow!"

"What happened?" Piper asked, her eyes wide.

"It's hot! Like burning hot."

"Let me try with my sleeve," Emma said, sliding her sleeve over her fingers and clumsily trying to raise the grating. She pressed her lips together as her cheeks bulged out from the effort. Her eyes squeezed shut, and she leaned her weight back, trying to dislodge the metal.

"Nope," she said with a grunt, plopping onto her rear. "It's wedged or bolted or something. We're not budging that."

Maggie tilted her head, pressing her ear closer to the grate. "Wow, that's hot. I think the water is down there. Sounds like it anyway."

She righted herself and glanced around the dimly lit space. "There has to be a way down."

"Check this out," Piper called from across the room. Her finger pointed to the faint outline of tiles on the wall.

Emma toggled on her flashlight again and pointed the light at the wall. "Wow."

Maggie's gaze scanned the large mosaic of tiles across the wall, filled with shapes and patterns. "What does it mean?"

Emma's brow crinkled as she ran a hand over one of the protruding tiles. "I don't know. I've never seen symbols like this before."

"So, it's not spelling anything or some kind of ancient language?" Maggie questioned, still studying the wall.

"If it is, I can't read it," Emma answered.

Maggie reached out toward the wall. "Wonder what happens if we–"

"*Don't* push them!" Emma shouted, slapping Maggie's hand away.

"Well, we don't know if they'll do anything, but maybe it'll help us solve this. Clearly, these mean something, and we don't know what that is."

"So let's leave well enough alone," Emma answered.

"I hate to be the Debbie Downer of the group," Piper said,

"but if we leave well enough alone, we'll just die down here of heat stroke or whatever, because in case you've forgotten, we're stuck."

"We're not stuck," Emma said. "We're just…"

"Stuck," Piper finished. "We don't know how to reopen the panel into the basement."

"If we get that desperate, we can figure out how to open it."

Piper crossed her arms, raising her eyebrows. "Really? Cause that hasn't worked so far, brainy."

"Okay, so let's press the buttons and hope that helps. Brilliant solution, *Rainbow Brite*."

"Well, that's low. You know that's the name my kidnappers like to use."

"Well, you keep calling me 'brainy.'"

"That's a compliment."

"All right, enough, ladies!" Maggie shouted, slicing her hands through the air. "Stop arguing. It's not helping."

"Oh, and what does the great Maggie Edwards suggest we do?" Emma said, with an exasperated sigh.

"Stop taking your frustration out on me," Maggie said, returning her gaze to the wall. "Be excited at the find!"

"I'll be more excited once I know the find won't kill me."

"Only one way to find out," Maggie answered. She reached forward and pressed one of the tiles into the wall.

"MAGGIE!" Emma said, slapping in the air a moment too late.

"What? It's fine. We're still alive."

Piper stared at the tiles on the wall. "You're playing a dangerous game, Boss Lady."

"No one else is doing anything. I had to do something."

"Contrary to your belief, you do not always *have* to do something. Sometimes we can just think or look for more clues."

"Okay, Sherlock Holmes, let's look for more clues. Everyone, spread out and start searching."

Maggie toggled on her flashlight and crossed the room, sweeping the beam across the far wall.

"I am really glad we ate before this," Emma mumbled.

"What? Did you say something?" Maggie asked.

"Nope," Emma said, her eyes trained on the tiles.

"She said she's glad you're just the normal snippy version of yourself instead of the hangry one," Piper answered.

"I didn't say that," Emma snapped.

"You did in so many words," Piper answered, squinting at a brick on the wall.

"Did you find something?" Maggie asked.

"No, just a stray mark," Piper answered, moving her beam to another area.

Maggie wrinkled her nose and returned to her own search. "This reminds me of the time we were looking for Marc Antony's burial chamber in Cleopatra's tomb. My hands were so sore."

"And then we got stuck," Emma said.

"And then we found Marc Antony and the Library of Alexandria. Look on the bright side."

"I'll look on the bright side when we're out of here," Emma answered.

"If you two are done sniping at each other, maybe someone can help me," Piper said.

Maggie snapped her head in Piper's direction, her jaw hanging open. "Help you with what? Did you find something?"

"Maybe," Piper said. "I can't tell."

Emma scrunched her eyebrows together and tried to follow Piper's gaze. "What is it? I don't see anything."

Piper tilted her head. "I'm not sure. Someone boost me up on their shoulders."

"Really?" Maggie asked, with a scrunched nose.

"Yes, really. You guys do this all the time. Why are you acting like it's a huge request?"

"Okay, okay," Maggie answered, shoving her phone into her pocket as she closed the distance between her and Piper. She squatted down and patted her shoulders. "Climb up."

Emma grabbed Piper's hand, steadying her as she straddled Maggie's shoulders. Maggie rose to stand, and Piper scanned the floor below.

"Whew, this is easy. You're lighter than Emma."

Emma stuck her hands on her hips. "Thanks, Maggie. You're a pal. You're not exactly light either."

"You should have tried Piper. She's a feather."

"Will you two shut up?" Piper said. "I found something."

"Really?" Maggie questioned, her chin tucking toward her chest as Piper wiggled around on her shoulders.

"Yes, really."

"What is it?" Emma asked, her brow furrowing as she tried to follow Piper's gaze.

"I think it's the password for that wall," Piper said. "It's spelled out in the floor tiles, but it's almost impossible to tell unless you're pretty high up."

"How is it spelled out?"

Emma squatted down, running a hand across one of the cobblestones. "Some of these are darker."

"Yep. The dark ones are spelling something out. If Maggie stops moving around, I'll get a picture of it."

Maggie pursed her lips, shooting a glance up. "Gee, sorry my slight movement while I hold another human being on my shoulders is too much for your photography needs."

"Well, we can't see anything if the picture comes out blurry. Just hold still a minute." The click of the cell phone's camera indicated a picture had been snapped. Piper held the phone up to her face and studied it. "Okay, good enough, I think."

Maggie blew out the breath she'd been holding and lowered down to her knees. Piper hopped off her shoulders.

"What's it look like?" she asked as she climbed to her feet, dusting her pants off.

They crowded around Piper's phone, staring at the picture. Maggie tilted her head, wrinkling her nose. "Wow, that's hard to read."

"I told you you were fidgeting too much. This is the best I could do."

"We'll have to make do and hope we can easily match the symbols on the picture to the ones on the wall," Emma said. She narrowed her eyes at the phone. "The first one looks like an 'S' with hooks on each end."

She flicked her flashlight beam toward the wall, studying it.

"There on the left," Maggie said, pointing to a tile with a similar symbol.

"No, that's only got one hook on the top. This has a hook on the top and bottom," Emma said.

"You're right."

"Good going, Boss Lady. You almost got us killed."

Maggie shot a sour look at her employee. "I did not. We have no idea what happens if we press the wrong ones."

"Probably a giant stone ball will roll down from somewhere and squash us."

"Here it is," Emma said. "I managed to find it while you two were arguing."

Her fingers brushed one of the stone tiles near the bottom of the wall. She bit her lower lip.

"Push it," Maggie said.

"Wait, don't push it," Piper said.

"Push it."

"No, wait!"

"Wait for what? What are we waiting for now? Oh, let me guess, we should wait for the guys to get down here before we push it."

"No," Piper said, with a shake of her head, "but you already pushed one. Maybe we need to toggle that off before we do anything else."

Emma raised her eyebrows, glancing up to the center of the mosaic pattern, where the depressed tile sat. "Hmm, good thinking."

"What if I managed to press one we need to press anyway?" Maggie asked. "We should check that first."

Emma rose to study the tile flush with the wall. "It looks like a number one."

Piper stared at her phone's display, flicking various spots to enlarge and study them. "Like this?"

Emma glanced at the screen, then at the tile. "Yep. Unbelievable. What luck you have."

Maggie crossed her arms and lifted her chin. "That's skill."

"Bull," Emma said. "There no way you could have known that one needed to be pressed."

"Educated guess," Maggie said.

"Okay, okay, let's just push that one and move on," Piper said, slapping the rune into the wall. "The next one looks like a backward three."

Maggie and Emma scanned the tiles in search of the next rune. "Here!" Maggie said, pointing at a tile. Emma and Piper checked, comparing it to the symbol on her phone.

"Yep, that's it," Emma said, with a nod.

Maggie pressed it.

"Two more to go," Piper said. "Next one looks like a weird eight with horns."

"An eight with horns," Maggie murmured as she scanned the tiles in front of her.

"Got it!" Emma said, pointing to a tile. After verifying it, she pressed it in with a long breath. "One more."

"It looks like a…" Piper wrinkled her nose and tilted her head. "Uhhh…like a faucet, maybe, sort of."

Maggie scrunched her face and slid toward Piper, glancing at the screen. "Oh, yeah, like a weird, curvy faucet."

Emma glanced at the picture before they set to work searching the tiles for the odd object. Maggie found it near the top. Her hand hovered over it as she glanced at Emma and Piper.

"Ready?"

"Not really, but go ahead," Piper said.

"Wait," Emma shouted, grasping Maggie's wrist. "What if pressing that is a trap?"

Maggie bit her lower lip, scrunching her forehead. "Why would they put symbols on the floor to trap people?"

"To keep idiots like us out," Emma said. "Because the real members would know the password."

"So, what will happen if we press it?"

"Cleansed by fire," Piper murmured.

"Ohhhhh," Maggie grumbled, as her lips formed a grimace. She shook her head after a moment. "I don't see another choice. We're either going to press it and take our chances or be stuck. I vote press it."

"I vote stuck," Piper said.

All eyes turned to Emma. She swallowed hard and rolled her shoulders back. "Press it."

Before anyone could react, she slapped her hand against the tile, depressing it into the wall. Piper squeezed her eyes shut, bracing herself for whatever came next. Maggie sucked in a breath, a grin playing on her lips as they waited to find out their fate.

CHAPTER 10

"Whoa," Maggie breathed, her heart skipping a beat.

A hissing noise sounded, and a puff of cooler, stale air rustled their hair as a panel slid open, leading down a set of crumbling stone steps.

Maggie playfully slapped Piper's arm. "And you were worried."

"I still am. This looks like a giant stone ball city."

"Come on. There's no stone ball," Maggie said, looping her arm around Piper's and tugging her forward.

"There still could be. Just when we get inside, the door will slide shut, and a stone ball will come out of nowhere."

"Even I think that's far-fetched," Emma said as they stepped inside the door and descended the stairs. "I'm more worried about the stairs giving way than a stone ball."

"I really thought it'd be colder down here since we're going underground, but it is hot," Maggie said, swiping at a bead of sweat that rolled down her face.

"Yeah, it is," Emma agreed, raising her voice. "And the water's definitely louder down here."

Maggie nodded as she pointed toward the glowing red light at the end of the stone corridor. "Sounds like it's coming from there."

They crept forward. The sound of water grew louder with every step. The passage spilled into a wide chamber beyond it.

Maggie stepped through first, her eyes going wide at the sight. In the center of the chamber, a large red river cut through the floor.

"Wow," she whispered as the frothy water roiled past them at a quick clip.

"Well, there's one question answered," Piper said, frowning down at the water.

"Yep," Emma agreed, her eyes trained on the quick-moving liquid. "There is a river of blood underneath your apartment building."

"And it's hot," Maggie said, wiping at her forehead again. "It's like a steam room in here."

Piper twisted away from the wide river, staring at the wall behind them. "Wow," she murmured.

"What?" Emma asked, peeling her eyes from the swirling red water to glance over her shoulder. Her eyes widened as she stared at the wall.

Maggie glanced at them before twisting her neck to eye the wall. "Oh, wow, this is incredible."

She lifted her phone, snapping several pictures of the wall.

"What is it?" Piper asked, pointing to a boxy structure drawn on the wall.

"A Confederate ironclad," Emma murmured as she stared at the drawings.

Piper wrinkled her nose. "What's it doing?"

Maggie studied the image. "Looks like it's sailing up a river."

"But what river?" Emma murmured. "It doesn't say. It shows it at sea, presumably." She pointed to a crude illustration showing the vessel in the water off a coast.

"And then in a river," Maggie said, pointing to another area on the wall showing the ship with banks on both sides of it.

"It couldn't have been far," Emma said. "Ironclads were not the best at sea."

"So, what? They rounded Florida and headed up the Mississippi, do you think?" Maggie inquired as she leaned closer to another portion of the drawing.

"That'd be my best guess," Emma answered, still studying the drawings.

"I'd say this ironclad had the gold on it," Maggie answered. "Check this out." She illuminated a portion of the massive mural with her flashlight. It showed cases of gold bars being carried to the ship.

"Okay," Emma said with a nod as she placed her hands on her hips. "So, they load the gold, then bring it up the Mississippi."

"How did he get to Rosemont? Did they branch off on a tributary or dump the gold somewhere else before they continued north?"

"Maybe they sank the ironclad somewhere in the river," Emma postulated.

"I doubt that," Piper answered.

"Why?"

Piper lifted an arm in response, her finger pointing at something across the room.

Maggie followed the direction she indicated, her eyebrows flicking up. "The story continues."

She raised her camera, focusing it on the far wall and snapping pictures. "It's hard to see these from this distance."

"Yeah, but even so," Emma said, "Piper's right."

"It shows them unloading the ironclad," Piper said. "Clear or not, that much is obvious."

"Where?" Maggie asked.

"I don't know," Emma answered, "but the drawings that follow that do not look American."

Maggie snapped a few more pictures depicting crudely shaped creatures with wide eyes and circular mouths.

"Native American?"

"Those don't look Native American," Emma answered, her eyes still trained on them.

"I've got pictures. Maybe Uncle Ollie will have some idea."

"Yeah, if we get out of here to ask him," Piper said.

"Think positive, Piper," Maggie said, flicking her gaze around the room as she slid her phone into her pocket. "There's got to be a way out."

She wandered to the end of the space, pressing her hands against the stone walls there.

"What's that?" Emma asked.

Maggie shot a glance over her shoulder, finding Emma staring up at the ceiling. "I don't see anything."

Emma shone her light in the air. It glinted off something suspended from the ceiling. Maggie shuffled closer, narrowing her eyes at the object. "What is it?"

"I can't tell. It looks like a box," Emma said.

Maggie tilted her head, staring up at it from another angle. "How do you get to it? It's hanging above the river."

"Is there a switch or something that will move it to us?" Piper asked.

"We can look for one," Maggie said.

"Whatever you do. If you find one, don't touch it," Emma warned.

With a roll of her eyes, Maggie stalked away, searching the chamber for anything that would move the box closer to them. After twenty minutes of searching, they found nothing and regrouped near the box to stare at it.

"Maybe it's on the opposite side of the river," Maggie suggested.

"I don't see anything over there," Emma answered.

"Well, there are a few dark spots not lit up by the glowing river. Maybe it's in there."

Piper stared down at the water racing past them. "How are we going to find out? I'm not wading into it."

"Maybe I can jump across," Maggie said, rubbing her chin.

"Are you crazy?" Emma questioned.

"No," Maggie answered.

"It's pretty wide, Maggie. And there's not a lot of room to get a head start."

"I jumped that big pit in the tomb. I can do it. I'll get a running start from the hall."

Emma heaved a sigh and waved a hand in the air. "Whatever. It's your life."

Maggie passed her phone off to her. "Here, hold my phone just in case."

Emma grabbed the device, still shaking her head. "Don't fall in the river of blood, okay?"

"Obviously," Maggie said, rolling her neck around and stretching her shoulders then her quads. She stalked from the room into the hall, swinging her arms back and forth as she sucked in deep breaths.

She stretched her neck from side to side again before she crouched into a runner's lunge. "Okay, here I go."

She launched off her back foot and raced down the hall, approaching the room at a fast clip. She thundered through the doorway and sprinted toward the stone bank of the river. Her foot hit the rectangular stone making up the edge, and she flung her body in the air, flying across the rushing water and landing hard on the opposite side.

She sucked in a breath, her eyes wide before a laugh escaped her. "Ha! I made it!" She spun to face the women across the river. "I made it!"

"Yay," Piper said, her face a mask of boredom. She whirled a finger in the air.

"Is there anything that will lower that box?"

Maggie scanned the surfaces, running her hand along the darkened corners in search of a trigger to move the box. Her shoulders slumped. "No."

Emma rolled her eyes, slapping her thigh with her hand. "So that was a waste."

"Plus, you're stuck," Piper said.

"What? I'm not stuck," Maggie said, her forehead crinkling.

"You are so. You had to run, like, a mile to make that jump. There's nowhere to run over there."

Maggie grimaced as she realized she had limited space to make the leap. "I'm sure I can make it. Somehow. Anyway, we should focus on getting that box."

"How?" Emma asked.

"I don't know. You're the archaeologist; you figure it out."

"Archaeologist, Maggie. Not expert in how to get boxes from ceilings in underground river chambers."

Maggie spun to study the drawings on her side of the river, tapping her foot against the floor as Emma's last comment rang in her head. "Hey, toss me my phone, and I'll get better pictures of this stuff."

"Seriously?"

Maggie twisted to face Emma. "Yes, toss it." Emma stared at her. "What? I'll catch it."

Emma raised her eyebrows as she stepped toward the edge of the river and swung her arm back. She lobbed the phone over the roiling water to Maggie.

"Told you," Maggie said as she toggled on the camera and

snapped a few more pictures. "Now…how can we get that box?"

"Maybe we can throw a rock at it and knock it down," Piper said.

"It'll likely fall into the river, and then we'll never get it," Emma answered.

Maggie inched toward the edge of the river and stretched her hand in the air. She stood on her tiptoes, reaching for the box.

"Maggie, you can't reach it," Emma said.

"I'm not trying to reach it. Just gauge how far up it is."

"And that helps us how?" Emma questioned.

Maggie flicked her eyebrows up, curling up the corners of her lips. "I have a plan."

"What plan?" Emma asked.

"Yeah," Piper added, crossing her arms, "I'm not sure I want to know, but I almost have to ask."

Maggie held a finger in the air. "Just a second, let me get back over there."

"Are you seriously going to jump it?" Emma asked.

"Yes, I can make it. I've got enough space to get my running start." Maggie backed up, shoving her phone into her pocket. She waved the other two women away. "Give me some room."

They inched back into the passage leading to the chamber. Maggie stared at the rushing river, biting her lower lip. Her heart thudded in her chest, and she blew out a long breath before she sprinted toward the river and flung herself to the opposite side. She landed on the edge, flailing her arms as she struggled not to fall backward into the river.

Emma dove forward, grabbing her and pulling her back.

"Whew," Maggie said, wiping the sweat from her brow. "Thanks."

"I had to save you. I *really* want to hear this plan of yours."

Maggie spun and faced the box, raising her hand in the air. "This is just above my hand if I stretch it."

"Right," Emma said, settling her arms over her chest.

"So, we just need to be a little taller, and we'd be able to reach it."

Emma's eyes widened. "You're not actually suggesting one of us climb on top of the other's shoulders to grab it?"

Maggie laughed and waved a hand at Emma. "Of course not. It's way too unstable."

Emma chuckled along with her. "Right. Well, thank goodness, I was worried it'd be something crazy like that."

Maggie continued laughing, pressing her hand to her nose as the giggling continued. After a moment, she wiped at the tears that dotted her cheeks from her laughter. "So, here's my plan. We do a cheerleader lift with Piper, and *she* leans forward and grabs the box."

Emma's arms dropped to her sides, and she let her jaw slide open. "You *are* crazy."

"I am not. You said doing the shoulder lift was crazy. But this is so much more stable. Two of us as a base holding Piper in the air. It's safer."

"Oh, yeah, totally. A lift from two people who were never cheerleaders of a person who was surely never a cheerleader for her to lean forward and grab a box."

"Hey," Piper objected. "What's that mean?"

Emma shot her an incredulous glance. "What? I just...you don't seem the type."

"Oh, thanks."

"Were you?"

"Was I a cheerleader?" Piper asked. "No, of course not, gag me."

"Then why did you take so much offense to me saying you weren't?"

Piper shrugged. "I just hate for people to assume stuff about me."

"Ladies, ladies, that's enough. I have cheerleading experience. I can totally get us through this."

"Of course you do."

"Varsity squad, three years in high school," Maggie said, with a nod. "We won nationals both times I was co-captain."

"Of course you did," Emma said, with a roll of her eyes.

"Wait, are we seriously entertaining the pyramid scheme?" Piper questioned.

Emma heaved a sigh, throwing her arms out to the sides. "In the absence of other ideas, I guess so."

"Well, why don't one of you be the top?"

"Because you're the lightest of all of us. You'll be easiest to lift," Maggie said.

"I'm stronger than I look. I can totally hold either of you."

"You may want to retract that statement," Emma said. "Maggie's heavier than she looks."

"Hey!" Maggie said, sticking a hand on her hip. "You're not exactly a feather either."

"I didn't say I was."

"Okay, okay, that's enough. I'm clearly the lightest. I'm also the youngest."

"By, like, a handful of years," Maggie pointed out.

"And what's that even have to do with anything?" Emma questioned.

"Clearly, my dexterity trumps either of yours. At your age, you'll be *way* more unsteady on your feet."

Maggie scrunched her nose at the woman. "I'm perfectly steady, thank you." She shook her head and waved a hand in the air. "Okay, here's what we need to do. Cup your hands together, lacing your fingers, and Piper will put a foot into each of our hands. Then we'll lift her up. Ready?"

"Hold on, let me put down my cane," Emma grumbled as she readied her hands for the maneuver.

They laced their fingers together and squatted lower. Piper stepped into Maggie's hand, then Emma's, balancing herself on their shoulders.

"All right, on three, we stand straight," Maggie said. After a countdown, they rose to stand. "Can you reach, or do we need to go higher?"

Piper wobbled a bit, trying to reach for the box. "I'm just shy."

"Okay," Maggie said, with a grunt. "Emma, pivot your hand so you can grip her foot and then lift straight up."

Emma groaned out a breath. "Oh, sure, easy."

"Do you need your cane, Grandma?" Piper taunted her from the top of the tower.

"Yes, to beat you with," Emma snarked as she wrapped her fingers around Piper's foot and leveraged her arm to shove her further into the air.

"Almost there," Piper said through clenched teeth. "Just another inch."

She stretched forward, wobbling to keep her balance as her fingers grazed the metal box.

"Reach!" Maggie said.

"Grab it!" Emma growled.

Piper pulled her lips back into a grimace and stretched another inch until her fingers curled around the edge of the box. "Got it. Now, I just need to wiggle it out of the holder."

She shimmied it from side to side as she tugged it toward her. "Almost there."

"Hurry up. You're not as light as Maggie claimed."

"Got it," Piper said as it popped out of the metal holder hanging from the ceiling. The force of the box releasing sent her arching back. Maggie and Emma adjusted their footing to hold her steady as she wobbled on top of the pyramid.

"Whoa," Piper said, leaning forward in a desperate attempt to catch her balance as her arms flailed.

"Steady," Maggie said through clenched teeth, her leg muscles flexing to keep her own balance.

"I can't hold her much longer. Let's put her down."

"Wait!" Piper shouted as she still tried to balance herself while they lowered her. The downward motion made her even more unstable, and she pitched forward again, her heels lifting from their palms.

"Keep hold of her!" Maggie shouted, but gravity proved stronger than their grasp.

Piper pitched forward, toppling over headfirst and plunging into the steamy, red waters.

CHAPTER 11

"Piper!" Maggie shouted as she stumbled back a few steps.

Emma's eyes went wide, and her hands flew to cover her gaping jaw.

Piper rose, gasping and choking as she floated downstream in the racing water.

"You jerks!" she shouted as she was swept away.

Maggie raced after her with an arm outstretched. Their fingers brushed together a few times, but she failed to grasp hold of her.

Emma rushed past them and kneeled against the wall where the water disappeared into the blackness, reaching her hand out. As Piper surged past, she tried to grab ahold of her wrist.

The water made Piper's hands slick, and her fingers slipped as she fought the raging waters that tugged at her friend.

"No!" Emma shouted, pounding a hand against the stone floor as Piper floated into the blackness beyond their reach.

"Idiots," floated back over the raging waters.

"Great," Emma said, her head hanging limply between her shoulders.

Maggie rose to her feet and tugged her phone from her pocket, holding it over her head.

Emma glanced up at her. "What are you doing?"

"Going after her," she answered before hopping into the water with her arms outstretched to stop her cell phone from getting wet. The racing current swept her toward the dark hole in the wall. Hot water swarmed around her, and her feet failed to touch the bottom.

"Are you insane?" Emma shouted, fear raising her voice to a higher octave. She stared after Maggie, with her eyes wide.

"I'm not letting her go who knows where alone!" Maggie shouted as she disappeared.

Another splash sounded as she continued floating through the dark cavern in the warm water. The red river carved a winding path through the underground cavern. She glided in darkness for several moments, with the walls pinching the river on either side.

The water spilled into a wider chamber, forming a large pool before disappearing under a wall on the opposite side.

With the current slowed, Maggie kicked her legs toward the bank, where the waters lapped. Piper lay in the dirt, coughing and sputtering.

"Piper!" Maggie called as she crawled from the water, her clothes dripping.

Emma floated in a moment later, her hands raised in the air, with her phone clutched in her right hand. She kicked her way over to the edge and climbed from the water.

"Thanks a lot, Boss Lady. Now, I can add 'almost killed by a river of blood' to my life experiences."

Maggie glanced around the inside of the chamber as Emma rang out her soaked shirt and squeezed her pant legs to the best of her ability. "You're welcome. Glad to add to your adventure. What is this place?"

"I think the more important question is, can we get out?" Emma said, straightening.

Piper climbed to her feet, brushing at her soaked clothes. "Actually, the most important question is, what is this red stuff all over us, and is it harmful? It's like sludge. Also, you owe me a new phone."

Maggie stared at the soaked device as Piper waved it in the air. "Put it in some rice when we get back. I'm sure it'll be fine."

"Right. I just floated through a river of blood and completely submerged my brand-new iPhone, but you're right, rice will probably do the trick."

Maggie smiled and nodded at the comment as she continued to scan the new chamber.

"She has a point," Emma said. "This is pretty slimy."

For the first time after climbing from the river, Maggie glanced down at her clothes. She wrinkled her nose as she ran her hand over her T-shirt. "Eww."

"It's like slime," Piper said, stepping closer. "I've been slimed, dude."

"It is like slime. What is it?" Emma questioned.

"Ew!" Maggie shouted as she peeled some of the red jelly-like material from her bare arms. "Is this actually blood? Like, coagulated blood?"

"Ewwww, gross," Piper cried, squeezing her eyes shut. "We bathed in blood."

"Blood from what?" Emma questioned. "That's ridiculous. What are they doing? Sacrificing virgins upriver to fill the water with blood?"

"Maybe. They did that in the past," Maggie answered.

"That's ridiculous," Emma said, wiping the sludge from

her arms. "This isn't blood. It's some kind of natural phenomenon, but it's not blood."

"What kind of 'natural phenomenon?'" Piper asked. "The kind that could eat through our flesh and kill us?"

Maggie's eyes widened. "Ewww, do you think this is a flesh-eating bacteria?" She wiped at her skin, trying to rid herself of any of the gelled substance.

"I don't know," Emma shouted. "But so far, so good. We all still have skin. So, maybe we should work on finding a way out of here."

"Wait," Maggie said, grabbing ahold of them.

"Now what?" Emma questioned.

"We should check and see what's in the box."

"Right now?" Emma asked. "We can look inside it when we escape from this creepy place."

"I feel like we should look. So Piper's sacrifice doesn't go to waste."

"Sacrifice?" Piper questioned.

"Well, yeah," Maggie said. "You fell into the killer river for this. And we should check it out while you're here to see it."

"Why wouldn't I be here later?" Piper asked.

"Because of the bloody flesh-eating bacteria stuff."

Piper thrust her hand at Maggie. "You have it all over you, too!"

"But you fell in. So you probably got it in your mouth and up your nose. So if anyone's not making it," Maggie answered with a crinkled nose, before lowering her voice to a whisper, "it's you."

"That's nice," Emma said.

Maggie swiped a hand through her hair. "Look, let's just open the box, okay?"

"Fine, fine. We'll open the stupid box before we search for a way out."

Piper thrust the box between them, holding it out with stained hands.

Maggie studied it from a few angles. "Looks like the top just pops off. Who wants to do the honors?"

Emma lifted a shoulder as she shot a glance at Maggie.

Maggie nodded, blowing out a breath. "Okay, I think Piper should do it. She fell into the river for this. She should do it."

"What? No way, dude, Piper is not opening a creepy box that was hovering over a river of blood. What if there's, like, a body part in it or a skull or something gross?"

"Didn't you used to love skulls?" Maggie questioned.

Piper screwed up her face. "Uh, like, not in a box over a river of blood."

"Okay, okay, fine. I'll open it," Maggie said.

She slid her shoulders down her back, arching an eyebrow as she stared down her nose at the box. With a deep inhale, she grabbed the top and shimmied it. Her lips twisted into a grimace as she worked to remove the lid from the swollen metal.

It popped loose after a bit of work, flying upward and causing Maggie to stumble back a step. The three women leaned closer to the box to peer inside.

"Another coin," Emma said, pulling the gold piece from inside the metal box and studying it.

"And a key," Piper added, removing the ornate metal object.

Maggie retrieved the last item. "And a scroll. Does the coin match the one Leo had?"

Emma studied it, using her cell phone's light. "Looks like it."

Piper raised her chin to study the object in Maggie's hand. "What's the scroll say?"

Maggie untied the twine holding it shut and unrolled the

parchment. "It's a map!" She spun it around to show the other two women. Five Xs connected by a dotted line marked vague spots on the sparsely drawn illustration.

"*That's* a map?" Piper asked.

"Yeah," Emma added, "it's more like a vague suggestion."

Maggie frowned, spinning the paper around to study it again. "It's got a trail and some Xs and everything. It's a treasure map."

Piper shook her head. "That's a pretty bad map. There are no references or anything."

"There's something written on the back." Emma pointed at the reverse side of the paper.

Maggie spun it over and read as Emma shined the light on the scrawled handwriting. "Find the keys, find the temple, find the gold."

"Keys? As in plural?" Piper questioned.

"That's what it says. Keys."

She held up the scrolly metal item she'd retrieved from the box. "So, we have one. Where are the others."

Maggie flipped the paper over. "Where the Xs are."

"Oh, great, so we'll never find them," Piper huffed, flinging her hands in the air.

"Maybe we should concentrate on getting out of here first, then give this some more thought," Emma suggested, dumping the coin back into the metal box.

Maggie rolled the scroll and placed it inside. "Okay."

With a sour expression, Piper dumped the key inside, and Maggie slid the lid back onto it.

"Okay," Maggie said, toggling on her cell phone's flashlight, "spread out, and let's see if we can find a way out of here."

Maggie shined the light across the river, squinting into the darkness at the far wall. "If we don't find anything over here, we can check out the other bank."

"I'm *not* going back into that water," Piper said.

"Jump across," Maggie suggested, waving the flashlight around but finding nothing.

"Let's hope we find it on this side," Emma said as she explored one corner of the cavern.

They searched the stone walls, using their flashlights and their hands to find any openings they could fit through.

"I haven't found anything," Emma said with a sigh as she wiped the sweat from her brow. "And it's still really hot."

"Yeah. I'm not feeling so good," Piper responded, plopping into a cross-legged sit on the dirt floor.

"Like from the heat or the…blood water?" Maggie asked, with a grimace.

"Both, either. I don't know. Maybe I'm just hungry."

Emma lowered herself to the ground next to Piper, drawing her knees to her chest. "Me, too."

"Hungry or sick?" Maggie asked as she joined them.

"Hungry," Emma answered.

Piper traced the outline of the box sitting between her thighs. "Do you think anyone noticed we're missing yet?"

"Who knows," Emma said as she sank her head into her hands.

Maggie tugged her shoes off and squished water from them. "It's been a while. And between the five of them, someone should figure out where we went."

"Oh, yeah, I'm sure. One of them is bound to have guessed we jumped off the balcony," Emma said, flailing her arms in the air.

"Tarik might," Maggie said, narrowing her eyes to stare into space.

"Oh, good, we're pinning our hopes on the idea that Tarik will somehow magically know you've jumped over the railing of your balcony," Emma said.

"*If* they've even noticed we're gone yet," Piper reminded them.

"Well, it has been a while."

Emma kicked her legs out in front of her, leaning back to rest on her hands. "Not that long."

Maggie flung herself back to lay flat. "Long enough."

"Henry will probably stop anyone from even knocking on your door if he thinks we're doing wedding stuff," Emma said.

Maggie rolled her eyes as she started to speak. "That's–" Her voice cut off, and she wrinkled her forehead.

"That's what? Ridiculous? Please don't say that, because it's not–"

"Shh," Maggie said, waving her comment away.

"What is it?" Emma asked.

"Are you having a medical emergency?" Piper questioned.

"No," Maggie answered, shooting her an annoyed look as she scrambled to her feet. "I see something."

"What? Imminent death when no one finds us?" Emma asked.

Maggie squeezed her lips together and shot a glance over her shoulder at Emma, shaking her head. "No, a way out."

Emma's eyes went wide, and she clambered to her feet. "What? Where?"

Maggie pointed a finger high on the stone wall. "There. See that dark spot? I think it's a hole."

Emma squinted at it. "Maybe."

"Big deal," Piper answered, still sitting on the ground. "We can't reach it."

"I think we can with my cheerleading ski–"

"Don't say it. Don't even say it. I am *not* getting on top of another pyramid with you two as the base. Pass."

Maggie ignored her, trying to judge the height of the hole.

"What do you think? Could we climb it with some teamwork?"

"No," Piper shouted behind them.

"Maybe," Emma said. "That's about the height of the exit when we were stuck in the tomb, and we made that."

"That's what I was thinking."

"Tell someone to come and get me," Piper said, flinging herself onto the ground.

"No way, Piper. We're all in this together."

"I won't get kidnapped from down here. No one will ever find me. I'll just wait down here for someone to rescue me. Oh, tell them to bring a slice of pizza or something."

Maggie rolled her eyes at the woman before stalking over to her and grabbing her hand. She tugged her upward, but Piper went limp.

"Come on, Piper," Maggie said, continuing to tug on her arm. "It's not that bad. We'll boost each other up and then pull the last person up to the hole."

Piper sat up and flicked her gaze to the hole. "It looks small."

Maggie glanced over her shoulder. "It's not that small."

"Are you sure? Can you really tell? You go up and check it out first."

Maggie slid her eyes from side to side. "I'm sure it's fine. It's probably–"

Emma approached, her brow furrowing. "Piper, are you claustrophobic?"

Piper wrinkled her nose and flicked her gaze to the floor. With a shrug, she said, "Maybe."

"Ohhhhh," Maggie murmured, squatting down next to Piper. "Here's the thing, Piper, it doesn't look *that* small. We may need to duck. Or crawl a little, but–"

Piper's shoulders slumped, and she let her head fall.

Emma cracked Maggie's arm, lowering her voice and

growling through clenched teeth, "You're making it worse, shut up."

"Well, I can't help it!" Maggie hissed. "I'm trying to be realistic but comforting."

"Telling a claustrophobic person you may have to crawl through an underground passage isn't comforting."

"Well, I–"

"Ugh, please, both of you shut up. I understand I have to go up there into the creepy underground passage, where I may become stuck and die with a rock pressing against my back. I just…need a minute."

"Okay," Maggie said as she rose, holding her hands in front of her. "Whenever you're ready."

Piper stared up at the hole, wrinkling her nose before she shoved herself up to standing. "Okay. Let's go. Let's do this. Let's die stuck in the creepy hole instead of stuck near the creepy river of blood."

Maggie chuckled at her. "Emma, you go first, then I'll send Piper, then you two pull me up."

"Why do I have to go first?" Emma asked.

"Because Piper's afraid of small spaces, but she can't boost me up. That means one of us has to go first. You want me to go first? Fine, I'll go first. Boost me up." Maggie lifted a foot in the air to punctuate her demand.

"Okay," Emma agreed, cupping her hands. "On three."

Maggie placed her foot in the makeshift stirrup, and after a countdown, Emma lifted her higher. Maggie caught ahold of the edge of the hole and scrambled up the rock face and inside.

She spun and stared down at her two friends below. "Come on up, the water's fine."

"Don't make bad water jokes after the blood river run, please," Piper said, with a grimace.

"Sorry. Okay, come on, step on Emma's hand, and let's go."

Piper let her shoulders slouch as she grimaced. "How small is it up there?"

"I don't know, I've got some room, and I'm kneeling. But I could almost stand."

"Good, not great," Piper lamented as Emma cupped her finger again.

"Up you go," she said as she launched Piper upward. Maggie grabbed ahold of her arms and pulled her into the cavern.

Piper's nose wrinkled as she glanced around the cave. "It's worse than I thought."

"Concentrate on helping me pull Emma up," Maggie said, laying on the ground and dangling her arms. "Jump!"

Piper grabbed Maggie's legs, holding her steady as Emma stretched her arms overhead and hopped higher to connect with Maggie's outstretched fingers. With Maggie bracing her, she scrambled up the rock face and into the cavern with them.

"Please tell me there is an opening," she said as she flung herself onto the ground and sucked in some deep breaths.

"I think there's one in the back," Piper said. "I can't tell because my phone is broken, so I have no flashlight, but I thought I felt air."

Maggie tugged her phone out of her pocket and toggled on the light. "Cool it, Piper, I've got mine."

"Air?" Emma asked, picking up her head. "Like, fresh air?"

"No, stale, dank, nasty air," Piper answered.

"Perfect, we're going deeper into the mess we've gotten ourselves into," Emma said, pushing herself up to her elbows. "The next time you decide to jump off your balcony, Maggie, you're going alone."

"You're loving it. You're up to your eyebrows in dirt and discoveries, and you couldn't be happier."

Emma stuck her tongue out at Maggie as she climbed to her feet and crept forward, hunched over to avoid hitting her head on the ceiling.

"Looks like there's an opening," she said.

"Great, let's see if it leads anywhere." Maggie stepped into the slightly shorter passage, crouching down more to fit. "It's getting lower as I go."

She knelt down and shuffled forward on her hands and knees, checking the space every few feet with her flashlight.

"Do you see anything?" Emma asked from behind her.

"No. I'm going to ditch the phone and keep crawling," Maggie answered, toggling off her light and slipping the phone into her pocket before proceeding ahead.

"Ugh," she grunted as she lowered herself down to her belly and army-crawled forward. "It's worse. Way worse."

"Oh, come on," Emma groaned behind her.

"Better check on Piper."

"Piper?" Emma called. "You still behind me?"

"Yep. Quit kicking dirt all over me."

"Sorry," Emma said with a grunt as she used her elbows to creep forward. "This isn't easy."

Maggie slithered forward in front of her. "Whew, this is tight. Piper's going to freak out."

"Stop saying that, Boss Lady!" Piper shouted from behind. "I'm thinking of wide open spaces with lots of air and no rocks."

"Sorry," Maggie called. "It's opening up a little. There's just one really tight spot, and then I think we're in the clear."

"Not quite," Emma said.

"Stop being a spoilsport," Maggie answered as she continued to shimmy forward. "It's literally, like, one spot that's tight, and then you can get back on your hands and knees to crawl."

"Not going to happen," Emma answered.

Maggie stopped and twisted her neck to glance behind her. "Why?"

"Because," Emma answered, a note of worry in her voice, "I'm stuck."

CHAPTER 12

"What?" Maggie exclaimed, craning her neck to see behind her. She reached for her phone and toggled on the light, shining it toward Emma.

Emma stared back, with narrowed eyes. "I'm stuck."

"Just shimmy a little."

"I can't shimmy a little," Emma spat. "I'm *stuck*."

"What do you mean you're stuck?" Maggie asked.

"Hey, brainy, keep going!"

"I can't!" Emma shouted. "I'm stuck! I'm stuck! What I mean is, I'm stuck. I cannot move. There is a rock pressing my butt, and I can't move it."

"Are you joking?"

Emma shot Maggie a stony stare. "Yes, Maggie. I'm joking. I'm not really stuck. I just figured now would be a great time for a prank."

"It just sounds…" Maggie held back a giggle.

"It sounds what?" Emma snapped.

"There's a rock on your butt," Maggie's features crinkled, and she pressed a hand to her nose, covering her mouth.

"Yes, there's a rock on my butt, and it's crushing me, and I can't move. I can't go forward. I can't go back. I can't move."

"Now's not the time to freak out, brainy. I'm doing my best to stay calm and collected here, and you're ruining it."

Emma rolled her eyes. "Well, I'm so, so sorry that my being stuck is ruining things for you."

Maggie's features crinkled further as she tried to maneuver her way into turning around. She crawled forward and studied Emma. "Okay, ummm, just…just…" Her facial muscles twitched.

She flicked up her eyebrows, settling her face and sucking in a deep breath. "Squeeze your cheeks." The comment caused her to burst into laughter. Tears filled her eyes as she chuckled.

Emma glared at her, her jaw flexing and eyes narrowing.

"Not those ones. The other ones," Maggie said, waving a hand toward her rear.

"Don't you think I've tried that? Squeezing them will hardly work. That'll just make them bigger."

"Right, so…let them go. Relax them."

"Oh, why didn't I think of relaxing my butt to see if it would magically get smaller?" Emma slapped the dirt under her.

"Shouldn't have had that extra slice of pizza," Piper taunted from behind her.

"Thank you, judgy peanut gallery," Emma said. "It's neither helpful nor kind."

"It's all I can do to stay sane, Fanny Mae. If I don't think about how funny it is that your butt is literally stuck between a rock and a hard place, I'm going to lose it in here. It is way, way, *way* too tight of a space. And–"

"And what, Piper?" Maggie called.

"Nothing," she called in a shaky voice. "Just trying to breathe through my panic."

"You're okay. It's fine. There's plenty of air and stuff. It's fine," Maggie answered.

"Why did you have to say the air thing? Now all I can think about is running out of air."

"Sorry, I was trying to be helpful."

"If you want to be helpful, help Fanny McTushie move her keister so I can get out of here."

"I'm trying, I'm trying. Just…close your eyes and think of open spaces." Maggie reached forward with one hand, balancing on the other. "I'll try to pull you."

"Maggie, you can't pull me. I'm stuck."

Maggie rolled her eyes. "There is no way you're stuck, Emma. Your butt isn't *that* big."

Emma let her forehead fall into the dirt below her. "It is. Piper's right. I shouldn't have had that extra slice of pizza. And I picked the one with extra cheese."

Maggie shook her head, her shoulders slumping. "It is not. It's not much bigger than mine. Maybe like half an inch."

Emma snapped her gaze up to Maggie, an irked expression on her features. "Well, that half-inch is costing me."

"I think you're just stuck because you can't really get any traction with your legs or arms because of how tight the space is. Here, give me your hand, and I'll pull. Hey, Piper!" Maggie shouted.

"What?" a weak voice answered.

"Push on Emma's feet when I say go. We need to get her moving so she can crawl the rest of the way out."

"This isn't going to work," Emma said, with a shake of her head.

"Okay," Piper's muffled voice answered.

Maggie shimmied her legs closer, resting her belly on her thighs. She stretched forward and grabbed both of Emma's hands. "Okay, on three!" she called to Piper.

After a countdown, she yanked back against Emma. Her features pinched as she strained to move her friend forward.

"Are you pushing?" she yelled to Piper.

"Yeah, I'm pushing! She won't budge."

Maggie puffed out a breath, easing up on her tugging. "Okay, just a second."

"I told you. I'm stuck," Emma said, with a shaky voice. "All you're doing is tugging my arms out of the sockets, and Piper is shoving my legs up until they hurt."

"You're not stuck."

"Maggie, just go for help, okay? Maybe they can send a search-and-rescue team."

"I'm not leaving you and Piper here alone. No woman left behind. Like in the army."

"That's the Marines, Maggie. And this isn't the Marines."

"Whatever. Look, I'm not leaving you here. Anything could happen. Like a cave-in, or an animal or something."

"Ugh," Piper groaned from behind Emma. "Please stop talking."

"Sorry!" Maggie yelled. "Okay, we'll try again. Try shimmying or something."

Emma rolled her eyes. "Fine. I'll try to shimmy my big butt loose."

"I really hope it doesn't cause a cave-in," Piper lamented.

Emma's features turned stony, and she shook her head. "Remind me *never* to jump off a balcony with you again."

"Just be quiet and shimmy," Maggie said, grabbing ahold of Emma's hands again.

She shouted the order to Piper and tugged backward. Her muscles stretched and strained as she shifted her hips and legs back to leverage the pull. Her cheeks puffed out from the effort.

She almost gave in until Emma exclaimed, "I'm moving!"

Maggie continued yanking on her arms until Emma

scrambled from the tight hole. Maggie collapsed to the dirt below, sprawling as far as she could in the small space.

Emma panted as she let her forehead rest on her hands. "Oh, that was so way too close for comfort."

"See, I told you I'd get you out," Maggie answered as Piper's head appeared at the opening.

She wrinkled her nose, her rainbow hair covered in dirt. "It's still too small. Keep going, I hate it in here."

"Okay, okay. I think we'll be able to almost stand up soon," Maggie said, crawling forward through the larger passage. They continued on their hands and knees for several more feet before Maggie was able to move forward hunched over instead of crawling. After another long stretch, the passage widened and ceiling rose, allowing them to stand up straight.

"Thank God," Piper said.

"Where are we?" Emma asked, glancing around.

"I don't know, but it looks like it opens up into a room up there," Maggie said, pointing her flashlight forward.

"Can't wait to see what's in that one!" Piper groused.

They continued forward spilling into a large chamber hewn into the rock. "What is this place?" Emma asked.

"Are those..." Piper began, her voice trailing off.

Maggie flicked her light in the direction of Piper's gaze. "Train tracks."

Emma wrinkled her nose. "Train tracks? Underground?"

"Was there ever a subway in Rosemont?" Piper questioned.

"How should I know?" Maggie questioned. "If there was, it wasn't while I was alive."

"I'm almost afraid to say this, but maybe we should follow them. We may find a way out."

"Hopefully we don't find an abandoned train filled with

bodies," Piper said as Maggie flicked her light back and forth, searching up and down the tracks.

"Which way?"

Emma followed the flashlight's beam back and forth. "Uhhh, that way is back the way we came."

"Let's go the other way," Piper suggested.

Emma and Maggie exchanged a glance. "Fine by me," Emma said, throwing her arms out.

"Okay, this way it is." They stepped onto the tracks and crept forward through the darkness.

"So," Piper said, her voice echoing off the walls after a few minutes of walking, "why don't you want to marry Henry?"

A chortle escaped Emma's lips at the question.

Maggie stopped walking, swinging the flashlight toward Piper, then Emma. "No one said that."

"I mean you sort of did when you wouldn't pick a date," Piper said when they resumed walking.

"I did not. I just…didn't pick a date yet."

"Because?"

"Because I didn't, okay? It's not a crime. There's no time limit on picking dates after you're engaged."

"Hmm," Piper murmured.

Maggie swung the flashlight toward her, shining the light in Piper's eyes. "What?"

"I didn't say anything."

"You made a noise. Like a 'hmph.'"

"I did not."

"You did, too," Maggie shot back.

"Can we just concentrate on finding a way out of here instead of arguing about who made what noise?" Emma asked.

"Fine," Maggie said, swinging the flashlight beam forward again.

They took a few steps forward before Emma spoke. "She has a point, though."

Maggie's jaw dropped open as she heaved a sigh, shooting an incredulous glance at Emma.

"What? She does. You had dresses planned years in advance for winter formals, fall balls, and more. But you can't settle on a date for this wedding?"

"Completely different," Maggie claimed.

"How?"

"There's a lot to think about. Like other people's schedules and stuff."

Piper squeezed her lips together, furrowing her brow. "Riiiight, sure there is. You haven't picked a date because you're worried about some random guest's schedule."

"What is the big, hairy deal? Why is everyone all over my case about this? It's fine. We'll pick a date, and it'll be fine."

Both women nodded their heads at her as they exchanged a glance.

"Just don't pick Tuesday, June fifteenth," Emma said before she and Piper burst into a cloud of giggles.

Maggie crinkled her nose, turning her features stony. "Very funny, you two. Really humorous."

"Are you sure you want me to be your maid of honor?"

Maggie blinked at the question. Emma held up her hands. "Just asking. I just…wanted to be sure it wasn't a rash request made in a desperate moment."

"I can't believe this. Really? Desperate moment?"

"You kind of needed to save yourself from the whole Tuesday, June fifteenth thing," Piper said.

"Well, I didn't ask you to be my maid of honor just to get out of talking about the date I picked by accident."

Emma shot up her eyebrows. "Okay. Fine. Just thought you may want someone…swankier."

"And with a smaller butt?" Maggie questioned wryly.

Emma wrinkled her nose. "Yeah, then the butt bow you get on the dress won't be so huge."

"No one is getting butt bows on their dress. I want something classy. Refined. Dignified. And besides, who would I ask? You're my best friend. And you're plenty swanky."

Emma shrugged as the chamber around them widened. "Cate?"

"Kensie?" Maggie asked, with a guffaw.

"She is a countess."

"That's pretty swanky," Piper pointed out.

"Do you think she'd let us get married at the castle if I asked her to be my maid of honor?" Maggie asked.

"I knew it," Emma said. "I'm just a placeholder for someone way better."

"I'm kidding. I don't want to get married in Scotland. At least, I don't think so. Even if I did, I want you to be my maid of honor. We've survived way too much together for you not to fix my train on my wedding day."

A wistful expression crossed Emma's features, and she tugged her lips back into a half-smile. "Yeah, I guess we have. Well, then, if that's what you really want, I'm happy to be your maid of honor."

Maggie smiled at her friend.

"If you ever pick a date and get married," Emma added.

The smile faded from Maggie's face.

"Hey, if you two are finished with your heartfelt moment, maybe you'd realize we're approaching something up here."

"A way out?" Maggie asked, hope filling her voice.

Piper shrugged and shook her head. "I don't know, it looks like a big room."

"A station," Emma answered with a grin, running forward to look around.

"Maybe there are stairs going up to the street level," Maggie said as she rushed forward.

Emma climbed the crumbling steps leading up to the platform. "Wow, this looks really old."

"Can it be that old?" Piper asked as she stared at the old tile on the floor and walls.

"Eh, the first subways were built around the turn of the twentieth century, so yeah, it could be a century old."

"No escalator to the top, then," Maggie said as she shined her light around the space.

"It's creepy in here," Piper said, with a shiver. "Like Silent Hill creepy."

"Ugh," Maggie said. "I hope there are no monsters."

"There are no such things as monsters," Emma said, with a roll of her eyes. "I found stairs!"

They hurried toward her and stared up the long staircase leading into blackness.

"Race you!" Maggie said with a grin as she launched up the stairs.

"This is childish! You cheated!" Emma called.

"You two are losers," Piper shouted, bringing up the rear.

They scrambled up the stairs, expecting to find a locked entrance at the top. Instead, they found nothing but more blackness. The stairs spilled out into a small space. Dirt and tree roots built a wall between them and any entrance that may have existed in a previous century.

"What did they do? Bulldoze the entrance and plant trees?" Emma questioned.

"Looks that way," Maggie said, with a pout.

"Now what?" Piper said, flinging out her hands.

"We need to find another way out, that's what," Emma said, pressing her palm to her forehead.

"Where? This was our best shot!" Piper shouted.

"No," Maggie argued. "These tracks keep running. We can keep following them, or we can go back the way we came and continue in the other direction."

"Less than stellar plan," Piper said.

"But still a plan," Emma answered. "Which way do you want to try first?"

"Let's keep going straight," Maggie said.

"Why not," Piper said, flinging out her arms. "Maybe we'll find another closed station that's been buried underground."

"Maybe we can claw our way out of that one," Emma murmured as they clomped down the stairs and crossed to the tracks. They slid off the platform down to the rails and continued in the same direction.

"It's creepy in here," Piper said as they left the station behind them.

"Yeah," Maggie said, a shiver snaking down her spine. "Cold, too."

"Right? It turned icy real quick after that bloody river," Piper agreed.

"We'll catch our death in here," Emma murmured, creeping forward between the two of them.

"Ugh, please don't say that, Fanny."

"Please stop calling me Fanny."

Piper shrugged as she laced her arm through Emma's. "It's Fanny or brainy, take your pick."

"If we're voting, I like Fanny. It's cute. And it would be a fun story at parties," Maggie said.

"No one asked for your opinion," Emma said. "Besides, it's not cute or fun. I'm not explaining to someone over a cocktail that Piper calls me Fanny because my butt got wedged while crawling through an underground tunnel."

Emma shook her head as they continued to inch forward in the cold, dark tunnel. "Okay, I'll take Fanny over brainy. At least I don't sound like a smurf."

"Good choice. Now, like I was saying, don't say death in here. It's creepy enough."

"Yeah, I'm waiting for a ghost train to roll through."

"Just like *Ghostbusters II*," Piper said, bobbing her head up and down.

"Are you two serious? There are no such things as ghosts!"

Maggie side-eyed her as the tunnel narrowed again. "Whatever you say."

"Do you have something different to say?"

"Well, you know Lenora's great-grandmother communicated with the dead, right?"

"That's ridiculous," Emma said, with a roll of her eyes.

"Tell that to Lenora. Oh, speaking of, I really should invite her to the wedding."

"I'm sure she'll want to race right across the pond for it."

Maggie swung her light to the side. It glinted off something shiny. "Hey, what is that?"

"Looks like a door," Emma answered.

"Should we try it?"

Piper wrinkled her nose and crossed her arms. "Do you actually think it'll still be open?"

Maggie twisted the knob and shoved. The door swung open with a creak. She twisted to face her friends, with a triumphant grin. "What do you say? Should we find out where this goes?"

CHAPTER 13

"Sure, let's go through the creepy door to nowhere," Piper said. "We've come this far."

"Can't be any worse than the creepy abandoned subway tracks," Maggie said as they entered a long hall.

Emma tugged her phone from her pants and toggled on her own flashlight, swinging it around. "Must be some kind of maintenance tunnel."

Maggie continued forward. "Do you think it leads anywhere? Like a control room or something?"

"Guess we'll find out," Emma answered, stowing her phone again.

They wandered through the straight corridor, finding no branching tunnels or signs of life. The meager light from Maggie's phone only allowed them to see a few steps in front of them. After a few more yards, the passage took a sharp turn to the right.

They inched along it until Maggie's light reflected off something in the distance. "I see a door!"

She raced ahead toward it and shoved it open. Her flashlight beam illuminated the interior in bits and pieces. A few tables dotted the space. Old wooden chairs sat haphazardly around them.

Maggie shuffled around the room, stumbling over one toppled chair. "What is this place?"

Piper wrinkled her nose. "I don't know, but it's creepy."

"It's not creepy," Maggie said, "just dusty."

"It's creepy. Why are all these chairs around here like people were sitting in them and then suddenly ran? And this one that's knocked over," Piper said, righting it. "Gives me the creeps."

Maggie approached the wall. Curled papers, covered in a layer of dust, filled a bulletin board. She ran her light over them, squinting to make them out. The beam illuminated a shiny piece of paper. Grim faces stared back at her, lined in front of an old-fashioned subway car.

"Emma, check this out."

Emma joined her, staring at the photograph at which Maggie pointed. She leaned closer, reading the handwritten caption. "Rosemont Subway Maintenance Workers, nineteen twenty-four."

"Wow," Maggie said, sweeping the beam across the room again. "Nineteen twenty-four. I wonder how long this has been abandoned?"

Piper ran her fingers over one of the tables, grimacing at the thick layer of dust. "Looks like since nineteen twenty-four."

"What are these other papers?" Emma questioned.

Maggie flicked the beam across to them again. "I'm not sure. I can barely read them."

Emma blew away some of the dust. It billowed into the air in a thick cloud. She and Maggie coughed and gagged, sniffling as the large particles tickled their nasal passages.

"Ohhh, this is a schedule," Emma said. "Look. The names are down the side, and the dates at the top."

"Oh, yeah," Maggie said, turning up the corners of her lips, "Tom Thomson worked Monday, Wednesday, Thursday, Friday, and Saturday. Walter Wilson worked Monday through Friday."

"Thanks for the report on work schedules," Piper said. "But could we concentrate on finding a way out instead of who worked what shift a hundred years ago?"

"We have no idea if this was a hundred years ago," Emma said.

"Uh, actually, we do. Look at the dates. The schedule starts on March tenth, nineteen twenty-four." Maggie's voice trailed off at the last words. She snapped her light toward the picture, then back to the schedule. With a final flick back to the picture, she leaned in to study it. "So this picture was likely taken before the last work schedule was posted."

"Probably."

"Which means this has been abandoned since nineteen twenty-four."

Piper wrapped her arms around her waist and shivered. "Let's get out of here. I feel like the ghosts of those guys are floating around everywhere."

"We have no idea what happened. Maybe they used a different space for posting schedules or…"

"Maybe they all died in a tragic accident," Piper said. "Let's not waste time debating it while we're still trapped underground, huh?"

Maggie snapped a few pictures of the bulletin board, zooming in on the photograph and a few other areas before her light caught something else pinned to the board. "What is this?"

Emma leaned closer to take a look. "It's a key."

Heat washed over Maggie as she tugged it from the

board. "It's a key just like the one we found in the box hanging over the blood river."

Emma held her light over it, studying the ornate top. "It does look similar."

"Piper, bring that box over here."

Piper, a frown still affixed to her face, wandered over, tugging the metal box open. Maggie picked the key out from inside and held it up next to the other.

"Different metal," Emma noted, "but similar shapes on the top."

"Yep," Maggie said.

Emma flicked her flashlight back to the board. "There's a note here." She blew off a cloud of dust before she gently pulled the metal pin from the board and freed the note. "Tom found this key last week in the ventilation shaft. Do not touch it. It's cursed."

"What?" Maggie asked, wrinkling her nose.

"Great going, Boss Lady. You touched the cursed key."

Maggie flashed her a glance before returning to study the note. "That's ridiculous. There are no such things as curses. Does it say anything else?"

Emma turned the paper over before spinning it back. "No, that's it."

"What? Who finds a cursed key and hangs it on the bulletin board with a note? Probably just some stupid joke." Maggie dropped both keys into the metal box Piper held.

"Hey! I don't want the cursed thing." She snapped on the lid. "You take it."

"Just carry it, Piper. We're doing important things, like searching for clues and using our flashlights to find a way out."

"Ventilation shaft," Emma murmured as she swung her flashlight around. "Hmm."

Maggie returned her light to searching the bulletin board for more information.

"Hey," Emma called as she approached a dark corner. "I found something."

"A way out?" Piper asked, hope filling her voice.

Emma shot a glance over her shoulder. "Maybe, though, I don't think you'll be happy with it, even if it is."

Piper let her head fall back between her shoulders. "Is it another tunnel? Please tell me it's not another tunnel crawl."

Maggie approached the supposed exit, sweeping her flashlight over it. "Is that a hole?"

"Yeah," Emma said. "The wall caved in around it, but it looks like it used to be a ventilation shaft. Probably used to bring air down into the room from the outside."

Maggie flicked up her eyebrows, squinting into the darkness. "Do you think it's still connected to the outside?"

Emma tugged her lips back into a grimace. "I don't know. I don't smell any fresh air, but maybe there was a fan that drew it down. Maybe it's too far to catch a whiff."

"We can try it. Worst that happens is we have to turn back and try another route."

"No," Piper argued, joining them to stare into the hole. "Worst that happens is this thing collapses with us in it and we die."

"Way to look on the bright side, Piper," Maggie said, climbing into the large shaft and waddling forward on her hands and knees. "You can wait down here while we check it out if you want."

"Pass. I'm not getting left in the creepy ghost chamber alone underground while you two escape." She pushed ahead of Emma and crawled into the shaft after Maggie. "I'm going before you in case your butt gets stuck again, Fanny."

Emma grumbled something unintelligible before she clambered into the shaft. The shaft creaked and groaned as they crawled through the thick metal box. Maggie stopped and held her phone up to shine the light ahead.

"How much farther?" Piper asked.

"It goes on forever. Keep your eyes peeled for any branches, even above us. I can barely see, and I can't keep holding the flashlight."

"How do you expect us to see anything without it? At least the light reflects somewhat."

"Fine, fine," Maggie said. I'll put it between my teeth. Just keep looking for a way out."

"No kidding, Boss Lady. I've been looking for a way out since we got down here."

"Hey, Maggie," Emma called from the back.

"Yeah?" Maggie mumbled, pinching the phone between her teeth.

"Please don't tell me you're stuck again," Piper said.

"Very cute, Piper. This thing is a mile wide. I'm not stuck. But I found something."

"A way out?" Piper questioned.

"Maybe. There's a hole in the seams of the shaft here. And it looks like there's a tunnel behind it. I'd have to pry it open more, but I'm pretty sure there's a passage."

Maggie swung around, aiming her flashlight toward Emma. "Really? Should we try it?"

Emma sat on her haunches and shrugged.

"No," Piper answered. "We should not. We should keep going and see if this gets us to the outside."

"All right," Maggie said. "If we get stuck, we can hit that on the way back."

They continued on their hands and knees until the shaft ended. Maggie pounded against the metal sloping upward before she tugged her phone from between her teeth and shined it around.

Her nose wrinkled as the light illuminated what hovered above them. "Dead end."

"Like, completely?" Piper groaned.

"No, I meant the kind of dead ends that aren't really dead. Yes, completely. There is a giant fan above my head, and there is no way we can get past it."

"Can we move it?" Emma asked.

"No," Maggie answered.

"Can we slide between the blades?" Piper questioned.

"No, Emma's butt won't fit."

"Hey!" Emma shouted.

"I'm kidding. There's a grating over it. It's thick." Maggie wrapped her fingers around the grill and yanked. "I can't move it. Can't bend it. This is a no-go."

Piper let her head hang between her arms. "Back to the death room."

"We can try the tunnel," Maggie said. "Maybe we'll get lucky."

Piper scrunched her body to spin in the tight space. "Oh, great. That sounds just as bad as the death room."

"Maybe it'll lead to a way out," Maggie said as they retreated down the tunnel.

"Gosh, I hope so," Emma said. "Because I don't think continuing up and down the tracks is going to do us any good."

"Really? You don't think we'll find any other stations that may lead out," Maggie questioned, her hands banging against the thick metal as she crawled down the shaft.

"No, I don't. I know I just moved here, but have you ever heard about this subway? Or seen or heard of any old entrances to it?"

"No," Maggie answered, "never, and I've lived here for years."

"Exactly. And why is that, do you think?"

"Because something terrible happened, and now no one talks about it," Piper called from the front.

Maggie wrinkled her nose. "Really?"

"Maybe not as tragic as Piper's suggesting, but I would say it's no longer used and they closed it off for a reason. That's why there are no old entrances anyone knows about."

Maggie stopped crawling, pinching her brows together. "What reason?"

"Everyone died!" Piper yelled.

"But why would they seal it? Even if everyone died."

"Who knows, but I'd bet they did," Emma said.

"Here's the stupid death tunnel," Piper said. "Are we going in or what?"

"My vote is to go in," Maggie said. "Especially after Emma's theory. We'd be wasting time, probably a lot of it, if we keep going up and down the tracks."

"So, into the macabre tunnel. If Fanny can fit her backside between the two pieces of metal."

Emma heaved a sigh, grabbing hold of the metal seam and tugging on it to let Piper slip inside. She twisted to face Maggie. "Hold it open, while I take my gigantic backside through."

Maggie held back a laugh as she tugged the metal back to create a space for Emma to slide through.

"Can you make it?" Emma called.

Maggie slid her legs through, elbowing the joint back as she tried to fit her hips. "I think so," she grunted, turning sideways and wedging herself between the two seams. She popped free, falling a few inches to the ground below. "Made it!"

"Looks like the passage continues straight for a while."

Maggie swung her flashlight beam around as they walked. "What is this place?"

Emma ran her fingers over the jagged stone walls. "This

looks like a natural tunnel. There must be a cavern system down here. They probably used some of the structure to create the subway."

"Let's hope it leads to a natural exit, though I'm not aware of any cave entrances in town," Piper said.

"I hope they didn't seal this one up, too," Maggie murmured.

They continued in silence for several feet before Maggie's leg muscles began to tire. "Are we going up?"

"Yeah," Emma said, pressing against her thighs with each step. "We're going up a grade."

"I really hope it ends in a cave right next to the Shop'N'Go. I could really use a Slurpee right about now."

"Honestly, I could drink an entire mega-sized cup of that blue foam," Emma said.

Maggie squinted into the darkness ahead of them, detecting the faint outline of a hump on the ground. "You'll get a brain freeze. What is that?"

"Gosh, I hope it's not some kind of weird underground creature," Emma puffed out.

"It looks like…dirt," Maggie said, with a wrinkled nose. They closed the gap between them and the unidentified object. Maggie shined her light beam on the pile of soil at their feet. "It is dirt. Why is there a pile of dirt here?"

"From there!" Emma said, pointing in the direction she shined her own light. "Looks like something caved in."

Maggie let her gaze float up to a dark hole above them.

"Can we get out through there?" Maggie asked, rising to her tiptoes to peer into the hole.

"Smells weird," Piper said, her nose wrinkling.

Maggie toggled her flashlight off and slid her phone into her pocket. "Smell is good. Maybe it means we're near the outside. Boost me up, I'm going in."

Emma cupped her hands, and Maggie stepped into them,

sticking her head into the hole and pulling herself deeper inside.

"What do you see?"

"Nothing yet," Maggie said. "It's dark."

Her hand hit something hard, and she shoved it aside, crawling further forward on her stomach as she kicked her feet to find purchase.

"Anything?" Emma called.

"Give me a second to get my flashlight once I crawl a little further in. There's some kind of rough fabric or something. And it stinks."

"What does it smell like?" Emma asked.

"Ugh," Maggie said with a groan, turning her lips down into a grimace, "awful. Like rotting flesh."

"Ewwwww," Piper called.

"Okay, just a second. I feel something else. It's smooth and round. Let me get my flashlight." Maggie strained to reach her pocket, stretching her fingers until they wrapped around the phone's edge.

"Well?"

"Just a second. I'm turning my flashlight on now, and–" Her voice cut off, replaced by a shriek.

"Maggie! What is it? Are you okay?" Emma shouted.

Her scream died down, replaced by a silent murmur as she stared at the object her hand had just touched. "I'm…okay…it's…not great."

"What's not great?"

Maggie twisted to shine the light above her, peering around. "The thing is…okay, so there's good news and bad news. What do you want first?"

"Good," Emma said as Piper said, "Bad."

"I'll go with good. I saw some light when I was crawling in. Not a lot, but with some work, we may be able to get out of here."

"What's the bad news?" Piper asked.

Maggie pressed her lips together, scrunching her nose as she shined her light on the object that had caused her to scream. "The bad news is, I seem to be inside a coffin with a dead body."

CHAPTER 14

"Uhhh, I'm not sure I heard you right," Emma answered as Maggie stared at the skull lying in front of her. "Did you say coffin?"

"Yep," Maggie called. "Coffin. The thing must have rotted away or something and caved into the tunnel. There's a dead guy in here. But when it rotted, the whole thing must have shifted, because I can see some light. If I can just shift the lid off, maybe we can get out."

"Correct me if I'm wrong, but aren't coffins usually buried?" Piper asked. "So, won't shifting the lid off just trap us below, like, six feet of dirt?"

"I saw light," Maggie said. "Maybe this one is in a mausoleum."

"Wow, did we go all the way to the cemetery?" Emma asked.

"That's what I'm guessing. Wonder what poor person this is?"

"A rich one if they have a mausoleum," Piper answered.

"What's he wearing?" Emma called.

"Uh, it looks pretty old, so I'm not sure I know the labels, but–"

"No," Emma interrupted, "I don't mean is he wearing Fendi or Gucci."

"Neither of those. That much I'm sure of."

Emma huffed out a sigh. "Maggie…"

"What?"

"Stop talking. I don't care what brand he's wearing. Is it old-fashioned or modern?"

"Oh, ahhhhh, old-fashioned."

"Why do we care?" Piper asked.

"She wondered who it was. I was trying to figure it out."

Piper huffed. "It's Bob Smith from eighteen-oh-five. Who cares! Just find a way out."

Maggie puffed out a breath as she pressed her back against the thick stone above her. "If I can just move this an inch, I should be able to get my fingers through and try to push the lid off."

"Hurry!" Piper called.

Maggie released the pressure on the lid. "Why? What's happening?"

"I want to get out of here!" Piper answered.

Maggie fluttered her eyelashes as she stared down at the skull below her. "No kidding."

She pressed her spine against the stone again, pinching her features as she pushed against the coffin's bottom and shifted to the side. The lid slid a tiny bit.

She panted out a few breaths and wiped at her forehead with the back of her hand. After a few more gulps, she threaded her fingers through the tiny slit, wincing as the stone scraped at her knuckles. "I can get my hand out. I'm going to try to push."

"Push with everything you got, Boss Lady!"

Maggie rolled her eyes as she shoved against the stone lid.

A strained scream emerged from her lips, but the stone did not budge. She eased off, panting with effort before she glanced down at the skull again. "Sorry, buddy, we're going to have to get up close and personal.

Maggie nudged the former head over to make room for her shoulder and wedged it against the bottom of the coffin. With his clavicle digging into her ribs, she pushed at the lid again, squeezing her eyes shut.

The lid shifted an inch. Maggie let off, gasping for air before she tried again, shifting it another inch. She lay on her side, squeezing both hands out and pushing. The stone lid toppled away, crashing to the floor with a resounding clap that echoed in the dimly lit mausoleum.

"I did it," she choked out through gasps. "Climb up, and we'll blow this joint."

"Please stop saying ridiculous things," Emma said.

"Oh, air. I smell dank, stale, nasty air, but still…air," Piper exclaimed. Her head popped through the hole, and Maggie offered her a hand to climb out of the coffin. "Eww!"

Maggie reached through the hole to tug Emma upward.

She clawed at the corpse's pants to steady herself before she grimaced. "Ugh, this is gross."

Maggie climbed from inside the stone coffin, joining Piper, who already searched for an exit. "You unearth mummies."

"They're preserved and wrapped. Not just…dead and sitting in a broken stone coffin I'm climbing through." She hopped out to the floor and glanced at the askew casket. "Wow, this thing really sunk, huh?"

"Yeah, lucky for us."

"Mmm," Emma said, with a roll of her eyes, "yeah, real lucky."

"Found the doors," Piper said, pointing to two large stone slabs sandwiched between two stained glass windows.

"Oh, good," Maggie answered, wandering toward her. "Open 'em up and let's blow–"

"Don't say it," Emma interrupted.

Piper pushed against the doors, with a grunt. She leaned back, dusting her hands off. "Locked."

"Locked? Who locks a mausoleum?" Maggie questioned, giving the doors a quick shove.

"People who don't want their loved one's grave robbed."

"Who robs the grave of some random person? This isn't the Pharaohs of Egypt, buried with jewels and gold and whatever."

"Still, some people might," Emma argued, pressing against the doors.

Maggie leaned a shoulder against the slab. "There's got to be a way to open these, right?"

"I would think so. What if you wanted to come in and leave flowers or say a prayer?" Emma asked.

Piper crossed her arms. "You'd come in from the outside. With a key."

"I think we just need a little more effort," Maggie said, standing back with her hands on her hips.

"What do you suggest?" Emma asked.

"Kick it?" She flicked her gaze to Emma, eyebrows raised in question.

"Can't hurt."

"On three," Maggie said. After a quick countdown, they both slammed a foot into each slab. The doors shimmied but held. Maggie squeezed her lips together, tugging back her head. "Close."

"Again," Emma said.

They kicked them again. Sediment rained down from the ceiling above them.

Emma raised her leg. "Again."

After another kick, the doors inched open but didn't give way entirely.

"One more," Maggie said before they slammed their legs into the stone slabs again. This time, they flung open. Fresh air whooshed in past them.

Maggie let her head fall between her shoulders. "Oh, thank God."

They strolled out into the bright sunshine, shielding their eyes with their hands as they stepped onto the grass.

A mortified couple with a young child stood in front of a gravestone a few feet away. Their jaws hung agape as the women emerged from the mausoleum.

"Hi!" Maggie called, with a friendly wave and smile. "Sorry about the noise. We had a hard time getting out. Luckily, the coffin wasn't sealed all the way."

The mother tugged her young son closer toward her before they hurried away.

"Nice going, Boss Lady."

"What?"

"Maggie, we're covered in dirt. We're a disheveled mess after we've been soaked in a blood-red river, our clothes are stained and grimy. And then you basically told them we just crawled out of a coffin."

Maggie turned pensive for a moment. "Oh, right. Oh, well." With a shrug, she tugged her phone from her pocket and toggled it on. "Ah, finally, a signal…and eighty-seven missed calls. Looks like the guys figured out we were gone."

She flicked her eyebrows up as she tapped her screen before pressing the phone to her ear. The line trilled on the other end once before a frantic voice responded.

"Maggie, where the hell are you?" Henry's worried voice answered.

"Well, hello to you, too, babe."

"Where are you?" he repeated.

"Well," Maggie began, "funny thing is…we're at the cemetery."

"How did you…never mind. They're at the cemetery." Another voice sounded, saying something unintelligible. "Yep. Hang on." A loud scraping noise filled her ears, and she pulled the phone away from her ear, scrunching her features.

"Maggie?" Henry said.

She pressed the phone to her ear again. "Yeah."

"Don't move. Stay exactly where you are. We'll be right there."

"Okay, I mean, there's no…" The line clicked, and Maggie yanked the phone down, staring at the display with a wrinkled nose before finishing her statement. "Rush."

"What did they say?" Emma asked as Maggie shoved her phone into her pocket.

"Don't move. We'll be right there." She rolled her eyes and shook her head. "Let me see the map we found."

"Was he mad?" Emma asked.

"Did you talk to Charlie?" Piper questioned.

"Yes and no." Maggie wiggled her fingers at Piper.

"Wait, yes, he was mad, or yes and no, he was both mad and not mad?" Emma questioned as Piper tugged the box from her hoodie pocket.

"Yes, he was mad. No, I did not talk to Charlie."

"Great," Piper lamented, passing the box to Maggie, who sat on the grass to open it. "I will never hear the end of this. But I'm blaming you." She jabbed a finger at Maggie, scrunching up her nose.

"Fine, fine, blame me. Although…does Charlie get mad?"

"Oh-ho-ho, yeah."

"Really? I can't picture it."

"Picture him when that hacker hacked his computer in Venice."

Maggie squashed her features while tugging the lid off

the metal container. "He was frustrated. I've seen Charlie frustrated. I've never seen him mad. Anyway, just blame me. It'll be fine. Let's see if we can figure this map out while we wait."

Emma stalked a few steps back toward the mausoleum. "I don't think it's a coincidence that the blood river connected to this tomb."

"Oh? Why's that?" Maggie murmured as she stared at the spare map scrawled in black ink on the yellowed paper.

"This is the tomb of Thomas Tilton," Emma answered.

Maggie craned her neck to stare at it. "Oh, wow. It is."

Emma joined Maggie on the ground, peering over her shoulder. "I'd bet the key we found in the death room was in his coffin and fell out when it shifted."

"Speaking of," Maggie said, tugging her phone from her pocket after handing the map off to Emma, "I'm going to look into what exactly happened down there, if anything."

She pounded both thumbs against her phone's virtual keyboard. A list of results populated on the screen, and she scanned them.

"Well?" Piper asked as she plopped onto the grass next to them.

"Uh, I haven't found anything cohesive yet."

"What does that even mean?"

"It means I don't know, okay? I don't see anything yet, but–" Maggie's voice cut off, and her eyes narrowed.

"Yeah? But?"

"Ummm," Maggie murmured.

Emma glanced up from the map, squashing her eyebrows together as she lifted her chin to peer at Maggie's phone.

"So, there's a reason why there are no remnants of the subway entrances anywhere."

"What's the reason?"

Maggie wrinkled her nose, her lips tugging back in a

wince. "They closed the subway and covered them all up because…it was cursed."

"What?" Emma questioned, scrambling closer to Maggie to stare at her screen.

"I knew it!" Piper said. "Vindicated! They all died down there, didn't they?"

Maggie flicked her eyebrows up as she scanned her screen again. "Not exactly."

"Oh, what, one of them escaped?"

Maggie wiggled her head back and forth. "Mmm, no, not that either."

Piper's eyes went wide, and she sat up on her haunches. "Then what?"

"Well, this site talks about the lore of Rosemont, including the blood river. Anyway, it mentions the subway in another post. It says the men smelled something odd coming from the ventilation shaft."

"The one we climbed through?" Emma asked.

Maggie nodded. "Yeah. When they investigated, they found the key." She pointed to an old photograph of the key on the webpage. "And shortly after, they started to experience bad luck. They said it was cursed."

"Like the note said."

"And we took it," Piper said, flinging her arms in the air. "That's just perfect. Now, *we're* cursed."

"That's ridiculous, there are no such things as curses, Piper," Emma said. "What happened to them?"

Maggie licked her lips as she continued reading. "Ben Williamson, the guy who actually found the key, tripped over a crack in the sidewalk, stumbled into the street, and…oh, wow, was hit by a bus."

Piper's head dropped back between her shoulder blades. "OMG."

"Bad luck, nothing more," Emma said, with a shrug.

"And the next guy who was with him when he discovered the key…first his wife left him, then the bank foreclosed on his house…"

"All things that were likely already snowballing well before the key was found," Emma said.

"And then he went to visit his brother in Akron and died after falling from a carnival ride."

Piper's eyes widened, and her jaw dropped open.

"Well, we all know carnival rides aren't well-built or tested!" Emma argued.

Maggie scrolled further. She tugged her lips into a frown and slid her eyes shut. "Oh."

"What is it?" Piper gasped.

"Tell us, so I can scientifically refute it," Emma added.

Maggie opened her eyes, sliding her gaze back and forth between the two women. She bit her lower lip, squeezing her eyebrows together. "The rest of the crew present when the key was found also died…all at the same time, when a subway train derailed, killing all passengers and maintenance workers."

CHAPTER 15

"Say what? A billion people died down there?" Piper rocketed to her feet, pacing the grass, her hands on her hips. "OMG."

"Not a billion," Maggie corrected, "but a lot."

"Ew!" Piper exclaimed, rubbing her arms as they turned to goosebumps. "I can't believe it. And now *we* have the cursed key."

"Piper," Emma said, her head dropping to the side, "there are no such things as curses."

"Yeah? How do you scientifically refute that?" Piper asked, flinging her hand toward Maggie's phone. "Every single person died in a massive train derailment."

"Maybe because there was something wrong with the tracks. It could have been the damp heat that caused them to become slick or warped."

Maggie continued scrolling through the article before she clicked off the phone.

"Did it say what caused the accident?" Emma asked.

Maggie shook her head. "No."

"What did it say?" Piper questioned. "It said something, didn't it? Something weird and unexplainable."

Maggie tugged her lips to one side, staring at the grass as she traced one blade with her finger. "It said no cause could be determined. And then the city ordered the subway shut down and all entrances shuttered because it was cursed."

Emma let her head fall between her shoulders. "Ugh."

Piper flicked up her eyebrows. "I told you. Even the town council knew what was up. We are so screwed on this."

"They were just superstitious," Emma countered. "It was over a hundred years ago. They didn't understand things like we do now."

"They understood all right. They understood that a billion people died because of a curse and took appropriate precautions." Piper ran her hands through her rainbow-colored hair. "Okay, there has to be something we can do. Look up how to break a curse on your phone. Maybe if we return the key to the dead guy and burn sage or something."

Maggie's thumb hovered over her display.

Emma shot her hand out. "Don't search that. This is ridiculous."

"It can't hurt. At least we'll be passing the time until the guys get here. I should have asked them to bring takeout."

"We're not Googling how to break a curse. There is *no* curse."

"Maggie!" Henry's voice shouted from a distance.

"Thank goodness," Emma murmured, her chin dipping to her chest.

Henry stormed toward them on the horizon, with Charlie and Tarik on either side of him. Leo jogged to catch up as Ollie brought up the rear, strolling at a distance behind the rest of the group.

Maggie rose to stand, brushing off her pants. Piper raced

toward Charlie, flinging herself into his arms as Henry passed them and hurried toward Maggie.

"What the hell happened?" Henry asked.

"Maggie stole a cursed key, and now we're all screwed," Piper said.

Henry screwed up his face. "What? What is she talking about?"

Leo caught up, puffing for breath as he leaned forward on his thighs. His gaze flicked between Emma and Maggie, resting on Maggie as he sucked in a deep breath. "You girls okay?"

"We're fine. Piper's being dramatic."

"It's the only way to live, chicky. Now, what's all this about a curse, fair maiden?"

"Wait, before we get to any curses, how the hell did you get here?" Henry questioned. "We banged on the door, and when Charlie stuck his head, in you were gone. What's going on here, Maggie?"

"I can explain," Maggie said.

"I sure as hell wish someone would," Henry answered, his hands on his hips.

Ollie caught up to the group, his eyebrows shooting up as he studied the women. "Interesting look. How'd this happen?"

Maggie grinned at him. "We found the river of blood!"

Ollie drew his chin back to his chest. "Really? Is this the source of the red stains?"

"Yep," Maggie said, biting her lower lip but still smiling, "we fell into it. Well, Piper fell into it, then Emma and I jumped in."

Henry waved his hands in the air. "Whoa, whoa, whoa. Back up. How did you find the river? How did you get out of your room?"

Emma crossed her arms and cocked a hip. "Maggie made us jump off the balcony."

Henry's eyes went wide, and his jaw dropped. "What?"

"It's a long story. Can we maybe head back home so we can change and get dinner, then explain?"

Henry stared at her, unblinking before he threw a hand in the air. "Yeah, sure, whatever. I guess it can wait."

Maggie frowned at the stinging tone. She sucked in a deep breath and nodded, choosing to let it go. "Great. We're all hungry. And this story deserves to be told right."

She picked up the metal container from the ground, collected the map from Emma, slid the top on, and started toward the parking lot.

Within an hour, they had returned home, showered, changed into fresh clothes, and sat down with Chinese takeout in Maggie's living room.

Leo poked around at his noodles with his chopsticks. "So, why'd you jump off the balcony, Mags? Wedding planning got you down already?"

Henry glared over the top of his takeout container, jabbing the chopsticks into his meal.

"No, we didn't even talk about the wedding," Maggie said as she snagged a piece of shrimp from her box.

Henry's gaze shifted to Maggie, his eyebrows raising.

Piper waved her chopsticks toward Maggie. "Yeah, pretty quickly after we got in there, Maggie jumped off the balcony."

Charlie rubbed her shoulders before returning to his meal.

"I didn't jump. I dangled and dropped."

"Why?" Ollie questioned. "You could have told us."

"We would have been happy to help you dangle." Tarik grinned at her.

"Not really," Maggie said. "No one wanted to hear it. And

I had a lead I wanted to follow up on. I couldn't parade past you without explaining, so I had to get creative. Anyway, I had an idea, and it panned out."

"What was the idea?" Leo asked.

"There's a window with a broken latch on the side of the building. We hopped down to the ground, pried it open, and slipped into the basement."

Ollie leaned forward, his eyes gleaming with curiosity. "Really? And you managed to find the river of blood? Do you think you could do it again?"

"Definitely," Maggie said. "Though I'm not sure all of you will fit through the window."

"And there's no way all of you will fit through the escape route we had to take," Piper said, thumbing toward Emma. "Fanny over here–"

"Don't say it," Emma grumbled.

"Fanny?" Charlie questioned. "Why the new name for brainy?"

"Never mind," Emma answered. "We have pictures of everything, so we can assess from here without having to go back down inside the secret chambers."

"Oh," Ollie said, his voice breathy, "I'd like to see them."

Piper whispered something in Charlie's ear. His eyebrows shot up, and he glanced over at Emma before nodding, his eyes falling to her backside. Emma glared at Piper, shaking her head.

"I'd be happy to show you if we can find a way inside that doesn't use the window," Maggie said. "Until then, we're stuck with these."

"I'm happy to use the pictures Maggie took," Piper said. "I have zero desire to go back into that death cavern and crawl through tunnels to escape."

"You couldn't get back out the way you came?" Ollie asked.

"Well, we tried, but it wasn't immediately obvious how to reopen the passage. And then after Piper fell into the river, we didn't have much choice but to follow her and hope we could escape somewhere else."

Ollie rubbed his chin. "And you came out in the tomb of the Confederate soldier who hid the gold. Fascinating."

"That's not all that's fascinating," Maggie said, shoving her takeout container to the side and dragging the metal box across the table. "We found two keys, a map, and a wall mural seeming to show the gold being unloaded from an ironclad."

Ollie's eyes widened, and he rubbed a napkin across his lips as he set his order of Sweet and Sour Chicken on the side table. "Really? Let me see."

Maggie toggled her phone on and brought up the pictures, sliding it over to Ollie. Henry and Tarik circled behind Ollie, studying the display over his shoulder. "Fascinating. And this is the river? Look at it. Breathtaking."

Charlie climbed to his feet and joined the group studying the pictures. "Is it glowing, or is that an artifact from the flash?"

"It glows," Maggie answered before biting into a piece of shrimp.

"Amazing," Ollie murmured as he swiped at the display.

"What's that?" Henry questioned, poking a finger at the screen.

Ollie zoomed in on the area. "Looks like some sort of statues nearby the site where they unloaded the gold."

Emma closed the lid on her takeout container. "It looks like they took the Ironclad up a river before unloading it. But those drawings do not look American, not even Native American. What do you think, Ollie? Does it look like anything you've seen before?"

"It has to be American, right?" Leo asked. "Thomas Tilton

came here after securing the gold. So, they probably came up the Mississippi, right?"

"It's a safe bet," Emma answered.

"Why is it a safe bet again?" Piper asked.

"Ironclads aren't seaworthy. They couldn't have sailed very far in one," Leo answered.

Emma shot a glance at him, her eyebrows raised. "That's right."

Maggie offered him an impressed stare. "Look at you with the historical facts."

"What? I watched *Sahara*."

"But in *Sahara*, the Ironclad *did* make it across the sea," Ollie said, with a wag of his finger. "And I'd wager this one did, too."

"Really?" Emma questioned. "To Africa?"

Ollie shook his head, flicking his gaze to the screen again. "No. By the looks of these illustrations, I'd put money on Columbia, maybe Venezuela."

"Really, Ollie? That's interesting," Charlie said before settling next to Piper and pulling his laptop onto the table. He clacked around on the keys as the discussion continued. "So, that means the river could be the Amazon or the Orinoco."

"Yes," Ollie answered, rubbing his chin as he stared into space, "but which one?"

"Can we check 'em both?" Leo asked.

Henry scoffed at him, rolling his eyes. "That's thousands of miles of river to check, and that's just one of them. And I doubt they put out a sign that says 'we left the gold here.'"

"You said there was more. Keys and a map?" Tarik asked, straightening.

"Yeah," Maggie said, digging into the box and pulling out the two keys and the map. She passed the map over to Tarik.

"We found another coin like Leo's, one key, and the map in a box over the river."

"I found it," Piper said. "Which is how I took the plunge into the crimson waves."

Leo picked up the coin and studied it. "And the other key?"

"We found that hanging in a workroom."

"With a note that says it's cursed," Piper said. "So, now we're all doomed."

Leo tossed the coin on the table, slouching back in his chair with a chuckle. "Doomed? Seriously?"

Piper shot Maggie a pointed look, arching her eyebrow. "Tell them."

"Wait, I'm a bit confused," Ollie said. "What do you mean workroom? Was this off the river area?"

"Yes and no," Maggie said. "Piper fell into the river, and we floated quite a ways down before we were able to escape it. We found a tunnel to crawl through–"

"That Emma got stuck in," Piper shouted.

"Right, but we got her unstuck, and we came out on some tracks."

"Tracks?" Henry asked as he took his seat on the couch again.

"Yeah," Maggie said, glancing over her shoulder at him before focusing on Ollie. "Did you know there was a subway in Rosemont?"

Ollie's brow furrowed, and he shook his head. "No. I've never heard of it."

"No wonder," Piper said. "After what happened?"

"What happened?" Henry asked.

"One of the trains derailed and killed a bunch of people, including most of the maintenance workers present when they found the second key. They hung it in the workroom, with a note saying it was cursed," Maggie explained.

"Most of them?" Tarik questioned. "So, not all of them?"

"Two of them died before the derailment in bizarre accidents," Emma said.

"The two who actually found the key," Piper added. "The others were there when the key was found but didn't do the finding."

"And then the town closed the subway and never spoke of it again," Maggie said.

Leo grabbed the coin from the table, rolling it between his knuckles. "When did this happen?"

"Nineteen twenty-four," Maggie answered.

"How interesting," Ollie said.

"How did you get to the cemetery?" Leo questioned.

"Oh, in the workroom, there was an air shaft. We crawled through it to try to get to the outside, but we couldn't. But we found a tunnel leading off the shaft and used that to get to the Confederate soldier's mausoleum."

"Right," Emma added. "His tomb collapsed into the tunnel, and we climbed through it and out into the cemetery."

Leo crinkled his nose. "Ew, was his body still in there?"

"Yep," Piper snapped.

"My poor maiden," Charlie said, stroking her hair.

"And now I'm worried that I'm cursed."

"There are no such things as curses," Emma assured her.

"So, what are our next steps?" Maggie questioned as she collected empty takeout containers and stuffed them into a trash bag.

Ollie stared down at the map again. "I think we'll need to do some research into this. See if we can pinpoint any of these vague locations."

Maggie stuffed the bag into her trash can and dusted off her hands. "Sounds good. Where do we start?"

Ollie snapped a picture with his phone before climbing

from the chair. "I think I'll start with a steaming cuppa and my laptop at home."

Maggie shot up her eyebrows. "Oh, you're leaving? I can make you tea if you'd like."

"No, thanks, Maggie. I'm going to head home, do some grading, then dig into this little treasure. Oh, can you forward me your pictures from the blood river?"

"Sure," Maggie said, snatching her phone from the coffee table and tapping around on it. "And you'll let me know if you come up with anything?"

"Of course," Ollie said. "You have a good night. You girls did some great work. Kick your feet up and relax."

"I'm hardly in the mood to relax, but–"

Ollie kissed her cheek, silencing the rest of her words before he waved to the group and headed for the door.

Piper and Charlie climbed to their feet, too. "I've got those images running through a database to see if we find any matches to help nail down the location. I'll give you a holler if we find anything, and you can run right over, chicky."

"You're leaving, too?"

"Yep, me and my fair maiden have a movie marathon planned." He wrapped his arm around Piper and squeezed her.

"Oh," Maggie said, a frown settling on her face, "okay. Enjoy."

Tarik, Emma, and Leo rose from their positions.

Maggie spun to face them. "Is everyone leaving?"

"I've got a few things to do, like laundry and stuff," Emma said as she snapped a picture of the map. "And I have a few places I can check for this."

"Oh, laundry. Right."

"We don't all have a laundry service," she said.

"Well, text me if you find anything."

"Sure, you do the same."

Maggie twisted to face Leo, offering him a weak smile. "I'll text you, Mags." He grabbed her hand and squeezed it before following Emma out the door. The two chattered on their way to the elevator.

Tarik clapped Henry on the shoulder. "See you at home, my friend." He offered Maggie a wave before palming his keys and heading for the door.

"Well, I guess that's that," Maggie said with a sigh, plopping onto her sofa cushion. She reached for the map. Henry slid it away, taking a seat on the coffee table across from her.

"I think we need to talk, Princess."

Maggie let her head rest in her hand, balancing her elbow on the side cushion. "Yeah, we do. I don't even have the slightest clue as to where to start with this map thing. It's so vague."

Henry chewed his lower lip as he flicked his gaze to the side. "Not about that."

Maggie let her head fall back into the cushion behind her. "Not again."

"Yes, again. Because you wouldn't talk about it before. We need to talk about this wedding, Maggie."

"No, we don't. It's a good ways off yet. We have plenty of time. There's no need to rush into anything."

"I'm not rushing into anything. But it feels like you'd rather postpone indefinitely."

"That's not true."

Henry leapt to his feet and paced around the room. "Isn't it? You jumped off a balcony rather than plan the wedding."

"Because we have other things to do right now. I wasn't going to start picking out flower arrangements when there's a river of blood to find!" Maggie exclaimed, flinging her hand out.

"Well, we don't right now, and you still won't talk about

it. You're putting me off. The same way you did in the desert. And you do this when you don't want to deal with something."

"You're reading into things," Maggie said, letting her head fall back into her hand as she shook it.

"Am I? Really? Then let's pick a date right now. There's nothing else going on. Let's just look at a calendar."

"Why do I have to pick the date? Why is this all up to me?"

"Because it's your wedding."

"Oh, it's my wedding. *My* wedding," Maggie snapped, jabbing a finger toward her own chest as she leapt from the couch. "Only mine. You have nothing to do with it."

"Apparently not, since you won't even discuss it with me."

"I'm giving you the opportunity to pick the date. You don't want to."

"Look, Maggie, when I say your wedding, I mean I want you to have the wedding you want to have. I know the dresses and the venue and the flowers and all that stuff are important to you. I'd just as soon go to the JOP next week and get married if it were all the same to me, but I know you don't want that."

"No, I don't," Maggie answered, crossing her arms and flicking her eyebrows up as she let her gaze fall to the floor.

"Okay, so this is why the details are up to you."

She dropped her hands to her sides, balling them into fists and shooting her gaze to Henry. "I don't want all the details to be up to me."

"You don't want anything! That's the problem. You want to avoid this. What's going on with you, Maggie? Just tell me. Do you have cold feet? Is there someone else?"

"Is there someone else?" Heat rose into Maggie's cheeks as she repeated the words. "How dare you accuse me of cheating! And you wonder why I'm reluctant to marry you."

"So you are reluctant?"

Maggie shot him a stony stare. "Get out."

"Come on, Maggie," Henry said, throwing his hands out to the sides.

"Get out!" she shouted at him.

He raised his hands in defeat. "Fine. Whatever. Don't marry me. I don't care anymore." He stormed to the door and whipped it open before spinning back to eye her for a second. "You know, maybe there's a reason you and Leo never stayed together. Call me when you're ready to talk."

He stepped into the hall and slammed the door shut behind him.

"Jerk!" Maggie screamed as she flung her remote at the door. It smacked off the wood and skittered to the floor. Maggie sank into the soft couch cushions as tears formed in her eyes. She flicked them away, annoyed at her own upset and hurt by his final words.

A pout formed on her lips as she fell sideways and pulled her feet up onto the couch, curling into a ball. She sniffled as thoughts skipped around in her mind. Working to push them all aside, she let her eyes slide closed. They popped open again, and she reached for her phone. Her thumb hovered over the call button next to Henry's name. With a sigh, she shoved the phone into her pocket.

A knock sounded at the door, stirring her from her own thoughts. She pushed herself up to stand, sniffling again and wiping at her cheeks as she hurried to the door.

"Couldn't stay away, huh?" she asked, pulling the door open, expecting Henry.

Her heart leapt into her throat as she stared at what faced her. She bit hard into her lower lip, raising her hands in the air and backing a few steps away from the door as three men charged inside, all of them holding guns.

CHAPTER 16

"Whoa," Maggie said as she continued to back away from the men who stormed into her apartment, guns drawn. "Easy. If it's money you want, I don't have cash, but I have jewelry. It's—"

"We don't want your jewelry, Ms. Edwards," one of them snapped.

"O-okay. What do you want?"

"You've been nosing around where you shouldn't have been."

Maggie's heart thudded against her ribs, and she swallowed hard, fighting to maintain her composure. "I don't know what you mean."

"Really?" the lead man said, his eyebrows furrowing as he skirted the couch. He tapped his gun against the map, still spread on the table.

"Oh, that? That's nothing," Maggie said, slicking a lock of hair behind her ear. "It's from a game my friends and I were playing."

"A game?" he asked, closing the gap between them. "A game called Find the Confederate Gold?"

"No," Maggie answered, holding steady eye contact and struggling to stop her lower lip from trembling.

The man kept his dark eyes trained on her as he reached back toward the table, scooping one of the coins into his hand and holding it up between his fingers. "No? This sure looks like Confederate gold to me."

He tossed the coin to another man behind Maggie. "Does this look like Confederate gold to you, Ryan?"

Ryan snatched the coin in mid-air and glanced at it. "Sure does, sir."

The man waved his gun in the air as he circled the couch. "I think Little Miss Maggie has been telling fibs." He pressed the barrel of the gun into her temple. "Have you been telling lies, Maggie?"

"No," she said, her voice quivering as she blinked back the tears stinging her eyes.

"Are you sure? Because I'd like to think we're friends. And friends don't lie to each other, do they?"

Maggie wiggled her head, gasping for breath.

"No, they don't. So, let's try this conversation again, shall we?"

"C-could you please take that gun away from my head?"

"Is it making you nervous?"

Maggie bobbed her head up and down.

"Aww, it's making her nervous, boys. She doesn't know what an excellent weapons handler I am."

A few chuckles went up from the other two men, and the lead man grinned at her.

"You said we're friends. And my friends don't hold guns to my head."

The man cocked his head, pulling away the weapon. "You make a good point. I won't point this at you again unless you lie to me again. I don't like liars."

Maggie licked her lips and nodded.

"Have you been searching for the Confederate gold?"

Maggie nodded again. "Yeah."

The man turned down the corners of his mouth before stepping back to the table. He slid the map off the marble top and waved it around. "And you found this."

"Yeah," Maggie answered again, her voice shaky.

"What else did you find?"

"Two keys," she said, her voice hiccuping.

"Easy, Maggie, there's nothing to be nervous about as long as you keep telling me the truth."

She squashed her lips together in a thin line as her forehead crinkled.

"Are these the keys you found?" the man asked, swiping them from the table.

"Yes," Maggie said. Her knees began to wobble, and she shifted her weight to ease the knot growing between her shoulders. "Look, just take them if you want, okay?"

The man raised his eyebrows as he studied the keys. "Oh, I will be taking them. Along with the map. And a few other valuable items. Did you find anything else?"

Maggie shook her head, swallowing hard. Her phone pressed against her tense leg muscles, and she wondered if she could somehow toggle it on to make a call.

"Really? The great Maggie Edwards hasn't found anything else?"

"We were doing more research. Trying to figure out where that map led. But we haven't figured anything else out yet."

The man stalked closer to Maggie. "That's a shame. But these things happen. Progress isn't always what we hope, is it?"

"Maybe you'll have more luck."

"I doubt that. I'm not the figuring type." He waved the gun in the air. "More brawn than brain. You know what I mean?"

"Sure. Figuring isn't for everyone," she said, her hand caressing the bulge in her pocket.

"You're a smart cookie, Maggie. And that's why, in addition to the map and the keys," he said, waving them in the air before stowing them in his pocket, "we'll be taking you, too."

He lunged toward her and grabbed hold of her arm before she could get away.

"No!" Maggie cried. "Let go of me. I can't help you."

"Oh, I think you can."

Maggie struggled against him, finding herself unable to wrench her arm from his grasp. She snaked the other down toward her phone in the hopes of dialing a number for help.

"Easy, easy," the man said, pulling her closer to him. He let his hand travel down her hip, tugging her phone from her pocket. He tossed it onto the couch. "You won't need this, darling. Now, let's go nice and easy to the elevator and out the front door, okay?"

Maggie wrestled against him, trying to yank her arm from his grip. "No!"

"Now, Maggie, I thought we were friends."

"I'm not going anywhere with you," she growled between clenched teeth. She strained against him, leaning back before shouting, "Help!"

The man tugged her closer, whipping her around and pressing himself against her back. His hand clamped down on her mouth. She tugged at his fingers, trying to free herself. The barrel of the gun poked into her side. "I wouldn't do anything stupid," he warned her.

"Now," he hissed in her ear, "nice and slow, we get on the elevator and walk straight out of this building with no trouble, okay? Real simple."

The gun stabbed into her ribs. "Got it?"

She nodded, sucking in a sharp breath as pain bloomed in her left side from the pressure of the weapon.

"Don't do anything stupid. Or you won't live to regret it."

Maggie nodded her acquiescence, and the man waved her to the door with his gun. With a shaky breath, she slid her eyes to her phone, face down on the couch cushion.

Fingers wrapped around her chin and tugged her face to the side. "What did I just say about doing something stupid?"

Maggie flicked her gaze to his steely eyes. "Sorry, won't happen again."

"It had better not." He grabbed her elbow and shoved her forward.

Maggie stumbled a few steps, sniffling as she sought any escape. She found none as the man marched her to the door. One of his associates pulled open the door. Her captor shoved her through it, hiding his weapon in his blazer after using it to poke at the elevator's call button.

Maggie bit her lower lip. She side-eyed Charlie and Piper's door, hoping they would peek out the peephole or open it. Her eyes flicked back to the floor indicator above the two elevators. One of the cars rose slowly from the ground floor.

Maggie exhaled a shaky breath, letting her eyes return to her neighbor's door. She licked her lips, a shaky breath escaping between them.

The number above the right elevator changed from two to three. Maggie's heart thudded against her ribs as she prayed for Charlie and Piper's door to open.

A shadow crossed under the door. Maggie's heart skipped a beat. Had they seen her? Would they open the door?

The elevator chimed as it reached their floor and the doors slid open. The man tugged her forward into the confines of the elevator. She shot a teary-eyed final glance at the still-closed door.

The elevator doors slid shut a moment later, trapping her inside the small car and sealing her fate. Her stomach turned as the cables worked to lower them to the ground floor.

She wrapped her arms around her midriff, trying to keep her breathing steady. She bit hard into her lower lip to stop it from trembling.

The elevator chimed, and the man slid his arm around her shoulder. "Nice and easy."

Maggie bobbed her head up and down, sniffling as he led her out of the car and toward the lobby. Reggie sat behind the desk, scrolling through social media on his phone. He glanced up as they passed.

"Going out, Ms. Edwards?"

"Yeah," Maggie said, with a shaky breath. "Just heading out with some friends."

"All right, well you have a great night."

"Thanks, Reggie," she said, plastering a smile onto her lips, "you, too. See you tomorrow."

Maggie waved as her breath caught in her throat. The evening air smacked her in the face, blowing her hair back as they strolled out the front door.

"You're good, sweetheart. I don't think he suspected a thing. Which is a good thing, because now we won't have to kill him."

Her features pinched at the idea as they led her to a large SUV. She scanned the parking lot, hoping to find Henry's car still in it and him behind the wheel. Instead, the spot he'd parked in when they'd returned from the cemetery sat empty.

He'd gone home after their fight. Why would he stay?

His last words stung her as the man popped open the rear door and shoved Maggie inside. She climbed into the seat, meeting a gun barrel as she settled into the hard leather. Ryan leveled his weapon at her from the front as the lead man slid into the back seat on the opposite side.

"Give me your hands."

"What?"

"Your hands, Ms. Edwards. Give me your hands."

"Why?"

"You don't get to ask questions. Give me your hands, or Ryan will knock you out with the butt of his gun."

Maggie offered him her wrists, and he snugged them together with a zip tie. "Ow," she complained, wincing as the plastic cut into her skin.

"You'll be okay," he assured her as the second man fired the engine. Maggie swallowed hard when the car lurched forward. She'd memorize the route. If she could get away, she'd remember where they'd kept her.

She shot a glance out the dark, tinted window, eyeing her apartment building as it slid by before disappearing behind her.

A thick black cloth cut off any more of her view. "Hey!" she exclaimed as the bag closed around her head.

"We wouldn't want you to know where you are. It'll ruin all the fun."

They drove for twenty minutes as Maggie worked to keep her breathing steady and memorize the turns they had taken. The car finally eased to a stop. The smell of fresh air wafted through the thick cloth.

The vehicle bobbled around before air swept across Maggie's forearm. A hand grabbed her roughly. "Nice and easy," the lead man said as he tugged her from the car. She slid onto the ground, her knees buckling.

Her captor's iron grip stopped her from falling to the pavement.

"I know I tend to make the ladies weak in the knees, but I thought you were a stronger woman, Maggie," the man said, with a gruff laugh.

His fellow accomplices chuckled over his poor joke. "Come on, let's go. We've got important business."

"Can you take the blindfold off now?" Maggie asked as he pulled her arm forward.

"Not just yet, sweetheart. We've got a surprise for you."

"I don't like surprises," Maggie answered, stumbling forward as she struggled to walk blindfolded and bound at the wrists.

"You may like this one. The boss is convinced you will."

"You have a boss?"

"I do, darlin'."

"I want to see him."

"And he wants to see you. We just need to have a short conversation with him first. And after that, he's all yours." The man gave a sharp laugh. "Well, I guess you're all his."

The three men chuckled again. Darkness consumed her, and no air blew across her bare forearms. She assumed they'd stepped out of the parking area and into a building of some kind.

"You wait here," her captor said. "Watch her like a hawk. She's slippery. Don't let her get away, or I'll personally shoot you myself for screwing up."

The man's shoes squeaked across the floor as he stalked away. Unintelligible voices floated from far away. Maggie strained to listen to the conversation, trying to pick out any words that could help her, but she couldn't make out anything.

"Could I get this bag removed from over my head yet?" she asked.

"No," one of the men answered.

"Come on. What can it hurt?"

"I said no," he barked at her.

Maggie pursed her lips at his words, wiggling her wrists

in the restraints. "How about the zip tie? Can you take that off?"

"No."

Maggie winced, sliding her wrists up and down again. "They hurt."

"I don't care. I said no. Stop asking for things."

The squeak of a man's shoes on the cement floor squashed any further conversation.

"Any trouble?" Maggie recognized the lead man's voice again.

"She's whiny and demanding," the other man said.

"Yeah, the boss said she was. Don't know why he didn't just want her offed, but he didn't."

Maggie's brow furrowed. How did the boss of these men know her? She swallowed hard, grateful he didn't have her killed outright. A chill snaked down her spine, though, as she considered what it was he wanted from her in return.

"She's his problem now," Ryan answered.

"Yep," the man said. His fingers curled around Maggie's elbow. "Come on, Ms. Edwards. Time for you to meet the boss."

"Wait, wait," Maggie said. "I-I need to use the bathroom."

"No," the lead man said, tugging at her again.

"Come on. I've got to go."

"You can go after you've talked to the boss. Not before then."

"But–" Maggie started, digging her feet into the floor as he yanked her forward.

She lost the battle, stumbling forward a few steps until she fell into stride next to him. He led her through a doorway. Her arm scraped against the cold metal as he tugged her into the room.

"Here she is, Boss. She's all yours. I'm glad to be done with her."

Maggie stamped a foot on the floor. "I have to go to the bathroom, and your goon won't let me."

"See what I mean," the man said.

He ripped off the bag from over her head. She sucked in a long breath, shaking her head to clear the fly-away hairs from her face. She focused her eyes on the man standing across the room from her. He rubbed his thumb along his lips, which curved at the corners into an amused smile.

His grin broadened, and he lowered his chin as realization struck her.

"Hello, Maggie."

Maggie swallowed hard as her heart hammered in her chest. She licked her lips, biting the lower one to stop it from trembling as her eyes focused on Brent Bryson.

CHAPTER 17

"Bryson?" Maggie gasped, her pulse racing as she broke out into a cold sweat.

"Did you miss me?" He threw his arms out to the side, wincing a little and sucking in a sharp breath.

"Not at all," she answered, a frown settling on her lips.

He approached, rubbing his fingers along her jawline as she tugged her face away from him. "Aww, come on, darling. We've been through so much together."

Maggie flicked her eyes back to his face, glaring at him, her nostrils flaring.

He held her gaze for a moment before he stalked away. "You really should thank me. I could have just let them kill you after they took the map and the keys."

"Why didn't you?" Maggie questioned.

"Where's the fun in that?" Bryson purred, with another cocky grin.

"I could have plenty of fun if you cut these zip ties," Maggie said, holding up her wrists.

"Maybe later, not quite yet."

"They hurt."

"Oh, how tragic," Bryson answered, unbuttoning his shirt and tugging it down past his shoulder. An angry red scar marred his arm. "How do you think this felt?"

"I didn't do that to you."

"No, your little Scottish friend, double-oh-duchess, did it. On your behalf."

"You were trying to kidnap me. It was only fair."

"Well, now I have kidnapped you. So, the zip ties stay." He narrowed his eyes and lowered his chin. "It's only fair play."

"Hardly amusing."

He closed the distance between them again, letting his fingers brush her cheek. "I wasn't amused either when I was shot. But let's not spend our time together rehashing the past, shall we? I'd hoped to move forward together."

She snapped her face away from him again, refusing to make eye contact. "Then why am I here?"

"Because I would like you to help me solve the clues and find the Confederate gold."

"No," she said.

He grabbed her chin in his hands, squashing her lips together as he squeezed her roughly. "Don't press your luck, Maggie. I don't like you *that* much."

Maggie wrestled her face from his grasp, stumbling back a step. She glared at him. She shifted her tongue, pooling her spit before launching it from her mouth. It smacked him in the cheek, sliding down to drip from his jaw.

Bryson wiped at his face with the back of his hand, his jaw clenching. He fluttered his eyelashes as he used his fingers to wipe away the final traces of saliva that clung to the stubble on his chin.

He raised his eyes to meet Maggie's, his nostrils flaring before he lunged at her, spinning her around and slamming her against the wall. Maggie winced as he pressed into her, smashing her cheek against the unfinished drywall.

She groaned as she struggled against him, but he crushed her with his bulk. "Let's be clear about one thing, Maggie. I will not tolerate this behavior. Do you understand?"

Maggie pushed back against him, digging her feet into the ground as she tried to escape again. He grabbed her hair and pounded her head against the wall. "I asked you a question."

She sucked in a shaky breath and gasped out, "Yes."

He jiggled her head again. "Yes, what?"

"Yes, I understand."

The pressure released against her back. Maggie pulled herself away from the wall, gasping for breath.

"Good," Bryson said, tugging down his sleeves and adjusting his shirt. "Now, let's talk about that gold."

Maggie stared at the floor, heat still washing over her from the encounter. "I don't know anything about finding it. We didn't make any conclusions about where it could be."

Bryson cocked his head, narrowing his eyes at Maggie. "I've never known you to be so bashful, Maggie."

"I tend to be less confident after someone's thrown me against a wall and threatened me."

"I didn't threaten you. I merely made a point. But you bring up a good idea. Perhaps you just don't have the proper motivation to help me."

Maggie shrugged. "I don't have any motivation to help you."

"Not even to stay alive?"

"I don't believe you're going to let me live, even if we find it. If you think I do, then you can't possibly think I'm smart enough to figure this out."

Bryson wandered to the metal desk, spinning a laptop around on the laminate top. "The great Maggie Edwards stumped? I'm shocked."

Maggie grimaced at him as he tugged open the device and tapped around on the keys.

"Perhaps this will motivate you."

A video feed filled the screen. A grainy black-and-white video showed the exterior of a building. Maggie let her eyes slide closed as she recognized it.

"Open your eyes, darling, you're missing the best part."

With a sigh, she snapped her eyes open and stared at the screen. A shadow crossed the pavement before its owner appeared. Bryson tapped the space bar, pausing the feed on Henry's face. Bryson smiled at the image before cutting his gaze to Maggie.

"I do not know what you see in this man, but...the fact remains, you are engaged to him. I assume that means you'll do whatever it takes to keep him alive."

"Henry's not stupid. He'll see you coming from a mile away."

"Will he? It's interesting that he didn't already. You were fairly easy to take. I really thought we'd be in for more of a fight, but he doesn't seem to even notice you're missing yet. This was taken only twenty minutes ago." Bryson waved to an object clutched in Henry's hand. "Burger Bub. Seems like he's happily enjoying his meal."

Maggie fluttered her eyelashes, clicking her tongue. "Why would he know I'm missing? He's not with me."

Bryson perched on the edge of the desk, crossing his arms. "Nor is he talking to you, it seems. One might think your fiancé would text you. Or share dinner with you."

"We planned to eat separately. I have wedding stuff to do."

"Really?"

Maggie jerked her head to the side, flicking a lock of hair over her shoulder. "Yep. Busy, busy. Flowers, invitations, guest lists. Henry's not big on wedding details."

Bryson rose and stalked toward her. "No?"

"No," she answered, holding his gaze.

"Do you know what I think, Maggie?"

She flicked her eyebrows up, prompting him to continue.

"I think you're bluffing. I don't think he knows you're gone yet, and I don't think he's going to be checking in, which gives us some time to play together uninterrupted."

Maggie bit into her lower lip, flicking down her eyes. Her brain scrambled to come up with the best solution to her current situation. Would admitting Henry didn't know help her or hurt her?

She sucked in a deep breath, making her final decision and meeting his gaze. "Okay, so maybe he doesn't know yet, but he will find out eventually."

"Eventually, yes, but when? My man tells me he overheard some arguing before Taylor stormed from your apartment. So, Maggie," Bryson said, sliding a lock of hair behind her ear, "we may have more time together than I anticipated."

"What makes you think seeing Henry will motivate me? If your guys overheard the argument, they should know we're not exactly on the best of terms."

"Please don't try to tell me you wouldn't care if he ceased to live."

Maggie offered a coy glance, pretending to be uninterested.

"Really?" Bryson questioned, taking a step backward and staring at the frozen image of Henry on the screen. "That big of a fallout, was it?"

Maggie lifted a shoulder.

He lowered his eyes to Maggie's bound hands. "Yet you're still wearing your ring."

Maggie wiggled her eyebrows. "Probably should have thrown it at him when he left."

Bryson offered her a coy smile. "How interesting."

Maggie returned his expression.

His grin broadened. "Do you really expect me to believe you wouldn't care if I killed Taylor?"

Maggie stared into his green eyes, assessing her answer carefully before giving it. "I wouldn't say don't care at all, but care a hell of a lot less than I did."

Bryson puckered his lips and nodded, letting his gaze fall to the floor. "You're angry with him. But not enough to want him dead."

"But maybe angry enough to work with you."

Bryson wagged a finger in the air. "You weren't fifteen minutes ago, which is why I think you're bluffing."

"I was shocked. And you weren't exactly nice. But the more I think about it, maybe we should work together."

"You are such a tease," Bryson said, with a shake of his head.

"At least you're interested in finding the gold."

"Taylor isn't?"

Maggie shrugged. "Not as interested as you."

"Hmmm," Bryson murmured, flicking his gaze sideways to the image of Henry. "All right, let's work together to find it. But if I find your interest is fake and you're undermining me in any way, I'll kill Taylor, and I'll make you watch."

"Understood. Now, how about removing these?" Maggie waved her wrists in the air.

"I don't think so," Bryson said with a sniff, slamming the laptop closed and sliding it off the desk. "We haven't come that far yet."

Maggie sighed, squashing her lips into a thin line.

"Don't worry," he said as he approached her, "you'll have the chance to earn your freedom." He winked at her before he pushed past her into the empty outer room.

"You coming?" he called over his shoulder.

Maggie's gaze followed him into the empty warehouse. She flicked her eyes to the desk in front of her, sucking in a deep breath as she prepared herself for what lay ahead.

With a roll of her shoulders, she lifted her chin and followed Bryson out the door.

"Oh, good, I thought maybe you were planning to be stubborn," he said. "If you are, there's a comfy seat in the back of this van for you. If you promise to play nice, you can ride with me."

He swung open the door of the ostentatious red sports car that had nearly run her down once outside of the museum.

Maggie eyed the two options. She'd have a better chance of escaping with Bryson. With a hard swallow, she forced a smile onto her face and stalked toward the car. "I'll take this one."

Bryson held a hand out, blocking her from sliding into the low seat. "You've got to promise to play nice."

Maggie slid her eyes sideways to stare at him. "I promise."

The corners of his lips curled, and he waved her inside, easing the door shut behind her. After a few spoken words to his compatriots, he slid in behind the wheel. Maggie struggled to tug on her seatbelt and latch it with her wrists bound together.

Bryson grabbed the buckle, sliding it into the receiver with a resounding click before he fired the engine. It sprang to life with a throaty growl. He revved the engine a few times as a garage door trundled up in front of them.

Maggie held back rolling her eyes at the behavior. As the door finished its circuit, Bryson shifted. The tires peeled against the smooth floor before finding purchase. The car shot forward. Bryson swung the wheel hard, and the vehicle fishtailed into a sharp turn before he straightened it.

"I hope you're not afraid of a little speed, darling."

"You're as bad a driver as Henry," Maggie answered.

Bryson flicked his gaze sideways as he shifted again. "So tell me, what did you and Taylor argue about?"

"None of your business."

"Oh, touchy, are we? Personal, then?"

Maggie stared down at her lap, weighing her answer.

"Did he cheat?"

"No!" she said, snapping her gaze to him.

"It was a fair guess. Perhaps with that mousy red-headed friend of yours. Ella, was it?"

"Emma. And she's not mousy." Maggie flicked a lock of hair over her shoulder with her bound hands. "She's just not as fabulous as me."

They drove a few more miles, any traces of civilization disappearing as the town of Rosemont faded behind them. "So you're really not going to tell me?"

"Are you actually interested in my personal drama with Henry?"

Bryson shifted again, urging more speed from the vehicle. "I'm always interested in drama involving Taylor."

Maggie eyed him as their surroundings zipped by the window. "Really? Relationship drama is your thing?"

"Sometimes a well-placed verbal assault can do more damage than a well-placed bullet. And I've already shot him once. I need new tactics."

Maggie glanced out the window, wondering where they were going. "Well, you're not getting them from me."

"I thought we agreed to play nice?"

She flicked her gaze back to him. "Playing nice means I'm not going to claw your face off and wreck this car to escape."

His eyes met hers. "I'll leave the clawing of faces between you and Taylor. I haven't done anything to incur your wrath."

"Oh, no," Maggie said, with a chuckle and fake smile, "you've only kidnapped me at gunpoint, tied me up, and held me hostage. And that's just this round. I'm not counting what happened in Scotland or Egypt. Oh, and threatened to kill my fiancé."

"A fiancé you don't care what happens to. By the way, I've given that some thought. If Taylor isn't enough motivation for you, let's add your little friend Rainbow Brite to the mix. I know how far you're willing to go to save her."

Any traces of amusement disappeared from her face. She set her gaze out her window. Through the reflection, she caught sight of him glancing at her.

"I see that seems to have provided the proper motivation."

She snapped her angry gaze back to him. "What do you want from me?"

"I told you. Your help finding the gold."

"But I don't know anything." She shifted to study their surroundings, searching for a clue to their destination.

"I may know something. We'll discuss it further when we arrive at our destination. Until then, tell me what you know already. What happened when you and your girlfriends did your trapeze act from your balcony?"

"We found a few keys and a map. You know this. Or at least I assume you do." She cut her gaze sideways. "Or did your guy not tell you?"

Bryson chuckled, slowing the car as he made a turn onto a narrow but paved road. "He told me. There is nothing to exploit there, Maggie. Move on."

"There's not much more to tell."

"I beg to differ. How did you come across these keys? How did you know to search there?"

"Leo told us a story about a river of blood. Charlie managed to track down an article claiming it flowed underground beneath our apartment building. On a hunch, we checked it out."

Bryson slowed the car, easing onto another paved road. "And found it."

"Yes."

"And?"

"The map, key, and a Confederate coin were in a box hanging over the river."

"Any other clues?"

Maggie bit into her lower lip, considering his question.

He flicked his gaze sideways. "Maggie?"

"Illustrations on the walls showed an ironclad being unloaded somewhere. The location had some sort of symbols around it none of us recognized."

"What did they look like?"

"Odd faces and heads. I had pictures, but your guys weren't smart enough to bring them."

"Where are the pictures?" he asked as a brightly lit house appeared on the horizon.

"On my phone. I wanted to bring it, but your guy insisted we leave it at my place."

They passed through a large iron gate flanked on either side by stone columns. Bryson eased the car to a stop outside of the modern house, killing the engine. "And I suppose you want him to go back and retrieve it."

Maggie shrugged. "It may be helpful. I mean, I saw them, but I don't know if I remember exactly what they looked like."

Bryson huffed out an aggravated sigh before he kicked the door open and climbed from the car. He waited as the van trundled up the driveway behind them and came to a stop. After a few spoken words, two of the men climbed out in the night air, while the others remained in the vehicle.

Bryson stalked to the passenger side of the car and yanked the door open. "Let's go."

Maggie winced as he pulled her from the car and led her to the house. After fiddling with a keyfob, he unlocked the door and shoved her inside.

She stumbled forward a few steps, catching herself before she fell to the flagstone floor below her.

"Let me know when Ryan and Jones return," Bryson barked at the other men. "Until then, do not disturb me. Ms. Edwards and I have business."

Maggie's stomach turned over at the words as he wrapped his arm around her elbow and pulled her forward with him. After a command to his virtual assistant, lights sprang to life around the living room. Bryson led her to an armchair, leaving her there and crossing to a bar.

"Sit down, Maggie, make yourself comfortable," he said as he poured two brandies.

"I can't get comfortable with my wrists bound together," she answered, waving her hands in the air.

"Try," he said, with a smirk. "You haven't earned your freedom yet."

He crossed back to her and waved a glass at her as she plopped onto the chair.

"No, thanks," she said, her lips tugging down.

He wiggled the glass in front of her face. "Come on, Maggie, I'm being polite. The least you can do is return the favor. We agreed to play nice."

Maggie ripped the glass from his hand, sloshing the amber liquid inside. He clinked his glass against hers before taking a sip. "To new partnerships."

Maggie wrinkled her nose as she stared into the drink.

"Now," Bryson said, sinking onto the couch adjacent to her. "Let's discuss our next steps."

Maggie slid the glass onto the marble coffee table in front of her. "Let's discuss how we're not a partnership."

Bryson eyed her over the rim of his tumbler as he took another sip of brandy. "I am becoming very much concerned about your motivation, Maggie."

Maggie cast her gaze at her feet as she considered her response.

"Maybe you have a point, though. I haven't been a very

good host outside of the drink. Aren't you the one who loves food and becomes...what was the word again...hangry?"

"I do *not* get hangry."

"Still, a late meal may be in order." He rose from the couch and stalked back toward the front door. Maggie scanned the room as he spoke to the men guarding it.

Several glass panels overlooked the desolate yard. The lights of Rosemont glimmered in the distance. Could she make it back to town if she escaped? She had to try. She launched from the seat and scurried across the room to the large sliding glass doors.

She tugged at the handle. The door did not budge. With a huff, she clumsily tried to flick the lock to a new position with her bound hands. A curse slipped between her lips as she fiddled with it, unable to flick the lever to the unlock position.

"Claustrophobic?" Bryson's voice said from behind.

She jumped, biting her lower lip and squeezing her eyes shut. She spun to face him, forcing another smile onto her lips. "I needed some air."

"Really?" he asked, the smirk returning to his mouth as he stalked toward her. She readied herself to be yanked away from the door, but he slid his arm behind her and flicked up the lock. His foot kicked a floor lock, disengaging it before he slid the door open. Cool night air tickled her bare forearms.

"Ah, much better, thanks."

Bryson smiled at her as she faked deep breaths of the fresh air. "You know, there is a six-foot fence surrounding this property on all sides. So, if you had thought of opening this door and fleeing into the night, you'd find yourself stuck. Particularly in your situation." He flicked his gaze to her wrists.

"Oh," Maggie said, feigning shock, "no. It just felt stuffy in here. I wouldn't run. Where would I go?"

They both laughed for a moment before Bryson tugged her closer to him. "Exactly. Remember that, because if you try to run, you won't be the only one who pays the price."

Maggie swallowed hard as Bryson's cell phone rang. He fished it from his pocket and swiped to answer the call. "Yes?"

His eyebrows flicked upward as someone spoke on the other end. His gaze cut to Maggie. "Really? How interesting. Thank you. I'll text you instructions."

He ended the call and opened his messaging app. His thumbs flew across the keyboard before he toggled off the device and slid it into his pocket as he stared at Maggie.

"Good news?" she asked.

"Interesting news."

"Care to share?"

"Yes, I think I will." He wrapped his fingers around Maggie's elbow and guided her back to her seat. "That was Jones. He's retrieved your phone."

"Oh, good," Maggie said, sounding a bit too excited as she tried to fake her way through the conversation.

"Yes, very. He sent me the pictures in question, so now we'll have all the information."

Maggie forced a smile at the words.

"And he found something else very interesting."

"Oh?" Maggie asked.

"Yes. It appears perhaps I have been applying the wrong pressure to gain your cooperation."

Maggie swallowed hard, then licked her lips.

"It seems you have rekindled your relationship with one Leo Hamilton."

CHAPTER 18

"I don't know what you're talking about," Maggie said, avoiding eye contact and setting her gaze on the floor.

"Don't you?"

"No."

"Really? How interesting. It would appear there is some rather damning evidence on your phone. It would also appear we need to move more quickly than I anticipated, since the group will likely be alerted to your absence thanks to your failure to show up at a clandestine meeting with Mr. Hamilton."

"It wasn't clandestine."

"It wasn't?" Bryson asked as a smile played on his lips. He toggled on his phone and tapped around before reading from it. "Where are you, Mags? You're late as usual. Didn't get rid of the old ball and chain yet, huh? Maggie, are you coming? We planned to meet an hour ago. Text something mundane if you can't talk."

He clicked off the screen and set his gaze on Maggie. "Sounds rather clandestine to me. I hadn't realized Taylor had become so unappealing. Though I certainly understand. I almost feel sorry for the bloke."

"That's none of your business."

"It is when I'm targeting the wrong man. But I've fixed that. If Taylor can't motivate you to help me, perhaps Mr. Hamilton can. Cooperate, or I'll make sure he doesn't survive."

Maggie pressed her lips together in a thin line. "I'm cooperating. Did you get the pictures we needed? Or did your guys spend all their time searching for a scandal in my text messages?"

"No, I've got the pictures. And as soon as we've finished our meal, I would suggest we get on the road. I wouldn't want any of your friends to track us down, though I'm quite sure they won't know the first place to look."

"Henry's not stupid."

"No, but is he motivated enough to find you? That is the question. If the information comes from Mr. Hamilton, he may not be."

"Whatever. I don't know where we're going to go, because I have no idea what any of this means. You would have been better off kidnapping Uncle Ollie."

"Oliver isn't nearly as pretty," Bryson answered as he collapsed onto the couch.

"But he has a lot more information about where this may be."

"If we need dear old Uncle Ollie, we'll nab him. Until then, we'll work together on what we do know."

One of Bryson's thugs wandered into the room, carrying a brown paper bag. The aroma of Italian food filled the air.

"Which is nothing, I keep telling you that."

Bryson accepted the bag, tearing it open and sliding the contents from inside. "Perhaps some food will help your mind work."

He slid one of the Styrofoam containers toward Maggie. She wrinkled her nose at it. "Sorry, my stomach just isn't cooperating for some odd reason."

"I would suggest you coax it. If you don't eat now, I make no promises on when you'll eat next."

Maggie glared at him, tugging the container closer and flipping it open. Her stomach growled as the scent of spaghetti reached her nose. "I can't eat with my hands like this."

Bryson eyed her bound wrists as he twirled strands of spaghetti around the tines of his fork. He reached into his pocket and withdrew a switchblade. With a flick of his wrist, he snapped it open.

Maggie swallowed hard as he lunged toward her, only letting out a barely audible sigh of relief when he sliced her restraints and returned the knife to his pocket. She rubbed at the angry red marks on her skin before she picked up her fork and dove into the meal.

"You know, I'm not being difficult," she said, lifting the garlic bread to her mouth for a bite, "I don't know where to start with this."

Bryson poked at the noodles in his container. "I may be able to help with that."

"How?"

"I have a lead on one of the keys."

Maggie froze, snapping her gaze to him. "Really?"

"Oh, it seems now I have your attention."

"You've had my attention since your goons waved a gun in my face. This is the first time I'm actually intrigued, though."

Bryson lifted his fork to his lips. "Good. That will help when the time comes to retrieve it."

"Where is it?"

"That's not information you need," Bryson said before taking a sip of his brandy.

Maggie set the fork down, balancing it on the edge of the Styrofoam container. "I disagree."

"I don't much care."

She tensed her jaw, flaring her nostrils as she considered her response. "You will if I can't solve this. The location of the next key may be able to tell me where it is in relation to these two. Which may lead me to discover the fourth key's location on the very vague map. So, its location is the information I need."

Bryson snapped his gaze at her, raising his eyebrows. "You make a compelling case."

"I usually do," she said, with a coy smirk.

"All right. I suppose it won't do much harm. New Orleans. French Quarter."

Maggie furrowed her brow as she spun more spaghetti around her fork. "Let me see the map again."

Bryson wiped his hands on the napkin draped over his thigh before passing it over.

Maggie unrolled it and studied it. "Okay, so these two Xs that are almost on top of one another must be the two keys in Rosemont. One buried with the soldier, and one over the blood river."

She traced a finger down to the next star. "So, is this the one in New Orleans, or is it this one?" She moved her finger down to poke at the lower star on the page.

Bryson rose from his seat, circled behind her, and leaned over her shoulder to peer at the map. "If this one is the New Orleans key," he said, poking a finger at the middle X, "where is this?"

"We need a map."

Bryson pulled his phone from his pocket, opened a map, and zoomed out to include New Orleans.

Maggie glanced at it, pressing her fingers against her temple. "This is completely out of proportion. There's no way to tell. If the first one is New Orleans, the other guy would be somewhere here, maybe? Panama?"

"What if the lower one is the New Orleans key?"

Maggie grabbed the cell phone from his hands, repositioning the map and zooming in. "So, my best guess for the other key would be Memphis, maybe?"

"Memphis," Bryson repeated, pulling the phone from her hands and settling on the couch again.

"Which one is it, though? We have no way of knowing."

"Not unless we find another clue."

"And if we don't?"

"We'll make an educated guess," Bryson answered, staring into the darkness beyond the glass across the room as he sipped at his brandy.

"Maybe Uncle Ollie–"

"What do *you* think, Maggie?" he interrupted.

"I don't have an educated guess. This is why I have an archeologist on my team."

"Where do you believe a Confederate soldier would have hidden the keys? Memphis or Panama?"

Maggie shot him an irritated glance. "When you say it like that, Memphis. But…"

Bryson flicked his eyebrows up as she stared into space. "But what?"

"The drawings don't look like anything American. Not even Native American. I asked Emma, and she doesn't believe it indicates a place in the US." Maggie squashed her features, biting into her lower lip.

"But?"

Maggie sighed. "But Ironclads weren't seaworthy. So it couldn't have gone anywhere else."

"Yet the drawings seem to illustrate that it did," Bryson said.

"But it couldn't have, which means we have nothing to go on."

"We have what we have. We'll need to do some research. Perhaps there is a legend in Memphis or Panama."

"Panama?" Maggie asked, with a wrinkled nose.

"A Confederate soldier appearing in Panama in the mid-eighteen hundreds would likely not have gone unnoticed."

Maggie shook her head as she closed the lid on her takeout container. "I really think we need Uncle Ollie or Emma."

"No," Bryson said. "You two women are more trouble than you are worth, particularly when you're together. The bickering never ceases."

Maggie chewed her lower lip as she stared into space. "Can't imagine she'll be very happy with me if she finds out I was meeting with Leo either."

"I wondered how long it would be before you tired of Taylor."

"I didn't tire of him," Maggie shot back.

"Really? Can't choose, then? A bit of having your cake and eating it, too, is it?"

"A bit of none of your business," Maggie said, shooting a glaring glance at him as she wadded her napkin and tossed it on top of the styrofoam box.

"Ohh, we're touchy about this. Which makes me think we're guilty of something."

"How are we going to research the other key?" Maggie asked, changing the subject.

"Let me worry about that for now. We'll focus on retrieving the New Orleans key."

"And how do you propose we do that?"

"Simple. We'll steal it from the current owner. I know

exactly where it is. It surfaced a few years ago. Of course, they never made the connection to this tale, but I'm fairly certain this is one of the four keys."

"What makes you so certain?"

"It was found with a Confederate coin, just like the one in the box."

Maggie leaned back, sliding down the chair's supple leather. "That's pretty compelling evidence, I guess. So, where is this key?"

"In the private collection of one Ronald Royce."

Maggie fluttered her eyelashes, her eyebrows shooting high. "The senator?"

"Correct."

"And how do you propose we get it? Rob a senator's house?"

"More or less," Bryson said, rising from his seat and crossing to refill his drink.

"Please tell me we get to watch your thugs do this from a van parked far, far away."

Bryson grinned at her, carrying the brandy snifter across the room to refill the drink in her hand. "Nothing quite so boring."

Maggie shot him a glance as her stomach turned over. "Please do not tell me you expect me to do this."

"I expect you to help," he called over his shoulder from the bar.

"Ugh. You should have left the brandy."

"It won't be difficult. We have our way in already. We'll only have to nab the key."

"Oh, is that all? What's our in?"

"The good senator is hosting a lavish soiree at his home tomorrow night. And guess who's invited?"

Maggie took a long sip of the brandy. "We are."

"That's right, darling. We are." He clinked his glass against hers before he slumped onto the couch again.

"You know it's never as easy as you think it will be."

"Ah, but I'm teaming up with the great Maggie Edwards. So, I expect we can pull it off."

She settled back in her chair again, taking another sip of the amber liquid as she mulled it over.

"We are going as Mr. and Mrs. William Richardson."

Maggie arched an eyebrow and shot him a glance. "I'm going to need a lot more brandy to pull that one off."

"I have every faith in you, Maggie. William Richardson is a wealthy businessman. And his beautiful wife is devoted to him."

"Like I said, I'm going to need *a lot* more alcohol. Tell me you at least got me a killer dress."

Bryson sipped his brandy before leaning forward, balancing his elbows on his knees. "How does a red Valentini sound?"

Maggie's eyes lit at the designer's name. She took a sip of brandy and licked her lips, playing coy. "It's a start."

"A start? Darling, I spared no expense for the glamorous Maggie Edwards. That dress set me back thousands."

Maggie lifted her eyebrows and leaned forward. "But I need shoes, too."

Bryson guffawed before swallowing the last of his brandy. "Don't worry, I took care of that, too. I don't remember the brand name offhand, but they're the ones with the red bottoms."

Maggie's lips curled on the edges. "And surely you took care of the jewelry your oh-so-devoted wife would be wearing."

Bryson rose to his feet, leaning closer to Maggie. "Don't worry. You will be appropriately outfitted. You may even leave both Mr. Hamilton and Taylor for me after you see the rubies I've acquired for the occasion."

"I wouldn't go that far," Maggie answered as Bryson offered his hand to pull her to stand. "I don't like you."

"How tragic. And here I assumed showering you with gifts would work. Come along, we need to leave now."

"Do I get to keep the outfit?"

Bryson shot a questioning glance over his shoulder at her. "Really? I assumed you wouldn't want to keep it. You don't like me."

"It *is* a Valentini," Maggie said. "But maybe I should reserve judgment for after I see it. You may have horrible taste in dresses."

Bryson scoffed at the statement. "I assure you, I am far better than Taylor in these matters."

As they entered the foyer, one of Bryson's guards approached, his cell phone clutched in his hands. "Sir, we have a problem."

"I don't like to hear those words, Ryan," Bryson barked at him.

Maggie chewed her lower lip, wondering if the so-called problem would be the answer to her prayers.

Before they went any further, Bryson waved a hand toward Maggie. "Jones, take Ms. Edwards upstairs for a few moments."

"What? No!" Maggie shouted as the man approached her. She danced away from him, dodging his grasp.

"Come on, darling, let's not make a scene," Jones grumbled at her.

"Get him off me. Bryson!"

Bryson slid his eyes closed and shook his head. "Go upstairs, Maggie."

"No! I'm not going anywhere with him! Look what he did to my wrists the last time," Maggie said, flashing her bruised arms. "And I'm pretty certain he bruised a few more places, too."

"Didn't you say something about having to go to the bathroom hours ago? Perhaps now would be an appropriate moment."

"Then I'll go alone."

"I don't think so."

"I'm *not* going with him," Maggie snapped, jabbing a finger at the burly man.

Bryson's features turned stony. "You'll do as you're told. Do not mistake our partnership for friendliness, Ms. Edwards, or you will be sorely disappointed. I like you, but I won't tolerate this behavior. Go upstairs with Jones, now."

Maggie pouted at him as the burly man reached for her again. "Don't touch me."

"Let her go," Bryson instructed him.

Maggie raised her chin and stalked past Bryson, mounting the stairs, with Jones following closely behind her.

"Don't dally, Maggie. We leave as soon as I've dealt with this issue," Bryson warned as she stomped up the thin wooden planks.

Maggie bit into her lower lip as she processed the statement. She preferred not to leave. The further they went from Rosemont, the less likely her friends would be able to find her. She needed a plan, and she needed one fast. She had to use this moment to escape. Her life depended on it.

CHAPTER 19

"Which way?" she spat at her captor as she reached the top of the stairs.

The man shoved open the first door on the right and waved her inside. She stepped into a posh bedroom and scanned it for a door leading to the bathroom.

"Over there. Don't be too long," Jones grunted as he pointed across the room.

Maggie followed the line of his finger, finding an open door leading to a dark space. She hurried toward it, snaking an arm around the jamb to feel for a light. Her fingers hit the switch, and she flipped it, flooding the bathroom with a warm, yellow glow.

She stepped inside and started to close the door. It caught midway through her swing. She glanced back, finding a meaty hand wrapped around the edge.

"I don't think so," Jones said.

"Are you kidding?"

"Nope. Door stays open."

Maggie let go of the handle and crossed her arms,

offering the man an unimpressed stare. "Now I'm the one who doesn't think so."

Jones didn't budge.

"I'm not going to the bathroom with you watching me."

"And I'm not letting you out of my sight."

"Fine," Maggie said, balling her hands into fists. "Turn around."

"Uh-uh," Jones said with a shake of his head.

Maggie's eyes went wide. She pressed her lips together and tried to dart past Jones. "Bryson!"

"Boss isn't going to help you. He's busy, and he already told you to do what you were told."

"By him, not by you," Maggie said, poking a finger at the man's chest. "I'm sure he'd agree a little privacy is warranted."

Jones narrowed his eyes at her. "Door stays open. Don't even think of trying anything." He spun, placing his back to her and blocking her exit.

Maggie heaved a sigh at the small win, swiveling to scan the bathroom for any way of escaping or a weapon. She found nothing. She crossed to the toilet at the far end of the room, hoping to find a window, but only a solid wall met her.

No way out. She licked her lips as her heart thudded in her chest.

"You done yet?"

"No! I haven't even started. Look, I can't go with you listening to me. It's gross and weird."

"Too bad. Try harder."

"I can't. Can you just stand over at the door to the room? Please?"

"Nope. Turn on the water."

Maggie wrinkled her nose at him before she stalked to the sink and turned both handles on full blast. She tugged open the doors below the marble top and scanned the contents. A spray bottle of cleaner, a toilet brush, and a plunger sat inside.

"Gotta make do," she murmured to herself, grabbing the cleaner in one hand and plunger in the other.

"Hurry it up," Jones said as she tiptoed closer to him.

"Oh, I'm ready," she said.

She lifted the plunger and swung down hard, cracking him in the head as he twisted to face her. He cried out as the wood handle cracked him in the head. She squeezed the spray bottle, sending a stream of cleaner at his face. Another cry escaped him as he stumbled back a step, rubbing at his eyes and temporarily blinded.

Maggie darted past him, doing a quick scan of the room for a way out. She'd have to break one of the floor-to-ceiling windows, then jump to the ground below, and she preferred not to do that.

Her heart hammered in her chest as she raced into the hall and ran toward an open door at the far end. Jones crashed into the door jamb behind her.

She glanced over her shoulder before slipping inside the room. Jones clutched at his face, still rubbing his eyes as tears streamed from them. "Somebody help!" he shouted.

Footsteps pounded up the wooden stairs. Maggie shoved the door closed behind her, searching for the lock and pressing it. The door wouldn't hold for long, but maybe long enough for her to make an escape or formulate a plan.

She scanned the oversized space. A wooden valet stood near a dresser against the far wall. A man's jacket hung from it. Maggie swept her eyes past it toward the bed standing in front of a floor-to-ceiling window.

Her heart pounded faster as she failed to find a better weapon or a suitable escape. She stepped farther into the room and shot a glance in the opposite direction. Warmth rushed through her, and she hurried forward toward the sliding glass door hidden behind sheers.

She shoved aside the white linen drape and flicked open the lock. Cool night air hit her face as she slid the door open and stepped onto the grey composite deck boards. She slammed into the railing on the far end and peered over it to the ground below.

Her pulse quickened as she studied the drop. The distance to the ground was greater than it had been at her apartment building. She couldn't afford to break an ankle, or worse.

A *boom* sounded behind her, stopping her heart. She glanced over her shoulder again as the wind tossed her hair around wildly. The bedroom door would not hold for long. She had to go. *Now.*

After tossing down the cleaner and plunger, Maggie swung a leg over the railing, straddling it. Her fingers clutched at the plastic-like material. The sweat drenching her palms made it difficult to maintain her tight grip.

She hoisted the other leg over, wedging her feet underneath the railing. An ear-splitting bang exploded from the bedroom.

Bryson raced inside, glancing left, then right. He swung his head in her direction, locking eyes with her. His eyes burned with fury.

Maggie glanced at the ground below her, swallowing hard and biting her lower lip. Bryson raced toward her, and she lowered herself down, letting her legs dangle while she clung to the rungs of the railing.

Bryson hovered over her, clutching at the railing. "I will give you one chance to surrender yourself and receive only a partial punishment for your rash behavior."

Maggie craned her neck to stare up at him. "I don't think so."

She released her grip on the railing and fell backward,

rolling into a ball as she landed in an attempt to reduce her injuries.

Her lungs stung as the ground forced the air from them. She rolled onto her back, trying to suck in a breath. Bryson slammed a hand against the railing and spun around, racing toward the bedroom and hollering for help.

Maggie moaned, climbing to her feet and staggering a few steps away. The screen on the sliding door leading to the living room skittered open behind her.

Tears filled her eyes as she pushed herself to sprint forward, despite the ache in her muscles from the fall.

Voices shouted behind her as the group worked to catch up to her and prevent her escape. She ran headlong down a grade, hoping to find a grove of trees in which to hide.

The gentle slope gave way to more flat grass. She swallowed hard as she caught sight of the fence trimming her in but continued to barrel toward it. She slammed into the wrought iron, wrapping her fingers around the pickets and squeezing a foot between two.

Her foot slipped as she tried to scramble up the high fence. She slid back toward the ground below. A glance over her shoulder showed her captors closing the gap between them. She had to make it over the fence, or she'd be trapped.

She dug her feet into the iron bars, squeezing her fists as tight as they'd go around the metal picket. "Come on," she groaned as tears stained her cheeks. Her feet slipped and slid, gaining no ground. She landed on the ground again.

Three men raced toward her. She leapt up, trying to catch hold of the top rail, but she fell short. As she landed, one of the men slammed into her, smashing her against the metal fence.

She cried out as the metal pressed against her cheek and ribs.

"Not smart," he growled at her as he spun her to face him.

She refused to make eye contact, heaving in breaths as sobs threatened to bubble up.

Ryan crushed her into the fence. "Not smart at all." He grabbed ahold of her arm, yanking her forward.

They trotted her up the hill and into the living room. Bryson sipped at his brandy as they entered and shoved Maggie forward toward him. One of them slid the glass panel closed behind them.

Bryson shook his head at her. "Very, very foolish, Maggie."

Maggie caught her breath, wiping at her tear-stained cheeks with the backs of her hands. "Hey, I had to try. You would have thought less of me if I hadn't, right?"

Bryson scoffed, taking another sip of brandy. "I appreciate the attempt at humor, though I'm afraid it does little to rectify the situation."

"You got me back, and I learned my lesson," Maggie said, with a shrug. "No harm, no foul, right?"

Bryson closed the gap between them, offering her a weak smile. "I'm sorry to say there will be quite a bit of harm on your part, Maggie."

She swallowed hard, forcing herself to maintain eye contact.

"I gave you a chance to come back. You refused. Had you listened, I would have merely bound your wrists again. But you chose not to."

"Figured you'd appreciate my tenacity."

"I did not. And now," he said, arching an eyebrow, "you'll pay the price."

Maggie fought to steady the tremble that threatened to make her knees give out and lower lip quiver.

"Look, I panicked, and Jones," she said, flailing an arm toward the man, "wouldn't give me any privacy when I went to the bathroom, which felt like a gross overstepping of his bounds."

Bryson flicked a hand in the air. "Enough. I have heard enough excuses. For once, you're not going to talk your way out of this. You made a conscious decision to leap from a balcony. You made another when you decided to race into the night, in the hopes of escaping."

"You can't honestly expect me not to have tried to get away, can you? I didn't think you were that stupid, Bryson."

Bryson stalked away from her, skirting the bar and refilling his brandy from behind. He poured a second glass and waved it toward Maggie. She sidled up the marble counter and hopped on a stool.

He sipped at the brandy, leaning on the bar and studying her over the rim of the glass. After a long swallow, he set the glass down and spread his hands across the marble. "You didn't think I was that stupid. Hmm."

A smirk crossed his chiseled features as he scoffed, "You know, Maggie, I didn't think you were that stupid either."

Maggie took a sip of the amber liquid, letting the caramel flavor roll across her tongue. She squashed her eyebrows together as she lowered her glass to the bar. "What do you mean?"

"You just tried to escape, and then you thought it wise to insult your captor. I'm really beginning to question whether or not you are worth the effort."

Maggie offered him a coy smile as she spun her glass around. "Of course I am."

"That remains to be seen. Until then, I plan to prove to you that I am, in fact, *not* that stupid." He waved his fingers toward one of his bodyguards.

Maggie shot a tentative glance over her shoulder, expecting to see the man approaching with a zip tie in his hands.

Bryson grabbed hold of her wrist and yanked her over the bar toward him. "I hope you'll find this a very valuable learning experience, Maggie. Betray me, and you will always pay the price."

"What are you going to do?"

Bryson flicked his gaze to the approaching man.

"Don't do anything to Henry or Leo...or Piper. I'll cooperate, I promise."

"Yes, you will. But for now, we'll have a quiet plane ride. I had hoped to enjoy your company, but you've put me in a rather sour mood, and I'd rather be alone with my thoughts."

"I'll keep quiet. I–"

"Yes, you will," Bryson said, letting go of her arm. She plopped back onto the stool. Before she could move, Ryan grabbed her from behind, sliding his arm around her neck and pinning her against his chest.

A sharp pain jabbed her in the arm, followed by a burst of cool liquid under her skin. She sucked in a sharp gasp, digging her fingers into Ryan's forearm.

"No!" she cried. "Please don't huuuu–"

Her words cut off as her voice slurred and wooziness overcame her. She struggled to keep her eyes open but lost the battle. Her arms fell to her sides, feeling like lead as sounds grew further away.

Her vision blurred, and the room slipped away.

CHAPTER 20

Maggie's eyelids fluttered open. Bright sunshine streamed through a thickly-draped window in front of her. She moaned, pressing her hands against her eyes as she squeezed them shut. Her head swam and stomach rolled as a wave of nausea washed over her.

She panted a few breaths, waiting for the sickness to pass. "Ugh," she moaned as the ill feeling finally waned and she forced her eyes open.

She sucked in a deep breath, scanning the room. Her elbows dug into the soft mattress as she pushed herself up. A soft, velvety blanket covered her. She flung it off and swung her legs over the edge of the tall bed.

Wooziness flooded over her, and the room spun. She massaged her temple, sinking her head between her knees.

"Come on, Maggie. You're not this weak," she told herself. "You've got to get up and get moving. Find a way out."

She slid to stand. Her legs wobbled under her. She forced herself to stumble to the foot of the bed, leaning against it to steady herself as her vision cleared. She raced to one of the room's windows and tried to raise it.

It didn't budge. She flicked the lock and struggled to lift it, bracing her foot against the crumbling paint on the sill.

The window didn't move. She could break it, she thought, searching the space for something to smash the glass.

She grabbed ahold of the small lamp on the mahogany bedside table, ripping the cord from the wall socket behind it and wrapping it around the thick brass base.

Maggie approached the window, shoving aside the thick drape. She lined up her shot and lifted the heavy but small lamp over her shoulder. As she swung down, her arm stopped, then was wrenched backward.

She stared with wide eyes over her shoulder, finding Bryson with a firm grasp on the lamp. He yanked it from her hand and tossed it on the bed. "I did not think you were this stupid."

"You drugged me," Maggie shouted, jabbing a finger at him. "What did you expect? I'd have been stupid *not* to try to get away this time."

"I drugged you because you could not follow the rules."

"I don't play by your rules."

"Except right now, you do. Unless you want me to end the life of one of your precious friends. Perhaps neither Taylor nor Leo is enough. Not even the demise of Rainbow Brite strikes fear into your heart. Let's try another. How about dear old Uncle Ollie?"

"Leave Uncle Ollie alone."

"Would be a terrible shame. He reaches a ripe old age and then is snuffed out because of your failure to follow instructions."

"Leave my friends and family alone. Isn't it enough that I'm already here working with you?"

"And trying to escape at every turn. I can't trust you. So, you must be forced into compliance."

Maggie huffed out a sigh, holding up her hands in defeat. "I'm complying. No more escape attempts."

"Forgive me for not taking your word for it," Bryson said, pulling his phone from his pocket and toggling on the display. "So, to be sure, I'll keep tabs on your friends, and if you should step out of line again, I will end one of their lives."

Maggie wrinkled her nose as she grimaced, her jaw flexing.

Bryson tapped around on the phone before sliding it back into his pocket. "If I don't send the all-clear every hour, someone will die. Is that understood? That means if I am distracted by chasing you around and fail to send a message, someone may not survive it."

"I understand," Maggie said. "No more trouble. I promise."

"Wonderful. Well, I hope you feel refreshed from your long nap, because it's nearly time for the gala."

Maggie flicked up her eyebrows. "Where's my dress?"

"All in good time, darling. First, we must discuss a few operational details."

"Such as?" Maggie questioned.

"Such as how we will secure the key."

"Simple, you distract people with your wit and charm, and I'll steal it," Maggie said, with a shrug.

"No, darling. You won't be out of my sight. We need to discuss how we plan to get from the ballroom and dining area, where the party will be held, to the private collection."

"You need my help with this? Aren't you a criminal extraordinaire? Shouldn't you have the means to pull this off?"

"I have the support in place to gain access, yes. However, there are guards at various stations throughout the mansion. I shall need your help to distract them."

"What do you want me to do?"

"Be the beautiful and beguiling Maggie Edwards I know you can be. Charm them enough to get close, then plant one of these on them." Bryson waved a clear sticker in the air.

"What is that?"

"This little sticker packs quite a punch. It will incapacitate the wearer in seconds of coming into contact with the skin."

"How do you expect me to get it on them?"

"Carefully," Bryson answered, with a smirk. "There is a tab you can touch, but I would recommend you keep your satin gloves on whilst applying them, just in case."

"Them?"

"They work in pairs. You'll need to be quick once you get close enough."

Maggie rolled her eyes. "Oh, wonderful. What do you think I am, a miracle worker?"

"A very skilled woman. I aim to test those skills. And with the stakes as high as they are for you, I imagine you'll succeed."

"Why don't you put the knockout stickers on them?"

"I would, but I'm simply not as pretty as you."

"You're selling yourself short, Bryson," Maggie said, with a coy smile.

"I think I'll leave it to you. And on that note, I shall leave you to get ready." He stalked to the door and tugged it open, waving in one of his bodyguards, who carried two boxes and a shopping bag.

"Enjoy the dress. And don't dally. I will collect you in ninety minutes."

"Ninety minutes? Wait a minute. I need make-up and hair products. I can't go looking like I just spent twelve hours drugged after being kidnapped. No Valentini is going to cover that up."

Bryson smirked at her and flicked his gaze toward a

closed white door across the room. "You'll find everything you need in there. Ninety minutes, Maggie."

Maggie's shoulders slumped, but she couldn't keep her gaze from falling on the box. She arched an eyebrow and wandered to it, running her hand along the corner of the lid.

She sucked in a breath. "Well, may as well make the best of it."

She shimmied the lid until it popped off. Inside, a spray of white tissue paper covered a splotch of red fabric. Maggie pawed at it, shoving it aside and running her fingers over the satiny material as she chewed her lower lip. The corners of her lips tugged upward, and she pulled it up, studying the dress. A thick, folded band formed the off-the-shoulder collar. Ruched fabric ran down one side to a slit up to the thigh.

"Hmm," Maggie said as she considered the style, spinning to hold it up against her and study it in the mirror. "Not bad, Bryson. Sadly, you were correct in saying you're better at this than Henry."

She spun back to the bed and tossed the dress on it. She tugged open the smaller box and grabbed one of the shoes. She twisted it at various angles, studying the heel, ankle strap, and rhinestone details.

"Perfect. Well, I guess I'd better become the beguiling Maggie Edwards."

She stalked to the bathroom. At a large vanity, a variety of makeup and hair products were sprawled across the marble. She perused the items before she plopped onto the stool.

Within sixty minutes, she was satisfied with her makeup. Her hair, still up in Velcro rollers, would have to wait. "Time to try on that dress. Let's see how good you really are, Bryson."

She stood, leaning closer to the mirror for one final inspection of her eye makeup before she hurried into the bedroom. She dug into the bag, finding all the necessities for under her dress.

She slid off her pants and carefully wiggled her top over the large rollers, tossing aside the clothes. After shimmying into all the necessary underthings, she picked up the dress, unzipping it before she stepped in. She slid it up, pulling her arms through the off-the-shoulder collar and reaching behind herself to zip it.

The stretchy satin hugged her curves. She twisted, smoothing the fabric down over her backside and arching an eyebrow. "Not bad, Bryson, fits like a glove. A Valentini never disappoints."

She checked the clock across the room. Ten minutes to finish her hair and get her shoes on. She hurried into the bathroom, tugging curlers out as she went. After removing them all, she fluffed the style, tucking one side into a red rhinestone-studded pin before misting hairspray all over.

After a few final flicks of the ends, she lifted the atomizer from the vanity and sprayed a few pumps of perfume before she returned to the bedroom and collapsed on the bed. She slipped one foot into her shoe, buckling it before moving on to the second.

A knock sounded at the door. "Come in!" she called.

The door swung open as she finished buckling the second shoe. She rose, shoving the dress down her thighs, and sucked in a deep breath.

"Well, you certainly did not disappoint," Bryson said, eyeing her from head to toe. "I suppose I didn't need the tux, as I doubt anyone will be looking at me."

"You got that right," Maggie said, with a final glance in the mirror. She spun to face him, sticking a hand on her hip. "I thought rubies were supposed to be involved?"

Bryson swept a hand from behind him, showcasing a velvet box. "I'm a man of my word."

"That's questionable," Maggie said, with a scoff.

He approached her, popping open the box. A thick ruby necklace sparkled inside, alongside a pair of drop earrings.

"Impressed?" he asked her.

Maggie wiggled her eyebrows. "It's not bad. It'll do."

She lifted the earrings out and turned to the mirror to fasten them. Bryson swept the necklace around her neck when she'd finished. She swallowed hard, lifting her hair for him to secure it. His warm breath wafted across her bare skin, and she suppressed a shudder.

"I just need to grab my gloves," she said, ending the moment as quickly as possible.

"Oh, you just need one more thing before that."

Maggie grabbed the matching red elbow-length gloves from the box. "What's that?"

He caught her left hand, tugging her ring finger forward before he slid a gold band onto it. "Your wedding ring."

Maggie wrinkled her nose as she stared down at her hand. "What, no glitzy diamond engagement ring?"

"It's being cleaned," Bryson said.

"Great excuse," Maggie answered, tugging the gloves on and grabbing the red evening bag off the bed.

Bryson waved the knockout strips in the air before he popped open the handbag and slid them inside. He offered his arm. "Shall we?"

"If we must," Maggie answered with a sigh, slipping her arm into the crook of his.

He led her down a set of wooden stairs to a small foyer. Warm air washed over them as they stepped in the waning heat of the New Orleans day. The sun already hung low on the horizon in a deep shade of red.

A town car awaited them at the curb. The driver popped the door open, and Bryson waved Maggie inside. She slid across the seat, allowing him to join her in the back.

As the car eased away from the curb, he checked his phone's display, his forehead crinkling.

"Remember," he said as he stowed it in his pocket again, "don't mess up. Or one of your friends pays the price."

"Got it," Maggie said, holding her hands up in the air before she flicked her gaze out the window at the passing landscape.

She sucked in a breath, trying to stop her legs from shaking and return her heart to a normal rhythm before it threatened to pound out of her chest.

No matter what happened at this party, she couldn't leave with Bryson. She had to find a way to escape. This may be her only chance.

CHAPTER 21

Maggie slid her eyes sideways toward Bryson. Her fingers tightened around the red evening bag on her lap. Inside, two stickers, capable of knocking out the wearer in seconds, slid around.

Could she get them on both Bryson, then the driver fast enough? Maybe. But would the car wreck? Would she be worse off than she was now?

She bit her lower lip. She may need to bide her time and wait until they were alone at the party. When they snuck off to retrieve the key, she'd used the knockout sticker on him and slink away into the night. He kept his phone in his breast pocket. She'd grab it and use it to call Henry once she'd gotten away from the senator's mansion.

She sucked in a shaky breath, pleased with her plan. Bryson glanced over at her, and she forced a smile onto her lips.

"What is going on behind those beautiful brown eyes?" he asked her.

"Nothing," she answered.

He flicked up his eyebrows. "I find that hard to believe."

His phone chimed, and he slid it from his pocket. His forehead wrinkled, and he tapped it before pressing it to his ear. "Yes?"

Maggie glanced down at her lap, straining to make out any words from the speaker on the other end. She could hear nothing distinguishable.

Bryson cut his gaze sideways to Maggie. "Really? How interesting."

Maggie's posture stiffened, and heat rose into her cheeks.

He returned his eyes forward. "Keep me informed via text. We're almost at the senator's."

He clicked off the phone's display and slid it into his pocket.

"Care to share?" Maggie asked.

He shook his head, turning down the corners of his lips. "It's nothing you need to worry your pretty head about."

"If it affects what we're about to do, I think it's something I deserve to know."

"It doesn't," he answered as the car slowed to a stop outside the lavish mansion.

Maggie narrowed her eyes at him as the driver popped open his door. He offered her a smile that bordered on a smirk before sliding from the car and offering his hand to help her out.

Maggie grabbed it, allowing him to pull her to stand before she wrapped her arm around his.

"Ready?" he asked.

"As I'll ever be," she answered.

"You don't look ready," he said.

She plastered a smile onto her lips. "How about now?"

"Perfect."

He led her to the front door, where he gave their names to the security guard, who checked them off the list and waved them to another man. With a large, flat wand, he checked Maggie, then Bryson for any weapons. He glanced into Maggie's purse.

Her heart thudded in her chest as she worried he'd question the two strips tucked in the zippered compartment. The man shoved the lipstick to the side, glanced underneath, then shifted his gaze to Maggie.

She offered him a nervous smile. A grin spread across his face as he flipped the flap closed and handed the bag back to her. "It's a great shade of lipstick on you."

Maggie's smile broadened, becoming genuine. "Thanks. Red's my color."

"It most certainly is." He waved them inside. "You're one lucky man, Mr. Richardson."

"Don't I know it," Bryson said with a smarmy smile as he slipped his arm around Maggie's waist and guided her inside.

"Well," he said as they entered and scanned the throngs of guests milling around the entryway and sitting room, "this should be easy for you. You're already charming them with just your lip color. Let's get the lay of the land and say hello to our hosts, shall we?"

"Whatever you say, let's just get this over with."

"Relax, Maggie, we aren't making a move anytime soon. We need a clear path to our target, and we don't have one yet."

"When–" she stopped as Bryson approached a tall man with salt-and-pepper hair and an award-winning smile.

"Senator, lovely to see you again. William Richardson, we met at the library gala last fall."

"Oh, yes, of course, Mr. Richardson, so pleased you could join us tonight. Your contributions to the library have made all the difference."

"Oh, how lovely to hear. I don't believe you've met my wife, Miranda. She was in Paris, so I was flying solo at the gala last year."

The senator flicked up his eyebrows as he extended his hand. "Oh, Paris? Work or play?"

Maggie offered a demure smile as she pumped his hand up and down. "A little of both."

Bryson chuckled, wrapping his arm around Maggie's waist. "Don't let her fool you. She's a world-class fashion buyer and was in Paris for a show. Though, she'll tell you that's all play."

The senator threw his head back, with a laugh. "Isn't that always the way with women?"

Maggie held down a gag as the two men clapped each other on the back over the less-than-funny joke.

"Well, I'm afraid it's I who is flying solo tonight. Mrs. Royce is abroad at a UN conference. It's a shame you couldn't have met her, Miranda. She'd simply love your dress."

"Oh, thank you," Maggie said, with a lift of her shoulder. "Too bad. Maybe next time."

"Indeed. Well, if you'll excuse me, please help yourself to the refreshments, and maybe we can speak later about getting you involved in our little museum here."

"I look forward to it," Bryson said, with a bob of his head.

The senator flitted away from them, extending his hand to another man, who smiled broadly at him.

"Popular guy," Maggie said as he left.

"And powerful."

"Oh, great," Maggie lamented as Bryson passed her a flute of champagne. "Just what I always wanted to do. Rob a powerful senator."

"You've robbed museums, darling. Not to mention one very powerful British lord. This is child's play for you."

"Sir Richard? Ugh, that guy was a jerk. Did you know he didn't even call Emma back about the museum loan?"

"Well," he said after a sip of champagne, "you *did* rob him."

"So? What's that have to do with the deal he was making with Emma?"

"Would you have loaned your collection to the people who robbed you?"

Maggie lifted a shoulder as she scanned the crowd. "Maybe. I'm working with you."

"Under protest. Or am I to understand that the offering of the dress, shoes, and jewelry has made all the difference in our relationship?"

"Let's not go crazy. I still don't like you."

His phone chimed in his pocket. He slid it out, toggling on the display and reading a message. His lips curled into a satisfied smirk, and he pocketed the device.

He slid the champagne flute from her hand and placed it on a passing waiter's tray before leading her to the dance floor.

"But you don't hate me," he said with a wiggle of his eyebrows as he slid his arm around her and led her around the floor.

She forced an irritated smile onto her features. "Let's not split hairs on this. Hate, don't like. Different, but not really."

"I think you're going to have an easy time pulling off your end of this heist, Maggie. You are a most intriguing woman."

Maggie rolled her eyes as he flung her backward into a dip before righting her. "Don't fall in love with me Bryson. We'd just never work out."

"And here I thought you liked a man with money and power."

"I didn't say I don't, but the key is, he also has to have a conscience."

"Ouch," Bryson said. "So, what is the deal with you and Taylor? Are you kicking him to the proverbial curb or not?"

"Still not your business."

"Well, it is. I need to know which trigger to pull when the time comes."

"None. How about that?" Maggie asked as they danced their way across the floor.

"Are you promising the time will not come?"

Maggie clenched her jaw as she considered her answer. She flicked her made-up eyes up to meet his. "I'm promising you don't need to threaten my friends. Now, when can we get moving and grab the key?"

"Anxious?"

"Very."

Bryson spun her around before pulling her close again. "Not enjoying our dance?"

"You're not that good of a dancer."

Bryson tugged her hand closer to his chest as they swayed. "Really? This is the first I'm hearing of my deficiencies. And I can't imagine Taylor is much of a dancer."

"I'd take him over you any day."

Bryson's phone chimed again. "Saved by the bell." He led her from the dance floor.

Maggie grabbed a full flute of champagne and sipped it as he studied his screen.

"It seems the time has come to make our move," he said as he clicked off the display.

Maggie took another sip of the bubbly liquid. "Good. I'd like to get this over with and get out of here. We've still got another key to find before I can be rid of you."

Bryson shoved the phone into his pocket. "I may have a lead on that other key."

Maggie flicked her eyebrows up as she drained the glass of its contents. "Really? Where?"

"Let's discuss it later," he said, slipping his hand around her arm and leading her away.

She dumped her empty flute off with a waiter as they

stepped into a long hall. "This way," Bryson said, leading her away from the din of the other guests.

He peered around a corner before tugging her along with him toward a set of double doors at the end.

From his pocket, he removed an earpiece and placed it in his ear. "I'm ready."

He slid a keycard from another pocket and shoved it into the security panel to the right of the door. "I'm in."

Numbers raced past on the screen before they began to fill in a code. The light on the keypad turned from red to green, and Bryson grabbed the handle and swung open the door.

"All right, darling," he said as he pressed his other hand against her back to guide her through the opening, "you're up next."

Maggie's heart pounded in her chest, and her throat went dry.

"I hope you're a better actress than you're letting on right now, because that face will get you nowhere."

"Why can't you do it? Or both of us. If there are two of them, I'll never get to them both fast enough."

"Don't degrade yourself so, darling. I have every faith in you."

"I don't."

"I do. And I would prefer not to be identified."

"You will be anyway! My dress is a dead giveaway. All they have to do is describe it, and they'll know it was me, and hence you."

"Doubt it," he whispered as they approached the corner. "These are bodyguards, Maggie, not fashionistas. They won't even remember your dress."

He peeked around the corner before flattening himself against the wall. "They are both at the end of the hall. Go."

Maggie swallowed hard, her knees threatening to buckle under her.

"Go!" he hissed.

She held up a shaky hand as she opened her purse and retrieved the stickers. She peeled them from their backing, clutching one in each hand. After a silent prayer, she slid her eyes closed for a moment, then blew out a long breath. "Okay."

She lifted her chin, shimmied her shoulders back, and marched around the corner.

Two bulky guards stood at the end of the hall, guarding a doorway. Maggie's heart pounded with every step.

One of them spotted her, his brow furrowing.

Maggie plastered a grin onto her face. "Hi! Wow, it's like a maze in here! I am so turned around."

"You can't be in here."

"Tell me about it. I have been wandering around this place for thirty minutes and can't find my husband. Knowing him, he's probably talking sports with the senator."

"Back that way," the man said, waving his hand to signal Maggie to turn around.

She glanced over her shoulder but continued toward them. "Oh, thanks. Let me just give you a tip for your trouble."

"No need, ma'am, just head back to the party."

The grin faded from Maggie's face, and she stormed toward them, closing the gap quickly. "What did you say? Did you just call me *ma'am?*"

"Uh—"

"How old do you think I am? That's insulting. I work very hard to project a youthful appearance. Hasn't anyone taught you any manners? You jerk!" She slapped the man across the face, affixing the sticker to his cheek.

His neck twisted from the impact, then his eyes rolled back in his head.

"Karev?" his partner shouted. He shifted his eyes to Maggie. Her hand already swung forward to plant the knockout sticker on his forehead. His eyes crossed, glancing upward toward the plastic before they rolled back, and he slumped to the floor.

Maggie stumbled back a few steps, clearing the way for him to hit the floor. She swung around to glance behind her. Bryson strolled toward her, loosening his tie.

"You are an impressive specimen, aren't you, Maggie? I'm beginning to envy Taylor." He flung one man's jacket back and palmed his weapon. He slid it into his waistband before he climbed over him to the door and shoved the keycard into the slot on the security keypad. "Or Hamilton. Whichever is your flavor of the month." He shifted his eyes sideways to glance at her as the numbers raced on the screen to create the code.

"Still none of your business," she said, setting a hand on her hip.

The light changed from red to green, and Bryson tugged the door open. "After you."

Maggie stalked into the large room, a shiver running up her spine as cool air caressed her skin. Her skin puckered into gooseflesh as icy air swirled around her when Bryson stormed past.

"We're in," he reported to his colleagues. "Where are we looking for this?" He pressed the earpiece further into his ear. With a nod, he said, "Got it."

"Key is housed in a cabinet in the rear," he said to Maggie, grabbing her arm and tugging her with him.

They wound around to an alcove. A rich mahogany cabinet rose against the wall. Maggie hurried forward, tugging on the door handles. "It's locked!"

"Give me your hairpin," Bryson said.

Maggie reached for the ruby barrette. "Seriously?"

He flicked his gaze to Maggie. "Yes, why do you think I gave it to you?"

"Looks," Maggie said as she slid it from her hair. "Minus a point for you on fashion savvy."

"Don't worry, the gold will make up all the points I need," he said, sliding the rubies off the pin and inserting it into the lock. The door popped open a few seconds later.

"Do I get to keep some of it?" Maggie asked as she pulled open the door.

Bryson shot her a stony glance.

Maggie held up her hands in defeat. "Just asking." She peered over his shoulder as he squatted down to search the drawers inside. He slid one of the lower drawers open. Inside, limned against a red velvet backdrop, was an iron key.

"There," Maggie said, jabbing a finger at it.

Bryson grabbed it and shoved it into his pocket as he rose to stand. Maggie closed the drawer and secured the cabinet doors with clammy hands. They just needed to escape the house, and they'd be clear.

Her heart thudded in her chest as they made their way across the room. "The guards will still be out, right?"

"Yes. Those strips will last for at least an hour."

She blew out a long breath, pulling the door open to find two bodies still sprawled in the hallway. She stepped over them, teetering on her high heels to balance.

As she cleared the second body, Bryson's hand wrapped around her arm and tugged her back against him. He wrapped an arm around her neck, squeezing it and bending her back at an awkward angle.

"Hey, what the–" Maggie began, when she spotted another figure down the hall, blocking their exit.

The cold metal of the nose of the gun Bryson had scooped up earlier pressed against her temple.

Her eyes went wide as she clutched at Bryson's arm, tugging it away from her throat. Tears formed in her eyes as they stared at the well-muscled figure in front of her. He raised his weapon, leveling it at the person.

Bryson's voice growled in her ear. "Hello, Taylor."

CHAPTER 22

"Henry!" Maggie choked out as Bryson continued to squeeze her windpipe.

"Let her go, Bryson," Henry barked.

"I don't think so. We're having a lovely time together." He craned his neck to glance at Maggie. "Aren't we, darling?"

Maggie tugged at the arm pressing around her neck. "I haven't been impressed so far."

"Oh, come now, Maggie. Admit it. We're having fun." He grinned as he tugged her closer to him.

Henry glared at him. "Let her go."

"All right. I'll let her go. For a price."

"Name it," Henry said, the muscle in his arm bulging as he gripped the gun tighter.

"The Memphis key."

Maggie's forehead crinkled. "You found the fourth key?"

"Oh, they found it, all right. And now I want it."

Henry pointed the gun toward the ceiling, holding both hands up in defeat. "It's yours."

He reached into the waistband of his pants and pulled out the iron key. He waved it in the air.

"Gently toss it to your lady love. Maggie, don't drop it."

Maggie's forehead crinkled. "What? I can't catch it like this."

"Try harder," Bryson hissed.

"It's okay, Maggie," Henry said. "Whenever you're ready, just tell me, and I'll toss it right to you. This is almost over."

"Enough blabbering. Throw the key."

Henry locked eyes with Maggie. She reached her arms in front of her as he lobbed it through the air. It landed on her wrists, and she fought to steady it before it clattered to the floor.

She wrapped her fingers around it and held it in the air with a gasp. "Got it."

"Excellent. Now slip it into my pocket."

Maggie reached behind her, sliding the key into Bryson's pocket before she returned to tugging against his arm.

"You got your key, now let her go," Henry demanded.

"Mmm, I've changed my mind. We're leaving now. Together." He pressed the barrel of the gun into Maggie's temple again. "Now stand back, or I'll go alone *after* I put a bullet in her brain."

"Easy, Bryson," Henry said, tucking the gun into his waistband and holding up a hand. "You don't need her. No one's standing in your way."

"Au contraire, Taylor. She's quite bright, and very useful. I think I'd like to keep her. Now, hands up and against the wall, while we take our leave."

"No way. Let her go. We had a deal."

"And now I've changed it. And if you don't want me to change it again, I would stand aside."

"Don't hurt her, Bryson."

"Don't make me, Taylor." He leveled his weapon at Henry. "Or you. I wouldn't mind putting another bullet in you. This time, I'll make sure it's the last you ever get."

"Stop! Just stop!" Maggie shouted as tears brimmed in her eyes. "I'll go with him."

"Maggie-"

"Oooh, there's a good girl," Bryson said. "You see, Taylor, even Maggie agrees."

Henry held up his hands, shuffling toward the wall and pressing his face into it. "You're forcing her hand."

"Mmm," Bryson answered as he pushed Maggie forward, "I'm not so sure about that. It seems our little Miss Edwards has a straying eye these days."

Henry shot Bryson a glaring glance.

Tears spilled onto Maggie's cheeks at the words. "You're an ass."

"Maybe so, but I'm winning," he said as they slipped past Henry down the hall.

Maggie took a step toward the party when Bryson pulled her back. "I think not. We'll use the back entrance. Wouldn't want you causing a scene."

He yanked her further down the hall. As he circled to face Henry again, Maggie lifted an arm to elbow Bryson in the gut. He grabbed it, preventing the attack. "I don't think so, darling. I've learned from the last time we tangled."

His hand clamped over her mouth, and he wrapped the other around her waist, lifting her from the ground. She issued a muffled scream as he backed down the hall.

"Goodbye, Taylor."

He darted around the corner and raced forward toward a frosted glass door. He pushed through it, stumbling onto a gravel path in the garden. A white van sat at the corner of the house. He set Maggie down, roughly grabbing her arm and pulling her toward the van.

"Sorry for the lack of swanky transportation, but we needed to pivot when your boyfriend showed up." He slid the door open and tossed her inside before slamming it shut.

Darkness enveloped her as a front door slammed shut and the engine revved. As the van lurched forward, Maggie pulled her knees to her chest, resting her chin on them as tears streamed down her face.

With all four keys in his possession, they would be moving on to find the gold. Her life span shortened with each step closer they took. She bit into her lower lip and sniffled. She'd have to find a way to get away from Bryson.

At least Henry had been searching for her. Or were they searching for the key?

A scraping noise interrupted her thoughts. She snapped her head up, holding her breath as she searched the darkness of the van for the source.

"Maggie?" a voice hissed.

Maggie's heart skipped a beat as she scrambled forward toward the sound. "Emma?"

"Yes, it's me."

"Oh, no, did Bryson get you, too?"

"No," Emma answered. "I heard the conversation between him and Henry. I spotted the guy leave the back of the van, and I slipped inside. I have a tracker. They can follow us wherever we go."

"Emma!" Maggie exclaimed, slapping her hands together. "You're a genius."

A warm hand grabbed Maggie's and squeezed.

Maggie returned the gesture. "And an idiot."

Emma dropped her hand to the floor, pulling away from Maggie. "Thanks. I thought you'd at least appreciate the save."

"I do," Maggie said. "But when Bryson finds you here, we're going to be in big trouble. I'm not sure what he'll do."

"Well, at least you won't be alone. I can't imagine how frightening this must have been for you."

"I wasn't happy to have a gun waved in my face nor to

find Bryson was the person pulling the strings, but he hasn't been too awful. He'll be grouchy now, though, I'm sure. Especially with you popping up."

"It's fine. We won't be with him long."

"What? Look, I've tried to escape multiple times. He's always one step ahead of me."

"I told you. I have a tracker. Charlie can track me wherever I go."

Maggie's heart skipped a beat as hope filled her. She shook her head a moment later. "They won't able to track us far once Bryson finds out you're here. I'm sure he'll put a stop to that."

"At least the team will have a start. Everyone came."

"Yeah. And they're pretty resourceful. We just need to stay alive long enough for them to get to us. But if there's an opportunity, we take it, and we get away from Bryson." Maggie grabbed Emma's hand again and squeezed.

"Agreed," Emma answered as the van took a sharp turn. "I just couldn't let you go it alone. Not even after the whole Leo thing."

"What?" Maggie asked, snapping her gaze toward Emma's voice, even though she couldn't see her.

"Oh, come on, Maggie. We all know now."

"Know what?"

"That you've been seeing Leo again. I'm not mad. Really, I'm not. I should have known better than to date your ex. I should have known you two would get back together. You always did in the past."

"We're not back together," Maggie said.

"Give it up, Maggie. The cat's out of the bag. And like I said, I'm not mad. Okay, I'm a little mad. But not enough to let you die at Bryson's hand."

"What cat? What bag? Leo and I aren't together."

"Uh, yeah, okay, sure. I mean, he tried to deny it, too, but the reason we knew you were missing is that Leo said you didn't show up to meet him and weren't returning his texts. Which led Henry to question why you were meeting Leo secretly. And Leo said it was just a friendly thing. After some arguing, he just refused to provide any details and said we were wasting time. But I think we all can figure out what's going on here."

"Uh, no, obviously you can't, because nothing is going on." They swayed as the van sped up.

"So, you two were not supposed to meet each other after we all left your place?"

Maggie pressed her lips together into a thin line as she weighed her words.

"Maggie? Have you or have you not been meeting Leo in secret?"

"Yes, okay, yes. I have been meeting him in secret. But not for the reason you think."

"Then for what reason?"

"I can't talk about it. It's private."

Emma tugged her hand away from Maggie's. "Wait, you're engaged and meeting another man...a man who I happen to be dating, and you're refusing to tell me? Wow, some friend."

"It's not what you think," Maggie said.

"Forget it. You're right. Not my business."

"Emma..."

"No, it's not. It's not my business what you and Leo are doing. Leo and I are over." Silence settled between them. "Oh, and find a new maid of honor, because I'm out."

"Emma!" Maggie shouted. "Yeah, you're right, some friend. You just assume the worst of me."

"Of course, I assume the worst of you. You're meeting my boyfriend in secret, and you tell me the reason is private and you can't talk about it. But I'm just supposed to trust you and be okay with it." Emma's head thunked against the side of the van. "You are always ruining my life."

"I am not ruining your life."

"Yes, you are. First, you almost got me fired. Then you almost got me killed. Then you almost got me killed again. And then you made me move and take the job in Rosemont and introduced me to Leo, and then you start secretly dating him again."

"We're not dating, OMG! And plus, I didn't *make* you move." Maggie scoffed at the statement.

"Okay, fine, you encouraged me. Why? So you could ruin my life again?"

"I'm not ruining your life. Leo and I are not secretly dating."

"Right, sure. This is why you won't set a date for the wedding, isn't it? Because you don't know which one you want."

"That's not–"

The van eased to a stop, brakes screeching, and Maggie fell silent. She grabbed Emma's hand as doors slammed in the front. The door slid open, and light streamed in from a nearby streetlamp.

Maggie squinted against it as she shoved Emma behind her. "Bryson, I can explain. Don't get mad."

"Explain what, darling? I knew Taylor was coming. I think I handled it rather well, wouldn't you agree?"

Maggie winced as he motioned for her to climb out. "Wait."

"I'm not letting you go, so if you're planning to beg for your freedom, save your breath."

"It's not that…it's just…"

Bryson flicked his gaze to her, his forehead crinkling. His posture stiffened, and he reached to his waistband to withdraw the gun he'd stowed there.

He leveled it at Maggie. "Who is that?"

Emma shifted behind her, poking her head around Maggie with her hands raised.

"Emma, no!" Maggie hissed.

"Emma Fielding," Emma answered in a shaky voice.

Bryson's eyebrows shot up. With the weapon following Emma's movement, he said, "Well, well, well, isn't this interesting? Get out of the van now."

"Okay," Emma said, swallowing hard.

Maggie thrust her arm out to block Emma. "No."

Bryson shot Maggie a surprised glance. "You have no authority here, darling. Let Ms. Fielding out of the van."

"Not until you promise not to hurt her."

"My, you are demanding. It's a wonder Taylor came after you."

"Save it, Bryson. Put the gun away."

Bryson scoffed at the demand, replying with a flat, "No."

Maggie slammed her hand against the side of the van. "Yes."

His jaw flexed as he shot a displeased glance at her. He shifted the gun to point at Maggie's head. "Do not test my patience. It is in very low supply after my encounter with Taylor."

Maggie's stomach dropped as the barrel pressed into her forehead.

"Maggie, it's fine. It's okay. I'll get out. I'm not going to do anything, I was just worried about Maggie. I didn't want her to be alone."

"You were worried about Maggie," Bryson repeated as he stepped back from the van, pulling the gun away from Maggie. "You? You two don't get along."

"I am her maid of honor. Felt appropriate," Emma mumbled as she pushed past Maggie and spilled out of the van on shaky legs.

"Maid of honor? You mean you're still going through with the wedding despite your attachments to Mr. Hamilton?"

"Really?" Emma asked, shooting a glance at Maggie. "Even he knows?"

"Don't start that," Bryson said, waving Emma away from the van with his gun. "The moment you two start fighting, everything goes to hell. Now–"

The screeching of tires interrupted his words. He crinkled his brow as LED headlights appeared in the distance from a car drifting around a corner.

Color drained from Bryson's face, and he aimed the gun at Emma, his muscles flexing. "What have you done?"

CHAPTER 23

"Henry?" Maggie questioned as she hung out of the van and stared at the approaching vehicle.

Bryson shoved her inside, barking orders at the other man. Before he slid the door shut, Emma dove back in the van. Bryson's nostrils flared when Maggie shifted her body to shield Emma from him. He flicked his gaze to the quickly approaching car before he slammed the door.

The front passenger door banged a second later, and the engine revved. Tires squealed as the van shot forward. Maggie toppled backward, smashing into Emma.

"You should have stayed behind."

"I couldn't leave you, Maggie. Besides, they can track me, remember?"

The van swung hard to the right, toppling them onto their sides.

"If we live long enough to be tracked," Maggie grumbled as she pushed herself back to sit.

Light streamed in as a window hinged open to the front. "Give me the tracker," Bryson's voice demanded.

"What?" Maggie asked.

Bryson's face appeared at the bars separating them. "Don't play coy with me. Ms. Fielding has a tracker on her person. I want it. Now."

"Is it really necessary at this exact moment? It seems like we have a more pressing issue," Maggie said as she swayed to stay upright when the van lurched around a sharp bend.

Bryson pressed the barrel of the gun through the bars. "Give me the tracker, or I start shooting."

"Okay, okay. Just a second." She glanced at Emma. "Where is it?"

Emma raised her voice so she could be heard by Bryson. "I can't give it to you. It's subdural."

"Are you serious?" Maggie asked.

Emma pressed her lips together, swallowing hard.

An object sailed through the window and clattered to the floor. Bryson's face appeared at the opening again. "Cut it out of her."

"What?" Maggie cried. "Are you insane?"

"No. Remove the tracker from her, now."

Maggie stared down at the knife, her lower lip trembling. "I can't do this! The car is moving all over the place. I could kill her!"

"Or I could." He trained the weapon on Emma.

Maggie wrinkled her nose, her shaky hand wrapping around the hilt of the knife. She opened her hand and shook her head. "No. I can't do it. You do it."

"You'd like that, wouldn't you? I'm not pulling the van over so Taylor can catch up. Now, remove it from her person."

Maggie's muscles trembled as her stomach rolled. She pitched backward when the van took another sharp curve.

"Cut it out of her, or I will shoot her."

Maggie's lower lip trembled as she grabbed the pocketknife and tugged it open. Tears filled her eyes as she stared at Emma. Her heart thudded against her ribs. "Wh-where is it?"

Emma bit her lower lip and pulled a small black dot from her pocket. "I lied. It's this."

Maggie's heart stopped pounding as she accepted the small device and held it toward the opening. Bryson snatched it from her palm. "If you've lied to me–"

"I haven't. I swear. That's it."

A gust of wind rustled their hair as Bryson opened the window and chucked the device into the night air. The barred peephole to the front swung shut again.

"Is that really it?" Maggie whispered.

"Unfortunately, yes," Emma said, with a sigh. "That's really it. There isn't a subdural tracker in me. I wish there was."

Maggie slumped to sitting. "I don't. I had no desire to cut you open in a moving vehicle."

The van picked up speed, its engine revving.

"He left you with the knife," Emma said.

Maggie stared down at the object in her hands, barely able to make it out in the darkness. "Maybe we can use it to free ourselves."

"Put it in your pocket. Don't use it right away when we stop. He's got a gun."

"Never bring a knife to a gunfight," Maggie said, reaching blindly for Emma. Her fingers bumped Emma's arm, and she slid them down to her hand. "Here, put it in your pocket."

"Why me? You'll be closer to him."

"I don't have a pocket, duh. Have you seen this dress?"

"I have actually. I cannot believe he got you a designer dress and all that jewelry."

"I can't help it. And think about what a disadvantage this puts me at. Not only do I have no pockets, how can I run in these heels?"

"You're Maggie Edwards. I'm sure you'll handle it."

"You're being an idiot, just put it in your pocket," Maggie said, shoving the knife at her.

"Of course," Emma said, snatching it from her. "Yes, I'm the idiot. And I'll just do whatever Maggie wants."

"Oh, stop it. Stop railing against me because you got kidnapped willingly. Try being in my position. I've been kidnapped against my will."

"Are you serious?" Emma snapped. "You're seriously sitting there in a million dollars worth of rubies and a designer dress and telling me I have it worse. The guy nearly shot me twice."

"Well, think of how many times he nearly shot me. I ran away, and then I got drugged by him."

"Are you serious?"

"Yes. I finally got the zip ties off my wrists, took the first chance I had to make a break for it, got caught, and then had a needle shoved in my arm. So, it hasn't been all butterflies and rainbows for me either. Plus, I've had the constant threat of who he'd kill if I didn't comply."

"Oh," Emma murmured. "I'm sorry, Maggie. You always put on such a brave face, it's easy to forget how terrifying this must have been for you."

Maggie sighed, letting her head fall back against the side of the van as it swayed again. "It's fine. Hopefully, Henry will catch up to them, and this'll be over."

"Yeah, about that," Emma started.

Maggie lifted her head, squinting into the darkness toward Emma. "What? Henry won't rescue us because of the Leo thing?"

"No," Emma answered. "I mean, at least it seemed like he still wanted to rescue you. Maybe only to wring your neck, but still…"

"Then what?"

"Well, let's think about this. How are they going to–"

A loud bang sounded, and the van swerved. Maggie scrambled across the floor, pressing closer to Emma. "Was that what I think it was?"

"Sounded like a gunshot."

"Yep," Maggie said.

"And that's what I was getting at before. How are they going to get us back in a car chase?"

"Uhhh," Maggie said when another blast sounded from behind them.

"That is if they don't shoot us accidentally."

"He's probably aiming for the tires."

"Yeah, well, he's not hitting them," Emma answered. "And even if he does, that's just a great plan. He'll blow the tire on our vehicle while we're traveling at high speed. If we survive the impending rollover, we'll be okay."

"You're right. And there's no other way to stop the vehicle, really. We're going to have to do something."

"Like what?" Emma cried.

Maggie shifted her gaze to the dim outline of the door. "Do you think we can get this open from the inside?"

"Are you crazy?"

Maggie ran her hands over the panel, searching for the release handle.

"OMG, you are," Emma answered. "Maggie, think about this. We can't open the door during a high-speed chase."

"I mean, we can. There's no law saying you can't open the door. And even if there was, I'm breaking it." Her fingers wrapped around the handle.

"Wait!" Emma shouted, clamping a hand over Maggie's. "Let's just talk about this. This is crazy. We're going to open the door and do what? Jump from a moving vehicle? We'll probably die at this speed or get run over by Henry, who is probably going a hundred miles an hour behind us."

"Okay, well, none of that was in my plan."

"Did you have a plan outside of opening the door?"

"Yes," Maggie said, fluttering her eyelashes. "I did, thank you."

"Oh, really? Care to share? What was it? And how did it not involve dying?"

"Well," Maggie said. She paused to suck in a long breath and lick her lips. "I figured we could open the door and then signal Henry that it's open. And then he could drive up next to the van and we could hop into the car."

"Are you joking?"

"No."

"You expect us to hop into a moving vehicle from another moving vehicle without Bryson shooting us?"

"Well," Maggie said, wrinkling her nose, "it seemed better than getting shot accidentally by Henry or dying in a fiery car wreck."

"Pass," Emma said. "I'm not jumping out of the van."

"We could at least signal Henry."

"Signal what?"

"I don't know!" Maggie said, throwing her hands in the air. "But I hate not doing anything. I feel so helpless just sitting here while whoever swerves around up there at breakneck speeds. He may not even be a good driver. We don't know. And if we don't get out of here, we're stuck with Bryson for who knows how long!"

"I think I may take my chances with Bryson before I take them with the pavement outside."

"I still think we should open the door. Then at least if we have the opportunity, we can bail."

"Don't open the door!"

"I'm opening it."

"No!"

Maggie batted Emma's hand away and grabbed the

release handle. She tugged but nothing happened. "Damn it. It's locked."

"Thank God. I can't believe I actually am glad Bryson locked us in."

Maggie slumped back to sit. She shook her head before she climbed to her knees and tried the handle again. "Damn it."

"Stop fiddling with that door. We don't want to break it."

"Yes, we do," Maggie said, jiggling the handle.

"No, because then we may not be able to close the damn door at all."

The van skidded to the right. Emma fell over on her side from the sudden move. Maggie flailed an arm, able to stay upright by hanging on to the door handle.

The vehicle made another sudden move to the left, slamming Maggie into the door. Emma slid across the floor, her feet smacking into the side.

"This is getting out of hand," Maggie shouted. She banged on the wall separating them from Bryson. "Take it easy up there before you get us killed, idiots."

"That'll help," Emma said, pressing herself up to sit.

"It might. Maybe–"

A gunshot cut off the remainder of Maggie's words.

"That came from up front," Maggie hissed. "He's shooting at Henry."

"Told you yelling at them wouldn't help."

Maggie huffed out a sigh as she pounded on the wall again. "Stop shooting, you ass!"

Another pop sounded as a gun fired from behind them. It smacked into the car somewhere.

"Are they kidding?" Maggie said, tugging at the door again. "Two idiot men with way too much testosterone. Why would they be shooting at each other while we're driving at, like, a hundred miles an hour?"

"I'm a little more concerned about Henry shooting at us than Bryson at him," Emma groused.

"Seriously? You're less concerned that Henry could get shot?"

"I'm more concerned that we could get accidentally shot, Maggie."

"Yet you don't want to escape."

"I didn't say that, I just don't want to–"

The sound of metal on metal tore through the air, cutting off the rest of Emma's statement. The door handle she held vibrated as the cars rubbed together.

The tires squealed, and the van swayed back and forth.

"You're kidding me," Maggie groaned through clenched teeth. "He did *not* just sideswipe the van we're in."

Maggie banged on the wall again. "Open the window! Open the–"

The panel squeaked open. "I'm a tad busy, Maggie. Are you both still alive?"

"Yes," Maggie said. "Open your window, and tell Henry if he hits us one more time the wedding is off."

"I'd prefer to open the window and shoot him. Would that work for you?"

"No, it wouldn't," Maggie said as the wind blew in her face when Bryson lowered his window and stuck his arm out. He fired three shots behind them before pulling his arm in and sliding the window up.

Tires screeched behind them, and Bryson swore under his breath. "Hang on."

He slammed the window shut, and the van swayed again.

"He's kidding."

"Uh," Emma groaned, "I don't like the sound of that."

"Me either. We need to find some way to brace ourselves in case this goes south."

"How? It's not like there's a seat belt back here!"

"No, but…there's a table. It's over here against this side." Maggie felt around in the dim light, rubbing her hand along the side panel until she hit the laminate edge. "Here."

She flung her arm out, smacking Emma in the head. "Ouch."

"Sorry." She swung her hand further down, grabbing onto Emma's shoulder and yanking her forehead. "Come over here and get under the table."

Emma crawled across, bumping into Maggie before she slipped under the table. The van fishtailed again. Maggie grabbed ahold of the table leg. Before she could duck underneath the top, the van made a sharp turn.

She struggled to hang on to the leg as the vehicle tipped precariously. Maggie bent backward when the passenger wheels left the pavement.

The front panel swung open, letting light into the dark rear. Emma's eyes went wide as Maggie tumbled away from her. She reached for her when the van lost its battle to stay upright.

The sound of crushing metal and shattering glass filled the air as the vehicle toppled on its side, rolling onto its roof and spinning.

A second later, the chase car slammed into the upside-down van. It pushed them several feet before the van caught the edge of the pavement and rolled over once more, this time landing on its side.

Maggie fluttered her eyelashes as she sucked in a painful breath. Her heart fluttered and she swallowed hard as she struggled to keep her eyes open. Pain radiated from her chest throughout her body. A shuddering sigh escaped her before her world went black.

CHAPTER 24

Maggie gasped in a breath, her eyes blinking open. She scanned her surroundings. A tear spilled from her eye, sliding down her temple toward her hairline as she lay on her back.

She tried to pick up her head, but pain radiated through her. The horrific car accident they'd just experienced played through her mind.

She groaned, forcing herself to roll onto her side and sit up. She glanced around, picking pieces of glass from her hair. Warm liquid ran down her cheek. She winced as she pressed her fingertips to her skin. She pulled them away. Red blood covered them.

With another grimace, she slid her legs up and shifted positions. "Emma?"

Wooziness and nausea swept over her as she climbed to her knees and crawled forward. "Emma?"

Her nostrils flared, and she sniffed. A groan pulled her attention forward. "Emma!"

She hurried forward on her hands and knees, ignoring the pain flaring in her leg. She found a crumpled body lying under an office chair.

Maggie flung the chair off her and pushed the hair from Emma's face. She thrust two fingers against Emma's carotid artery. A steady thump pounded back.

"Thank God," she murmured, pushing Emma's strawberry blonde locks further back. "Emma. Emma, come on, wake up. You need to wake up."

She slapped her cheeks lightly. "Come on, Emma."

She grabbed her shoulder and shook her, tears filling her eyes. "Come on, Emma. Wake up. You don't get to die."

The tears fell, splatting onto Emma's pale skin as Maggie shook her, desperate to wake her. "Emma, come on. We don't have time for you to play dead."

A moan escaped from Emma's parted lips. Maggie wiped at her cheeks and sniffled before patting her friend's cheeks again. "That's it, Emma, come on. Open your eyes."

Emma groaned again, her features pinching. Her eyes fluttered open, and she sucked in a sharp breath. She squeezed her eyes closed again, with another moan.

"Emma, no, don't close your eyes again. You need to wake up."

"Wh-what happened?"

"We wrecked," Maggie said. "Big time. And we need to get out of here."

"No," Emma murmured. "No, we should wait for emergency services."

"No, Emma, we can't. We have no idea if anyone's coming and..." She glanced behind her, chewing her lower lip. "We need to get out of here."

Emma reached toward her thigh. "My leg."

"Is it hurt? Let's see if you can put weight on it."

"No!" Emma shouted, slapping a hand against her forehead. "I can't move."

"Well," Maggie said, with a deep sigh, "I hate to tell you

this, but you're going to have to dig deep. We can't stay in here."

"Oh, Maggie, stop pestering me. We can't get out even if we tried. We're stuck."

"We're going to have to get unstuck."

Emma flung her arm out. "Why are you so insistent about this? We don't always have to be doing something. Sometimes waiting is the best thing to do."

"I'm insistent," Maggie said, sliding her arm around Emma's shoulders and trying to lift her, "because there is gas leaking in here, and I'd really like to not blow up."

Emma's eyes went wide, and she glanced toward her feet. "What?"

"Yes," Maggie said, with an emphatic nod, "now let's go."

Emma wrapped her fingers around Maggie's arm and squeezed. "Help me up. I don't know if I can bear any weight."

"Okay, let's just sit you up first." Maggie pulled Emma up to sit on the side of her hip. "Are you dizzy? Seeing stars other than me? Nausea?"

"No, Dr. Edwards, I feel fine. Just my leg hurts."

"Okay, sit there for a minute, and let me know if you start to feel sick. I'm going to try to pry the door open." Maggie rose to stand, ducking her head, and reached toward what was now the ceiling.

"Why are you reaching up there?"

Maggie grunted as she grabbed the handle and yanked. "Because that's where the door is now."

"Oh my God, we flipped."

"Several times," Maggie said. "Once during the initial crash, and again after Henry hit us."

"Ugh," Emma said, letting her chin sink to her chest.

Maggie dropped the handle and knelt next to Emma. "What's wrong? Are you sick?"

"No. Just disgusted. I knew one of these car chases would end in disaster. I only hoped to be far, far away when it did."

Maggie shook her head and returned to trying to wrench the door open. "At least it wasn't the one I drove in. That one ended in triumph, if you remember."

"We really need to stop doing car chases. I'm a museum director. How am I constantly involved in this much danger?"

"You're also a key part of a covert government team tasked with retrieving rare artifacts from around the globe."

Emma sighed and let her head thud against the van's roof. "Why are we always racing a bad guy for them?"

"Maybe we won't be anymore," Maggie said, wondering how the two men in the front of the van fared.

Metal creaked, and a sliver of light shined down on them. "Come on," Maggie grunted. She tugged at the door, prying it open little by little. The screech of metal on metal announced every small gain.

"Okay," she said, blowing out a breath. "I think that's big enough to climb out. Let's get you up to stand, and then I'll climb out and pull you up."

She reached for Emma who struggled to rise. She hopped on her right leg, her left stiff.

"How is it?"

"My hip's killing me, but I can manage."

"Okay," Maggie said, leaving Emma to balance against the van's wall. She reached up through the opening and heaved herself up. She kicked her legs as she shimmied through the small opening she'd created.

The warm night air swept past her skin as she scanned the outside. A body lay sprawled on the pavement in front of them. Maggie swallowed hard, identifying him as their driver. Where was Bryson?

She swiveled her head, finding the other car sideways in

the street several feet from the van. She could not identify the status of any occupants with the airbag deployed.

With her teeth digging into her lower lip, she pulled her legs out and lay on the van, dangling an arm inside. "Grab my hand."

Emma's fingers wrapped around Maggie's bicep. Her other hand reached for the opening, clasping onto the edge as Maggie pulled.

"Come on, climb," Maggie said through clenched teeth.

"I'm doing my best," Emma grunted.

"Make your best faster. We're sitting on a powder keg."

Emma shot her an irritated glance as she shimmied out, wincing when she bent her leg to tug it through the small opening.

"Okay," Maggie said, standing up and scanning the pavement below. "We need to find a way down. This is probably the best way." Maggie pointed to the front end of the vehicle.

"Oh, my God," Emma said, staring at the nearby car with the crumpled hood.

"Emma, come on."

Emma shifted her eyes away from the mangled mess, turning her eyes toward the front of the van. "Oh, my God!" she shouted again, clamping a hand over her mouth.

"I think that's the driver of the van," Maggie said, following her gaze to the body. "Come on, we need to get away from this van if we want to stay alive."

Maggie clambered across the passenger door. Her gaze fell inside as she crawled across the window on her hands and knees. She froze, chewing her lower lip.

"What?" Emma asked.

"Bryson's inside."

"So? Keep going!" Emma said. "You said this van is going to blow. We need to get away from it."

"I know, but he has the keys."

"Really?" Emma questioned, limping forward toward her. "You're worried about the keys?"

"I did not get kidnapped and nearly killed in a car accident to come out of this with nothing to show for it," Maggie said with a grunt as she shimmied backward and tried to pull open the door.

It creaked up before it slammed shut again.

"Help me," she grunted.

"Maggie," Emma said as she lowered herself to one hip and shimmied forward. "I may have a broken hip or leg. I'm not going to worry about the keys."

Maggie lifted the door again but could not swing it open. "It's never going to work this way. We can't swing it."

"Let's just get away from this van. We survived the crash. I don't want to die in an explosion."

"Okay, okay." Maggie crawled across the door again and slid down the front bumper, landing in a heap on the pavement. "Come on!"

Emma wrinkled her nose as she hovered on the top of the passenger door, balanced on one knee. "I can't do that with my leg!"

"I'll catch you. Come on."

"Fine. You'd better catch me." Emma wagged a finger in the air as Maggie nodded before she shimmied forward. With a wince, she swung around and held on to the bumper's side, letting her legs dangle. "Oof, that hurts."

Maggie reached for Emma's hips when the windshield caught her attention.

"Maggie! Help!" Emma shouted.

"Yeah, yeah, I've got you," Maggie said, returning her attention to her friend.

"Yeah, barely," Emma huffed as Maggie eased her to the pavement.

"Can you bear any weight?"

Emma tugged her lips back in a grimace as she tested her hip. "A little. It's pretty sore."

"Okay, ummm," Maggie murmured as she twisted to face the van again.

"What? Help me get over to the other car. We need to see how the guys are."

"Just a second. I think I can get Bryson out through the windshield."

"Are you serious? The man lives to exact revenge on us, and you're going to save his life?"

"Well, and get the keys."

"Leave the damn keys. Don't risk your life over a stupid treasure, Maggie."

"I'm not risking my life. But–" She pressed a hand to her forehead and squeezed her eyes closed.

"But?" Emma asked, bobbing her head as she flung her hands out to the sides.

"I can't let him die. I know it's stupid, but he may still be alive. He won't survive if the van blows, though."

"And neither will you."

"Just hobble over there. If I can't get him, at least I tried." Maggie shooed Emma toward the other vehicle.

Emma shook her head as she hobbled away. "This is stupid."

"Yeah, I know," Maggie said. She kicked a spiked heel through the broken windshield, freeing a few more pieces before she stuck her head inside the van. Bryson dangled from his seat belt. Blood dripped from his nose and mouth.

Maggie pressed a hand toward his jugular, surprised to find his flesh warm and a pulse thudding against her fingers.

"You're alive," she murmured. With a groan, she stretched toward the seat belt and pressed the button to release it.

Bryson fell in a heap, landing on the driver's broken window. She grabbed him by the shoulders, untangling his limbs and dragging him back from the van through the broken windshield. Blood ran from a gash on his forehead and another on his wrist.

She struggled to tug him a safe distance away before she let his body collapse to the pavement and knelt next to him, searching his pockets. She retrieved the four keys and his cell phone.

As she rose to leave, his hand grabbed her wrist. She gasped, staring down at his bloody face. His blue eyes, now open, contrasted with the red liquid.

"Maggie," he gasped.

She tugged her wrist back toward her, but Bryson held firm. "You're going to be fine. I'll call someone for you."

"Maggie!" Henry shouted from behind her.

She twisted to face him. He hurried toward her, pulling a gun from his waistband.

Maggie shifted her gaze back to Bryson. "I'd let go unless you want to be shot after surviving a car accident."

He gasped in a sharp breath before he released his grip on her arm. She rose and hurried toward Henry. He wrapped her in a tight embrace before he pulled away, cupping her face in his hands. "Maggie, are you okay?"

She nodded, blinking away the tears in her eyes. "I'm okay. What about you?"

He winced as she touched a large gash on his forehead.

"I'm fine. It's nothing. We need to get out of here."

"Yeah," she said, with a sharp nod. "I think Emma needs to get checked out."

"We need to get out of here before any of Bryson's backup shows up. We've been here too long." Henry wrapped his arm around her shoulders and led her away from Bryson.

"Is your car usable?" Maggie asked as they started toward the vehicle.

Henry nodded. "Yeah, I think it'll run."

"That's good, because we need–"

A loud boom interrupted her statement as the van behind them exploded. A fiery burst shot from its rear end, blowing it into the air before it slammed back to the pavement.

The force of the blast smashed Maggie and Henry to the ground. Maggie's ears rang as Henry scrambled to his feet.

Bright lights blared in her eyes. She squinted against them as fingers wrapped around her arm and tugged her up.

"Maggie," Henry's voice called, sounding distant.

Maggie crinkled her forehead, struggling to get her breath after the fall.

"Let's go."

"Henry! Let's go!" Tarik shouted.

An engine roared to life as Maggie regained her feet. She stumbled forward with Henry's help. The headlights of another car raced toward them. She stared at them, moving slowly as she tried to recover from the explosion.

Her hearing began to return to normal.

"Come on, Maggie," Henry yelled, dragging her with him. "We've got to get out of here. That's Bryson's backup coming."

CHAPTER 25

The car aimed at them. The engine revved and headlights blinded Maggie as she struggled to hurry after the blast knocked her down.

The back door flung open, and Henry shoved her forward. She dove into the car, sliding into the seat next to Leo. He wrapped his arm around her and pulled her close as Henry leapt inside and pulled the door shut.

"Go!" he shouted, banging on the headrest.

Tarik slammed his foot on the pedal, and the tires squealed before the car surged forward.

Henry's hand clamped on the back of Maggie's head, forcing it between her knees. "Get down."

Gun shots sounded from behind them. A few bullets peppered their vehicle.

She grabbed her shins, her face inches from Leo's, who crouched next to her. "You okay, Mags?"

"Yeah," she said.

Wind gusted in from the rear window as Henry opened it. He thrust his arm out, his hair blowing wildly. His muscles flexed as they fired return shots.

The chase car skidded sideways shortly after passing Bryson's limp form. Someone darted out of the back seat and raced to him, feeling for a pulse.

Henry slid inside the vehicle, raising the window.

"Are they still chasing us?" Emma asked in a shaky voice from the front passenger seat.

"No, they stopped to help Bryson. Keep going, Tarik. Don't let up."

"I have no intention of it, my friend," Tarik answered, his dark eyes never leaving the road.

Maggie slouched back in the seat and blew out a long breath, running her fingers through her hair.

"How's your hip?" she asked Emma.

"It hurts," she said, shifting in her seat with a wince, "but I don't think it's broken."

"We should get it checked out."

"No hospitals," Henry said, slicing his hand in the air. "We have no idea how quickly they'll be after us again."

"Especially since you took those keys," Emma added. She let her forehead fall into her hand.

Tarik flicked his eyes at Maggie through the rearview mirror. "You got the keys?"

"Yes," Maggie said, opening her hand and shifting her palm forward. "Bryson had them. I pulled him from the van and took them, along with his phone."

Henry snatched the phone from her hand and lowered the window again. He tossed it outside before closing the window. "I don't want them tracking us."

He twisted to face Maggie. "That was stupid to pull him from the car. He could have killed you."

"I wanted to get the keys. I didn't just survive a kidnapping and car crash for nothing, Henry."

Henry shook his head, his nose wrinkling as he turned his attention forward.

"You did good, Mags," Leo said, snaking an arm around her. "Are you sure you're okay? Did you hit your head in the crash?"

"I may have, but I'm fine. We need to move fast. I'm sure Bryson will be after us in no time. He has nine lives. We need to hole up and talk about next steps."

Emma crinkled her brow and twisted to shoot Maggie a glance, wincing as she leaned on her hip. "Did I just hear you say 'hole up?'"

"What? Henry says it all the time."

Henry shook his head. "She's right. As much as I hate to admit it."

"I'll find a place," Tarik said. "I see signs for the airport. I'll follow them."

"Good thinking, mate."

Maggie placed her hand on Henry's knee as he flicked his gaze out the window. She puckered her lips at his reaction. "Hey–" She stared when his phone jangled.

He dug it from his pocket and jabbed at the display. "Charlie, we got 'em…yeah, they're both fine more or less, but we're going to need some medical supplies…basic stuff for cuts and bruises. We're looking for a place to hole up now…"

"Tell him to get me some normal clothes," Maggie whispered.

Henry waved away the comment. "Also, grab something for Maggie to change into…yeah, I'll call you as soon as we've found one."

He clicked off his display and shoved the phone into his pocket as Tarik merged into the light traffic on a highway. "I'll put a few exits between us and the crash, then find a motel. We'll need to hide the car."

"Yeah, it's too easy to track with the smashed hood," Henry agreed.

They drove in silence for several miles before Tarik veered off the highway and threaded through the streets, following signs for a hotel. He pulled into the lot. After a few minutes inside, Leo, the least banged up of the group, emerged with a key.

"Asked for a room around back," he said as he slid in next to Maggie.

"I texted the address to Charlie, they're en route," Henry said as Tarik pulled the car around the back of the rectangular building.

"I'll dump the car a few parking lots over and head back," Tarik said as they climbed from the car.

The rest of the group hurried in through the back door of the hotel. Emma limped, walking better than she had at the crash site. They pushed into the small room.

Maggie hobbled to the bed and plopped onto it, tugging her shoes off before flopping back on the mattress. "Ugh. I can't wait until Charlie, Piper, and Uncle Ollie get here, so I can get out of this dress. I have never wanted out of a designer dress more than this one."

Emma sprawled on the other bed, with a wince. "I hope they get painkillers. I need a fistful."

"Are you sure we shouldn't get her checked?" Leo asked. "I can take her."

"You'd be sitting ducks for Bryson. We stick together. That's final," Henry said, tapping around on his phone.

Maggie sat up and patted the bed next to her. Henry glanced at her before returning to study his phone and stalking to the opposite side of the room.

Maggie followed him with her eyes before she snapped her gaze at Emma and Leo. "Do you want anything?" Leo asked.

"Nope," Emma said, rolling onto her side.

Leo glanced at Maggie and raised his eyebrows. She

shrugged and shook her head, trying to signal that she hadn't told Emma anything.

"Should we discuss next steps?" Maggie asked.

"We'll wait for Charlie, Piper, and Ollie to get here. Then we won't have to rehash anything," Henry snapped.

"All right," Maggie said, with a wiggle of her eyebrows and flutter of her eyelashes. "Well, I'd like to wash my hands and clean up a little. Anyone need the bathroom before I head in?"

With no answers from anyone else, Maggie pushed herself to stand and shuffled toward the bathroom while holding up her dress. She squeezed past Henry, who made a move to claim the bed she'd just left.

Maggie clamped down on his arm. "Come with me. We need to talk."

"I don't think we do."

"Henry," she said, with a tilt of her head.

"Maybe later," he answered, tugging his arm from her grasp.

She pressed her lips into a thin line, realizing his reluctance not only stemmed from the recent revelation about her secret meetings with Leo, but also from a desire to pay her back for refusing to talk to him earlier.

With a heavy sigh, she reached for him again when a knock at the door sounded. "It's Tarik."

Henry darted toward the door to let in the man.

"I hid the car. Hopefully, no one will find it, but we should move as quickly as possible."

"Agreed, mate," Henry said as he closed and locked the door behind them. "As soon as everyone else arrives, we'll make a plan and head out."

"Henry," Maggie insisted again, with a stamp of her hosiery-clad foot on the floor. "I need to talk to you."

Henry flicked his gaze to her, his jaw flexing. His nostrils flared, and he narrowed his eyes before he clicked off his phone and shoved it into his pocket. "Fine."

Maggie lifted the bottom of her dress and strode to the bathroom. She approached the mirror as Henry leaned against the door jamb, his arms crossed.

"Wow," she said, with a wince. She ran a finger along a cut on her jaw and one on her cheek before she turned to stare at a large bruise forming on her shoulder.

"You sure you're okay?"

She glanced at him through the mirror. "Physically, yes." She spun to face him, balancing herself on the pedestal sink. "Close the door."

"Maggie–"

"Just close it," she said.

Henry flicked his gaze to the side, refusing to step inside the bathroom. "I assume Emma told you how we knew you were missing."

Maggie stuck her hand on her hip, her other fingers tracing the bowl of the sink. "She did. That's what I want to talk to you about."

Henry refused to meet her eye. "We don't need to do this now."

"Yes, we do. But I'd like to do it in private." She flung her hand toward the open door. "Henry, come on!"

He puckered his lips and took a step inside, swinging the door shut behind him. He flung his hands out. "There. Happy?"

"Thank you." She heaved a sigh. "It's not what you think."

Henry's eyebrows shot up. "Really? Isn't it?"

"No," Maggie said, crossing her arms and cocking a hip. "And to be honest, I'm a little miffed you think that of me."

"You're miffed? You? You who have been sneaking around having secret meetings with her ex."

"Did he tell you why?"

"No. He refused to tell anyone why. When it came down to it, he insisted the better thing to do was search for you. I agreed. But that doesn't mean I wouldn't like some answers."

"And I was happy to provide those, but your attitude leaves something to be desired."

"I can't believe this. I cannot believe you're the one caught cheating, and you're going to cry about my attitude."

"Caught cheating? We weren't cheating. Again, I would have been happy to explain, but I cannot believe you'd think this of me. You! The man who told my at-the-time boyfriend we spent the night together, and then when he stormed out, you told me it was on him because he assumed the worst of me. Who's assuming the worst now?"

"What would you like me to assume, Maggie? Secret meetings with Leo that have been going on for quite some time, from what I understand. You're distant. You won't set a date for the wedding. What else should I think?"

Maggie pressed her lips together and tugged the corners into a frown. "Not that. You wanted Leo not to assume it when you told him we spent the night together. But you can assume. The almighty Henry can assume it, because he's special. He's smarter."

"These are two completely different scenarios."

"Are they? Really? They look pretty similar to me. My and Leo's meetings have nothing to do with us."

Henry screwed up his face. "How can you say that?"

"Because it's true. Believe it or don't," Maggie said, with a flick of her hair. New voices filled the room outside. "Sounds like Charlie, Piper, and Uncle Ollie made it. I'd like to get out of these clothes, so if you'll excuse me."

Henry shifted to block the door. "Are you serious? I thought you were going to explain."

"And I thought you were going to not think the worst of

me. But here we are. Like you said, this isn't the time to discuss it."

Henry firmed his jaw, flicking his gaze away from her before he shifted to the side. Maggie pulled the door open and strode into the bedroom.

"Hey, there, chicky. I've got the clothes you requested," Charlie said with a grin as he slid pizza boxes onto the laminate desk near the door.

"Ugh, thank you. I will be so glad to get out of this dress."

"Wow, Boss Lady," Piper said as she wrangled medical supplies from inside a plastic bag, "never thought I'd hear you say those words."

"Right?" Maggie said, with a smile. "I must admit, this is a killer dress."

"No kidding," Charlie answered. "It almost worked, too."

Maggie chuckled at the joke as Ollie wrapped his arms around her before he pulled back and studied her. "You okay?"

"I'm okay."

Piper approached her and studied her face. "You sure about that? Looks like you need a little medical attention."

Piper grabbed Maggie's chin and turned it to eye the cut.

Maggie winced. "Yeah. I'm a little worse for wear. But it could have been worse."

"So, who am I nursing first? You or Fanny?"

Maggie waved a finger at Emma. "Emma. Get her some painkillers and patch up that cut on her forehead. I'm going to change first."

"Here you are, chicky," Charlie said, handing a bag of clothes over to her.

She thanked him and spun to return to the bathroom. Henry turned sideways to let her pass. She grabbed his hand and glanced up into his crystal blue eyes. "Hey, I love you," she whispered before she kissed him on the cheek.

She took a step toward the bathroom when he snaked an arm around her waist, stopping her. She twisted to gaze up at him. "I love you, too, Princess."

Her lips turned up at the corners as she stared up at him. After another quick peck on his lips, she hurried into the bathroom. She shimmied out of the dress and draped it over the tub.

"You were a killer dress," she murmured before she pulled the clothes from within the bag.

As she tugged the pants on she studied the large welt on her thigh. She sucked in a sharp breath. "Yeah, that's gonna hurt tomorrow."

With a final glance at the large bruise on her shoulder, she pulled the T-shirt down and tugged the hoodie over it before removing the ruby necklace. After slipping into her shoes, she emerged from the bathroom.

"Tell me you bought the giant-sized bottle of pain relievers."

"You feeling it, chicky?"

"Adrenaline's still pumping, so it's not too bad, but I am going to feel this tomorrow."

"I can't believe this happened. If you'd have let me drive–" Leo began.

"Driving was just fine, my friend."

"Maybe you should have tried not shooting at the van we were in," Emma said with a wince as Piper dabbed the cut on her forehead.

"It wasn't the best result, but we got the girls back *and* the keys," Henry said. "Which means we have to get moving to find that gold, because Bryson won't be far behind."

"The slime survived, did he?" Charlie asked as he pulled a piece of pizza onto a plate and handed it to Maggie.

Maggie offered a sigh. "Thanks. Yes, he did. He's got nine lives."

"He wouldn't have if you didn't pull him out of the car," Henry said.

"I had to get the keys," Maggie explained after a bite.

"And you got them?" Ollie asked. "All four?"

"All four," Maggie said, grabbing them from the bed next to her and waving them in the air.

"Okay," Ollie said, pulling his cell phone out and accessing his map application. "So, two keys were in Rosemont, one was in Memphis, and one here in New Orleans. So, that takes care of four of the Xs on the map."

"Any luck tracing those drawings we found in the Blood River chamber?"

"Nothing definitive, but they have similarities to pre-Columbian cultures. I'd say something along a South American river given the drawings and the depiction of the ironclad moving up a river."

"It's still most likely that it was an American river, Ollie," Emma argued.

Ollie served himself a piece of pizza and perched on the bed next to Maggie. "If you're basing that off the notion that ironclads weren't seaworthy, you may want to re-evaluate."

"What do you mean?" Maggie said. "I thought they couldn't make it as far as South America?"

Ollie bit into his pizza and chewed, his eyes settling on it for a moment. "Thanks for not ordering hot peppers this time."

Charlie pointed a finger-gun at him and winked. "Anything for you, Ollie."

"And to your point, Maggie, this was the original thought. But there has been some evidence that ironclads may have been able to make the journey."

"It makes sense with the map, too. Does anyone have pictures of the map?"

"Didn't get to pull that off Bryson after the wreck, huh?" Emma snarked.

Maggie narrowed her eyes and shot a glance at Leo. "Get her something to eat, so the pain meds can work."

"Just remember who dove into the back of Bryson's van so you weren't alone," Emma answered as Leo retrieved pizza for them both.

"Just remember who pulled you from a van that was about to explode. Now, anyway," Maggie said as Tarik offered his phone with pictures of the map, "these two points that are together were the Rosemont keys. This one is Memphis. And this one is New Orleans. Which means the final X, likely the treasure's resting spot, is further south."

She spun the phone to show everyone her analysis, jabbing a finger at each mark.

"Or," Emma said after washing down a bite of pizza with a gulp of soda, "New Orleans is the last X, and the treasure is north. Memphis, maybe."

"That's ridiculous," Maggie answered.

"Why would it be ridiculous?"

"So, they dropped two keys, then dumped the treasure in Memphis, then kept going north to store the final two keys? That makes no sense," Maggie said, with a shake of her head.

"It doesn't *not* make sense," Emma retorted.

"Brainy has a point," Charlie chimed in. "Split the keys north and south. Centralize the treasure."

Emma shot Maggie a haughty glance, with her eyebrows raised.

"Yeah, but," Piper said after a swallow of soda, "it stands to reason the treasure was locked up and *then* the keys were distributed. Which would mean they'd have to travel up the Mississippi, offload the treasure, *and then* distribute the keys."

Leo bobbed his head up and down, pointing a finger at Piper. "Which would mean they'd have to backtrack."

"Unless they split up into two teams, one who went south, and one who went north," Henry chimed in.

Leo shook his head. "Which would make sense *if* Thomas didn't say *he* hid the keys."

"But did he?" Henry questioned. "I mean, this is a second-hand story passed down through over a century of people. How can we know he explicitly said he himself hid the keys?"

Leo glared at the man as he bit into his slice of pizza. "I guess you have a point."

Ollie shook his head, tossing his empty plate onto the nightstand. He slapped his thighs before waving a finger in the air. "The fact remains, the images depicted at the off-loading site look pre-Columbian."

Maggie poked a finger at him. "That feels like an important clue, yes. We really need to look at this as a whole."

"She's right," Leo said. "If you take these separately, you can make the case those Xs are anywhere."

Emma dropped her crust onto her plate, with a sigh. "Not really. We know where four of the five marks are. We're just debating the fifth."

Piper plopped on the end of the bed next to Leo. "Oscar's right. Without a scale or any landmarks, it's impossible to assess where it is."

"I'm going to let that one slide, since you said I was right," Leo said.

"So, we look at them as a whole. The whole package points to a river, which could be the Mississippi or in South America."

"Or the Nile," Emma said, with a shrug. "If you want to say ironclads could sail across the seas, why are we restricting it to just South America?"

Ollie leapt from his seat and paced the floor between the beds. "Because of the depictions shown near the off-loading site."

Silence fell over the group. Henry flicked his gaze to Maggie. "You're team lead. It's your call."

All eyes turned to Maggie as she weighed the information. "I trust Uncle Ollie's judgment. And my gut says it's not on American soil."

Emma pressed her lips together, flicking up her eyebrows. "Even if you're right, where are we going? South America's a big place."

"Uncle Ollie, were you able to pinpoint it down to any cultures, specifically?"

"No, there is nothing exactly like this. Only similarities with pre-Columbian art style."

"So, Columbia?" Piper asked as she grabbed another slice of pizza.

Emma shook her head. "Not necessarily. Pre-Columbian refers to architecture and art characteristic of people from North, South, and Central America."

"And even some of the islands in the Caribbean," Ollie noted.

"Right. So, that doesn't help us pinpoint it." Emma waved her empty plate in the air. "Can someone grab me another slice?"

Henry retrieved the plate and filled it with more pizza.

Maggie tapped around on Tarik's phone, pulling up a map and performing a browser search. "Okay, well, it looks like we've got two choices here. The Orinoco River, or the Amazon."

"Both are prime locations, as they both travel through dense rainforest areas where anything could be hidden and remain that way for centuries," Ollie said.

Maggie stared at the map. "We're going to have to make a call."

"Amazon," Leo said as all eyes turned to him. "What? Are we voting? That's my vote."

Henry poured more soda into his plastic cup. "It's not a democracy."

Maggie studied the picture of the map again before she studied the map of northern South America.

Ollie rubbed his finger along his beard. "What's your gut say, Maggie?"

She remained silent, flicking between the makeshift treasure map and real map. She zoomed in and out a few times before she narrowed her eyes at it. "My gut says Venezuela."

"Why?" Emma inquired.

"Because it's closer to where we know the ironclad left port in the U.S., and if you look at the treasure map and this one, it lines up."

Emma swung her legs over the edge of the bed and stood, with a wince. "What?"

She peered over Maggie's shoulder as Maggie toggled between the two maps.

Henry pulled up the picture of the map on his phone and handed it to Maggie. She held the two side-by-side. "These two are here," she said, pointing out Rosemont. "Then Memphis, then New Orleans."

"Oh my goodness, you're right," Emma said, with wide eyes. "That makes this X right about here. Deep in the rainforest, along the Orinoco River."

Maggie flicked her gaze to Emma and nodded before turning her attention to the rest of the group. She scanned their eager faces. "Looks like we're going to Venezuela."

CHAPTER 26

"Not again," Maggie said, with a wrinkled nose. She crossed her arms and shot a narrow-eyed glare at Henry. He hefted a bag of their things onto his shoulder, avoiding her stare.

He grabbed a second bag, slinging it onto the other shoulder before he straightened and slammed the trunk shut. He turned, finding Maggie staring at him.

With a nervous grin, he kissed the tip of her nose.

"It's a good thing I love you," she said, grabbing a strap of one of the bags.

"I've got it," he said.

"You sure?"

"I should make you carry it. But I won't."

Maggie curled the corners of her lips up as the others climbed out from the van and grabbed their gear. "Not even because you're mad at me?"

"I'm not mad…I'm just…" He heaved a sigh. "We need to have a serious discussion when we get home."

"I know. But I promise–"

"I believe you. You're right. I thought Leo was an arse to think the worst of you, so I have no right to do it."

"What about Leo?" Leo questioned as he shrugged a backpack onto his back.

"Nothing," Maggie said before turning to Henry. "There's no reason to think the worst of me. There's nothing going on." She planted a kiss on his cheek before she twisted to stare at the convenience taking them into Venezuela. "I still think this is a punishment for what happened though."

"It's the easiest way into the country," Henry answered.

"Why can Thomas never send a cushy private jet?" Charlie asked as he strode hand-in-hand with Piper to the cargo plane ahead of them.

"That's the same question I have," Maggie answered. "I may have to keep some of this Confederate gold and buy us one."

"It is faster than any legal channels, which the private plane would still need to go through. This flight is already scheduled, and we can arrive safely in Venezuela without any fuss," Ollie said as he strolled to the plane.

"And time matters," Tarik added. "Bryson will be right behind us."

"If not ahead of us," Henry said, spinning to face them as he backed toward the plane.

"If boss lady wouldn't have saved him, we'd be free."

Maggie rolled her eyes as they climbed into the cargo hold. "That's not true. Someone else would replace him."

"But be further behind," Emma retorted.

Maggie flung her hands in the air as she settled on the floor, sticking her hoodie underneath her for a cushion. "Oh, whatever. Sorry for being a nice person."

"Riiiiight, St. Maggie, saving criminals one car crash at a time," Emma said, with a shake of her head.

Maggie glared at her. Leo shrugged off his backpack and settled in next to Emma. She shimmied away from him.

He flung a hand in the air before he glanced at Maggie. She shrugged, shaking her head. "I'll fix it," she mouthed before pressing her lips together and offering a nod.

Henry eased into a spot next to Maggie, draping an arm around her. Leo narrowed his eyes at the scene before he slid his sunglasses on and leaned his head onto the crate behind him.

Maggie leaned into Henry. "You got a riverboat to take us upriver, right?"

"Yeah," Henry informed her. "We'll aim for the area on the map, but it's pretty vague. It may be difficult to find."

Maggie puckered her lips. "Hopefully, there will be some way to track this down. I mean, these Confederate soldiers found a place to put the gold in the eighteen hundreds. It can't be that hard, right?"

"Sure it won't be," Henry said, with a chuckle.

Maggie yawned, wiggling her stiff shoulders. "Hope you don't mind if I get some sleep on the flight. Despite the luxurious nap, I took thanks to Bryson's penchant for drugging people, I'm exhausted."

Henry kissed the top of her head. "Sleep away, Princess."

The cargo door closed, and the engines roared to life. Maggie's heavy eyelids fought to stay open as the plane trundled down the runway. She glanced across the cargo hold, smiling as she caught sight of Piper and Charlie settling in for a movie.

Uncle Ollie, his legs crossed at the ankles, leaned against a crate with his hat over his eyes. She shifted her sleepy gaze to Emma, who scowled at her before letting her head thud against the crate behind her.

I really need to fix things with Emma, she thought as the plane left the ground and she drifted off to sleep.

* * *

An obnoxious buzzing woke Maggie from her sleep. She fluttered her eyelids open as the plane dropped in the sky.

"What the hell? Did we hit turbulence?" she murmured before realizing Henry no longer sat at her side.

Shouting erupted from the cockpit. The plane climbed steeply before it rolled to the side. Crates and boxes toppled from the sudden move. Maggie slid across the floor. She kicked her feet out in front of her, bracing herself from moving more.

"What's happening?" Emma shouted, pushing up to sit.

"Turbulence?"

A few of the others, still groggy from sleep, glanced around to ascertain the source of the alarm.

"Where are Henry and Tarik?" Maggie asked.

The plane wobbled again before it dove down. Maggie rolled to the side, grabbing at anything to stop her movement.

"What the hell is happening?" Leo yelled.

Henry pushed open the cockpit door and staggered out. "We've got big trouble."

Maggie crinkled her brow. "What?"

"Is it a storm? Can't they go around it?" Charlie questioned.

Henry pressed his lips together in a thin line and shook his head. "Came out of nowhere. And it's pretty bad. We need to find a corner. The pilots are doing their best, but the cargo is going to be shifting around a good bit."

Maggie nodded as she scrambled to her feet. She scanned the space and pointed to a corner near the back. "Maybe there?"

"Good enough," Henry said, with a nod. "Hopefully, we

can fit everyone. With these crates sliding around, someone may get hurt."

Maggie rose to her feet, stumbling to the side as the plane lurched again. Henry reached out to steady her as the others hurried to seek shelter in the back corner.

Thunder boomed outside as rain continued to pelt the plane. It rolled, climbed, and dove. Piper squeezed her eyes closed as she pressed herself against the wall, her hands clasped together in front of her.

Charlie wrapped his arm around her shoulders. "We'll be okay, fair maiden."

"I hate flying in storms."

"Planes want to be in the air," Ollie assured her.

Leo slid in-between Maggie and Emma. "Until they crash."

Piper groaned, letting her chin fall to her chest.

Maggie smacked his arm. "Nice going, idiot."

"What? I think we should all be prepared for the possibility. It could happen. We're flying over the rainforest in what sounds like an epic storm."

Piper let her head fall back, thudding against the wall with another moan.

"Well, you don't have to keep talking about it," Maggie said through clenched teeth. "She's upset enough."

"Sorry for being a realist."

"That's not being a realist, it's being an ass," Maggie murmured, turning to face Henry. "Where's Tarik?"

Henry crouched on the floor next to Maggie. "With the pilots. He's a pretty good navigator."

"It makes me nervous that they aren't pretty good navigators," Maggie said, with a wince.

He offered her a reassuring smile. "We'll be okay, Princess. I'm certain these guys have flown through storms before."

"Then why is Tarik with them?"

Emma nodded. "For once, I agree with Maggie. It makes me *less* comfortable that he feels he needs to be up there."

Henry settled to the floor. "Think of Tarik as a little added insurance."

Emma narrowed her eyes at Henry as she hugged her legs to her chest. "Is there something you're not telling us?"

Henry licked his lips, letting his gaze fall to the floor. "No."

"Look me in the eyes and say that," Maggie retorted, with a bob of her head.

"There's nothing. It's just a really, really bad storm."

Maggie flicked her gaze up to the ceiling, drawing in a long breath. "Okay. Just a really bad storm. Tarik is added insurance."

Piper covered her face with her hands as thunder resounded again.

"How are you so calm in all of this, Ollie?" Emma asked as she studied the older man. With his legs stretched in front of him and crossed at the ankles, he leaned against the plane's side casually, as though they were flying through calm skies.

"Oh, I'm used to it."

"Flew through a lot of turbulence in your time, Ollie?" Charlie asked.

"Yes."

"And everything turned out okay," Charlie said to Piper, shaking her shoulders a bit. "Ollie's planes were just fine, and he's still here, see?"

"Oh, no," Ollie answered, wagging a finger in the air. "Two of them crashed."

Emma's eyes bugged out of her head. "What?"

"See, I told you I was the realist," Leo added, flinging a hand in the air.

"Uncle Ollie! You've been in two plane crashes?"

"Yes," Ollie said. He twisted to face Piper and patted her shoulder. "See, I've lived to a ripe old age."

Piper pulled her hands away from her face, running her fingers through her rainbow-colored hair. "After you almost died in two plane crashes."

"'Almost died' is a bit of an exaggeration. If the pilot is skilled enough, you have a good chance of surviving."

"Back of the plane has the highest odds, so we have the best chance of only being maimed," Leo chimed in.

Maggie swatted at him again. "Uncle Ollie wasn't maimed."

"Actually, I was," Ollie said, lifting his button down to showcase a large scar on his abdomen. "A piece of the wreckage went right through my gut here, and–"

Maggie held up a hand. "Okay, that's enough. Maybe we can discuss your war wounds after we're safely on the ground and sailing up the river on a beautiful cruise."

"Beautiful cruise?" Henry questioned. "This is–"

"Don't say it," Maggie interrupted. "Just let me picture a lovely river cruise until we're on the ground."

She squeezed her eyes closed and sucked in a breath as the plane dropped again.

Piper clasped her hands, balancing her elbows on her knees and letting her head rest against them.

Charlie rubbed her back. "Breathe through it, fair maiden. We'll be on the ground in a jif."

The crates shifted again as the plane peeled sharply to the side. Piper whimpered as they braced to stop themselves from moving, too.

Leo grabbed Emma's hand and squeezed it. She stared down at their intertwined fingers before she let out a sigh and shifted closer to him.

Maggie leaned into Henry, glancing up at him. He offered a tight-lipped smile and squeezed her shoulder.

They flew for a few minutes in relative peace. No loud booms, no lurching or dropping, no sliding cargo.

Maggie scanned the group. "Do you think we're coming out of it?"

A deafening crack answered her question. The hum of the engine on their left ceased.

"Uh, that doesn't sound good," Leo said.

Henry rose to his feet. "I'll go check."

"Henry!" Maggie exclaimed, reaching for him. "Don't go."

"It's okay," he answered, grabbing her hands and squeezing them. "I'll be right back, I promise."

Maggie crinkled her forehead and shook her head as he strode across the cargo area toward the cockpit. He disappeared into the small space. Maggie heaved a sigh as she kept her eyes trained on the door.

Henry emerged from it a moment later. Her stomach turned over as he strode toward them. "One of the engines is out, but they're trying to restart it."

"What does that mean?" Emma asked.

"The other engine is fine. We can fly with one, and if they get the second one restarted, it's not a problem," Henry answered.

"Did it get hit by lightning?" Maggie asked.

"Yeah. That's the loud boom we heard."

Maggie pursed her lips and nodded. "Hopefully, they'll get it restarted."

"Yeah," Henry answered as he settled on the floor. "But like I said, even if they don't, we'll be okay with just the one. As long as that one stays running, we've got nothing to worry about."

A sputtering noise sounded, and the constant drone of the motor cut out.

Maggie's eyes went wide, and she glanced over her shoulder. "Uh…"

Henry's brow crinkled as he began to push himself up to stand. "Let me go check–" he began as Tarik burst from the cockpit.

"We're in big trouble. Both engines are out, and we can't get them restarted."

"What?" Emma shouted as Piper covered her face again with her hands.

Tarik stared at them with wide eyes. Maggie's heart pounded against her ribs, and she swallowed hard. Her stomach rolled with Tarik's next words.

"We're going down. We need to prepare for a crash landing."

CHAPTER 27

"What?" Piper shrieked. "No!"

"Told ya," Leo said.

"I'm so glad you're proud about being right, Oscar."

"All right, easy, everyone, calm down," Maggie said. "Prepare for a crash landing. But they can try to restart the engines, right?"

"They can try," Tarik said, "but I doubt it's going to happen. We're going down."

"Are there any parachutes aboard?" Henry questioned.

"No," Tarik answered, with a shake of his head. "Even if there were, it would be too few."

"Omigod, omigod, omigod," Piper repeated as she hugged her knees to her chest and rocked back and forth.

The plane dropped suddenly, eliciting shouts from several of the passengers.

"We need to brace for impact," Henry said as they continued to glide forward, pelted by the rain and blown around by the wind gusts. He raced across the cargo space, grabbing their bags and dragging them toward the group huddled in the back. "We need to insulate as much as possible from things hitting us."

The plane tilted to the side, sending the crates sliding around again.

"We'd better hurry," Maggie said as more alarms rang from the cockpit.

Tarik nodded, shoving the bags against them. "She's right. That's a low altitude alarm."

"Oh, God," Piper groaned. Charlie wrapped his arms around her, bracing his legs against the floor.

"Everyone down, heads between your knees," Henry said as he collapsed to the floor next to Maggie. The plane rolled again.

Maggie slid closer to Ollie, grabbing his hand and squeezing. The plane shuddered and banged. Tarik took a seat against the wall, tucking his head between his knees and holding his duffel bag against his hip.

Maggie tucked her chin to her chest, burying her head between her knees. Henry pressed his chest against her back, shielding her as much as possible.

Leo wrapped his arms around Emma who clung to him, her features pinched with worry.

The plane continued to dive toward the ground. The pilots shouted from the front as they fought to land the plane with no engines.

Tears formed in Maggie's eyes as her stomach rolled with every movement and shake of the plane.

The plane lurched again, and they fought to brace themselves from sliding across the floor. Netting covering several crates tore under the stress. The boxes toppled across the space, crashing into the side of the plane with a splintering *crack*. The contents spilled from within, flying through the air and pelting them.

The sound of trees scraping the plane's bottom brought

the reality ever closer. Within another instant, one wing struck something. Metal scraped and wrenched as the plane twisted sideways.

Seconds later, it slammed into the ground, rear first, with a resounding *boom* as Maggie's world went black.

* * *

She fluttered open her eyes. As her vision came into focus, she found herself on her back. An ache in her leg thudded in time with her heartbeat. She groaned and rolled to her side, pushing herself up to sit.

"Easy, Maggie, you okay?" Henry asked from behind her.

"I-I think so," she murmured, tasting the metallic tang of blood on her tongue.

He slid his hands under her underarms and lifted. "Let's get you out of here."

"Wait, we have to get everyone else."

"I'll come back for them. I want you safe."

"No," Maggie said, struggling against him to crawl forward. "We have to get everyone. You get Leo, I'll get Emma."

Maggie shuffled across the debris-strewn floor toward the redhead. She pushed her hair back, assessing her with two fingers to her carotid. "She's got a pulse. Emma. Emma, come on, wake up."

Maggie nudged her as she scanned the plane's other occupants. "Where's Uncle Ollie?"

"I took him out already," Henry said.

"He's okay, right?"

"Unconscious, but with a steady pulse. No injuries that I could see."

Maggie continued to shimmy Emma's shoulder. "I can't get her to respond."

"Can you drag her?" Henry asked as Leo offered a murmur. "We need to move fast."

"Okay," Maggie said, shoving her hair behind her ears before she climbed around Emma and grabbed her hands, tugging her arms overhead.

"Come on, mate," Henry said to Leo. "Get up."

Leo's eyes fluttered open. His features scrunched a second later. "Oh, what the hell?"

"The plane crashed. Can you get up and walk? We've got to get out of here."

"I think so," Leo grunted, pushing himself up. He clamored to his feet and hobbled around. "Yeah, I'm good. I'm okay."

"If you're not hurt, check Piper and see if we can get her out of here," Henry said as he hurried to Charlie and checked his pulse.

"Got it," Leo said as Maggie tugged Emma past him. "She okay?"

"So far. She's breathing, with a pulse. She's a little banged up, but so far, so good," Maggie answered.

Leo stopped her and scooped up Emma. "I'll take her out. Check Piper and see if she's okay. I'll be back in to help you with her as soon as I get Emma out."

"Okay," Maggie said with a nod, hurrying toward the limp form of Piper. She felt for a pulse, finding a strong beat thrumming against her fingertips. "Got a pulse."

Henry bent over his British buddy. "Good, get her out of here. I've got Charlie."

"Is Tarik already out?" Maggie asked as she dragged Piper toward the open cargo door.

"I haven't seen him."

Maggie nodded as Leo raced back inside and hefted up Piper. She let go of her arms and hurried to help Henry drag Charlie from the plane.

They stepped outside into the pouring rain. Maggie squinted against it as large drops pelted her. They carried Charlie toward a canopy of trees. Ollie kneeled over Emma, assessing her injuries.

"Is she okay?" Maggie asked.

"Looks like no major traumas on the surface. I'd like to wake her up, though."

"Have you seen Tarik?"

"No," Ollie yelled over the rain that beat against the trees soaring above them.

"He must still be inside," Henry said as thunder rumbled overhead. "I'll go check for him."

"I'll go with you and check the pilots," Maggie said, with a nod.

"No, you stay here. Help Ollie with everyone else."

"No way," Maggie said, with a head shake. "We go in together."

"All right, come on," Henry huffed.

They sprinted through the rain, ducking from the deluge into the plane. Maggie scanned the area as they picked their way through toppled crates and spilled merchandise in search of Tarik.

Maggie sidestepped past a pallet with its cargo net nearly intact. Inside, the shipping containers leaned precariously to the side. The net stretched to its limit to stop them from spilling onto the floor.

A large crate blocked the small door leading to the cockpit. Maggie climbed on top and slid down into the small space between it and the open doorway. She peered inside at the two men, slumped in their seats.

Blood covered the pilot's face, and his eyes stared blankly ahead. Maggie squashed her lips together as she closed his eyes and turned her attention to the co-pilot. Facing away from her, she found it impossible to assess his condition.

She pressed a hand against his shoulder and gave him a shake. His body wriggled, but he did not stir. "Sir?" Maggie asked, giving him another shove.

She wrapped her fingers around his shoulder and pulled him back. His body flopped back on the chair. His arms hung limply at his side. She stumbled back a step, banging into the crate behind her. She gripped the door and pulled herself upright. Her stomach turned over as she stared at the large tree limb poking through his abdomen and large blood splotch around it.

"Maggie!" Henry called.

Maggie slid the eyes closed on the co-pilot's face before she climbed across the shipping crate and skirted around the other fallen cargo to Henry's location.

A booted foot poked from under the debris.

"I found him," Henry said, shoveling as much of the rubble from the body as he could.

Maggie dropped to her knees, tugging smaller pieces of broken containers and packing material from the pile.

She shimmied further up, uncovering his head and torso. After freeing his face and neck, she pressed two fingers against his clammy flesh.

"His pulse is weak."

"We need to get him moved."

Maggie nodded, shifting a number of plastic-wrapped packages off his chest. She froze as she exposed his black T-shirt and sat back on her haunches.

"Henry," she said, her arm flailing in his direction, while her eyes remained fixed on Tarik's abdomen.

"Huh?" he grunted, still trying to free Tarik's lower half.

"Henry," she said again, finally tearing her eyes away from Tarik and focusing on Henry.

"What?" he asked, sweat beading on his brow and his face red from the effort.

Without a word, Maggie flicked her gaze back to Tarik. Henry followed the line of her vision. The pieces of wood in his hands slipped to the floor below as he pushed past Maggie to assess the situation.

His hands shook as they hovered over the large piece of metal poking from Tarik's stomach. "We need to get him out of here."

"We need to be careful not to move that, though. We can't take it out until we know he won't bleed to death," Maggie said, shifting more debris off Tarik's legs.

Leo appeared in the doorway, his hair dripping and clothes soaked. "Did you find him?"

"We did," Maggie said. "We need help. He's hurt. Badly. We need to move him without jostling him too much. We have no idea how deep that metal is inside him."

Leo climbed across the wreckage-strewn floor and grabbed Tarik's ankles. "On three," he said as Henry shuffled to lift the man's shoulders.

After a quick countdown, they hefted his limp body between them, struggling to move him to the entrance across the detritus.

Maggie hurried ahead of them, climbing into the steady rain and hurrying to the canopy of trees.

"What happened?" Emma asked, sitting straighter.

"We found Tarik. He's hurt pretty badly."

Ollie climbed to his knees as the men approached carrying Tarik and eased him onto the wet ground. Ollie leaned over him, taking his pulse before he tugged a Swiss Army knife from the pocket of his soaked cargo pants. He sliced open Tarik's shirt and studied the wound.

"Can we remove it?" Maggie asked.

"We can't leave it in. But we risk infection or bleed out by removing it," Ollie answered. "We need to find something to stop the blood and a way to close the wound."

"There should be a first aid kit in the plane," Charlie said.

Henry rested his hands on his thighs, squinting into the rain. "We'll need to cauterize the wound. I've got a lighter. If we can find another piece of metal to heat, we can use that."

"There's plenty to pick from," Ollie said, with a nod.

Charlie scrambled to his feet. "Piper and I will go find the first aid kit."

"What about the pilots?" Piper questioned as Charlie pulled her to her feet.

"Dead. Both of them," Maggie answered. She dropped to her knees, grabbing Tarik's hands. "Hang on, buddy, we're going to patch you up."

Within minutes, they gathered their materials to perform the procedure. Charlie handed Maggie the pilot's jacket. "I thought this may help with the bleeding."

Maggie nodded, accepting the jacket, her features pinching with grief over their pilots.

"It's good that he's unconscious," Ollie said. "Because this is going to hurt. Maggie, get ready with the jacket. As soon as I pull the piece, put firm pressure on the wound until Henry can cauterize it."

Maggie nodded as Ollie leaned over Tarik. He slid his eyes sideways to Maggie and offered her a nod. She returned the gesture, wadding the coat and holding it over his body.

Ollie yanked the metal from his abdomen. Blood gushed from the wound. Maggie clamped the coat down hard over it, pressing to stop the blood flow.

Henry approached them with a red hot piece of metal. "Ready?" she asked.

He nodded, and she pulled the jacket away. Henry pressed the metal against the slice, searing the flesh closed. The scent of burning flesh filled the damp air.

The action yanked Tarik back to consciousness. His eyes snapped open as he screamed in pain.

"Easy, mate," Henry said, pressing his shoulders back into the wet ground. "Easy."

"Tarik," Ollie said as he assessed the cauterized wound. "You've been hurt in the crash. Lie still while we finish our work." He turned his attention to the others. "I need a few things. It'll help ease the pain."

Ollie rattled off a list of ingredients to collect and sent the others scurrying into the rainforest to find them. After their search, he mashed the items together into a thick, greenish compound and smeared it on the wound.

Maggie ripped open a package of gauze from the first aid kit, while Charlie held a jacket over her to shield the dressing from rain.

She pressed the square down over the wound and held it in place while Piper taped the edges. Tarik grumbled in pain as they finished their work.

"All right," Ollie said, sitting back on his haunches and slapping his thighs. "Now we'll need to form a makeshift stretcher to carry him."

"Stretcher?" Emma shouted over the still-pouring rain. "Surely, we should wait here near the plane for rescue."

"We are in the middle of the rainforest, likely miles off course."

"The storm pushed us severely off course, yes," Henry said with a nod, wiping water from his face.

"Surely, there's a black box in that plane. They can track us somehow," Emma answered.

Ollie climbed to his feet. "Like I said, we're in the middle of the rainforest. Rescue isn't coming anytime soon."

CHAPTER 28

Most of the group stared with gaping jaws at Ollie's last words.

"We need to try to navigate out of here and find help," Henry added.

"Ourselves? Go into the rainforest ourselves?" Piper questioned.

"We were always going into the rainforest, Piper," Maggie answered.

"But with guides and a boat and stuff. Not just walking around in some random location where anything could happen."

Charlie slid his arm around her. "It'll be okay, fair maiden. We shall endure."

"Unless we die of some weird rainforest disease."

Ollie rolled up his wet sleeves as the rain finally began to subside. "The person most in danger of dying from some random fever is Tarik. We need to make a stretcher and try to keep his wound as clean and dry as we can to prevent infection."

"At least it finally stopped raining," Maggie said, raking her fingers through her soaked hair. "What do we need to find?"

They gathered the necessary materials and used makeshift tools to put together a movable gurney. After rummaging through the plane for any usable items, they gathered in the clearing near the downed plane.

"Well," Maggie said as they prepared to move out. "I've got no signal on my phone, so GPS isn't going to work."

Ollie adjusted his glasses. "No, but we may be able to ascertain a general location using landmarks we find."

"How are we supposed to navigate, though?" Piper questioned. "There are literally trees in every direction you look. There are no landmarks."

"We need to find the river," Ollie said simply.

Henry peered over Maggie's shoulder, shifting the map around. "Last known location for the plane was somewhere around here."

"Which puts the river west of us," Maggie said.

"How the hell do we know which way is west?" Leo questioned. "Does anyone have a compass?"

Henry shook his head. "I arranged for all the stuff we'd need to be at the port and loaded onto the boat."

"Great," Leo groused, tossing his hands in the air. "Some Indiana Jones you are. You didn't even bring a compass."

Henry stuck his hands on his hips and glared at the man. "Did you bring a compass?"

"No, I'm the getaway driver. That's it. That is literally my one job. I am not the explorer who should have brought a compass and a machete and whatever we need to survive in the jungle."

Maggie rolled her eyes. "He couldn't possibly have known we'd be in a plane crash."

"Why not? Ollie has been in two of them–"

"Three now," Ollie said, rocking on his heels.

"Three crashes. This man has literally been in three plane crashes, so it seems expected. And given the events of the past few days, we probably should have anticipated it. I'm surprised Bryson didn't shoot the plane out of the sky." Leo chucked his hands over his head as he paced around the small clearing.

"It's probably the curse," Piper said, wrapping her arms around her midriff. "Nothing has gone right since we touched that stupid key."

"Stuff was going wrong way before that," Maggie answered.

Clouds gave way to peeks of sun.

"Sun's coming out," Henry said, glancing up. "That means it'll be heating up down here soon."

Maggie glanced at Henry's watch. "What time is it?"

Ollie checked his watch, too. "Nearly eleven in the morning."

Maggie scratched her head. "Okay, so, the sun should be overhead, more or less."

"Which helps us not at all," Emma said, crossing her arms.

"Well, sort of it does. Because it should be descending in the west, so we should head toward it once it reaches solar noon."

"We were flying southwest," Piper said. "Can we use that to pinpoint direction?"

"We were, but the plane hit something and spun," Maggie said, her forehead crinkling.

"Does anyone know how many times it spun? Was it a full circle? Two?" Charlie questioned.

Maggie scrunched her eyebrows together. "We hit and spun backward before we crashed. I'm not sure after that how the plane skidded, but it was a roughly half-turn. Something knocked the tail."

"Okay, so we assume the nose is pointing northeast," Henry said. "Which means we should go this way." He turned to his left, pointing west.

"All right. Let's grab Tarik and head out before it starts to get hot."

"Wait, wait, whoa," Leo said, waving his hands in the air. "Before we go trotting off into the jungle, we need to be sure we're going the right way. We could be lost in here for days. Turned around, going in the completely wrong direction. We have no food, no water, nothing. I vote we wait with the plane until we can make a definitive assessment of direction."

"Definitive assessment of direction?" Maggie said, crossing her arms and arching an eyebrow.

"Yes. We shouldn't go wandering off into the jungle. We are ill-prepared."

"We know how to survive," Henry said, with narrowed eyes.

"I don't. She doesn't," Leo countered, thrusting an arm toward Emma. He flung his other arm toward Charlie and Piper. "They don't."

"Now, wait just a minute, mate. Old Charlie's got a trick or two up his sleeve for survival."

Leo let his head fall back between his shoulders. "Oh, come on! I can't be the *only* one thinking this." He turned to Emma, his eyes wide.

Emma lifted a shoulder, shifting her gaze between Leo and Maggie.

"Emma, Henry wouldn't risk our lives. You know that."

"I guess," Emma said, lowering her gaze to the ground.

"No! Don't let her bully you into agreeing," Leo pleaded.

"I'm not. Ollie thinks we should move, too."

"I'm not one hundred percent on board with the plan to trek into the jungle," Piper said.

"Thank you!" Leo interrupted, throwing his hands in the air.

"But…I'm also not one hundred percent on board with the plan to stay here either."

Leo flailed his arms at the plane. "Are you kidding me? We have shelter here."

"But no food and no water," Henry said.

Maggie nodded. "And two dead bodies, which may attract animals."

"Ugh," Emma groaned.

"What? I'm being honest. Do you not think predators will smell that? The last thing we need is some jungle cat prowling around here, picking us off one by one, like some horror movie."

Leo crossed his arms and shook his head. "Perfect. So, instead, let's go prowling around the jungle cat's territory and hope that works better."

"Stay if you want, mate," Henry said. "No one's forcing you to go."

"Unbelievable," Leo said as the group prepared to set off. With Henry and Ollie in the lead, they skirted around the plane and entered the dense canopy. Leo and Charlie balanced the stretcher between them.

"So, you're going, huh?" Maggie asked as Leo stalked along behind Emma.

"Well, I'm not staying here by myself. That's the stupidest decision. It's dumber than going into the rainforest completely unprepared."

"With any luck, we'll find the river soon. Then we can follow it to civilization."

"However long that takes," Leo said, with a roll of his eyes.

"Get over yourself, Oscar," Piper said, pushing past him to be in the middle of the group. "Just because we didn't want to sit around at the wreckage and wait to be rescued, doesn't mean we're stupid."

"It could," Leo shouted after her.

She twisted to eye him over her shoulder. "Dude, we just survived a plane crash. How much worse could it get?"

"You're the one who said we were cursed!" he shouted after her.

They trekked along through the dense foliage. Within the hour, sweat soaked their clothes as temperatures, and humidity soared. They came to a stop in a small clearing. Emma plopped onto the ground, fanning herself.

"Hot? Just wait," Leo said, setting the stretcher down on the ground and wiping the sweat beading off his brow.

Henry circled a few of the tree bottoms before he scrambled up one. Something thudded to the ground moments later near Ollie's feet. He collected them and returned to the group.

"Coconut," he said as Henry slid down to the ground, landing in a crouch. "Water and sustenance."

"Oh, yes, please," Emma said, reaching for one as Ollie hacked it open with metal from the plane.

He passed another to Piper and Charlie.

Leo wrinkled his nose. "I'm not a huge fan of coconut."

"Just eat it and shut up, Leo," Maggie said with a groan as she knelt next to Tarik.

"We should try to get some coconut milk into Tarik," Ollie said. "It'll help with swelling."

Maggie pressed her hand to Tarik's forehead, then his cheek. She tugged her lips back into a frown. "Swelling may be the least of our concerns."

Ollie bit into a piece of coconut, tearing the flesh from the rind as he made his way over to her.

"He's burning up."

"Oh, no," Emma said, scrambling over to them.

Ollie knelt next to him, feeling his pulse. "Pulse is still steady."

Sweat beaded on Tarik's brow and soaked his hair. Henry approached and pressed a hand against the man's forehead. "Yeah, he's hot."

"Is there something we can do?" Piper asked. "Some sort of herbal remedy that may help him?"

"Achiote," Leo said as he stuffed his hands in his pockets, hovering over Tarik.

"What?" Maggie asked with a crinkled brow.

"Yes, he's right," Ollie said. "The indigenous peoples use Achiote for fevers, but finding it is another matter."

"How did you know that?" Maggie asked, staring up at Leo.

"I work for a cosmetics company. They're always interested in testing natural ingredients that can remove inflammation or provide some health benefit. That's one of the ones we looked at in the past."

"Looks like your skills aren't limited to getaway driving. Do you know what it looks like?"

Leo bobbed his head up and down. "Yeah. It's red and spiky."

Maggie glanced up into the trees.

"I haven't seen any," Leo informed her.

"Well, we should spread out and look," she answered. "Split up and go in separate directions."

"We can do that, but we shouldn't spend too much time," Ollie said, straightening.

Maggie offered him a blank expression.

"We need to keep moving, Maggie. I know it's difficult to hear, but we need to do what's best for the entire group. We need to keep moving."

Maggie pressed her lips together and glanced down at the lifeless form of Tarik.

Ollie squeezed her shoulder. "I know it's hard, Maggie. But we can't risk the entire group to save one."

"He's right," Henry said. "We also shouldn't leave him. We have formed groups to search for the Achiote, but no more than five minutes of searching and someone should stay with Tarik."

"I'll stay with him. I'll try to get some coconut milk into him," Ollie said.

Henry stuck his hands on his hips. "All right, the rest of us will fan out and search for this fruit. Remember, no more than five minutes of searching. We can't afford to get too tired out. We need to conserve our energy and our resources."

The group split, with Maggie and Henry wandering south of their current location. Maggie beat back the foliage as she studied the trees above her in search of the spiky fruit.

"I hope we find this," Maggie said. "I feel terrible for Tarik."

"I'm not certain he's feeling much of anything right now," Henry answered, his neck craned upward.

Maggie froze, twisting to face him. "He's going to make it, right?"

Henry leaned sideways, staring into the canopy above them. "I hope so."

"Hope?" Maggie questioned, her eyebrows shooting high.

Henry flicked his gaze to her. "That was a big wound. He may have internal bleeding we don't know about, and the fever isn't good."

Maggie lowered her gaze to the ground below as only the sounds of the jungle filled the air.

"Hey," Henry said, rubbing her shoulder, "we'll do everything we can for him. But sometimes…it just doesn't work."

"We can't let him die."

"We're not letting him die, Maggie. Things happen."

Maggie pinched her features as she fought back the strong emotion that threatened to spill over. "Not on my watch. I bring my team home every time."

"No one's blaming you."

Maggie flicked her glassy gaze up to his face. "That's not the point. Their lives are in my hands. I make the calls. We can't let him die."

"Then let's keep searching for the Achiote."

Maggie nodded, twisting away from him as she sniffled in a breath.

He caught her arm, tugging her back. "Hey, you okay?"

"Yeah," she said, without making eye contact.

"You sure?"

She raised her eyes to his, blinking back her tears, and nodded. "Yeah, I'm good. We can do this."

"If anyone can do it, Maggie, it's you," he said, with a grin.

She wrapped her arms around his middle and squeezed as he pulled her close. After a breath, she pushed away. "Ugh, okay, no, let's do this later. You smell."

"I do not," he said before giving his shirt a sniff.

"Yeah, you do," Maggie said with a chuckle as she pushed through more of the dense vegetation.

"Oh, like you smell like a bouquet of roses."

"Seriously?" she asked, shooting a glance over her shoulder. "You're seriously going to say I smell?"

"You said I did."

Maggie turned her gaze back to the trees above them. "Yeah, you're a guy. It's almost not an insult."

"It *is* an insult, regardless of gender."

"Oh, come on," Maggie said, with a laugh, "guys–"

Her voice cut off, and she froze, raising her hands high.

"Guys what?" Henry asked, trailing a few steps behind her. "Maggie?"

She slid her eyes sideways, barely glancing over her shoulder. "Uh, Henry…you may want to stop talking now."

Returning her focus forward, she pulled her lips into a nervous smile, raising a shoulder as she stared down the tip of a spear.

CHAPTER 29

"Hi," Maggie breathed out, with a grin plastered on her lips. She studied the face of the native, who appeared less than enthused to meet her. His scowl coupled with the spear shoved toward her made his displeasure clear.

"Whoa," Henry said as he spotted the man. He raised his hands up and slowed his steps.

"What do we do?" Maggie asked.

"Hope he doesn't kill us."

"Should we back away slowly?"

"Can't do that," Henry answered.

"Why?"

"We're surrounded."

Maggie's eyes went wide as she scanned the jungle around them. "What?"

"There are two just to your left, another two on the right, and I'm fairly certain someone's filled in behind us."

"Okay, well, we need to do something," Maggie said, lowering her arms.

The man thrust the spear closer to her with an angry grunt. She raised her arms up again, with a grimace. "Okay, sorry. But we're not going to hurt you."

"Obviously," Henry murmured.

She poked a finger at her chest. "I'm Maggie. Maaaaggggi-iieee," she said, drawing out the word. "What's your name?"

"Maggie, this isn't a social event."

"I'm being polite! And you don't seem to have any suggestions."

The man rambled something at her in a language she couldn't understand.

"Okay," she said, with a head shake. She raised her voice, speaking slowly. "I can't understand you."

"He's an Amazonian, Maggie. He's not deaf."

Maggie wrinkled her nose at him and shook her head. "*No comprende.*"

"Also not Spanish or Mexican."

"I'm doing the best I can do here. Thanks for hanging me out to dry." She turned her attention back to the native. "No hurt. Help. We need your help."

She held her hands out, palms facing up, and wrinkled her forehead in a pleading glance.

"What are you doing?" Henry asked through clenched teeth.

"Asking for his help. Maybe they have Achiote." Maggie straightened and pointed back at herself. "You help. You help me. Help."

The man glanced over her shoulders at one of his fellow tribesmen. Another man raced from behind them, hurrying to one of their captors and whispering in his ear. The man's eyebrows shot up, and he barked something at the man with the spear.

The man jabbered something back, glancing back at the

other man. The runner nodded his head up and down emphatically. The spear-holding native glanced back at Maggie and Henry before he lowered his spear and spoke to them.

"What?" Maggie asked.

He shooed them back with his hands.

"Okay, I guess he wants us to go back this way."

He continued to motion for them to return the way they'd come, offering small pokes with his spear to keep them moving. Maggie marched next to Henry, with her hands up.

"I wonder if they found the others?" she whispered.

"I'm not sure, but we're getting close to where we left Ollie and Tarik. Maybe we should make a stand."

Maggie glanced over her shoulder and winced. "Not sure we can make a stand. This guy's got that spear almost up my...you know what."

They approached the clearing, and Henry shook his head, his nostrils flaring. "There are too many of them. There's nothing we can do. Damn it."

"It's okay, Henry. We'll get through it."

They pushed through the last of the thick foliage, emerging in the small clearing. Ollie knelt next to one of the tribesmen. The others grouped around, having already returned to the site. He glanced over his shoulder, raising his eyebrows as he rose to his feet.

"Ah, there you are. These are the Awaguawa. They have agreed to take Tarik to their village for treatment."

Henry slid his head forward. "Treatment? Can we trust them?"

"They seem to be a peaceful bunch," Ollie said, crossing his arms. "And given Tarik's condition, I think we should risk it. I'm not sure he'll survive if we don't."

Maggie wrapped her arms around her midriff and slid

her eyes sideways to the men carrying spears. "I'm not sure we can refuse."

"Oh, we can," Ollie assured her.

"Ollie, they were fairly aggressive with us," Henry said.

"Well, sure. We're wandering around their home. They have to be safe. I don't speak their language very well, but I can communicate well enough to tell them we were in trouble and are merely attempting to get our sick friend to safety."

"And they offered to help?" Maggie asked.

"Yes. Though we are under no obligation to take them up on it. However, it would be rather rude not to accept their help."

Maggie nodded as she studied the men tending to Tarik. "Okay, let's go with them. He needs the help, and we could use a break, too. Maybe they can point us in the right direction."

"I agree," Ollie said.

"Okay, we'll follow them," Maggie said with a nod, turning to Henry. "Can you help with the stretcher? We can give Charlie and Leo a break."

Ollie wandered to the men kneeling near Tarik and spoke a few unintelligible words. They shook their heads and waved their hands in the air.

"What are they saying?" Maggie asked.

"I told him we'd follow them with the stretcher, but he's insisting they will carry it."

"Oh," Maggie said, flicking up her eyebrows. "That's nice of them. Okay."

Two of the men lifted the makeshift cot, and the group followed behind, surrounded on all sides by the tribe. With lowered spears, they meandered their way through the thick vegetation.

"Wonder how far away their village is?" Maggie whispered to Ollie.

"I'm not sure, but I didn't get the impression it was far."

Maggie crinkled her brow. "Not far? I can't imagine–"

Her voice cut off as they pushed past a large tree and into a clearing filled with huts. "Oh, wow."

"Amazing, isn't it? Completely hidden in the rainforest," Ollie said, with a grin.

Maggie glanced at him, with an amazed grin. "Yes, it is. Wow. I never expected this."

One of the men mumbled something to Ollie and waved toward one of the huts. Ollie nodded and motioned to Maggie. The man flicked his gaze to her, then back to Ollie before he nodded.

"What's going on?" Maggie asked.

"They're taking Tarik to the doctor's tent. The others are being asked to wait in another hut. I asked if you could come with us. I'm not certain he was convinced you should, but he agreed."

"Not convinced I should?"

Ollie tugged his lips back in a wince and cocked his head. "Well, you are obviously a woman."

"Yeah, so?" Maggie asked, with a shrug.

"Some of these cultures are extremely superstitious about women and their involvement in medicine."

Maggie's jaw flapped open. She clamped it closed, wrinkling her nose.

"Try not to take it as an insult. They are a different culture."

Maggie held up her hands. "I'm not insulted. It's just…different."

The rest of the group was led to another hut, while Maggie and Ollie shuffled behind the men carrying the stretcher. They ducked into a small, dark shelter.

The men laid Tarik's stretcher on a central slab made of a large tree trunk. A man with a painted face and straw headdress approached him. Ollie wandered closer, but as Maggie stepped over the threshold one of the men waved her back, murmuring something she couldn't understand.

Ollie glanced over his shoulder. "Oh, he's asking you to wait there and not cross the threshold."

"Oh," Maggie said, inching back to stand just outside, "okay."

"He says you can observe, but not enter. They do not wish to bring bad luck to the sick man."

"Right. Okay, neither do I, so I'll just stay here." Maggie held up her hands and nodded to the man. He returned the gesture.

Ollie closed the gap between himself and the village's doctor. The man waved a smoking branch of something Maggie couldn't identify over Tarik before setting it aside. An assistant pressed a damp cloth on Tarik's forehead.

The doctor spoke to Ollie, waving at Tarik's bandage.

"Injured," Ollie said, miming an object poking through his gut.

"Ahhh," the doctor said, before speaking in his native language again. He leaned over Tarik and pulled an eyelid open as Ollie answered him.

"Sick. Fever. *Fiebre.*"

The doctor snapped his gaze up to Ollie. "*Fieve?*"

Ollie nodded and pressed a hand to Tarik's skin. "*Fieve.*"

The doctor waved a hand to the bandage and spoke again. Ollie nodded at his statement.

He spoke again, poking a finger at the wound before he shuffled away, disappearing through a bead-adorned doorway into another room. The assistant continued to dampen the rag and press it to Tarik's forehead.

"Can they help him?" Maggie called from the doorway.

"Yes, I think so. I believe he said he will treat both the wound for infection and give him something to help with the fever."

"I hope it helps."

"So do I."

The doctor returned from the back room, carrying a wooden bowl. He lifted the bandage and slathered the concoction on the angry wound before covering it with large leaves. He spoke again to Ollie, then disappeared into the back room.

"Okay, the wound is treated, and now he will give him something for the fever."

"Let's hope it works." Maggie waved her crossed fingers.

"Until we can get in touch with Frank, this is the best hope we have."

Maggie nodded as the doctor returned and spoke to Ollie, who nodded and tilted Tarik's head back, pulling open his mouth. The doctor poured a thick liquid into his mouth before murmuring something else to Ollie.

"He says the serum will take a few hours to work. We may wait with him, but he prefers you to remain outside."

"Right," Maggie said. "Actually, if you're okay to stay with him, I'll go let everyone else know."

Ollie offered her a tight-lipped smile and nodded. "Yes, of course. I know staying on the fringes of the action isn't your cup of tea."

Maggie offered him an amused smile. "No, it's definitely not, but I will respect the doctor's wishes. Let me know if anything changes."

"Of course."

Maggie pushed off the door frame and twisted to scan the village. She studied the huts, trying to recall in which one her team waited.

She chewed her lower lip as she flicked her gaze from one hut to another almost identical building next to it.

"Which one was it?" she murmured as she patted her thighs.

"Ummm, let's see…we came in…" She spun in a circle, searching the dense rainforest that surrounded them. "Uhhh, there?"

She jabbed a finger in the opposite direction of the door to the hut. "So, they went into…that hut."

She offered a curt nod, reassuring herself that her choice was correct. She strode across the dirt path to the other hut and ducked inside.

Three sets of eyes flicked toward her from the females who sat on the floor sewing clothing.

"Oh, hi," Maggie said, with a broad grin and wave. "Hello."

The woman and the two younger girls stared at her with blank expressions.

Maggie pointed back at herself. "I'm Maggie. I'm looking for my friends."

She received no response.

"Obviously, this is the wrong tent. Do you know where they are?" She splayed her hands out at her sides.

The females exchanged glances before returning their stare to Maggie.

Maggie brought a flat hand up to eyebrow level. "I'm looking for my friends." She finished by clasping her hands together to signal friendship.

The youngest woman, a girl of no more than twelve, climbed to her feet and scurried toward Maggie.

"Ah, thanks," she said as the girl approached.

She wrapped her hand around Maggie's and tugged her forward. Maggie's brow crinkled as she resisted. The girl fixed her brown eyes on Maggie and motioned for her to follow.

"Oh, okay," Maggie said with a nod.

The girl led her to the other two, the older of whom already rose, setting her sewing aside and hurrying across the hut. She bent over a hearth for a few moments as Maggie eased herself to a cross-legged sit next to the younger woman.

The other girl, a teenager, stared, her hand frozen mid-stitch.

Maggie smiled at her. "Hi."

The oldest woman returned and offered Maggie a small wooden cup filled with a steaming liquid. The corners of her lips turned up as she motioned for Maggie to drink it.

"Oh, right," Maggie said, studying the murky liquid in the cup. "Okay."

She sipped at it, noting the gamey flavor of the broth and wondering what animal from which it was made.

"Thank you!" Maggie said, raising the cup in the air.

The woman motioned for her to finish it.

Maggie nodded and swallowed the last bit of the broth. "Mmmm," she murmured, with a bob of her head and smile.

The girl who had brought her in babbled something in a language Maggie couldn't understand as the woman took the cup from her and placed it across the room before returning to the group.

She picked up her sewing and continued her work. Maggie studied them for a moment before she spoke. "Can I help?"

All eyes turned to her again. She scanned the group. "Help. Sew?" She made a sewing motion with her hand.

The oldest woman's eyebrows shot up, and she nodded, waving a finger in the air. She collected fabric from the pile and offered it to Maggie with a sinewy thread on a needle.

Maggie laid the fabric, which seemed to be an animal hide, in her lap and attempted to thread the needle. It proved trickier than she expected. The youngest girl set aside her sewing to help Maggie achieve the task, then showed her a sample stitch.

Maggie nodded and practiced one. "Like this?" she asked, flicking her gaze to the girl. She gave Maggie a toothy grin and nod.

"Thanks," Maggie said as she set to work creating the stitching around the edge of the material.

"So," she said after a few stitches, "we really appreciate your help with our friend. His fever is pretty high."

They stared at her as she spoke in a language they did not understand. "Uh, my friend. He has a fever. *Fieve.*"

The oldest woman squashed her brows together, leaning away from Maggie.

"No, not me," Maggie said, with an emphatic head shake. "My friend. He's with your doctor."

She used her hands to simulate the headdress the doctor wore and poked a finger in the direction of his hut.

"Ahhh," the woman said, with a nod. "*Amica.*"

Maggie studied her for a moment, and the woman spoke again. "*Amica ta fieve.*"

Maggie knit her brows as she parsed through the statement before she nodded. "Yes. My *amica* has a *fieve.*"

She continued her sewing for a few minutes. "Do you happen to know where my other *amicas* are?"

She eyed them as she continued her work. "Other *amicas*. More *amica.*" She held up her hand and wiggled several fingers.

The woman nodded and spoke to the youngest girl. The girl climbed to her feet and held a hand out to Maggie.

"Oh," Maggie said, holding up a finger. "Just a second." She finished a few more stitches, then slid the work toward the oldest woman. "Done."

The woman picked up the hide and studied it, her fingers

tracing the stitch work. She murmured something in her native tongue before flicking her gaze to Maggie and giving her a nod.

Maggie smiled at her as she climbed to her feet. "Thank you," she said, with a bow of her head. "Thank you for the food and company." She mimed the food and then the circle of females.

The woman reached her hand out to squeeze Maggie's before the other teen repeated the gesture. The girl wrapped her fingers around Maggie's hand and tugged her toward the door.

Maggie followed behind her as she led her into the wide dirt street cutting through the village. She waved her forward, pulling her toward the edge of the town.

"Wait. *Amica*," Maggie said, leaning back against her.

The girl held a finger in the air. "*Secreti*."

"What?" Maggie asked.

The girl pressed a finger to her lips and shook her head. "*Secreti*." She murmured a few more words before she mimed in a similar fashion to what Maggie had used earlier to indicate *look*.

"Oh, you want to show me a secret. Okay," Maggie said, with a nod. "Then my *amicas*, okay?"

A smile spread across the girl's face, and she led Maggie toward the thick vegetation surrounding the village. She pushed through it, entering the rainforest.

Maggie chewed her lower lip as they wandered back through the dense flora. The girl let go of Maggie's hand as they approached a stone plinth with a face on it standing among the trees. The carving reminded her of the ones she'd seen near the blood river.

"*Amica*," the girl said, pointing to it.

Maggie crinkled her brow, wondering if they had misunderstood her request. Was *amica* not the word for "friend"?

The girl babbled on a few more words before she pointed again. "*Amica,*" she repeated.

Maggie started to shake her head when she noticed carvings on the stone. She narrowed her eyes at it, stepping closer and shoving aside a few leaves that clung to the stone.

Her eyes went wide as she recognized the symbols carved into the side of the stone. An ironclad sailed up a river.

CHAPTER 30

"Are there more of these? Anything else like this?" Maggie asked the girl as her fingers traced the rough edges of the carved symbols.

The little girl's shoulders rose to her ears, and she babbled words Maggie couldn't understand.

Maggie spun, searching the rainforest for any other markers. She found none and returned to studying the stone plinth in front of her. She knelt down, tracing the images before she puffed out a sigh and straightened.

"Can you take me to my *amicas* now?"

The girl's dark eyes stared up at her.

"*Amicas*," Maggie said again, pointing back toward the village.

The girl nodded and smiled before grabbing Maggie's hand and pulling her back toward the village. She navigated past several of the huts before she tugged Maggie toward one. "*Amicas*."

She motioned for her to enter.

"Thank you," Maggie said, with a nod and a smile. "Can you wait here with me?"

The girl's dark eyebrows knit together. Maggie grabbed ahold of her hand and tugged toward the hut. "Stay with me."

The girl nodded and allowed Maggie to lead her into the hut.

Henry leapt from a seated position and hurried toward her. "Maggie, any news?"

"Tarik has been treated for both his wound and the fever. I left after that, because I'm not permitted in the hut."

"Huh?" Piper asked.

"As a woman. They prefer me not to go into the hut."

Emma raised her eyebrows. "Wow, and you didn't pitch a fit?"

"No, I didn't. It's their culture. I respect that."

"Any indication on when we could expect results?" Henry asked.

"No," Maggie said, with a shake of her head, "but I found something for us to do in the meantime."

Emma adjusted her cross-legged position, drawing her knees to her chest and drumming her fingers against her shins. "What are you going to do, put on a fashion show for the village?"

"No. Come with me."

"I'm not sure we should wander around the village, Maggie. I'm not sure that would be welcome."

"It's fine. She can take us," Maggie said, waving toward the girl. She twisted to face her. "Can you take my *amicas* to what you showed me before?"

The girl wrinkled her nose and shrugged. "*Amicas*," Maggie said, pointing to the ground.

The girl nodded and spoke again, using the word *amicas* but nothing else Maggie could recognize.

"*Secreti. Amicas...secreti.*"

The girl's eyes lit, and she nodded. The smile faded from

her face as she stared at the group. She faced Maggie again and shook her head.

"No?" Maggie asked.

She babbled on for a moment before she pressed a finger to her lips.

"Oh, right," Maggie said, with a nod. "They won't say anything. I promise." She pressed a finger to her lips, then shot a glance at the group. *She wants you to promise to keep this a secret.*

"*Secreti,*" the girl said again, pressing a finger to her lips.

One by one, the other members of the team pressed their fingers to their lips in a silent promise to keep the secret. A smile formed on the girl's face, and she waved for them to follow her.

"What's this about, Maggie?" Henry whispered as they followed the girl from the hut, snaking around the other buildings toward the rainforest.

"You'll see," Maggie said, with a coy smile.

"A hint would be nice. We were just in a plane crash, and now we're stuck in the rainforest," Leo groused.

Maggie rolled her eyes. "Sorry for the inconvenience, but I think you'll be pretty pleased with her secret."

The girl twisted to glance over her shoulder at Maggie's last word and grinned. She pressed a finger to her lips. Maggie mirrored her behavior with a wink and smile.

They pushed into the vegetation surrounding the village.

"I hope she knows where she's going," Leo said.

Piper stomped along behind them, her arms folded over her chest. "I hope she's not leading us to get eaten by the local jaguar."

"We're not going to get eaten. Just give her a minute. You'll be excited when you see it."

"It's not a nice landscape scene or something, is it?" Emma asked. "I would have preferred to stay in the hut."

"It's not."

The little girl stopped in front of them and pointed ahead of her, twisting to face them.

"Check it out, gang," Maggie said with her hands on her hips.

"Is that—" Henry started, skirting past the girl and stooping to study the plinth.

"An ironclad," Emma finished for him.

Maggie nodded as she crossed her arms. "Uh-huh. And proof that the gold made it into this jungle."

"Probably not far from here either," Henry said, scanning the landscape. "Are there any more like this?"

Maggie shrugged. "I already tried asking her, but I can't understand her, and I'm not great at their language either."

"We should get Ollie," Charlie said. "He does pretty well at understanding them."

"I can run back and get him," Maggie offered, thumbing toward the village.

"I'll come with you," Henry said, rising to stand. "Emma, see if you can make any sense of this, we'll be right back."

Maggie glanced down at the girl next to her. "I need to go get my other *amica*." She held her hand out, and the girl wrapped her fingers around Maggie's.

They strode back to the village, seeking out the medical hut.

Ollie approached the door as they hovered in the opening. "He's resting comfortably. So far, the fever is still fairly high."

"Hopefully, the medicine works soon," Maggie said.

Ollie smiled down at the girl holding her hand. "Hello. Who are you?"

He squatted down to her level and spoke in another language. Maggie recognized his name as one of the words.

"Yarima," the girl answered.

Maggie patted her hand. "Is that her name? Yarima?"

"They don't use personal names, but this is how she is referred to," Ollie answered.

"We need your help with her," Maggie answered.

"Is she ill?" Ollie asked, straightening.

"No. She took us to a statue in the rainforest. She said it was a secret. It looks like the depiction of the faces we saw in the illustration and shows the ironclad sailing up the river and unloading the gold. We need to know if there are more of those or if she has any other information."

Ollie's jaw dropped open. "You found a clue to the ironclad?"

"We did," Maggie said, fluttering her eyelashes, "by pure chance. Come take a look."

Ollie glanced over his shoulder at Tarik. The doctor's assistant still attended him, dabbing a cloth across his feverish forehead.

"I can stay with him," Henry said.

"I think he'll be fine. Let me just tell them I'm stepping out." Ollie hurried across the room, murmuring to the man who sat at Tarik's head.

After a nod and clap on the man's back, Ollie returned to the door. "Lead the way."

Yarima tugged Maggie back toward the statue and within minutes, they rejoined their group. Ollie wandered to the stone carving, with wide eyes. "Incredible."

"Isn't it?" Maggie asked, patting the girl's hand again. "It must be close by or this was along the route. We've tried asking if there were more of these, but I can't understand her."

Ollie twisted toward the girl, still crouched. He spoke to her in what sounded close to her own language. She grinned and nodded, babbling an answer back to him.

"What's she saying?"

"From what I can make out, she says there is a legend passed down through the generations. White men came here many moons ago. They brought cursed gold. They placed it in an abandoned temple. The temple claimed many of their lives. Only two men emerged after unloading the gold."

"Is the temple nearby?" Maggie asked.

Ollie held his finger in the air. "Just a moment, I'll ask."

Ollie spoke to the girl again. Her eyes went wide, and she snapped her gaze to Maggie. She shook her head, her features pinching. Frenzied words spilled from her lips. She latched onto Maggie's arm, squeezing it.

"Ow, okay, it's okay," Maggie said, stooping down to her. She shifted her eyes to Ollie. "What has her so upset?"

The girl twisted to Ollie, speaking emphatically. Ollie translated it for Maggie. "She's worried about you going to the temple. She doesn't want anything to happen to you. She says you are a nice woman, very helpful."

Maggie smiled at the girl, sliding a lock of her dark hair behind her ear. "Aww, I'll be okay. We're strong and smart." Maggie flexed a bicep before she tapped her temple.

The girl's features pinched, and she shook her head. Ollie tapped her arm. She swung her head toward him. He spoke to her again. She wrinkled her nose, swallowing hard as she flicked her gaze back to Maggie.

She pressed her lips together and answered Ollie. He nodded, raising his eyebrows and offering her a tight-lipped smile. The girl pointed past Maggie, murmuring a few words.

"She says the temple is this way," Ollie reported.

"She told you?" Maggie asked, her eyebrows shooting up. "How did you convince her?"

"I told her you were a superhero."

"Close enough," Maggie said with a grin as Emma clicked her tongue at the statement. "Can she take us there?"

Ollie passed along the question. The girl shook her head as she responded.

"She says no. She says the ground there is cursed. She cannot step foot on it, or she will bring great shame and sadness to her village."

"Oh, right." Maggie patted the girl's hand. "That's okay. You were very helpful to show us."

Ollie passed along the sentiment.

Henry stalked forward, squinting into the rainforest beyond. "We should put together a search party."

"I agree," Ollie said, rising to his feet.

"Right," Maggie said. "But first we need to take her back to her family."

"I'll go with you," Henry said, tromping back toward them, "grab our stuff, and we'll head out."

"I'll stay with Tarik," Ollie said. "Someone should monitor him."

With nods all around, Ollie, Henry, and Maggie returned to the village. Henry continued toward the hut they'd waited in, while Maggie stopped with the girl outside of her family's domicile. The girl flung her arms around Maggie's neck before she darted into her hut.

Henry returned as Maggie rose to her feet. "We've got limited supplies, so we'll have to watch our resources."

"Right. I hope it's close. The carving suggests it would be."

Ollie hurried toward them, puffing with exertion. "Wait, wait," he called, waving his arms.

"Uncle Ollie, what is it? Is Tarik worse?"

"No," Ollie said, leaning forward on his thighs as he reached them. "No, he's showing signs of improvement. I spoke with the doctor. He wants us to speak with the village elders before you find the temple."

Maggie raised her eyebrows. "Oh, okay. Maybe they don't want us searching for it."

"Quite the opposite, I think. He seemed to indicate they would welcome the effort. According to him, the gold should be removed by *'blancagents,'* and then the curse would be lifted. I got the impression they would be most grateful to us if we pursued this."

"Really?" Maggie asked. "Wait, the gold has to be removed by who?"

"*Blancagents,*" Ollie repeated. "White people."

"The same as the people who put it there," Maggie said, with a nod. "That makes sense. Okay, lead the way."

They turned to find the doctor awaiting them. He waved for them to follow him, taking them to a large hut at the center of the village. The doctor entered first, with the others trailing behind him, and spoke in his native language to a group of three men sitting on the ground.

They conversed for a few minutes, with the doctor motioning toward Maggie, Ollie, and Henry. One man rose to his feet, his eyes wide as he spoke. The doctor nodded in return to confirm his previous statement.

"He's telling them we have come for the cursed gold and seek to remove it from the land. The elder is confirming that we have agreed," Ollie whispered.

"He seems surprised," Maggie said.

"He is. He says this gold has been a blight on their community since the men put it in the temple. The land there is cursed. They used to have a well near it, and it went bad and killed many. They cannot use it anymore."

"Chemicals leeched into the soil, most likely," Henry answered.

Ollie nodded at the reasoning. "The elder says they will send three men to take us to the entrance, but no further. He says they will not step foot on the ground."

"Right," Maggie said. "That would be helpful. We'll handle it from there."

Ollie studied the man as he spoke again. His features pinched, and he poked a finger at them.

"What's he saying?" Maggie asked.

Ollie winced and glanced at her. "He says...he says if we pursue this, we will most likely die."

"Yikes, I hope not. Tell him we'll be okay. We're trained for this."

"I'm not sure there is training against curses. He thinks we'll be cursed. He–"

Loud pops stopped any further conversation.

"What was that?" Maggie asked, instinctively shrinking lower.

"Sounded like gunfire. But who would..."

Shrieks sounded as another spray of the noise sliced through the quiet village. A man stalked into the hut, machine gun pointed in the air. He tipped up his hat, revealing his scratched face.

"Well, well, well," Bryson said, "we meet again."

CHAPTER 31

One of the elders shouted at him, trying to skirt around Maggie, Henry, and Ollie. Henry held a hand out, blocking him.

"Get out of here, Bryson," Maggie shouted at him, her hands on her hips. "You have no business here."

"Oh, I disagree. I think I very much have business here. We were in the middle of something when we were so rudely interrupted."

Maggie narrowed her eyes at him. "Okay, fair enough. But these people don't need to be involved."

"You thought they did."

"No, Tarik was injured, and they were kind enough to help us. We're going to find the gold now. Pull your team out of their village and come with us."

"Maybe I ought to leave a few people behind. As you said, Tarik is here. His life could become a useful bargaining chip."

Maggie set her jaw. "I should have left you in that van when it exploded."

Bryson smirked at her. "But you didn't. Interesting how you felt compelled to rescue me."

"More like felt compelled to get the keys back I'd worked so hard to retrieve. But if it makes you feel better, sure, you can think I like you enough to pull you out of a van."

"It makes me feel exceptionally better." He flicked his gaze to Henry. "I'm not certain how it makes Taylor feel, though it sounds like he's already on the losing end."

Henry's hands curled into fists, and he lunged forward, stopping in his tracks when Bryson leveled the weapon at him.

"Uh-uh-uh. Come now, Taylor, is she really worth dying for when she's already cheating?"

Maggie pushed in front of Henry. "Hey! I'm not cheating!"

Bryson tugged the corner of his lips down as he flicked up his eyebrows. "Really? Surprising given how cozy we were."

Maggie shook her head at him. "You've got to be kidding. You kidnapped me."

"You didn't seem to mind, in fact you were quite exhilarated by the adventure of it all."

"You're an idiot," Maggie shot back. "And this is beside the point. Do you want in on the gold or not?"

"Of course. You and I put so much work into this."

Maggie crossed her arms. "Give it a rest, Bryson. Get your men out of this village."

"You're hardly in a position to make demands, Ms. Edwards."

She sauntered toward him, lifting a shoulder. "I don't know. Given how cozy we were, I thought I could."

The corners of his lips turned up in a smirk. "These villagers seem to be a good bargaining chip for you."

Maggie flicked her gaze up at him through her eyelashes. "Do what you want, but if you split your team, it'll be far easier for mine to overpower yours."

Bryson scoffed. "Oh, please. That ragtag band of colorful

characters you refer to as a team couldn't overpower a chimpanzee."

"Go ahead and underestimate me. That'll be fun for you." She clapped him on the shoulder before she pushed past him. "Let's go."

She stepped outside, finding four gunmen at various locations in the village's streets. Frightened villagers hovered in the doorways of their homes, peering out at them.

The doctor hurried toward them as they appeared. Angry words spilled from his lips. Ollie shook his head as he spoke to him.

"Is there a problem, Professor?" Bryson asked.

"He is upset. He wants Tarik removed. He thinks we are all together."

Maggie crossed her arms, cocking a hip. "The problem is you. Things were going fine until you arrived."

"I told him we were *not* together. I think I convinced him to continue to treat Tarik for now."

"Get your guys out of this village," Maggie demanded again.

Bryson grabbed her by the wrist, yanking her forward. Yarima raced from one of the doorways, flinging herself against Maggie and wrapping her arms around Maggie's waist.

Maggie wrenched her arm from Bryson's grasp and wrapped it around the girl. "It's okay. I'm okay."

Bryson stared down at the girl. "And who is this?"

Maggie glared at him. "None of your business."

"She seems quite attached to you. I wonder...are you as attached to her?"

"Don't," she warned.

"Perhaps she should come with us. I would imagine she would keep you in line."

"That's not necessary," Ollie answered as Henry helped shield the child.

Bryson leaned his weapon against his shoulder. "Let's make a deal, shall we?"

Maggie sneered at him, her lips curled with disdain. "The deal is that you come with us, and let these people go."

"Mmm," Bryson said, wrinkling his nose, "I'm not happy with those terms. We'll need to renegotiate. Here are your choices. I leave two of my men in this village, and if you fail to cooperate, we begin executing people."

"Pass, here's your choice. You come with us. You get the gold. You leave these people alone. Your fight is with us, not them."

Bryson lifted his chin, staring down his nose at her. "That's not a choice. Here's your second option. We leave the villagers in peace." He dropped the nose of his weapon toward the girl still clinging to Maggie's waist. "But she comes with us."

Maggie tightened her grip on the child. "Are you insane? This is someone's child. She is not coming with us."

"Then I suppose two of my men will stick around here. I'll be sure they still pay special attention to this little beauty."

Maggie slid her eyes closed, clenching her teeth. "I really should have left you to die."

He took a step closer to her and traced her jaw. She snapped her head away from his finger. "What's your decision, darling?"

Maggie slid her eyes closed as she considered the impossible choice. With the first option, they had access to only half of his team and couldn't keep tabs on the other half. It left the entire village in danger. With the other, she purposefully chose to put someone's child in the line of fire.

She pressed her lips together until they hurt and snapped open her eyes. "Everyone comes with us."

Bryson's face twisted into an amused grin. "Really? We're choosing child endangerment? Bravo, Maggie, you continue to surprise me."

"The child is endangered either way. At least this way I can keep an eye on you and your mercenaries." Maggie hugged the girl closer to her as she turned to Ollie. "Can you tell her she's coming with us on an adventure?"

Ollie knelt in front of Yarima and passed along the message. Her eyes went wide, and she stared up at Maggie.

"It's okay. You help me."

She twisted to speak to Ollie, who winced as he passed the message along to Maggie. "She's excited to help, but she's worried it will bring shame to her village."

Maggie patted her hand. "No, it's okay. You will be a hero to them. And we'll make sure you don't do anything they don't want you to do."

Ollie passed along the message, which seemed to satisfy the girl. She squeezed Maggie's hand and smiled at her.

"All right, get your people out of this village," Maggie said to Bryson. "Now."

Bryson shouldered his weapon again. "So full of authority. How alluring." He raised his chin and shouted to his men over her head, instructing them to follow.

They trekked into the jungle, leaving the village behind except for Yarima and the three men from the village. After Ollie explained the new circumstances to them, they nodded, warily eyeing Bryson and his team.

"Tell them not to worry about him. We'll handle them," Maggie said.

With another wary glance, the men acknowledged Ollie's new comments before pointing further into the rainforest.

They pushed through thick vegetation, motioning for Maggie and her team to follow. Maggie tugged Yarima along with her, offering her a reassuring smile as they trekked further into the tropical flora.

Within minutes of walking, sweat beaded on Maggie's forehead. She wiped it away and fanned herself.

"Too hot for your tastes, Princess?" Bryson asked her.

Maggie wagged a finger at him. "Do not call me that."

"I thought you enjoyed it."

"Henry can call me that. You haven't earned the right."

"And how does one earn that right?"

"For starters, they stop pointing guns at me," she said, shoving the tip of his weapon away from her.

He slipped an arm around her shoulders. "Well, if that's all it takes–"

"It's not," she assured him, wriggling from under his grasp and pointing ahead of them. "Go find out how much further."

"My, my, you're bossy."

"I *am* the team leader," Maggie said as she stomped her way forward.

Bryson smirked at her as he strode ahead toward the front of the group.

Henry closed the gap between them, hurrying up from behind her. "We need to do something about him."

"I agree. There are only four of them. With any luck, we'll lose a few entering the temple, and then we can overpower the rest."

"I can't imagine Bryson will be that stupid."

"Neither can I," Maggie answered. "And they have all the firepower."

"This isn't going to be easy," Henry agreed.

"First things first, we need to make sure Yarima and the three villagers are safe. Once they're out of the way, we make a move. Not before then."

"Okay," Henry said, with a nod. "If you have the opportunity–"

"I know. Take it. Same with you. But not before we get these guys clear of the trouble. I don't want collateral damage."

Henry flicked up his eyebrows. "Maggie–"

"No! Get them clear, then we move on them. Period." She sliced her hand through the air before she increased her pace to stalk away from him. She sighed, pressing her lips together as she stared at the form of Bryson in front of her. She couldn't risk harming the innocent people who had been drawn into this fight.

She hoped her decision didn't cost her team their lives.

Shouts erupted from the front of the group. The three tribesmen ground to a halt, waving their hands at something on the ground.

They pointed toward the side near a large tree. Ollie wandered toward it, pulling a large leaf back. A stone face rose from the ground.

"This must be a marker for the temple. They will not go past this spot," he reported.

Maggie closed the gap between them, studying the marker before she stared ahead. The men bowed their heads, inching backward.

"What are they doing?" Bryson barked.

"This is considered cursed ground. They won't set foot on it."

"Well, that's just too damn bad. They'll have to get over it." He leveled his weapon at them and signaled for them to move forward.

"No. We have enough people to go without them. We just needed them to lead us to the temple," Maggie said, with a shake of her head. "Let them go."

"I don't think so. That wasn't the deal."

"Deal's changed. We don't need them."

"I disagree," Bryson said, his face close to hers. "I think they make a wonderful asset to ensure your cooperation."

"You already have my cooperation. I'm going into that temple."

Bryson smirked at her. "Yes, but I don't trust you. Having a few people to shoot holes into makes you all the more trustworthy."

"Take us," Piper said, stepping forward. "Use us as your hostages, and let these people go."

Bryson glanced over his shoulder at her. "Well, there's an interesting idea. Rainbow Brite has offered herself yet again as a hostage on your behalf. Oh, the choices." Bryson tapped his chin in mock thought. "Let the men go, zip tie Taylor and the rest. Maggie, Red, and this little one will go into the temple with me."

Maggie shook her head. "No, she goes with her people."

"No, she doesn't. She's the perfect hostage for our little trek into this temple. If you keep arguing, I'll bind her hands, too."

Maggie flexed her jaw, wrapping her arms around the girl's shoulders as Bryson's men poked their weapons toward the three villagers, forcing them into the jungle before they shoved Piper, Henry, Leo, Charlie, and Ollie to their knees, binding their hands behind them.

Bryson pulled a radio from his pocket and toggled it on. "Channel three. Keep me updated." He spun to face Maggie. "Let's go, darling."

"I'm not your darling. Leave that gun here."

"Ha!" Bryson barked. "I don't think so. I may need it."

Maggie pushed past the foliage surrounding the stone face. "Only you would be insecure enough to feel you need a gun against two women and a little girl."

"You do yourself a disservice, Maggie. It is because of the

two women I'm up against that I need the gun. You've both proven deadly when pushed too far."

Maggie slid her gaze sideways to eye him. "Remember that."

"Oh, I will," he said with a smirk as Maggie pushed back the final few leaves before a clearing. In the middle, a squatty stepped pyramid rose toward the sky.

She swallowed hard as she stared up at the imposing structure. Despite its small stature, the secrets it held could cost them their lives.

Yarima clung to her waist, hiding her face in Maggie's shirt.

Maggie rubbed her shoulders. "It's okay. It's an adventure. Fun!" She forced a smile on her face and glanced down at the girl.

Yarima buried her head again, murmuring in her native language.

"Bryson, she's terrified. Let her go home," Maggie tried.

"No," he answered flatly as he stared up at the pyramid.

Maggie sucked in a long breath as heat rose in her body. She clenched her hands into fists, her nose wrinkling as her mind processed an idea. Yarima tightened her grip on Maggie.

"Doorway must be on the other side," Emma said as she began to walk toward a corner of the structure.

"Whoa, easy, Red. We all go together."

Maggie shifted under the girl's grasp, shimmying down to kneel in front of her. "It's okay."

"Let's go, Maggie," Bryson called as he took a step toward Emma.

"Give me a minute. She's scared."

Bryson rolled his eyes as he stalked a few more steps toward the pyramid. "Don't make me come back for you."

Maggie cupped the girl's face in her hands. She flicked

her gaze sideways to Bryson, who studied the pyramid's facade. Both he and Emma craned their necks to find an opening near the top.

Maggie cut her gaze back to the girl's dark eyes. She slicked a lock of dark hair behind Yarima's ear. "I want you to run," she murmured. "Do you understand? Go home. Run home and don't stop running until you're safe. Do not go past the men there. Do you understand?"

"Maggie," Bryson called.

"Just a second," Maggie snapped.

Bryson narrowed his eyes at her before he turned his attention to the pyramid.

"Go now," she said in a low voice. She pushed the girl toward the thick vegetation.

"Go!" she hissed.

The little girl stared up at her for a moment before she spun and fled into the jungle. Maggie's heart thudded in her chest, partially with relief and partially with fear over the retaliation from Bryson.

She blew out a breath, convincing herself she'd made the right choice to save the girl's life, despite what may happen to her now.

"Mag–" Bryson called over his shoulder again as she stalked toward him. "Ah, there you are. We have–"

His words cut off, and he searched the nearby area. "Where is the girl?"

Maggie shrugged. "Ran off. I couldn't stop her."

Bryson's face reddened, and he lunged toward Maggie, grasping her arm and yanking her closer to him.

"Whoa," Emma said as she grabbed at his shoulder.

"Do you think this is a game? You sent her away."

"Yes, I did," Maggie growled at him. "And I would do it again. My team is one thing, an innocent bystander is another. She was a child."

"I don't care what she was. You don't make the decisions here."

Maggie wrinkled her nose, struggling against him. "Too late for that."

"Get off her," Emma said, jumping on his back. She wrapped her arms around his neck, pulling his head back. Maggie kicked his shin. He stumbled back a step. With Emma's weight on his back, he toppled backward. They landed in a tangle of limbs on the ground.

The machine gun bobbled around, smacking off the ground and sending a wild shot into the air. A shriek pierced through the jungle sounds.

Maggie stumbled back a step, grasping her arm. "I've been shot."

CHAPTER 32

Maggie stared down at her now-bloody fingers, with a grimace.

Emma shoved Bryson off her and scrambled to her feet. "Oh my God, Maggie!" she screamed as she rushed toward her.

The expression of shock on Maggie's face melted into one of anger as Bryson recovered and rose to stand. She marched forward and slapped his cheek with a blood-soaked hand. "You idiot. You shot me."

She raised her hand to land another blow, but he caught her wrist. "Let's not be hasty."

"Hasty? You shot me, you jackass. Don't you know anything about weapon safety? And you wonder why I let that poor little girl go. Good thing before she got accidentally shot."

"Maggie!" Henry shouted as he raced into the clearing, his hands still bound behind his back.

Emma flicked him a glance. "She's fine, apparently."

Maggie glanced down at the blood running down her arm. "Just a flesh wound. No thanks to Bryson."

"You shot her?" Henry gasped.

"Oh, please. The gun went off accidentally." Bryson grabbed the radio from his pocket and spoke into it. "Why the hell is Taylor here bothering us?"

A man raced into the clearing a moment later, leveling his gun at Henry. "Back to the line, Taylor."

Henry hesitated, staring at Maggie.

"I'm fine," she answered. "It just grazed me."

Henry glared at Bryson as the man waved his weapon at him again. "I said go!"

Henry flexed his jaw, allowing the other man to back him into the trees.

Bryson shoved the radio into his pocket and adjusted his collar. "Shall we proceed?"

"I think we should clean that wound first," Emma answered.

"With what?" Maggie asked. "Leaves and sticks?"

"Maybe the vil–"

Maggie sliced a hand through the air. "We're not going back there." She licked her fingers and rubbed at the blood on her arm. Emma pulled a tissue from her pocket and pressed it against the wound.

"Thanks. Let's find this entrance and get this over with. I'm in a terrible mood now," Maggie said, grimacing at Bryson.

"Funny, I haven't noticed much change in your attitude," he said, with a wrinkled nose.

"I think I saw a doorway at the top on this side," Emma said, waving her finger around the corner.

Maggie stomped in the direction Emma pointed. "Great. Let's go."

She rounded the corner with the others following behind her and stared up at the top. "Well, I guess we're climbing."

She mounted the first step and scrambled up. They reached the top, huffing and puffing.

Maggie's head fell back between her shoulders, and she flung a hand in the air. "It's closed."

She banged against the hard stone, with a muffled scream.

"You didn't think they'd leave it unlocked, did you?" Emma asked, with a coy grin.

Maggie snapped her gaze at her friend, her jaw hanging open. "Wow, did you just make a joke?"

"Very funny, Maggie. I'm fun. I'm funny."

"Not usually," Maggie said, arching an eyebrow. "Sorry, I'm in a terrible mood now that I've been shot." She glared at Bryson.

He rolled his eyes. "Barely. Get over it, Maggie. Think of all the fun stories you can tell at parties."

Maggie peered around the corner at the wall on the other side. "Nothing over here."

"I checked the side opposite of this," Emma answered, "nothing. This is it. This is the entrance. We just have to figure out how to open it."

"Dynamite?" Maggie asked.

"We don't have dynamite. And besides, we can't blow a hole in the thing, we could collapse it. This is an important piece of history."

Maggie crossed her arms and stared at the closed door. "Okay, so then we have to figure out how to open it. Can we pry it open?"

Emma studied the stone. "Maybe there's a trigger to open it. We should search for that first."

Maggie snapped her fingers, reaching into a pocket of her cargo pants. "The keys. Do you think these go somewhere to open it?"

Emma glanced at them. "Maybe. Let's search for a keyhole."

Maggie rubbed her fingers across the carvings in the stone around the door, while Emma searched the door itself. She glanced over her shoulder at Bryson as her fingers traced the outline of a jaguar. "You could help, you know."

"You two seem to be doing an adequate job."

Maggie blew out a disgusted sigh. "I didn't think I could dislike you any more than I already do, but you continue to find ways to surprise me."

"That's what keeps our relationship exciting," he said, with a cheeky grin.

Emma shot her a glance. "The weird semi-flirting between you two is creepy. Please stop."

"Keep your mouths shut and concentrate on the task," Bryson said, waving the gun at them.

"Are you kidding me? Maggie's allowed to tell you how much she hates you, but I say something, and you wave the gun in my face?"

"Every time you two girls start your bickering, I end up in a less-than-desirable predicament. Therefore, I would prefer you work silently."

"Unbelievable," Emma murmured under her breath. "Maybe you can date him, too."

Maggie balled her hands into fists and stamped a foot on the dusty stone beneath her feet. "You want to say that again."

"No," Bryson said. "Back to work."

"No!" Maggie said. "I want to hear what she has to say."

Emma rose to her feet. "I said maybe you can date him, too."

Maggie offered her an unimpressed stare with narrowed eyes. "I'm not dating Leo."

"Oh, the Hamilton situation rears its ugly head again. I'll say I do agree the evidence is rather damning," Bryson chimed in.

"No one asked you," Maggie said, crossing her arms.

"He's right. Secret meetings. You knew where his parents were. You've admitted you were together, and he told us he knew you were missing because you were supposed to have another secret meeting."

Maggie spun to face the wall, pressing on the carvings again. "I admit nothing."

Emma rolled her eyes as she continued her search. "Whatever. It'll all come out in the end. Once there's no longer a gun to our heads, the truth will be told. I don't understand why you're putting it off."

"I'm not putting anything off. But we're a little busy right now. This is hardly the time to talk about how I'm *not* dating Leo.

"What I find most interesting is that it seems Taylor isn't that bothered," Bryson said. "So, either he's already lost interest in you, or he is fool enough to believe you."

Maggie glared at him over her shoulder.

"What?" he asked, with a shrug.

She returned her attention to the wall, shaking her head.

Next to her, Emma dug her hands into the stone door, blowing dust out of the way. "I think I found something."

"Really?" Maggie stooped down next to her.

"Feels like an indentation. Maybe it's a keyhole. I need something to dig."

Maggie glanced behind her at Bryson. "Are you deaf?"

Bryson narrowed his eyes at her. "Go get it yourself."

"Fine," Maggie said, rising to stand and brushing off her pants. She scrambled down the stairs, retrieved a stick off the ground, and hurried back up. She passed it off to Emma as she puffed from the effort.

Emma stuck the end in the growing hole, digging dirt from inside. Her lips turned down as her bicep bulged with every scrape. "This is some sort of mud. I bet they sealed the lock with it."

"Keep going," Bryson told her as she slowed.

"Yeah, okay. Give me a second. This isn't exactly easy, and a stick isn't the proper tool."

"Cry me a river, Red. Just get it done."

"I'm really starting to agree with Maggie about you," Emma grumbled as she continued to dig the mud packing from the keyhole. She raked the back of her hand across her forehead as she pulled away the stick. "Okay, try one of the keys."

Maggie dug one from her pocket and leaned forward. She chuckled before inserting the key and turning it.

"What's wrong with you?" Emma questioned.

"You have dirt all over your face. You look like some sort of warrior queen."

"Seriously? That's what we're worried about right now? There's a crazy man pointing a gun at us."

"I'm not crazy," Bryson objected as Maggie twisted the key. It didn't budge.

"Nothing. I'll try another."

She swapped the key out and inserted another into the lock. It wouldn't move.

"Maybe there's still dirt in it," she suggested as she slid the third key into the hole. It spun easily. "Ha! It worked!"

The panel slid up from the bottom, leaving a space large enough to crawl through.

"Excellent work, ladies. I knew I picked the right team. In we go." Bryson pushed his foot against Emma's back.

She fell forward onto her hands.

"I'll go first," Maggie said.

"No, wait!" Emma shouted. "I should go first. I can spot triggers for traps better than you can."

"Maybe we should go together."

Emma shook her head. "It's fine. You go through the next one first."

"Deal," Maggie said, sitting back on her haunches as Emma crawled forward.

"Flashlight," she called to Bryson as she peered into the darkness. He pulled one from his pocket and handed it to her.

She flicked it on, shining it inside the space.

"What do you see?"

"A platform. Stairs leading further inside. I don't see anything that looks like a trap trigger."

Maggie crawled forward, sliding under the stone slab and into the pyramid.

"Maggie!" Emma shouted.

"What? You said it was clear."

"What if I was wrong?"

Maggie stuck her head out of the hole. "I trust you. You're the smartest person I know, next to Uncle Ollie."

Emma wrinkled her nose as she crawled inside. "Thanks. I think."

Maggie grabbed the flashlight off her as Bryson crawled inside. She shined it into the cool, dark space, illuminating the stone barrier blocking them from plunging into the temple's interior. She swung it around to the unadorned walls behind them.

Maggie climbed to her feet, peering over the stone wall. "I don't see any gold."

"I'm sure there are other chambers underground," Emma said. "Let's go down to the bottom and look around."

Maggie swept the beam over the stairs that ringed around the four walls, following them as they jutted from the pyramid interior. "That's a lot of stairs."

"I'm certain you ladies have the dexterity for the job. Let's go." Bryson waved them on with the nose of his weapon.

Maggie wrinkled her nose at him as she stepped onto the first step. "Probably should go one by one."

"Fine, but leave a space between you two of at least a few steps," Bryson replied.

"Oh, for heaven's sake," Maggie said as she trundled down the stairs. "If you plan on holding us both hostage at once, you'll need to–"

"What? Trust you? I don't," Bryson answered from above her.

Maggie glanced sideways at him as she turned the corner. "I was going to say man up, but we can go with trust if it makes you feel better."

"Don't push me, Maggie," he retorted as Emma started down the stairs and Bryson followed.

"If you think this is me pushing you, you'd hate to see me when I'm on my full game."

"You're not frightening me."

Maggie's fingers scraped against the rough wall as she continued down the stone steps. "No, just Emma and I being too close together does that."

"Don't make me shoot you again."

"So, you're admitting that you shot me on purpose?"

"I'm admitting to nothing."

"Will you two please shut up?" Emma shouted, flinging her hands in the air. The sudden movement caused her to wobble. She pitched forward, flailing her arms in a desperate attempt not to fall.

"Emma!" Maggie shouted, retreating up a few steps two by two.

Emma's descent halted. She sucked in a sharp breath, sliding her wide eyes to the side. Bryson tugged her backward by her shirt, righting her before he let go. She swallowed hard. "Thanks."

"Proceed," he answered, waving for Maggie to continue.

"Can you give her a minute?" Maggie cried.

"I'm fine. It's okay. I'm okay. Go ahead," Emma said, with a lick of her lips.

Maggie glared at Bryson as she spun on her heel and continued down the stairs. She reached the corner and took two more steps down when the stone under her feet broke away. Her stomach turned over as she plummeted into the darkness below with a yelp.

CHAPTER 33

"Maggie!" Emma screamed, hurrying down the steps between them.

Maggie clung to the edge of what remained of the step with only her fingertips. Sweat beaded on her brow as her hands slipped on the crumbling stone.

Emma crouched on the stair above her. "Take my hand."

Maggie grunted as she tried to reach for her, nearly losing her precarious grip on the chunk of remaining stone.

She reached out again but failed to make the connection. A groan escaped her as she hung by one arm, her shoulder joint aching from the effort to hold her weight up.

"You gotta reach for me, Maggie."

"I am reaching for you. Do you think I *want* to fall?"

Maggie clamped her hand down on the jagged stone step again. It gave way as she balanced her weight.

Emma lunged forward, grabbing her flailing wrist. "Gotcha. Give me your other hand."

Maggie bit her lower lip as she shifted her other hand from the sharp stone. After a slip of their sweaty palms, Maggie squeezed her fingers around Emma's.

Emma grimaced as she struggled to hang onto Maggie.

"Lean back," Maggie grunted.

"Easier said than done," Emma said through clenched teeth.

Maggie's body rose as she struggled to cling to Emma's hands. She glanced up, finding Bryson tugging them backward.

She scrambled up onto the step, kicking her feet to find purchase on the stone. With labored breathing, she rolled onto her back and wiped at the sweat on her brow.

Emma collapsed backward, breathing out a long sigh.

"Okay, that was…horrible," Maggie said.

"Be more careful going forward," Bryson said, wiping a bead of sweat from his forehead.

Maggie craned her neck to stare behind her, narrowing her eyes at him. "Oh, sure, sorry my near plunge to my death inconvenienced you."

"It would have put a damper on our plans, yes," Bryson said. "Now, come on. Let's keep moving."

Maggie huffed out a breath as she pulled herself up to stand. She stared at the black hole between them and the next step. "I'll have to jump it. At least it's not far."

"Don't fall," Emma said. "I have not survived a car crash and a plane crash, only for you to plummet to your death inside a pyramid."

Bryson wiped at his brow again and peered into the darkness below. "I'm not certain you'd actually die from it. It's high, but we're approaching the bottom. Perhaps you'd only break a leg."

Maggie glared at him over her shoulder before she focused on the gap in front of her. She licked her lips and lunged backward before leaping across the chasm.

She landed on the next intact step and stumbled forward

onto the one below it. With a sigh of relief, she spun to face the others. "Made it. Who's next?"

Bryson shoved at Emma. "You. I don't trust you over here alone."

He waved his hand at Maggie. "And you go down a few more steps. I don't want you together after she jumps."

Maggie rolled her eyes at him as she continued to tromp down the steps to the corner. Emma sailed across the gap, followed by Bryson. They continued down into the darkness, finally reaching the bottom.

Maggie hopped off onto the stone floor, shining her light around. "Now what?"

Emma joined her along with Bryson a moment later. "There's nothing here," he said, glancing around.

"I doubt they were going to leave it laying out in the open," Maggie said.

Emma grabbed the flashlight from Maggie and headed for one of the walls. "There must be another doorway somewhere. We have three keys left."

"Right. We need to find a keyhole. Do you have another flashlight?" Maggie asked Bryson.

"Not on me, no."

Maggie stuck her hands on her hips. "You're the worst tomb raider ever. Call one of your guys and have him bring a flashlight."

"Go search with her."

"Oh, am I allowed? I know you don't like us to be near each other."

"Go search with Red. Don't talk to her. Don't touch her. Don't do anything with her that is suspect, or I'll shoot one of you."

"Of course, you will," Maggie said as she stalked toward Emma. "Find anything?"

"I said don't talk to her."

Maggie let her head drop between her shoulder blades as Emma gave her a head shake. "But these paintings are fascinating."

"I said no talking!" Bryson shouted.

"I hope Uncle Ollie gets to see this," Maggie said as she studied the wall in search of a keyhole.

A loud bang ricocheted off the stone walls. Maggie and Emma ducked instinctively and spun to face Bryson.

He shouldered his weapon. "I said no talking."

"We have to revise that rule. How do you expect us to work in silence?"

"Fine," Bryson said. "Come here."

Maggie cocked a hip, setting a hand on it. "Why?"

Bryson leveled the weapon at her. "I wasn't asking."

She clenched her jaw as she stalked toward him with narrowed eyes.

"Give me your wrists." He pulled a zip tie from his cargo pants.

"You're not serious. How do you expect me to navigate this place with my hands bound?"

"Carefully. Now give them to me."

Maggie wrinkled her nose, holding out her wrists. Bryson tugged the zip tie tight around them, causing Maggie to wince.

"Now, off you go to find the next keyhole."

"I still don't see how you expect me to work like this," she said, waving her bound wrists in the air.

"Your eyes still work. Use them."

With a stony glare at him, she returned to Emma to continue their search. "I'm not seeing anything so far, which makes sense since these are outside walls."

"Yeah, but maybe they're insulated or something. Maybe there's a chamber between this and the stone we saw outside," Maggie conjectured.

Emma swept the beam around the room. "Maybe. Though it seems like the correct size in here. It doesn't feel smaller than it should, which would indicate rooms rimming the outside."

Maggie thudded against the stone with her fists. "So, if these lead to the outside, where would we find another passage?"

"Maybe we were wrong. Maybe the gold was here and someone took it away a long time ago."

Maggie glanced across the stone floor. "Really? Don't you think that would have made the news?"

"Not if tomb raiders grabbed it."

Maggie's shoulders slumped, and she covered her face with her hands and groaned. She lifted her head and shook her hair over her shoulders. "No."

"What?" Emma questioned as she continued to search the last remaining wall.

"No. We did not come all this way and survive a cursed subway, a car crash, a plane crash, *and* getting shot to find out there's nothing here. We're missing something."

Emma chewed her lower lip as she considered the statement.

"Come on, Emma, think."

"I'm thinking. I'm an expert in Egyptology, not pre-Columbian South America."

Maggie tapped her toes on the floor, puckering her lips. "It can't be that different from Egyptian stuff."

Emma shot her an unimpressed glance. "Seriously?"

"Yes, seriously. When you really break things down, most cultures did things in a similar way. Even those that evolved an ocean away, right?"

"Pyramid construction was quite different."

"Not really. They have a similar shape, just a slightly

different style. If this was an Egyptian tomb, where would you look next?"

"That's the thing, if it was it would have chambers that were…" Emma's voice trailed off.

"That were what?" Maggie asked.

"Built into the structure," she finished as she hurried to the room's center, sweeping the light across the floor. "But those are much larger than this."

"Okay?"

Emma waved a finger in the air as she stared at the floor. "This one is quite small. Which makes me wonder if a portion of it is underground."

"Oh, good thinking. You may be right. Where would the opening be?"

"I'm guessing in the middle here, but it could be anywhere. This is where my inexperience is going to cost us. I'm not certain how these cultures structured their pyramids."

"Okay, well, don't sweat it, we'll find it."

"But it'll take longer," Emma said, with a stamp on the stone floor.

"Okay, Speedy, calm down. Then it takes longer."

"I really wish everyone would stop calling me these ridiculous nicknames. My name is Emma. Not brainy, not Fanny, not speedy."

Maggie crinkled her brow and rubbed her bound hands along Emma's shoulders. "Okay, Emma. It's okay."

Emma heaved in deep breaths. Maggie stepped closer to her, lowering her voice. "Is this some kind of ploy? Like, to defeat Bryson? Because I'm not sure now is the right moment."

"It's not. It's not. But he's got a gun to our heads, and we're on a ticking clock. Every second we spend with him increases our chances of being killed." She eyed the bloody gash on Maggie's arm. "Or accidentally shot."

"It's okay. We'll find it. He's more bluster than anything."

Emma returned to sweeping her beam across the floor. "Really? He's kidnapped you, kidnapped a few villagers, and now shot you."

"Accidentally," Maggie said. "Look, let's just concentrate on finding this. Just ignore him."

Emma glanced over her shoulder at him. "Easier said than done."

"What's the holdup?" Bryson yelled.

Maggie twisted to face him. "We're trying to find a keyhole in the floor or some kind of trigger to open a passage underground. You could expedite things by helping. I mean we're searching with a handicap." She waved her zip-tied wrists in the air.

"It's not hurting your eyesight."

"It is. Because I have to lean funny to see over them."

"Just keep looking," Bryson said as he joined them to search for a keyhole.

Sweat rolled down Emma's forehead, and a drop dripped from the tip of her nose. "Oh, wow, is it hot in here?"

"Not really," Maggie said. "It's warm, but it's not hot."

Emma swiped at her face as she continued the search.

"You're having a hot flash."

"I am not," Emma snapped.

"Don't be so touchy. I'm not saying you're old. I'm saying you're overheated because you're stressed out."

"Will you two please stop babbling?" Bryson asked.

"I can't help it," Maggie said. "I like to talk."

Emma breathed out a huffy breath. "No wonder I'm stressed out."

"I cannot imagine a time when you two actually got along."

Maggie studied the floor as Emma swept the beam around and they inched forward. "You should have known us in college. We were the best of friends."

"Debatable," Emma called from the middle of the chamber, swinging the beam to the opposite side for Bryson to check the floor.

"See what I mean?" he said. "Nothing here. You two are like oil and water."

"Which is why we make a great team. Who else would have gotten into a van that you'd be getting into to save my life?"

"I'm still shocked," Bryson shot back as Maggie stared at the floor. "Especially since you've stolen her boyfriend."

The light beam wobbled as Emma swung it back toward Bryson, scanning the floor as she went. She wiped at her brow again, blowing out a long breath.

"I didn't steal her boyfriend. We're not dating. Look, I'm not explaining this to you. You don't deserve an explanation." Maggie sliced a hand through the air as the beam came back to her side, and she searched the floor. "Clear."

"She does," Bryson answered as Emma searched the middle of the floor before sliding the beam toward him.

"Now is not the time or place."

"He's right, though," Emma answered. "I kind of feel like I deserve more than the vague non-explanation you've given me."

"Really? You're going to take Bryson's side? At this particular moment, when we're stuck inside a temple searching for Confederate gold, you're going to demand an explanation about Leo."

"Well, it seems as good a time as any," Emma said.

"Maybe when we're safe and not being held at gunpoint would be a better time."

"Whatever, Maggie. Put it off all you want. It doesn't

change the fact that you're a crappy friend, and an even crappier team leader."

"What's that supposed to mean?" Maggie shouted. "I'm a damn good team leader."

"Oh, yeah, sure. So far, we've crashed twice, and now we're being held at gunpoint by the bad guys. Excellent job, Maggie."

Emma blew out a long breath, wiping at her forehead again.

"Will you get your panties out of a twist? You're going to pass out from being so overheated, and then I'll have to drag your body around the entire pyramid."

"Sorry my hot flash is inconven–" Emma's words cut off, and she scuffed her shoe against the floor.

"What is it? Did you find something?"

She dropped to a knee, rubbing her fingers over the stone in the floor. "Maybe."

Maggie hurried to join her as Bryson closed the gap from the other side.

"Hold the flashlight," Emma murmured, passing it off to Maggie as she dug into the stone.

Maggie aimed the flashlight down at the divot.

Emma used her fingertips to clear away some sediment. "This is a keyhole."

Maggie bounced on her toes. "Can you get it clear? Do you need a tool?"

"I think I can get it." She blew a sharp breath into the divot, spraying dirt and dust into the air.

"You're right. It's a keyhole," Maggie exclaimed. "Let's start trying keys."

She turned her hip toward Emma. "You'll have to grab them. I can't fish them out with my hands like this."

"Don't touch her," Bryson barked. "I'll get the keys."

Maggie rolled her eyes as Bryson approached and slid his

hand into her pocket. He wiggled his eyebrows at her as he fished them out.

"Your touch isn't exhilarating in any way, just get the keys."

Bryson pulled the three remaining keys from her pocket and passed them off to Emma. "Start trying keys."

Emma spread them out across the stone, selecting one and trying it. It turned easily, and the stone slid away. Maggie shone the beam into the hole. A set of stone stairs led down into the underground chamber.

Her heart skipped a beat as she stared into the darkness.

"Well," she said as she eyed her fellow explorers, "should we see what's down in the creepy basement?"

CHAPTER 34

"I guess we have no choice." Emma swiped at her brow again as she side-eyed the gun in Bryson's hands. She collected the remaining keys and shoved them into her pocket.

"Ladies first," Bryson answered, waving the weapon into the hole.

"I'll go first," Maggie offered, taking a step onto the first stone stair.

Emma grabbed her arm. "Maggie!"

"What?"

"There could be a trap."

Maggie glanced down at her feet. "So far, so good."

"Give me the flashlight," Emma huffed, grabbing it from Maggie's hands.

She knelt on the floor, swiping it around the hole's edges as she hung her head inside.

"Anything?" Maggie asked.

Emma sat back on her haunches, her face shiny and red. "I don't see anything," she said, her voice breathy.

"Emma? Are you okay?" Maggie climbed out of the hole and squatted next to her.

"Get in that hole," Bryson barked.

"Wait a second," Maggie answered.

"No, get in–"

"Something's wrong with her!" Maggie shouted, leaping to her feet.

Emma braced her hands against her thighs, heaving a few breaths. "I'm okay. I'm just…" She puffed out another breath. "I'm just…"

Emma pitched headfirst toward the hole as her words trailed off.

Maggie thrust out her bound wrists, catching her before she fell all the way in. "Help," she groaned.

Bryson backed a few steps away. "I don't think so."

Maggie winced, her features pinching with the effort to hold Emma back with her clasped hands. "She's sick. Pull her back."

"I think she's faking."

Maggie huffed out a sharp breath, clenching her teeth. "She's not, believe me. She's heavy as a rock."

Bryson grunted, tossing the strap of his weapon over his shoulder and reaching forward to haul Emma's limp form back.

"Cut my zip ties," Maggie said as he settled Emma on the stone floor.

"No."

"She needs help!" Maggie answered.

"I'll handle it. Just hold the flashlight."

Maggie retrieved it from the floor, where it had landed when Emma collapsed, and pointed it at her friend. Bryson knelt beside her, checking her pulse and pupils.

"She's burning up."

"Really?" Maggie squealed. "I told you she wasn't faking, you idiot."

Bryson stood up inches from her face. "And I told you to stay back."

Maggie refused to budge. "Take her out to get help."

Emma groaned on the floor, interrupting any further conversation. Maggie pushed past Bryson to kneel next to her. "Emma?"

"What happened?" Emma asked as her eyes fluttered open.

"You passed out."

"I wasn't having a hot flash," she argued as she squeezed her eyes closed again.

"I know. You're sick. You have a fever." Maggie glanced over her shoulder at Bryson. "Give her some water."

Bryson tugged a water bottle from his pack and handed it to Maggie. She offered him an unimpressed stare. "A little help?"

Bryson heaved a sigh, digging in his pocket to retrieve a pocket knife. He flipped it open and sliced off her wrist ties. Maggie breathed a sigh of relief as she flipped the top open on the reusable water bottle and passed it to Emma.

"Thanks," Emma said, pulling herself up to sit and taking a sip.

"You need to go back with the others," Maggie said.

Emma shook her head as she took another sip of the water and handed the canteen back to Bryson. "No, I'm good."

"Emma, you're burning up."

"I said I'm fine. I'm the best person to be in here…outside of Ollie, and I don't want to put him through this with Bryson." She shot Maggie a knowing glance.

Maggie nodded, reading the silent signal. "Okay. Well, I guess we should keep going if you think you can walk."

"I can make it," Emma answered, holding her hand out for Maggie to pull her up. She rose, stumbling forward a step and breathing out a long breath. She wiped at the sweat beading on her forehead again. "Okay, I'm ready. Give me the flashlight."

Maggie passed it over to her, and Emma took a shaky step down into the underground chamber. Bryson caught Maggie's arm before she descended after her. "No funny business."

"I wouldn't dream of it," Maggie answered, wrenching her arm away and following Emma's bobbling light deeper into the pyramid.

"Wow," Emma said as she shined the beam around the room at the bottom. Pictures on the walls painted scenes of the ironclad's unloading.

"Well, we're in the right place," Maggie murmured.

"Find the gold," Bryson barked from behind them.

"Okay," Maggie said, screwing up her face. "Let us have a minute to appreciate the history."

"You can appreciate it when I have my gold."

Maggie rolled her eyes. "Come on, let's find the next keyhole."

"I think it's down there," Emma answered, pointing her flashlight beam toward what appeared to be an ornate door on the opposite end of the room.

"That looks promising," Maggie answered, moving toward it. Her fingers traced the stone carvings before landing on a keyhole. A smile spread across her lips. "Yes, this is it. Keys?"

Emma dug them from her pocket and passed them over. Maggie slid the first into the hole, but it wouldn't budge.

"Let's hope it's the next one," Emma said.

Maggie slipped the first key into her pocket before shoving the next one into the keyhole. It spun easily. She pulled her hands away, still holding the key, as the door slid up. With a shaky breath, she glanced at Emma.

"In you go," Bryson said, shoving them both forward. They stumbled across the threshold into another chamber. The door slid shut behind them, cutting them off. "Hey!"

"Uh oh," Maggie said.

Bryson banged on the door. "Open this door."

"I didn't close it!" Maggie yelled.

"I don't care who closed it. Open it right now."

"Okay, okay. Hold on. I'm looking for a keyhole," Maggie answered as Emma swept the flashlight beam over the backside of the stone panel. "I don't see one."

"There must be some way to open it," Bryson answered.

Maggie set her hands on her hips. "Well, you tell me what it is, because I can't find it. We'll keep searching, but so far I don't see a way to go back."

"You'd better find a way to get this door open or…"

"Or what? You'll shoot me again? Through the wall?" Maggie snapped.

"I'll shoot Taylor."

Maggie scrunched her nose, and let her head fall back between her shoulder blades. "I really hate that guy."

"I'm not sure he knows that," Emma answered, with a click of her tongue.

"Oh, please," Maggie said as she felt around on the panel in search of a trigger to reopen it.

"Oh, come on, Maggie, you're a professional flirt."

"I am not," Maggie answered, with a wrinkled nose. "Hey, Bryson, we can't find anything on the door at all. Go get Uncle Ollie."

"No," he shouted back.

"Stop being a blockhead and go get Uncle Ollie. We're trapped in here. There's no keyhole on this side and no trigger."

"Then keep going. There must be another door to another chamber. Find it. Maybe that will open all the doors or lead to another way out."

Emma crossed her arms and glanced at Maggie. "He's right."

"Who's the flirt now?"

"I am *not*," Emma said as she swung the beam around.

"He's right," Maggie mimicked as she followed the light.

"Well, he is. We need to expand our search."

"Right, Emma wants to go further into the tomb—"

"Temple," Emma corrected.

"Whatever. Emma wants to go further in despite every other time wanting to do the exact opposite."

Emma huffed. "Well, necessity is the mother of all inventions."

Maggie rolled her eyes, running a hand through her hair. "Sorry, I should be the adult here. You're sick."

"I'm not *that* sick."

"You're burning up."

Emma stalked further into the room, waving the flashlight around on the other walls and floor. "Yeah, but I'm not dying. I just needed some water."

"Are you sure? Because now we don't have any water. I don't need you dying on me in here."

"I'm not dying," Emma snapped. "I'm just sick."

Maggie doubled over laughing. "You have jungle fever."

Emma shot her an icy glare. "Oh, sure, laugh it up. My weird rainforest illness is really funny."

"Sorry, it kind of is. Jungle fever, get it?"

Emma shot her a narrowed-eyed glance. "Why don't you go laugh it up with Bryson?"

Maggie let her shoulders slump. "I'm not flirting with him."

"You flirt with everyone," Emma answered, sweeping her hand over the wall.

"I do not."

"Just be quiet and search for the keyhole."

"Fine." Maggie set her lips in a frown as she scanned the space in front of her. "I don't flirt with everyone."

"Oh, that's right," Emma answered as she shuffled further into the chamber, "you don't flirt with your fiance anymore. He's been thrown over."

Maggie stamped a foot on the ground. "That's not true."

"Isn't it? You don't want to get married. You won't set a date. You've got a side piece."

"I do *not* have a side piece." She scanned the floor, sweeping her foot across the stones in search of any divots.

"Sure, sure," Emma answered.

Maggie snapped her gaze up. "Okay, fine. Do you really want to know why I don't want to set a date?"

"Because you're dating another guy?"

Maggie stuck her hands on her hips and shook her head. "Do you want to know or not?"

Emma glanced over her shoulder before flicking her gaze back to the wall. "Okay, fine, I want to know. Can't wait to hear it, actually."

"Okay, smarty, I don't want to set a date because..." Maggie pressed her lips together and shook her head.

"Yeah?"

"I just..." Maggie paused again, crinkling her nose as she stooped to study the floor tiles.

Emma flicked the flashlight toward her. "Well? Spit it out, tomb raider."

Maggie screwed up her face at the name but shrugged it off. "Okay, okay. I just...feel like when we get married, my life will end."

"What?" Emma asked in a high-pitched voice before she returned to her search. "That's ridiculous."

"It's not," Maggie said as she rose to stand. "I feel like... things will be expected of me. Like housekeeping and cooking. Children."

Emma shot a sideways glance her way. "That'll put a stop to your jungle treks."

"Right? That's exactly it. And the other day, you'll never guess what he said to me."

"What?" Emma asked, brushing away a spot of dried mud from the wall.

"He called me Mrs. Henry Taylor." Maggie stopped, flinging her hands out and sliding her eyes closed.

"O-okay, I'm not really getting a read on you here."

"Emma! How would you like your identity to be completely erased? Suddenly you're not Emma Fielding, Museum Assistant Director, and you're Mrs. Leo Hamilton."

Emma flicked up her eyebrows. "I guess I see your point."

"It's archaic!" Maggie exclaimed. "Suddenly, I just cease to exist and become attached to my husband."

"Did you say anything to him?"

"Uh, yeah," Maggie exclaimed. "Obviously. I'm Maggie Edwards, I'm not exactly a shrinking violet."

"And what did he say?" Emma squatted down to study a stone on the floor.

"He said he was fine with it."

"So, what's the problem?"

"Nothing. I don't know. It just feels...big. Life-changing."

Emma slid the beam to her again.

Maggie screwed up her face, shielding her eyes. "What are you doing?"

"Memorizing this moment. The one moment I've seen the great Maggie Edwards scared."

"I'm not scared," Maggie said, batting the flashlight away from her. "I'm just...okay, I'm scared."

"Maggie, it's not going to be that life-changing. You'll still be you, and he'll still be him. He loves adventure as much as you do. He loves tombs and travel and no roots."

"You'd think it'd be him not wanting to get married," Maggie answered, digging at a divot in the wall.

"I think he loves you. I don't think he wants to domesticate you."

"Good, because I'm staying feral."

Emma smiled as she continued around the corner to the back wall. "You know, this is the one time I think I've been surprised by you. All through college, we thought you and Leo would be married, and now, suddenly, you're afraid of marriage? Go figure."

"I'm not afraid of marriage. All through college, and a little after, I figured that's what I *should* do. That's what was expected of me. I dated Leo because he could provide the magazine lifestyle I thought I should aim for."

"And then?"

"And then I found my true self somewhere in that desert in Egypt, and I haven't looked back. I'm not made to *just* host cocktail parties and make sure his career goes well while mine's a hobby. I'm made to host fabulous parties and kick ass in the jungle."

"So, keep doing that," Emma answered. "No one's going to make you change. Certainly not Henry. He's the most supportive man I've ever met when it comes to your empowerment."

Maggie puckered her lips. "I guess you're right. Okay, fine. Let's see. June nineteenth."

"What?"

"June nineteenth. The wedding date. If June fifteenth was a Tuesday, that'd be the following Saturday. That'll work."

"Only you would pick the wedding date sans the groom and while trapped inside an underground temple and being held at gunpoint."

"He asked me to do it, and now it's done. What difference does it make if I do it now or not? At least we have something to look forward to."

"Mmm. I can't wait," Emma said, with a roll of her eyes. "It'll be interesting to see how Leo takes it, though I'm sure Henry will be thrilled."

"Leo shouldn't take it anyway. Why would he care?"

Emma shot her an icy sideways stare.

"Oh, stop it. We're not dating."

"Then what are you doing?"

"Stuff," Maggie said, squatting down to study the floor.

"What stuff?" Emma asked.

"I can't tell you."

"Oh, right. Because that's innocent."

"It is!" Maggie insisted. "Wait, I think I found something."

"Of course, you did. Even the universe has your back."

Maggie pressed her lips together and shot Emma an irritated glance as she unearthed a divot in the wall. "I think this is the keyhole. I'll tell you what's going on with Leo if you promise to act like I didn't."

"What?"

"I mean it's a secret, and if Leo knows I told you, he'll be really disappointed."

"I'll bet. I'm sure Leo would be extremely disappointed that you admitted you've been stepping out on Henry."

"I have not been," Maggie said as she pulled the key from her pocket and inserted it in the hole.

It turned easily, and the floor rumbled beneath them. "I've been–"

Her voice cut off as the stone slid away underneath them and they plunged into the darkness below.

CHAPTER 35

Maggie and Emma shrieked as they plummeted down into the dark hole. Maggie collided with something hard before she continued to slide further into the darkness.

Emma slammed into it seconds later. The flashlight fell from her hands, toppling further down and landing with a hard thud.

The light flickered, then went out.

Maggie tumbled onto a hard surface, with a groan. Emma slammed into her a second later, rolling her across the hard stone floor.

"Ow," Maggie said as she pushed herself up into the darkness. "Emma, are you okay?"

"No," Emma groaned.

"Seriously?" Maggie asked, flailing an arm in search of her friend.

"I'm fine. I'm not hurt, but that was…I don't know how many times I have to tell you not to do things until I check them out."

"Oh, like we could have known the floor was going to

open up," Maggie said. She slid her hands around in the darkness searching for the flashlight.

"There had to be some warning sign."

"And you dropped the flashlight," Maggie huffed.

"Oh, I'm sorry that after I fell through a hole and smacked into who knows what, I didn't keep hold of the flashlight."

"It's okay, I forgive you."

Emma scoffed in the darkness. Maggie crawled forward in search of the light source. She cracked her head into Emma's forehead, both of them scurrying backward.

Maggie pressed a hand to her throbbing temple. "Ow. Watch where you're going!"

"You watch where you're going. I'm trying to find the light."

"So am I," Maggie answered. "Okay, look, only one of us can move around at a time so we don't bang into each other."

"I guess since I lost it, I'll be the one to find it."

"I'll find it. You just sit there and be sick."

Maggie crawled forward again, with her hand outstretched and sliding across the stone floor.

"It's creepy in here," Emma said after a moment.

"I thought you loved this stuff?"

"Yeah, on a proper dig with lights."

Maggie inched forward. Her hand struck something cold and hard. She fumbled around its edges, a smile turning up the corner of her lips. "Emma, I think we may have found the gold."

"How do you know?"

"I think I'm touching a gold bar." She let go of the metal and continued her search for the flashlight. "If I ever find the flashlight, we'll know for sure."

"Maybe you should keep talking while you search. It's a little less disconcerting when there's sound in here."

"What do you want me to talk about? Oh, what colors do

you think for the wedding? I don't want to go too girly, but I don't want anything drab either. Maybe silver and gold. That's classy. Oh, or how about black and white?"

"I don't know. I was thinking you could finish what you were telling me about you and Leo."

Maggie froze, licking her lips before she continued forward. "Right. Sure."

"Now you don't want to, huh?"

"No, I'll tell you." She swung her arm around again as she crept forward. Her fingers touched something that rolled away. "Wait a second, I think I found the flashlight."

"Are you serious? What is it with this? Every time you're going to tell me, you get away with not having to."

"I think it's kind of sweet that you want to know."

"I don't. It's just passing the time."

Maggie's fingers wrapped around a cold barrel. "You do. You like him. A lot. And you want to make sure he's not still hung up on me. And let me tell you, he's not."

"Says you. Every man in the world is hung up on you."

"That's so not true. Okay, I've got good news and bad news."

"What's the bad news?" Emma asked.

Maggie squeezed her hand around the barrel of the flashlight she'd retrieved. "I've got the flashlight, but it's missing the batteries, so now I have to find those."

"Ugh," Emma said. "What's the good news?"

"That I got the flashlight," Maggie answered. "I covered both in one sentence."

"What's the Leo news?" Emma asked as Maggie returned to her search, this time for batteries.

"Do you really, really want to know, or do you just want to trust me when I say we're not seeing each other and he's into you?"

"I don't want to trust you. I want to know."

"All right, all right. Oh, found one battery." Maggie slid it into the barrel and continued searching for the next one.

"Stop putting it off."

"I find it disturbing that you don't trust me," Maggie said as her fingers touched the second battery. "Ha! Got the second battery."

"I find it disturbing that you won't just answer."

Maggie slid the battery into the tube and snapped the hinged back shut. "There's a reason I won't answer."

She flicked on the flashlight and swung the beam around the massive room. The light glinted off gold bars stacked over her head. The corners of her lips turned up as she reached out to run her fingers along the carefully stacked gold.

"Emma! Look! We found the gold!"

"Great. Now we can die down here with it, and I still won't know what you're doing with Leo."

Maggie wrinkled her nose, aiming the flashlight at Emma. She squinted against it, holding a hand in front of her eyes.

"I want to see your face when you hear this."

"That just makes it so much worse."

Maggie climbed to her feet and closed the gap between them. She puckered her lips and stared down at Emma. "Leo and I have been secretly meeting for a very special reason."

"You're getting back together."

Maggie shook her head. "What's an important event that's coming up next month?"

"Thanksgiving," Emma answered.

Maggie rolled her eyes. "No. Try again."

"Veteran's Day."

"Emma, will you be serious?"

"I am being serious. What important events come up in November outside of those?"

Maggie slid her head forward, rolling a hand in the air. "Come on. Think."

Emma let her head sink into her hands. "I can't think. I'm sick, remember?"

"Okay, fine, since you have a burning fever, I'll just tell you. It's your birthday next month."

"That's not really an important event–"

"And it's Henry's birthday next month."

"And you want to spring on us that you and Leo are back together on our birthdays?"

Maggie let her shoulders slump as she shot Emma an irritated glance. "No. We're planning a huge surprise party at the museum. Which has been really difficult trying to set up at the place you work at. Also, Leo is searching for the perfect present for you, and I'm fairly sure he's planning to test it out for another big purchase."

Emma screwed up her face. "What? Oh no, he's not getting me an iPhone, is he? I like my Android."

Maggie crinkled her nose. "No. He's getting you jewelry for your birthday. And then I think he'll assess how you like the style for another piece of jewelry."

"Do you mean like a matching bracelet?"

Maggie stuck a hand on her hip. "You really are dense."

"I am not."

"You are so. He's getting you a charm bracelet since you always liked mine in college. And I think for Christmas…" Maggie pressed her lips together, flicking her eyebrows up. "It's going to be a ring!"

"What?" Emma asked, her jaw dropping open. "Like an engagement ring?"

Maggie bounced on her toes as she nodded. "Yep. I told you he liked you."

"Enough to marry me?"

"Do you like him enough to marry him?"

"I don't know. Maybe." Emma's gaze darted around the space. "Maybe not." She shifted her gaze to Maggie. "Maybe you were right. Maybe we should just escape into the jungle and live our lives free of commitment."

Maggie reached a hand down toward her and pulled her to standing. "Let's just escape into the jungle first and then figure it out. Besides, what happened to 'it's not life-changing?'"

"Felt better when I was saying it to you than applying it to me."

Maggie shined the light beam around the space. "Let's just find a way out of here. Your fever is probably affecting your brain."

"That's a lot of gold. I'm surprised the ironclad didn't sink," Emma said as she studied it.

Maggie scoffed at the statement as she snaked around it toward the wall. "Yeah, Bryson will be rich."

She stopped dead, sucking in a gasp.

"What?" Emma asked, hurrying toward her. "Did you find an exit?"

"No, but…" Maggie spun to face her friend. "We could do a double wedding."

"What?" Emma exclaimed. "No."

"Wow, that was quick," Maggie said, returning to her search.

"Umm, a double wedding is a terrible idea. Terrible. You will want thousands of people. It'll be like a royal wedding. And I'll have two people in the back."

"Okay, fine," she said as she swept the beam around the walls. "Separate weddings. I guess it wouldn't be good to have my maid of honor also getting married."

"No. Who would fix the ten-foot train you'll probably have? Or make sure the tiara sits right on your head?"

Maggie narrowed her eyes and slid her gaze to Emma.

"Don't forget checking my hair and makeup constantly."

"Right, that, too," Emma said. "It's a full-time job. I can't be getting married, then."

"Well, you could. I mean, only two people are coming to see you so, not that big of a deal."

"Very funny. Just focus on finding a way out of here, or neither of us will be getting married - because we'll be dead."

"I don't want you to die before your party," Maggie said. "It's going to be epic. Oh, *and* you'd better look surprised. Not kidding. If Leo finds out I told you, he'll be super mad."

Emma dropped her jaw open and widened her eyes.

Maggie did a double take at her. "Are you sick? Do you feel worse? Is your throat closing?"

"No, I'm acting surprised."

Maggie puckered her lips and shook her head before she returned to searching the wall. "That's the worst surprised face I've ever seen. You look like you're dying."

"I do not."

"Try it in front of a mirror when you get home, and you'll see what I mean."

"Not all of us practice our faces in mirrors."

"Well, you'd better start. I'm not going to take the heat for your knowing this."

Emma pointed to an area on the wall. "Give me some light here. Are you going to tell Henry?"

Maggie centered the beam where Emma indicated. "No."

"It's nothing. Just a divot in the stone. Move on. Don't you think he's going to be mad?"

"He'll get over it."

Emma wrinkled her nose. "That's pretty cavalier."

"Will you stop grilling me and just be excited that we found the gold?"

"I'll be more excited that we found the gold when we're

out of here. Oh wait, I won't be excited because Bryson's going to steal it."

"Not if I can help it," Maggie answered as she continued to sweep the beam around. She tilted her head as the beam crossed something behind a stack of gold bars. "Is that a shadow or a hole?"

Emma studied it before she flailed a hand toward it. "I can't tell. And I can't reach it."

"We need to move the gold."

"You're kidding me," Maggie said, with a huff. "We should have brought Bryson for this."

"Like he'd lift a finger," Emma said, swiping at the sweat on her brow.

"Sit down, I'll move these."

Emma grabbed a stack of bars and shuffled them to a new spot. "I'm not *that* sick."

"Okay," Maggie said, with a shrug of her shoulders. She shifted a few bars of gold to a new location.

They whittled down the four stacks, finding another row behind them. "Ugh. How much gold did this guy have?"

Emma scanned the space with the flashlight. "A lot."

Maggie shook her head as they started to move the top bars from the remaining four stacks. After shifting a few off the top of the pile, she aimed the flashlight behind it. "Okay, this is a hole."

"Great. I hope it leads out of here."

"Me, too," Maggie answered as she hauled more blocks to their new spot. "If it does, we need a plan."

"Get out. That's my plan."

"Beyond that. We should try to find our way to the rest of the team and rescue them from Bryson's people."

"And how do you plan to do that?" Emma dropped a few more bars onto her stack.

"We'll have to get the drop on them."

Emma set the last of the bars from her stack on their new spot. "Will you stop saying things like that? We can't just get the drop on someone. You need to be capable of getting the drop on them."

Maggie rolled her eyes, dragging the remaining bricks out of the way. "I will not stop saying it, because that's exactly what we're going to do."

She blew out a long breath as she aimed the flashlight at the hole. "There's a passage."

"Great. Let's hope it leads to a way out." Emma swiped the flashlight from her and traced the outline of the hole with it. "Looks clear. But we'll proceed with caution."

They entered the corridor, creeping ahead. "Doesn't seem like they built these with as many traps as the Egyptians," Maggie said.

"Good thing. You'd be dead."

Maggie ran a hand along the side of the passage, ignoring Emma's comment. "This looks natural."

"Yeah, which worries me."

"Why?" Maggie snapped her gaze to Emma.

"Because they didn't build it. So, it may not be a back door."

Maggie winced as they continued forward. "Well, that's not good. Though what are the chances it's not? I mean, that's a lot of gold back there. Did they really climb all those stairs and wind their way down to the bottom of the temple to put it in, or did they unload it from somewhere much closer?"

"Like where?" Emma questioned.

"I don't know. Like the river."

"If the river connected to this, it would be underground. Did they sail the ironclad through an underground river?"

"How should I know? I'm not the brains of this operation,

I'm just the awesome leader. Maybe it wasn't underground in the eighteen hundreds."

"I just think that if this connected to water, there would be some indica–" her words cut off as their feet submerged in water, "–tion."

"Like that?" Maggie asked.

"Yep."

Maggie took a few more steps forward. "At least it's warm. And it's not very deep."

They continued forward, splashing through the water that filled the passage.

"You spoke too soon," Emma said a few moments later as the water rose to their shins. "The next time you want to pursue a treasure hunt, please make sure there is no water. We have been in more rivers than enough."

"Next time, we'll go back to the desert," Maggie promised.

"At least it's dry. Ugh," Emma moaned as the water hit her knees.

"Where is this water coming from?"

"Underground source? It must feed into the main river."

"Like I said," Maggie answered with an arched eyebrow as she waded forward.

"This is still a pretty far haul," Emma said.

"But it's not as far as climbing all those stairs and then going down all the other stairs and then going into the secret chamber and down to another secret–"

"I get it. This is getting deeper. I'm not sure how much longer we can continue."

Water rose to their thighs. "We may have to swim."

"I was afraid you'd say that."

"Well," Maggie said as the water engulfed her entire lower half, "you gotta do what you gotta do. And right now, this is our only way out."

After another few seconds of walking, Maggie dove

forward, plunging into the water and kicking her feet. "Come on."

"How do you propose I hang on to the flashlight?" Emma shouted, still fighting to walk through the water that hit her belly.

"Just kick with your feet and hold the flashlight up with one hand."

"Oh, right," Emma answered, "cause that's easy."

Maggie trod water, waiting for her to catch up. "I'll take it."

Emma walked forward with the water up to her chest and passed her the flashlight before plunging deeper and swimming forward. Maggie kicked her feet, paddling next to her.

"Hey, quick question: this isn't the place where those worm things swim up your…you know?"

"I think you mean a candiru fish, and yes, they are from South America."

Maggie winced as she swam forward.

"Don't pee in the water."

"Ugh," Maggie answered, her nose wrinkled.

"I'm kidding. They're not in Venezuela."

"Oh, thank goodness."

"Ew," Emma said, offering Maggie a disgusted stare.

"What? OMG, no. I didn't. But I don't want to take any chances."

They continued forward as the water spilled into a large cavern. Maggie swam into it, swinging the flashlight's beam around. She froze, her feet kicking to hold her up in the water as she focused the light on one thing. "Oh, wow, Emma, look."

Emma's eyes went wide as she stared at the object illuminated across the large space. "Wow."

CHAPTER 36

Maggie shined the light from side to side as she bobbed in the water. Her lips curled up at the corners, and she shot a glance at Emma. "This is amazing."

"I've never seen anything like it. I hope we can show Ollie," Emma said, splashing her way over toward the massive object.

Maggie swam toward it, too. "I don't think I've ever seen an ironclad up close."

"And in an underground cavern in Venezuela no less," Emma answered as she hoisted herself up and climbed on top of it.

"Take the light," Maggie said, surging out of the water to pass it off before she climbed on top of the rusty ship. She wandered to the armament and peered under the roof. "Where do you get in at?"

Emma led her to the access panel and flung it open. She shined the light inside.

"Let's go in," Maggie said.

"Pass. I'm not getting stuck in an ironclad in the jungle while being held at gunpoint."

"Technically, we're not being held at gunpoint anymore. Come on," Maggie said with a grin, sliding into the hole and dropping down to the floor below. "Emma! Come down here. There are cannons and stuff."

"Yeah, okay. I'll look when we're rescued."

Maggie's head appeared at the opening. "Come on! Stop being a scaredy cat."

Emma rolled her eyes but lowered her legs into the hole. "I just know I'm going to regret this."

"Look at the cannon. I can't imagine being up against another ship and firing this. They had to be in such close range," Maggie said, with a shake of her head. "That's crazy."

"Even crazier is where they lived. Come on," Emma said, with a slight smile. She found access to the living quarters. Maggie followed her into the tiny space.

"Oh, my goodness," she whispered as Emma shined the light around the space. Maggie shivered, her skin turning to gooseflesh. "People lived in here."

"Right? Tiny, isn't it?"

"It's not just that, but…over one hundred years ago, people lived in here and fought a war. It's just…strange being so close to their things."

"You were close to Cleopatra's body, and she lived thousands of years ago," Emma said as she swiped a finger along the dust in a sailor's cubby.

"Yeah, but that feels so ancient, it's like it's not real. But this…this is recent history. These are people's great-grandparents."

Emma tilted her head, furrowing her brow. "I never realized you were into modern history."

"Modern history. That sounds so weird." Maggie chuckled as she took a step forward. The ancient ship creaked under her. A bang thudded through the ship. "This old girl doesn't sound too good."

"I'm not surprised. An ironclad in this humidity?" Emma pounded against the wall. "Not too good on her joints."

Maggie mimicked her behavior, smacking a hand against the wall. "Do you have arthritis, old girl?"

Another creak answered her. Emma flicked up her eyebrows. "I think that was a yes."

Maggie pounded a fist on the side again. "Oh, no," she said in a deep voice, "I'm old, and my bones ache."

Emma offered a laugh before she gave a double knock on another wall. "I've been sitting in hot, humid weather for hundreds of years."

The ship creaked again and shifted.

"Whoa." Both women stumbled forward. "I think she's mad at us for pounding on her."

"Yeah, maybe we should give her a break. She carried all that gold down here."

Maggie patted the wall gently. "And now she's resting."

"I wouldn't be happy with this retirement spot. It's too muggy. And the bugs," Emma said.

Maggie snickered at the joke. "And sitting in a giant puddle of water. Maybe that's why she's so grumbly."

"Yeah. I would be."

"Okay, no retiring in Venezuela," Maggie said with a nod as Emma shined her light around the space.

She sucked in a sharp breath. "Well, I guess we should stop playing war and find a way out of here."

Maggie nodded and took a step. She stumbled. "Whoa. What's with this floor?"

Emma spun, wobbling a bit. The color drained from her face, and she snapped her gaze to Maggie. "Are we moving?"

"No. How would we be moving?"

Emma pressed her lips together into a frown. "We're in a ship."

"Yeah, but it's docked or whatever," Maggie said, with a laugh.

"Are we? What was all that creaking about?" Emma crossed the room, heading for the ladder to the armament.

"Just an old ship protesting us wandering around it," Maggie said with a shrug as she wobbled her way behind Emma.

"It sure feels like we're sailing."

"We can't be sailing. Ironclads are steamships, duh. Is there a ghost running the engine?"

Emma shot a glance over her shoulder. "I'm impressed you knew that, but that doesn't change the fact that we are moving."

She peered out the canon port. "See."

The walls of the cave surrounding them slid by, picking up speed by the second.

"Uh oh," Maggie said, with a wince. "How did that happen?"

Emma shook her head as she pushed out onto the deck. "Because we were stupid enough to get inside an ironclad and wander around. Now we dislodged it, and it's sailing down the stupid river."

"This is ridiculous," Maggie said as they stood on the deck. Stone surrounded them on both sides as the ironclad barreled along. "You stupid ship. How did you do this?"

"Well, it did. Calling it stupid does nothing to help us."

"Okay, we'll just jump off the back," Maggie said, with a shrug.

"And get pulled right along with it in its wake to heaven knows where?" Emma answered.

"I'm sure we'll be fine," Maggie said. "Just swim away."

Emma gave her an unimpressed glance before rubbing a hand against her forehead. "Okay–"

"Wait!" Maggie exclaimed. "I see light! We're coming out of here."

Emma crinkled her brow as she stared ahead at the speck of light that grew with each passing second. "What is that noise?"

"I don't know. It sounds like pounding or something."

"Yeah, loud pounding?"

"What the heck?" Maggie asked, peering ahead of them at the light. "Sounds like…"

The color drained from Emma's face. "Water. Lots of water. A waterfall."

"What? Like a real one?"

Emma shot her an unimpressed glance. "No, Maggie, like a fake waterfall. The kind without water or a fall."

"Sorry, it's not every day that we run into a waterfall." Maggie stared ahead. "I see it. It's at the mouth of this cave. We're going out into the river."

"Uhhh, okay, I think we better duck under the armament's cover before we get drenched with water."

"Right," Maggie said. She followed Emma into the armament as the front of the ship pushed through the waterfall into the bright sunshine beyond it. Seconds later, water pounded against the metal roof.

Maggie ducked instinctively as they passed under the waterfall. She breathed out a sigh of relief when the ship pulled clear of the cavern, continuing downstream as the current pushed them along.

"Whew," Maggie said, stepping into the light, "got out of there at least. I wonder where we are." She shielded her eyes and scanned the horizon.

"I'm not sure, but we need to find a way off this ship."

"I guess we could jump into the river."

"Maggie, this current is strong enough to push an ironclad. I'm not sure we can swim against it."

Maggie scrunched her face. "We only need to make it to the shore."

"I think we're moving faster. I guess we can chance it. I don't know."

"Maybe we can steer this thing over to the shore and run aground."

Emma crinkled her nose and shot a sideways glance at Maggie. "Do you know how to steer an ironclad?"

"No, I figured you would."

Emma narrowed her eyes. "I studied *ancient* cultures."

"This old girl's pretty ancient," Maggie said, patting the railing.

"You know what I mean. I can't pilot an ironclad."

"Well, okay," Maggie said, with a shrug. "How hard could it be? There's probably, like, a wheel or something. And then we'll turn it, and the ship will turn."

"I don't think it's going to be that simple, especially with no engine."

"Well, do you have a better idea? We either try to run this baby aground, or we jump."

Emma crossed her arms and tapped her foot against the metal floor beneath her feet. "Why is there never a good option?"

Maggie's forehead pinched, and she craned her neck to see ahead of them. She took a few steps forward, the crease between her brows deepening. "Uhhh…"

"If we jump, we're stuck swimming with who knows what in this river. Maybe getting bitten by a piranha."

Maggie shot a glance over her shoulder. "Piranha? Are you serious?"

"Yes. Though they don't attack humans often. Although, I am sick. That may attract them. They may smell the weakness."

"Well…" Maggie began.

"Or," Emma said, cutting her off, "we literally *try* to wreck this ship."

Maggie wobbled her way back to Emma. "You may want to decide faster."

"Why? Ohhhh, I get it," Emma said, crossing her arms, "now you set a date for the wedding, you're all excited to get back and tell Henry so he's not mad at you anymore."

Maggie shook her head, glancing over her shoulder at the front of the ship. "Mmm, nope. That's not it. It's–"

"Burning desire to see your other boyfriend, Bryson?"

"Bryson is *not* my boyfriend, and no. But I'd think fast if I was you."

Emma fluttered her eyelashes. "Whatever for, Maggie?"

Maggie thumbed behind her. "Because there's another waterfall coming up, and we're going to go over it if we wait too long."

"What?" Emma asked, wide-eyed. She pushed past Maggie, staring ahead at the mist rising from the pounding of the water. "Oh, crap."

"So, are we taking our chances in the water or on the ship?"

"Uhhh," Emma said, pressing a palm against her forehead. "Ship. Ship. The water's current will be stronger. What if we can't make it? We'll be dragged over the falls."

"Okay, so where's the wheel? I didn't see it by the cannon."

"No, it'd be in the front. In the pilot's house. Come on." Emma grabbed her hand, leading her through the ship to the small space.

Maggie raced to the ship's wheel and spun it. "Come on, come on," she murmured.

The ship continued its trek forward toward the waterfall.

"Why isn't it turning? It's broken."

"It's not like a car wheel, Maggie. It takes time for these big things to turn."

"This is what they felt like on the Titanic when the ship wouldn't turn."

"Yet it would have been better for them to hit the thing head-on," Emma said, crossing her arms.

"Wait, you don't think we should…"

"No! I don't think we should hit the falls head-on." Emma rolled her eyes and shook her head.

"Just asking. I don't know if an ironclad can withstand falling over a waterfall."

"I don't want to find out," Emma said. She bounced on her toes, wobbling her knees back and forth as she waited. "There. We're turning."

"Come on," Maggie said. "The one time you want to run into something, and there's nothing to help you out."

Emma shook her head, drumming her fingers against her thighs. "There we go. We're going sideways."

"How close is the bank?"

"I don't know. I can't see it."

"So, not close enough," Maggie said, with a huff. "How close is the waterfall?"

"Ahhh, like, way too close."

"What?" Maggie snapped, letting go of the wheel and racing ahead to look.

"Maggie!" Emma exclaimed, diving for the wheel as it spun back and holding it hard over. "You can't let go of it."

"OMG, we're way too close. We're never going to make it to the bank."

Emma shook her head as her biceps bulged while holding the wheel. "Not now, the stupid ship is going straight again."

"Sorry," Maggie said, slicking her hair behind her ear. "But I'm not sure it matters. I don't think we're going to make it. I think we're going over the falls."

Emma stared ahead at the mist rising from the pounding water. "We have to do something."

"What? We're not turning fast enough, and you're right. If we jump over, we'll get swept away."

Emma sucked in a few panicked breaths, pressing her hand to her head. "Uhh, the anchor. Maybe we can drop the anchor."

"Okay, that'll stop us from going over the falls, but then what?"

"I don't know," Emma shouted as she pushed past Maggie. "But we have to do *something* before we go over the falls."

Maggie ran her hands through her hair and followed Emma to the anchor. "Okay. Let's do it."

Emma glanced up at her and nodded. "Here we go." She released the anchor. The chain rattled its way down, dropping the heavy weight toward the river bed.

"Come on, come on," Maggie said as the ship aimed at the ever-closer falls.

The anchor thudded against the bottom, dragging along it. Their motion slowed, and a smile spread across Maggie and Emma's faces.

"It's working," Maggie said, biting her lower lip.

Emma shot her an excited glance, bobbing her head up and down. The ship continued to slow, almost to a stop.

Maggie blew out a long breath, slicking her hair behind her ears. "Okay, now we need a way to–"

The ship groaned underneath them, shimmying sideways and knocking them both off their feet. They began drifting down the river again toward the waterfall.

"What the hell happened?" Maggie asked, pushing herself up to sit.

"The anchor broke. Probably the chain rusted over the years." Emma glanced at the falls that rushed toward them. "There's nothing to stop us from going over."

CHAPTER 37

Maggie scrambled to her feet, her features pinching as she stared ahead. "We have to jump."

"Maggie, we'll be swept right over the falls, along with this ship. We'll never beat this current."

Maggie's shoulders slumped, and she scanned the horizon in search of help. "What else can we do?"

"We're going to have to hunker down inside the ironclad and hope we survive the fall. Maybe the impact will be cushioned by the metal exterior."

Maggie moaned and slapped her hands against her head. "Okay, where's the best place to ride this out?"

"Living quarters, maybe," Emma said, with a shrug. "It's in the middle. Maybe we'll be protected from being smashed against the rocks or the ground."

"I hope we can get out after this," Maggie said as they made their way toward the entrance.

"Oh, please," Emma groaned as they entered the living quarters. "Maybe get under the cots."

Maggie bobbed her head up and down as she dropped to the floor and slid under one of the stacked beds.

Her muscles tensed as she waited for the ship to pitch over the edge and fall to the rocks below. The ship picked up speed. Maggie squeezed her eyes closed and braced herself against the wall. An earsplitting scrape drowned out the thundering pounding of the waterfall. The ship shuddered and groaned.

Maggie lay under the cot, straining to listen for any other noises. "Uh, what was that?" she asked Emma.

"I don't know," Emma said, sliding out from under her stack of beds. "But we're not moving anymore."

"Really?"

"We can't be. We'd have gone over the falls by now." Emma scrambled to her feet, glancing around as Maggie climbed out.

They made their way up to the top of the ship. The falls rumbled beneath them. "OMG!" Emma shouted as they approached the front of the ship. "We're teetering on the edge."

"Let's get back before we tip it." Maggie glanced around on both sides of the ship. She jabbed a finger toward the starboard side. "We're stuck on a rock."

Emma glanced down at the large stone sticking up from the rushing water. "Great. Let's hope it holds."

"What good does it do us?" Maggie shouted. "We're stuck in the middle of the river on top of a waterfall. We can't get to land from here."

Maggie slapped her palms against her head. "We're going to die on an ironclad stuck in the middle of a river in Venezuela."

Emma ducked into the armament and settled on the floor. "Yep."

"Seriously?" Maggie asked, stamping a foot on the floor.

Emma snapped her gaze up to Maggie. "What?"

"That's it? You're just giving up?"

"What do you want me to do? Invent a land bridge? Part the seas?"

"Think of something. Brainstorm. We can't just sit here and die!"

Emma dropped her jaw open. "Uh, yeah, we can. And we will. Because we're stuck here."

Maggie slumped to sit, letting her forehead fall against her knees. "I can't believe this. I survived being shot by Bryson to die on this stupid ship stuck in the middle of this stupid river."

"On the upside, I'll probably die of jungle fever first. You can eat me to stay alive a little longer."

"That's disgusting. Why would you say that?"

"I'm feverish. I can't help it," Emma said, thunking her head against the wall.

Maggie listened to four thuds before she shook her head. "Stop doing that. It's annoying."

"Oh, I'm sorry to be annoying you in my final hours of life."

"I cannot believe there's nothing we can do. Piper was right about the curse," Maggie said, throwing herself onto the floor and curling into a ball. She squeezed her hands into fists and pounded against the rusty metal. "I'm too good to die like this!"

"Having a temper tantrum isn't going to help. The river isn't going to dry up because Maggie Edwards wants to live. A helicopter isn't going to descend from the skies to save us. No one is—"

"Shhh," Maggie said, sitting up and waving a finger in the air. "What is that?"

"The sound of us slowly dying."

"No, it's not that. It's like shouting or something."

Maggie peered over the edge of the armament's half wall and scanned the horizon. Her heart skipped a beat, and her eyes went wide. She pounded against the wall. "Emma, get up! We're saved!"

"What?" Emma asked.

"We're saved!" Maggie rose to stand and hopped over to Emma, tugging her upward.

"If you have another hare-brained scheme in mind–"

"No, shut up. They found us. Piper, Charlie, Henry, everyone is here. They found us. We're saved!"

"What?" Emma exclaimed, scrambling to her feet. She eyed the bank, finding the team along with men from the village gathering rope to reach them. "OMG! I can't believe this. They found us."

"And they're free. They got away from Bryson's guys."

"I can't believe it."

"Who says a temper tantrum never solved anything." Maggie rushed out onto the deck and waved her arms. "Henry!"

"Maggie! Stay put! We're coming for you."

"Okay, be careful. Take your time. We're not going anywhere. We're stuck on a rock."

Henry tied the rope around him, securing it with several knots. "I'm coming for you."

He waded into the water after the tribesmen secured the other end around a thick tree and held on to it. Piper, Charlie, Leo, and Uncle Ollie helped them steady the rope as Henry fought the current to get to the ship.

As they let more rope out, he drifted to the falls.

"Henry!" Maggie yelled. "Go back. You can't make it!"

Henry grabbed ahold of a nearby rock, clinging to it as he rested. "I'll make it," he puffed.

"You can't. Go back." Maggie waved him toward the shore.

The team on land, tugged the rope, pulling him back. He conversed with a few of the tribesmen, who gestured emphatically.

"Maggie," he called, cupping his hands around his mouth, "we're going to try up here, so I can swim to the middle and float down to you."

"Okay!" she yelled.

They untethered the rope from the tree trunk and shifted positions. Further from the falls, Henry had an easier time swimming toward the middle before he let the current drag him toward the ironclad.

Maggie hurried to the edge and leaned over, with her hands outstretched. They locked arms, and Maggie leaned backward, tugging him onto the ship with Emma's help.

She flung her arms around his neck as he pulled her close. He leaned away from her. "We need to get you off this ship. I'll tie the rope around us both, and they'll pull us back." He jabbed a finger at Emma. "Then I'll be back for you."

"Take Emma first. She's sick," Maggie said as he untied the knots on the rope.

He shifted his gaze to Emma and nodded.

"I'm fine. I can wait."

"It's fine," Maggie said. "You go first. Make sure Uncle Ollie knows she's sick."

"I will." He held out the loop in the rope toward Emma, and she climbed into it. After he secured it around her, they inched to the edge. Henry signaled the team on the bank before they slid into the water. They floated toward the waterfall before the rope snapped tautly, and they began their slow journey backward.

Maggie shielded her eyes as she followed their trek back. The ship groaned underneath her as they reached the bank. Dripping wet, Emma shimmied from the rope loop and plopped on the shore, falling backward and covering her face with her hands.

Henry dove back into the water as the ship groaned again. Maggie spread her legs wider to stay upright as it shuddered. The ship lurched forward, edging closer to tipping over the falls.

"Henry!" Maggie called as he reached the middle of the river. "The ship is slipping!"

He floated toward her at what seemed like an agonizingly slow pace. The ironclad inched forward again. The sound of metal tearing ripped through the air, and the ship shuddered.

Maggie fought to stay upright as the front end began to tip down.

"Maggie!" Henry screamed. "Jump!"

"I'll go right over," she shouted back. She scanned the water in search of anything she could cling to. The rock Henry had used earlier was too far away. She'd never reach it in time.

The ship tipped further as Henry closed the gap between them. She eyed his location. Could she make it to him if she ran and leapt off the back?

More metal sheared off the side of the rusty rig. She didn't have a choice. If she didn't jump now, she wouldn't make it.

"Henry! I'm going to jump!"

He nodded, stretching out his arms to grab on to her.

She slicked her hair behind her ears and raced up the incline toward the back of the ship. She flung herself in the air, splashing into the water moments later and falling shy of Henry's location.

The ironclad tipped behind her, falling in slow motion over the edge. Maggie barreled toward the falls, with nothing impeding her from going over.

She kicked her feet, fighting to stay above the water and

away from the edge, but it was a losing battle. The water whisked her along, just out of Henry's reach.

Desperately, she clawed at the water. Her foot kicked something hard, and she scrambled to find it again. She smacked into a rock underwater, knocking the air from her lungs. She managed to cling to its slippery surface. As her fingers started to slip, a strong grasp wrapped around her arm.

Henry wrenched her toward him. She wrapped her arms around him as they started to float backward.

"I got you, Princess."

"Thanks," she said, pressing her forehead against his as they were pulled back to land. "Guess what?"

"What's that?"

"I set a date for the wedding."

Henry laughed. "Somehow it feels appropriate to hear that at this very moment."

She smiled at him as they reached the bank. "How'd you get away from Bryson?"

"Your friend, Yarima. She alerted the village, and they came to help. They surrounded Bryson's guys and then found Bryson inside the pyramid. Don't worry, they're all under guard."

The little girl ran from the cover of the trees, flinging her arms around Maggie's soaked midriff.

Maggie hugged her, kissing the top of her head. "Thanks, Yarima. You saved our lives."

She flicked her gaze to the others. "We found the gold."

"So my great-great-grandfather was right," Leo said. "Thomas Tilton told him the truth."

"Yep," Maggie answered. "Get ready for some press. Because your family was a big part of this find."

"A find that I'm guessing just went over the falls," Ollie said.

"No," Maggie answered, with a shake of her head. "It's in the pyramid. I can show you. Too bad you didn't get to see the ironclad, Uncle Ollie. That was something."

"Until it floated away," Emma groaned as Leo stroked her hair.

Maggie wagged a finger at Emma. "She needs medical attention, she's feverish."

"I'm certain the villagers can help," Ollie said. "By the way, Tarik is up and talking."

"Oh, yay," Maggie said, with a broad grin. "So, we did it."

"That we did, chicky."

"Yep," Piper agreed, "we uncursed ourselves. Although, next time, can we maybe skip the plane crash?"

Maggie flicked up her eyebrows. "Yeah, let's skip that next time."

"What's on the docket for next time?" Ollie asked.

"Mmm, I'm thinking King Solomon's Mines."

THE END
(But there's more to come!)

* * *

Look for Book 5 coming in 2024! Until then, check out my other adventure series, Clif & Ri on the Sea. Book 1, *A Pirate's Life for Ri*, is filled with swashbuckling adventure!

* * *

Let's keep in touch! Sign up for my newsletter (and get three free books!).

A NOTE FROM THE AUTHOR

Dear Reader,

If you'd like to stay up to date with all my news, be the first to find out about new releases first, sales and get free offers, join the Nellie H. Steele's Mystery Readers' Group! Or sign up for my newsletter now!

All the best, Nellie

OTHER SERIES BY NELLIE H. STEELE

Cozy Mystery Series

Cate Kensie Mysteries
Lily & Cassie by the Sea Mysteries
Pearl Party Mysteries
Middle Age is Murder Cozy Mysteries

Supernatural Suspense/Urban Fantasy

Shadow Slayers Stories
Duchess of Blackmoore Mysteries
Shelving Magic

Adventure

Maggie Edwards Adventures
Clif & Ri on the Sea

Made in United States
Troutdale, OR
02/21/2024